THE FALL apart

L.M. WOLFE

Copy-edited by: Ten Thousand
Proofread by: Claire and J
Cover design and formatting by: Rotoscope Design
Developmental critique by: Bryony Leah

First printed and EPUB version: 2023
Paperback ISBN: 979-8-218-26823-7

READ BEFORE READING

This story portrays a realistic and raw approach to various topics and situations that could be upsetting to some individuals. There is adult language—like, a lot—and mature, explicit scenes. Every element is fictional and meant to be read that way.

A detailed list of potential triggers can be found on my website: www.lmwolfe.com. Please make the best choice for yourself, and your mental health, before continuing.

With all that being said, and if you're still here, I hope you enjoy the ride.

XOXO

~L

Playlist

SIDE A

SIDE B

*For anyone who's ever felt they're just winging
this whole mom, woman, or human thing…
Spoiler—everybody is.*

1. STAY TOGETHER FOR THE KIDS

I sit, cuddled up on the chaise of the couch, buried beneath my kids' blankets, sipping coffee. Well, it was coffee when they were here. Now it's mostly vodka.

On repeat is a song by one of my favorite bands. It goes into detail about a child's perspective of their parents fighting, the pain, the wonderings of why they can't get along. Oh, and the lyrics focus on the holidays, particularly this one.

Fitting.

Loose strands from my poor excuse for a ponytail fall over my face as I drown in the vodka. In the music. It *is* a great song, all things considered. The type of jam Jake and I would routinely blast, prompting serious eye rolls from our teenage daughters. Thankfully, our two younger kids still find us amusing. Nineties and early 2000s tunes—that's our style.

My style.

Tears roll in violent waves when I actually concentrate on the lyrics. I keep stopping and restarting, begging for the torture to continue.

I love and hate how music can evoke so many emotions. Emotions that, until today, I've kept stuffed into a box. Triple-taped for added security.

My dogs rest their heads in my lap, tails wagging, unaffected by the chaos that's become their life. My life. Their brown eyes are round with concern, their mouths hanging open, tongues dangling. They sport the goofy smiles that retrievers have down to a science.

"Go! Leave me alone. Everyone else does." I can't contain the sobs that have free flowed since the moment the kids left for Jake's parents' house.

The dogs ignore my dismissal and slip their wet noses under my hand, demanding I pet them. They're so in tune with every member of this household's feelings and can't stand to see anyone sad. It's like their actual life's mission to instill joy and happiness in people's hearts.

And I'm not about joy and all that bullshit right now.

Also, I'm being ridiculously dramatic. My specialty.

I want to sit here, sip my drink, and feel sorry for myself. My first Christmas Day without my children.

My first Christmas alone. *Ever.*

The first fucking Christmas in my life where I have nobody, minus the dogs, who don't count. Okay, that's not fair—they do.

Shredded boxes and carelessly torn paper litter the floor. The kids were so rushed, not taking time to enjoy their gifts. I got the odd obligatory *thank you,* but there was a schedule to keep. They were on a mission, desperate to be ready with their toys and clothes when they had to leave with their dad.

I couldn't bother to move my micro-managing ass off the couch to pick up a single scrap of paper. My house would've never been in such disarray in the past. Nope. I always had a trash bag out, ready to tidy up. Because, after the stress of finding perfect gifts, ensuring everyone got crossed off the list, then wasting hours on precise wrapping…

A messy house? No thanks.

Back to the pained song. The singer's high-pitched, almost whiny voice blasts from my speaker, and I bury my face in an oversized unicorn mug—a present from my son, Will—gulping another searing swig.

My cup's about empty. That was fast.

I make my way to the freezer, dismissing the dogs' short-lived consolation efforts. While ignoring the loud squeaks of their new toys, I pull out a bottle my friend Kelsey left several months ago.

On *that* day.

I've done well avoiding its presence, but *this* day calls for it. I shake the carton of dwindling OJ. Gonna have to raid the juice pouches soon; no shot I can drink this stuff straight. I'm not there yet.

The entire exchange of kids was so damn weird this morning. We've done the swap before, multiple times, but this one was different. For starters, it's Christmas. They have gifts they wanted to play with, gifts *supposedly* from both of us. Jake, my ex—well, not technically my ex. I'll get to that—and I decided we should attempt to maintain some normalcy for them. Try to make it easy. He came over early in his pajamas, so he'd be here when they woke up. Because… *that's* normal? Laughable. What's normal anymore? Nothing is easy. Everything's hard.

So, normal meant I still did most of the work. I made him get gifts for his side of the family, which felt shitty, but I couldn't bring myself to do it.

And why should I anyway?

Another wail. His family. Will I ever see them again? A mouthful of the botched screwdriver burns a path down to my stomach. I love my in-laws; we always got along. They were my family too.

And now… they aren't?

Jake and I were the success story. Met the day after high school graduation. Had a baby young, married for love, living in our dream house. Textbook perfection. We beat the odds. He was still the one.

Seriously? Shania Twain?

Sixteen years and three more babies later, everything is so far from perfect. Life is falling apart, the walls crumbling around me. I suppose they have been for a while now. The stress of work, the house, keeping up with bullshit appearances—all of it's been chipping away at us. It took one thing, one act of betrayal for the last thread we were hanging from to give way.

The remains of an overcompensating breakfast cover the island—French toast, bacon, sausage. Keep it the same. Change nothing. Make the kids believe we're going to be alright. But they're not stupid. Brynn and Jordan are teenagers, far too aware of how these scenarios pan out—they've seen it with their own friends.

Roo and Will appear to be fine with it, pumped to get new rooms at Dad's temporary house. Bunk beds. That's what they cared about. It's probably all I would've cared about at seven, Will's age. As for Roo, she's eleven but doesn't process the same as many of her peers. She seems good. I hope she is.

We'd sat them down three months ago and promised to put in the work. Explained that sometimes parents need a time-out. It is *not* their fault. This isn't permanent.

So full of shit.

Both of us held it together this morning. I begrudgingly bit my tongue while our offspring showered Jake with hugs and thanks for his amazing gifts. As if the contents weren't equally surprising to him. Yep, *that's* something I kept the same as every other year.

Merry *fucking* Christmas.

I submerge myself once more in the lyrics, which are difficult to listen to, yet spot on in such a disturbing way.

Okay. Let's give it a rest.

"Screw you, Alexa." My words garble together.

"Sorry," the reprimanding robotic voice booms. "I'm having trouble understanding you."

Me too. Me too.

As the song resumes, my gaze travels to the towering tree in the corner. A wide variety of mismatched ornaments accumulated over the years hang from synthetic branches. It's not one of those coordinating department-store jobs. Nope. This is random, messy, and chock-full of memories. The picturesque one is in the front room. I wish I was kidding.

An artificial tree. Matches *nicely* with my artificial life.

I pick at someone's unfinished plate, which is drowning in syrup. Gross. Why so extra with the condiments? A little can go a long way. The combo of hours-old food and the scent of a sickeningly sweet candle forces my stomach to churn.

Or that could be the vodka?

After abandoning my brief effort to soak up my liquid breakfast, I settle back on the couch, fixating on a funny seasonal classic. We watch it every December, at least twice. My kids can recite it. Last year, Will wished a cashier at the store Merry Christmas, then told her to kiss his ass, my ass, the girls' asses. Not my proudest mom moment, but what can ya do?

"Ugh! I'm definitely gonna need all the Tylenol."

The dogs tilt their heads from side to side, confused by the crazy lady taking up space on the sofa. I place my cup on the end table and scratch their ears, heaving a completely lost type of sigh. You can't pet one and not the other—they're a total package deal. Both snuggle into me, pleading with their eyes to return the owner they're accustomed to.

"You guys are stuck with just me today."

The hair on their backs spikes in response to a series of rapid bangs on the front door. They lunge into threatening stances, snarling and barking. As if they'd do anything but lick an intruder to death.

What in the—

I load up the door-camera app to see who's here because… who even looks out a window anymore?

Poor connection—check your internet settings.

Awesome. I have no clue how to do this stuff. Technology is Jake's deal. And, of course, he maxed this house out with smart switches, Wi-Fi boxes, voice-enabled lighting. So much unnecessary nonsense. Gotta keep up with the times.

The doorbell dings again and again. Repeated, heavy raps thunder through the foyer.

"I know you're in there," a muffled voice calls. "I hear your music."

Fantastic. Annie.

"Let me in, bi—"

I fling open the door, scowling at my impeccably together-looking best friend, who is shivering from the cold and gloomy weather outside. It's not much better in here. I stare at her, expressionless, before turning to retreat to my blanket fort.

No adulting today.

Adulting, ha! What a fun word. Close to adultery. That one makes my eye twitch.

"Wow!" Annie examines the uncharacteristic destruction all around us. "What the hell, Alex?"

My blank stare continues at her judgy face, and I raise the mug to my mouth. It's really not judgy. I'm just caught up in my own misery at the moment. After shoving food out of the way, she unloads presents onto the kitchen island, making disapproving sounds at my mess.

"I brought cookies," she says, extra cheery. Like baked goods are the answer to my problems. She plops down next to me, and I can feel her disgusted—okay, they're concerned—eyes piercing the side of my face.

"Thanks," I grumble into my ridiculous cup, fingers literally curled around a rainbow-tail handle. Well, it's the thought that counts.

"Damn, you're looking…"

I shoot her a death glare, and she chuckles with an unapologetic shrug. This chick is a wannabe comedian and thinks she's hilarious. She kind of is. But I'm in no mood for her antics today.

"You smell like syrup." Annie pinches her nostrils. "And a bar."

"Yep."

"What song are you listening to?"

The fast beats and angsty voice cry out from the speaker. Her eyes widen, jaw dropping in horror when she recognizes the mental torment I'm subjecting myself to.

It's not right… it's not right.

"Oh, hell to the no. Alexa!" she yells. "Power off."

2. I'LL BE THERE
FOR YOU

"So, how was this morning?" Annie asks with a cautious edge. Natural beach-waved chestnut hair hangs down her back. When did it get that long?

These last few months have blurred by. Between sporadic shifts at the hospital, sleepless nights, sports, Roo's therapy and medical appointments, meltdowns, plus the fifty-fifty split with the kids, it's been a million times more hectic than before.

Jake and I have communicated mostly via text lately, only when necessary. A quick hi and bye during the exchanges, but nothing more. Nothing since I snapped at him for stealing my friends.

He didn't. They're his friends too. I was being a dick. After finding out he'd hung with our besties—an invite never extended to me—the solid sting of yet another betrayal, while slightly misplaced, was undeniable. I get it. How do you choose? Who gets who in a split? It's a crapshoot.

But that's not the *real* reason the communication—I use the term loosely —puttered to near nonexistence.

I know why he stopped trying so much, stopped calling me fifty times a day. Now he resorts to late-night messages, though the groveling ones have grown less frequent. It had nothing to do with my… our friends. Jake saw my finger. He noticed the deep indentation from the rings that had lived on my left hand for over sixteen years—the symbols of promises we made to each other. He realized I'd taken them off.

His eyes had gone vacant as his bottom lip quivered, and like a switch, he'd hardened, his consistent optimism dissolving into thin air. It was a mortal wound. I'd wanted it to hurt.

At least, I thought I did.

"Hello? Alex? Did you hear a word I said?"

"No, sorry." I blow out a rumbling breath.

Annie tuts with another hearty laugh, but there's no masking the uncertainty behind her playful facade. I know a thing or two about putting on a show.

"Go take a shower and sober up. We have a long day ahead."

"Long day?" I whine. I just wanna be alone. She *always* pulls this shit on me, dropping by whenever she wants. I'm betting that between her and Kelsey, my closest friends in the area, there's some sort of check-in schedule for me. They worry I won't be fine by myself. Joke's on them. I'm totally fucking fine. "Why are you here, Annie?"

"Rude." She kicks festive paper out of the way then drags the ottoman closer. "I'm here because you're such a ray of sunshine and I wanna soak you in." She lets out a snort as she flings off her boots and props her legs on the footrest. "Also, here to have a leisurely cocktail. Though, how 'bout we take it down a notch?" Her finger flicks to my mug.

Not the worst idea.

She looks cute in jeans and a cream sweater, with her hair and makeup on point. "Don't you usually go to Jace's mom's today?" I ask with a frown, studying her outfit. She seems dressed for it. "Annie… your kids. Why aren't you with them? You should be with your family." I swallow the painful lump in my throat. No one should be without their family on Christmas Day. Not by choice.

Mine isn't a choice. I mean, not really… is it?

In the past, Jake and I seamlessly juggled holidays between our families, alternating here and there. We spent Christmas morning at home. Later came the mad dash to assemble the crew and somehow get everyone out of the house in one piece—difficulty level: ten—wrestling them into coordinating outfits that, of course, they hated. How dare I, right? After they were presentable, and I had a whopping five minutes to throw my shit together, we'd make the two-hour drive to celebrate with his family. Usually turning around at least twice for something forgotten.

I'd often felt overwhelmed and guilty for pulling the kids away from their new stuff. Not to mention, after all the prep, what would be better than to kick back and relax? A day in pajamas and a movie marathon? Yes please.

Funny… now I have exactly what I wanted.

Could I have gone with? Sure. Jake had invited me, multiple times. But maintaining a charade for more than a few hours, for more than only our children, seemed daunting. Everyone has their limits.

"You should be with your family, Ann." My shoulders slump, then I rest my elbows on my thighs.

She clicks her tongue and gives a dismissive wave. "This was a fantastic excuse. I *hate* going there. Jace told the mega-bitch I was sick." She yanks my prized ceramic from me and coughs after slugging a mouthful. Her nose crinkles and she wipes her lips. "Anyway, the kids will be fine. Liv can't stand me these days." Damn teenage girls. "And you know Pipes—she only cares about presents. They won't miss me for a second."

Liv is smack in the middle of my older two. Jord and her are closer, but she'll hang with Brynn… when she allows it. Pipes, or rather Piper, is her youngest.

Back when Jake and I started discussing the possibility of a third—he would've had ten kids if I'd agreed to it—Annie thought it'd be fun to have a matching set of babies. And we did just that. Pregnant together, miserable twats for an entire summer. I'm sorry, but pregnancy is not the glorious glowing crap you hear about. It's sweaty, messy, and near the end, it feels like a bowling ball is about to drop out your vag.

Either way, our mission was a success—two gorgeous baby girls, born only three days apart. Couldn't have planned it better if we'd tried. Well, we did try, but you know what I mean.

When Ruby—aka Roo—and Piper were babies, we were beyond extra, dressing them identically and constantly discussing all the trouble they would get into.

Destined to be besties, same as their moms.

A little after their first birthdays, I noticed Roo wasn't hitting the same developmental markers. She didn't babble, or say mama and dada like Piper; like our other two girls had by her age. She wouldn't wave or hold a spoon. It took a few more years to get a formal diagnosis: autism spectrum disorder.

We sought every specialist along the coast, throwing thousands of dollars into therapies. It's been a long road. The tantrums and setbacks happen from time to time, but we've learned to maneuver these unchartered waters. To a point. Annie's been there through each step. She's Roo's godmother and takes that role seriously.

"Earth to Alex!" her borderline-irritated voice rings out. "Are you, for real, that in the bag already?"

No. I'm just in my feelings today.

"It was a strange morning. I'm kind of having a—"

She scoops her arms around me and pulls me in, crushing my face against her pristine sweater. "I know," she whispers into my hair.

I am *not* a hugger. I have a shirt that says "don't touch me," compliments of Kelsey. Annie knows this. Everyone knows this. I get tagged in funny memes about it all the time.

I'm not a fan of touchy-feely or physically affectionate stuff. Except for my kids. Well, any kids. And Jake.

It *used* to be Jake.

"Don't." I wriggle in her grasp, desperate to peel her arms off me, but she keeps them locked tight. I hate the power of this hug. My eyes burn for the zillionth time today. I don't want to lose it because he doesn't deserve my tears. No, these tears belong to my children, my babies, and the emptiness that fills me when they're away.

"It'll get better."

After I stop fighting, she releases me and leans her side into the back cushions. I catch a fast dab beneath her eyes before she grabs my hand.

I fixate on the ceiling—it's safer there—and bite the inside of my cheek, attempting words that won't prompt yet another sob. "Just… I miss them."

"I get that." Annie nods. A smile spreads across her lips, and a single laugh jolts her shoulders. "They drive you nutty, right? But when they're gone, all you want is for them to be back. The mysteries of mom-life." She squeezes my fingers before letting go, then shifts her attention away from me, aware of my unstable state.

"Yeah," I agree. It's true too. Kids drive you up the wall daily. But when they're away? Well, it's how the song goes. You truly don't know what you've got…

I sigh and then stand, smoothing my rumpled clothes. Suppose I'll get my life together-ish. The floor is steady enough beneath my bare feet, which carry me to the mirror in the foyer, where I subsequently gasp at my reflection. I resemble a deranged raccoon. Deadass. The light mascara I'd swiped on earlier has melted from my lashes. My hair is flat and glued to my cheek from lying on the couch for so long.

Annie busts out laughing when she sees my expression. I get I'm having a moment here, but *damn.*

"Hot-ass mess," she says, no mercy. The truth is a thing, and my best friend speaks it.

She watches me wipe the black streaks from my face. My eyes are so puffy and swollen, even the bags under them have bags. I mean it. Could pack those suckers full for a month-long vacation.

I inhale a deep breath then glance at her. She's worried, and not without reason. But I also know there's a serious determination to see me happy. Isn't that the way of genuine friends? Don't get me wrong, Annie allows me to be my flawed self, and how important is that? To have a person you never have to fake it for. Because, truth, some would inspect your dirty laundry the second you hung it out to dry. I appreciate her.

"You love this mess," I finally reply, showcasing my body with open palms. I pinch the middle of my ratty tee. Opted out of the family pajamas this year. "Not everyone can pull this off." Humor is our go-to, one of the best meds out there.

"That's right."

Her teasing, slow clap eggs me on. I pout my lips and stare off to the side, mimicking the poses our teens have down pat. Annie whistles, shrill and ear-piercing, while I continue to work the invisible runway. Or, in this case, the foyer, where I stride to the door to release my rowdy hounds.

"You're *my* hot mess. Now go clean yourself up, slap some fresh clothes on your beautiful butt, and nut up. We've got stuff to do." This is her version of a pep talk.

A scoff rumbles from my throat. "Stuff to do?"

"Yup. I brought all kinds of goodies." She tips her chin to her stash on the counter. "We can binge-watch whatever. Dance. Sing. The possibilities are endless."

I groan, but she continues despite my protests.

"I'll brew us a fresh pot of coffee. And then, if you're good"—her eyes narrow, gauging my intoxication level, which, trust me, isn't too bad—"then maybe a mimosa or two?"

I'm sure there will be more than two.

Annie flips through the channels as I make my way into the open kitchen. "I can't deal with any more Christmas movies. What are you in the mood for?"

To wallow in self-pity, table for one. Sadly, I don't think that's an option anymore.

"No preference. You choose." I resist the temptation to pick nasty leftovers off a plate. Lesson learned. I get to it, cleaning the counters, marveling at the surplus of food. Can't believe the dogs didn't sniff it out and swipe what they could reach.

Small victories.

After tying the trash bag shut, I hesitate. The thought of carting this to the bin is less than ideal. My next-door neighbor is ultra-meddlesome, and I don't need to be headlining any more local gossip.

"Leave that. I'll handle it."

"You don't have to, Ann."

"If you go out there like that…" I can tell she's lining up for something by the way her lip curls. "Pennis—"

"His name's Dennis."

She smirks. "I like my version better. Whatever the fug his name is will go TMZ on you. Probs snap a pic for shits and giggles."

She's not lying. He takes nosey to new heights. You know the type that conveniently only grabs the mail when you're outside? Perhaps a telling blind off-kilter from their peeping? Or one who does yardwork when there's a party happening, hoping to eavesdrop the latest scoop?

Yeah, that's him.

Back when the text I saw on Jake's phone had blindsided me, I went ballistic and flung his clothes on the front lawn. Hurled his beloved hockey gear into the street. Isn't that what you're *supposed* to do? The ability to rationalize became null and void. I couldn't even begin to get my chaotic thoughts in order. Insensible words of hate rocketed from my mouth—I was on the brink of losing my shit.

Okay, in reality, I was *definitely* losing my shit.

Sarah, a different and completely supportive neighbor, ushered the kids out of my house. She's the best, always helpful. Roo was going off from my screaming, banging her head into whatever she could find. I couldn't stop. The hurt struck so deep and flooded my vision with rage.

Jake pleaded with me to take a breather. To hear him out, explaining that it wasn't what it seemed.

He wanted me to listen. And I wanted to rip his balls off.

I've harbored excruciating guilt since then, knowing I caused my sweet girl's meltdown. But we can't change the past.

Sarah ensured she could handle Roo. She didn't tell me I was out of line. She heard what I was yelling, knew my reaction was on point. Jake, on the other hand, continued begging me to calm down.

Never in the history of asking someone to calm down will they *actually* fucking calm down.

Dennis called the police, but by the time they arrived, some other neighbors had already made their way over to separate us. The cops asked Jake to leave so I could cool off. D-bag then posted a proclamation on the neighborhood social media page about our domestic disturbance, providing photo evidence of our decorated lawn. Thanks so much for that. Hope your spouse never pisses on your marriage and flushes your entire life down the drain. We should all be so lucky.

"God, that guy is such a prick."

"Yeah," Annie says. "Straight up douche czar."

I can't help but laugh. Czar is high up there. Close to emperor. Not as low-key as lord.

She raises her palms in the air, blue eyes incredibly large. "Well? What are you waiting for? Times tickin'."

"Okay, okay. But I'm not getting fancy, so don't expect it." I surprise us both with a smile. A *genuine* smile.

"Never."

I head up the steps, stopping on the second. "Annie." I turn to face her. "You should be with your family today."

She raises her brows and shoots me a smirk. It falls. "You *are* my family."

3. MR. BRIGHTSIDE

Wow. I needed that. The alcohol was doing a number on my thought process. Or lack thereof. My head's far less foggy now. Sometimes a shower is a cure-all.

Getting drunk? Bathe in a sobering rinse. Got a hangover? Let the stream soothe your swollen brain. Smelling funk? You guessed it—scrub on up. Need sex? Turn that sucker on cold. Or hot. Not that I'm referring to a detachable showerhead or anything. But since my mind is wandering, may as well follow it down that twisted path.

Not saying I *need* need it. However, when you go from having it available twenty-four-seven to not at all, there's a big difference. And I said *available*, not that it was a constant occurrence. Anyway, when that mood strikes, no amount of battery-operated toys make up for the real deal. Trust me, I've tried.

And yeah, I get it… am I seriously thinking about sex right now? What can I say? The human mind is a bizarre place.

Been a while though—like a long while. Before we split, it was at least two or three weeks. Not that he didn't want to. Jake was constantly up for it. Every single morning.

If I wasn't already awake and out of bed—you know, someone has to corral the kids—he'd rub his erection against my ass, hands going wherever they pleased. Nine outta ten times, I left him to his own devices.

He was always in the mood to get down; been that way since we met. His sex drive never faltered. Mine—probably the same as most women, at least the ones who are honest—well, mine is a different story.

* * *

In our younger days, we had sex so much. Anywhere. Everywhere. We weren't exactly exhibitionists, but sometimes it toed the line.

With every pregnancy, my libido was as turbulent as my hormones. After each baby was born, Jake referred to the months that followed as the *newborn sex phase*. Which meant… there was none. Because being sleep deprived, feeling like a damn cow, and changing shitty diapers is enough.

Who has the energy for sex? What even is sex?

The years ticked by, and the roller coaster continued. For a while, it would be four to five times a week. Gotta keep that spark. Then maybe once a week. The decline in our bedroom extracurriculars started after Will came into the picture.

I was satisfied with three, fulfilled, didn't care they were all girls. I hated when people asked if we were going to try for a boy. As if my reproductive life was any of their effing business.

Roo's diagnosis had been recent. There was no magic mirror to show us the future and what it would bring—if only. We were struggling to adjust to her needs, trying to help her the best we could.

She was four and only said about twenty words, a stark contrast to the average fifteen hundred for her age group. Socialization was nonexistent. She wouldn't make eye contact and was tough to understand. Day-to-day activities, such as getting dressed, proved far more challenging than we could've imagined.

We went back and forth for a while, weighing the pros and cons, coming to the ultimate conclusion that our focus would best be served on our girls. All of them.

Time for the snip.

Jake wasn't excited about it. I doubt any guy wants a scalpel within ten miles of their precious jewels, but I'd pushed out three babies and swallowed years of birth control in between.

My work here is done.

He reluctantly had the procedure then boohooed nonstop after. Frozen peas kept his lap company for days. Damn guys and their junk. Betty White said it best: "If you wanna be tough, grow a vagina." Accurate words.

A couple months and a missed period later, those two distinct blue lines showed up for the fourth time. On all four tests. *Yup*—99.9 percent effective, my ass. Of course we had to be the exception to the rule.

In October, Will joined our family. He was the best newborn and scarcely cried. We toted him everywhere. Brynn and Jordan had their own personal baby doll—they were like his other moms. Still kinda are. Our girls adored their brother; Roo became obsessed with him. Life was alright.

Just keep swimming.

Once you have three, four is only a number. Another mouth to feed, an additional peanut to kiss you goodnight… till the preteen nonsense starts. If you're not there yet, buckle up. Such a treat.

Moving on.

Will had recently turned one when our lives drastically changed *again*. We were at a school function for Jordan, and he wouldn't stop screaming. That first-year, subdued behavior was trickery. Kids can fool you like that. Jake did his best to keep him quiet, wrestling him onto his lap to stay still. Jordan had a chorus solo, and why should she miss out on a rare fifteen minutes of fame because of her brother?

Brynn repeatedly grabbed my arm, trying to get my attention, and I snapped at her. But then I realized what she was trying to show me. Roo had peed herself, right in the middle of the jam-packed auditorium, sitting there zoned off into space.

I'd made it my life's goal to have her potty trained before Will came, and dammit if I didn't succeed. She hadn't had an accident in over a year. We rushed outta there… after Jordan's performance.

This happened more and more, and it was agonizing to watch her lose the minimal words she had. Back to the specialists, who ran every test possible. Turns out, it was epilepsy for the win. The universe's cruel joke. As if sensory and learning issues weren't enough, let's throw in a serious medical condition.

Why not?

I beat myself up for not deciphering the signs. I'd been a nurse for close to eight years at that point, but my specialty was emergency and trauma. Neuro had never been my strong suit. Roo was having absence seizures, sporadic fits of staring, not the tonic-clonic, grand mal versions you see on

TV. We thought she was an avid daydreamer. Sometimes it's tough to tell the difference. Still, I should've known.

We made it work though.

Divide and conquer, failure simply not an option. Not for the Everett family.

I cut back at my job. Despite being stressful, I could be myself there—not Mom, but Alex. I missed the adrenaline rush, and I missed my friends. Hell, I missed *me*. But one of us had to take Roo to her appointments and get the girls where they needed to be. Someone had to watch Will. Anyone! Daycare and epilepsy don't exactly go hand in hand, so something had to give.

Jake was busy with his advertising firm, partnered up with our friend Luke—Kelsey's husband. After some financial help from their parents, they built the business from the ground up, outsourcing media spots to large clients, making decent money. We could afford for me to stay home.

It wasn't what I wanted, or maybe it was. Either way, I immersed myself in my kids.

It didn't take long till I lost myself in the mix.

Jake's hours away took a toll. Not just on me but on the kids. They adore their father. He's the most fantastic person on the entire planet to them, the fun one. I've gotta be the one to hold it down, the rule enforcer.

It doesn't seem fair.

Combine years of that with all the other happenings, and this is where it can lead, my friends.

* * *

The bass from a new tune is bumping through the floor, yanking me back to reality. I try not to pick at my appearance for too long in the mirror. Grown-out highlights show roots that were once blonde but have darkened over the years. Some strands of gray have budded from my temples. Gotta get that touched up.

I dab on a little concealer, because when you're in your mid—cough, cough—thirties, you need it. A flick of mascara, slight brow fill in. Yeah, those suckers thin out with age—something to look forward to. I gather my shoulder-length hair into a sad excuse for a messy bun. Good enough.

"What the hell is taking so long?" Annie shouts up to me.

"I'm comin', I'm comin'."

I trudge downstairs. She's made herself at home, lazing on the couch as if she lives here. I genuinely love that my friend is so comfortable. I feel the same at her house.

"Seriously? You always watch this show." I scrunch my nose after glancing at the TV. "Why don't you have the volume on?" I flop down next to her. Annie has a hard-core obsession with this coffee-drinking, quirky group of friends.

"Whaddaya mean?" She chomps on a cookie then washes it down with champagne that must've been in her bag of tricks. Guess she forewent the coffee. "This shit's timeless. A classic. I don't need to hear it because I know what's happening. Plus, I'm listening to our fave." She nods at the overused speaker on the kitchen counter, playing a completely unrelated song. Such a multi-tasker.

I cringe at the infamous line when it hits. Yeah… I certainly wonder how the hell it ended up like this.

"Love this song," I say, refusing to let the lyrics set up shop in my head.

"Another timeless classic," she mumbles through cookie crumbs and climbs onto the ottoman, rocking out as we occasionally do. "Come on." She tugs the sleeve of my shirt with a mischievous smirk.

"Not in the mood." Monotone would be an appropriate descriptor.

"It's not an option. Your ass. Up here. Now! Plus, you get a nip of this as a reward for taking a shower."

Her excessive volume makes me wince as she tempts me with the bottle in her hand. She's jumping up and down like a maniac, belting out the words severely off-key, reminding me of our midnight dance sessions in the early days of our friendship.

I give in because… it's Annie. She won't take no for an answer. We thrash around on the oversized footrest in my now spotless house. She really is the best flipping friend you could ask for.

"Thank you." I pause my uncoordinated, outdated moves. We always play this song twice, at a minimum—as if we couldn't sing it a cappella. I grab her forearms to snag her undivided attention. She knows if I'm making physical contact, it's deep.

For a rare handful of seconds, Annie is serious. She stares back at me, and I can see the sadness in her eyes, the understanding that things just aren't the same. After a few beats of this wordless communication, she guzzles from her bottle and releases a long exhale before passing it to me.

"I got something for you." She wiggles her brows, swerving the potential path of our conversation, then bolts off the ottoman, swipes whatever from the kitchen countertop, and runs back, popping up to where she left me like it's a box jump. Her and that damn CrossFit. She shoves a small blue bag into my hands.

"Annie! We said no gifts. Only for the kids."

"Oh, shush. It's nothing."

I sift through white tissue and pull out a thin silver bracelet. "Aw, this is beautiful. Thanks so much."

"Wait." She stops me before I can cram it on my wrist. Once you get one of these in place, you're committed. "Read it," she says, pinning me with an abnormal dose of sincerity.

I study the plain-looking band, squinting to make out the four tiny words etched along the inside.

You Fucking Got This

Typical Annie gift.

The corners of my lips curve ever so slightly. It feels strange to smile, but… it's nice.

I needed this. 'Cause I definitely *don't* fucking got this.

4. DON'T SPEAK

The festivities continue well into the evening.

We keep doing what we do best—when the kids aren't present of course. We're good moms. Do everything for those tiny people. But for shit's sake, we all deserve a break from time to time.

Is alcohol the wisest choice? Doubtful, but sometimes the temporary escape is a necessary evil.

We've passed that borderline *funny talk, dance around like idiots* phase, and now we're into the *totally wasted, gonna get deep* phase. I hate this stage of the game. This is when genuine emotions slip out, and I don't like to reveal my weaknesses. But when it's just Annie, sometimes I let them show. Even if I try to hide the truth, she knows.

The two of us are planning our next tattoo. Yup, so cliché, I'm aware. Best friends with matching tattoos, and we got 'em. Several. The puzzle pieces on our feet, obviously for Roo. Jake and Jace have them as well.

My favorite, though, is a heart within a heart.

The small design we intended is actually a decent-sized marking. Black ink spans the inside of each of our wrists. We'd explained the inspiration to the tattoo artist, who went freestyle with it. When she transferred the stencil onto my skin, I couldn't say no, and Annie followed suit.

Her mom, her best friend, became suddenly ill back when I was pregnant with Will. Five days and three hospitals later, they couldn't figure out what was wrong with her.

She was fine. Then she wasn't.

She died. *She fucking died.* And nobody knew exactly why. Still don't.

Wanna see the light go out in someone? Watch them as their hero disappears. Not for the faint of heart.

Annie became a recluse and refused to speak to anyone. I tried for weeks. Jace tried, Jake tried. I know, it's annoying that their names nearly match, but we didn't plan *that* one. After all my conversation efforts failed, I'd sent her a card with my favorite E. E. Cummings poem "I Carry Your Heart with Me" on the front. It might seem cheesy, but it's true. I meant it, every single word. Hence the tattoo.

This woman is my soulmate, and I can't imagine my world without her. She's always been there for me. Case in point, she's missing her family Christmas to hold my hand. Annie is the absolute best.

Anyway, after that, and for the first time in weeks, she left her bedroom and re-entered society. It took months for her to find a new normal, but we made our way there… *together.*

Jake always went with us whenever we got some ink. He got his first tattoo the day he turned eighteen, on his chest, directly over his heart. I lost my shit when he showed me the neatly written, cursive word.

My name, Alex, branded on his body.

Talk about a grand gesture. He was so sure of things, so confident in his actions. I had trouble committing to a nail polish color at eighteen.

Years and kids expanded his artwork. When he's buttoned up in his custom suits, you'd have no clue he's a walking canvas. But when the shirt comes off, the real Jake is on display.

Enough about him. Where's my drink?

"So, what are ya gonna do, Alllle?" Annie slurs. This chick is plastered. Words are tough to understand. Fortunately for her, I'm speaking the same language.

"Who knows?" I pop a shoulder, sitting next to her at the kitchen island.

I don't know.

What do you do? Do you throw everything away? Do you consider the fact that he's probably one of the most picture-perfect humans and fathers in the world? Or do you dwell on the shortcomings? The clothes on the floor, the dishes in the sink?

Can you ignore the feelings that exist deep down? Ones you want to hide? The notion that you might not truly be happy anymore? The complacency?

Oh, yeah… and do you forget the minor detail that you had to see a text from some skank?

Yup, his phone lit up on this very counter during evening homework hell. Good times.

And it was a sext, not a text.

Angela DeMarco, some trashy national buyer from New York, couldn't wait for his cock to be inside her. Couldn't wait to see him the next week. Couldn't wait for them to fuck.

Verbatim.

Nice… right?

So, yeah, what would you do?

We decided, or I decided, he was going to get a six-month lease on a townhouse around the corner. If it were up to me, at that exact moment, I'd have signed divorce papers without a second thought. After a while, I simmered… kinda. Plus, there's a year waiting period from the time of separation until they grant a divorce in our lovely state. I would re-evaluate the situation when *I* was ready.

Jake told me it was someone he did business with; had met up with her during his last trip to the city. He felt he could talk to her. Said I was emotionally unavailable and had been for years. Tried to flip the script.

I'd briefly considered moving beyond the text, but in his tell-all confession, he admitted they'd kissed.

And *that* was the fucking deal-breaker.

I refused to listen to any more on the matter. Picture figurative fingers stuck in my ears. Mature… I get it. Since then, today is the first time we've been in the same room for longer than a minute without spitting fire. Without *me* spitting fire.

"You gotta forgive him, Al," Annie says in a liquor-induced plea, covering my clenched hand with her palm.

My tongue smacks against gritted teeth, and I glare at her before turning away. I know she wants the band back together in the worst way, but I just can't move on. Though, this is the first time she's said the words out loud.

"Okay, sure. All's forgiven. No big deal." I stare straight ahead at the fridge, unable to look at her again without another bout of tears. Honestly, I'm over the crying.

"He loves you, Alexandra. Jake adores you and the kids. You know he does. He messed up." Her grip tightens, and so does my fist.

I shift my attention from the exhilarating kitchen appliances back to her. She can barely stay upright on the counter-height stool, and if she scoots her ass any further, she'll be on the floor. With excessive puppy-dog eyes, she pouts at me.

"Oh, yeah… he adores me." My jaw clenches, and I receive a perturbed grunt in return. I give her the bitchiest look I'm capable of, hoping she notices the way all three—probably—of me are lofting daggers at her.

She continues making a case for Jake. "It was only a kiss."

Since when does Annie defend him? Why is she doing this? She's supposed to be Team Alex. Suddenly she wants Jake to be absolved? I don't think so.

"It was only a kiss? You have *got* to be kidding me." Heat sprints up my neck. "If Jace *only* kissed someone, would you be okay with that? Would you be cool and forgiving if he'd set up an actual fuck date?" I'm aware my voice is growing borderline hysterical loud.

"He said when he tried to talk to you, you—"

"He *said?*" I clip, on the verge of bursting a blood vessel.

"Alex, listen—"

I don't let her finish. "So sorry we ruined things for you. So sorry you have to pick a side. It's clear which one you're *actually* on." Every single syllable packs a hefty dose of anger, but I grasp the severity of what I'm insinuating only after I say it.

Isn't that the way it always goes?

Annie is one of the most selfless people in the world, but once those words come out, you can't ever get them back.

"That's the problem," she mutters. "You only hear what you want."

My arms slam across my chest. "Well, I promise you it's not fucking this."

"Don't act like this, Alex! Don't be such a child." A distinct crease forms between her eyebrows.

Me? A child?

I gear up to spit more venom. It's apparently open-mic night, and I'm about to take her to the chop shop. Even though, in reality, it's not intended for her. Well, the anger's not.

The dogs go wild—Cujo mode—as Jace lets himself in, strolling through the front door towards us.

"You're supposed to be my person," I whisper, thankful for the interruption that prevented me from saying something I'd regret.

Also… *Grey's Anatomy?* Yeah, I've hit my limit.

"Hey, ladies." Annie's husband's smooth voice diffuses the obvious tension in the room. Wrinkles line his forehead as he takes stock of the current situation.

We don't fight. Banter? Yes. But shouting matches with each other? Only lovingly.

His brown eyes dart between us, ultimately landing on his wife. He rounds the counter and kisses the top of her head. I tear away my gaze, wishing that tiny gesture didn't make me think of *him.*

"Hey, Jace. Merry Christmas," I mumble, finger swirling over an imaginary nothing on the tan countertop. I can barely bring myself to glance at him. He and I have a friendship on its own, but he's Jake's *Annie.* Team Jake till the end.

He gives my shoulder a one-armed squeeze, letting out a sigh. "Merry Christmas, Alex." The sadness, the remorse for how things are, it's there in his voice. In the way he says my name.

I miss you too, Jace. Wish I could admit it out loud, but I gotta keep up the act. Gotta keep everyone thinking I'm fine.

"Wow, you two." He quickly changes gears, examining the counter contents while running a hand through his dark waves. A low whistle leaves his lips as he takes in the various empty bottles, and the drunken stupors on our faces. "You're both lit up like Christmas trees!"

We snicker. I love hearing the guys use our lines. Annie's eyes meet mine, and hers brim with the same as my own—an apology neither of us needs to say out loud.

"Can we stay for one more?" she asks. At least I think that's what she asks.

Jace studies her, skeptical brow-raise in place. "You've probably had enough," he answers after catching my subtle nod.

He's right. I couldn't drink another drop if I wanted to. The room is getting spinny, and I already feel the makings of a monstrous hangover.

"'K… ten morrre mennates." She sucks the last noisy sips through her straw.

Jace stares at her for a moment, amusement playing on his lips. "I'm gonna have a smoke," he says before walking out to the back deck. That's his unspoken five-minute rule.

I'm sure he feels like it'd be betraying Jake if he stays here and hangs out. Or perhaps he doesn't want to be thrown into the discomfort of me potentially bashing his best friend, while he has to sit here and take it. Because any way you slice this… Jake's the one who messed everything up.

Five minutes later, they're headed out the door, and I'm back to being alone.

I stumble upstairs, getting into our bed—my bed—and stretch across the cozy flannel I love so much. I spread out as far as humanly possible, enjoying the ample room. Couldn't ever use these sheets before; Jake complained they made him too hot.

Now I can sleep on them whenever I want. It's awesome.

My subconscious—maybe they're conscious thoughts, or let's call it a dreamlike state—slips to visions that they should *not* be slipping to.

Where are the sugarplums?

I guess it's from months without actual intimate contact… from someone else. Whatever. Despite what my intoxicated brain and wounded heart have to say, my body is craving a release. Not to mention that it's been him, solely Jake, for the past two decades. I don't have a large basis for comparison. And I hate that my mind is going here because I don't understand it. I shouldn't think about him that way… right?

As I drift off to sleep, all I can see is that flawless and stupidly attractive face. The permanent five o'clock shadow along his sharp jawline taunts me. Not to mention, his thick, almost black, hair, styled to perfection— it's aggravating, every strand in place. That chiseled body he's maintained by playing hockey, snowboarding, and coaching the kids' basketball, baseball, lacrosse, you name it. And the intricate ink that creeps down his defined torso, leading to the glorious V-line he's kept impeccable after all these years.

No dad bod here.

And his tongue. Capable of unspeakable acts. He could do things; we used to do things.

Ugh. I toss and turn under the covers, unable to get his haunting fucking face out of my head.

And the voice? Don't even. Though, in my dreams, he doesn't need to say a word, and that's probably for the best. Trust me, his mouth, lips, body… they're all capable of speaking for themselves.

5. MISERY

I can hardly open my eyes, and there seems to be some sort of vise grip drilling into each temple.

Oh no, that's right—I got piss drunk yesterday, and this is the aftermath. It's not gonna be an easy recovery either.

Nope. When you get older, it's a two-day minimum. That's why I never drink.

Alright, that's a lie. Though I only cocktail it up on the weekends when I don't have the kids. Makes it a little easier to adjust to the downtime. And what the hell is downtime with kids anyway? It doesn't exist when you live together twenty-four-seven. But when they're shuffled back and forth between parents, you get that coveted peace.

Honestly, it's super lonely.

I release a louder than necessary groan. The dogs' heads bobble left and right, unable to make sense of the monster in my bed. *Same.* I cover my head to stop the rude morning light from forcing me out of my cocoon. Stray sunbeams filter in through the slats of my blinds, like the actual assholes they are, burning my skin.

What did I do to myself?

I sit up slowly, and every ounce of blood whooshes to my brain, making me smack a palm over my face. Have I been chomping cotton balls all night? I reach blindly towards the bedside table for something—anything. My hand connects with a glass, and I breathe a sigh of relief. I don't hesitate or sniff or examine. Desperate times. I chug the warm contents like it's my job.

Holy shit!

The liquid scorches the back of my throat, and I promptly spit it out. What kind of heathen brings a cup of vodka to bed?

I fly off the mattress, gagging, and hoof it to the bathroom. With a hasty flip of the handle, I gulp straight from the faucet, desperate to wash away the disgusting taste clinging to my tongue. Why would someone willingly drink this stuff?

Bad. Decisions.

Also, thank you, sweet baby Jesus, the clamminess that was slithering up my neck retreats. You know, that ick sensation that makes you wanna go fetal on the floor? Dodged it. This head though.

And… my back?

When I attempt to stand up straight, a nagging pain ricochets up and down my spine. Getting old is total bullshit—you can injure yourself by sleeping the wrong way.

My phone buzzes, vibrating against the wood of my night table. I didn't look at it all day yesterday; didn't want to be tempted to go on social media and post a revealing quote. It's not as if I have a stockpile saved for every occasion.

Twenty-eight new messages. *Fantastic.*

Five from Jake:

> *Yesterday 2:05 PM*
> Thanks for this morning. Pulled out all the stops as usual. Hope you have a relaxing day. I know you always hated all the running on Christmas.
>
> *Yesterday 7:55 PM*
> What's going on? Jace said you and Annie were fighting? That's not like you guys.
>
> *Yesterday 11:32 PM*
> I'm so sorry, Alex. So fucking sorry. I'll live the rest of my life in misery. Text me back.
>
> *Today 12:05 AM*
> Typical. Can't even respond.
>
> *Today 8:21 AM*
> Sorry about the texts. My fault. Leaving now. Be there around 10:30.

Ugh, okay. Shit, it's already nine. I slept, what, twelve hours? I'm a fan of sleep, but this might be a new record.

As for the texts…

First: Yup, always bitched about the traveling.

Second: Fucking Jace.

Third: Been a few weeks, but this is probably the five thousandth message like this.

Fourth: This one too.

Fifth: Yeah…

I type an acknowledgment of his last text, ignoring the others, then sift through the rest of my notifications. With a single-eyed squint at the bright screen, I fight to focus through a wicked headache. Wow, I need to get a grip before the kids come home. I smell like I just got done with a full-day bender.

Oh, wait.

I swipe through more messages real quick. Several from my parents, all sent yesterday, wishing me a Merry Christmas, various emojis and misplaced text lingo—someone needs to break it to Mom that LOL does *not* mean lots of love. There's one asking if I want to come visit sooner, and another suggesting they could change up our traditional plans and make the trek here. Super grateful *that* didn't happen. While they don't live crazy far, it's a couple hours south, not a simple drive around the block. The last says they're worried about me, the usual.

I shoot back a short, hopefully convincing response.

Today 9:02 AM

Merry Christmas. Love you both. Had a nice relaxing day with the pups. Kids had a fantastic morning. Can't wait to see you. I'm doing fine. Promise. LOL

I can't resist the last part. Shame on me.

Just envisioning getting everyone packed increases the throbbing behind my eyes. We're headed to visit my family tomorrow to spend a few days after the holiday, and it's always a big to-do. I *am* excited to see my parents and siblings, but the prep is exhausting. My mom still wanted me to invite Jake. Sometimes I'm convinced they love him more than me.

If only they knew.

But they don't. No one does, except our close friends… and several neighbors. I couldn't bring myself to tell my parents. They fell in love the second I brought Jake home all those years ago. There's an air about him that's infectious—he can make anyone fall for him. I guess that's why he thrives in sales. I guess that's why twat-waffle Angela DeMarco was sniffing around.

There are five messages from my oldest, Brynn, mainly asking to hang out with friends. Three from Jordan, same thing. These girls are social butterflies.

Seven from Kelsey:

> *Today 7:03 AM*
> **What the hell did you bitches get into yesterday? Wish I coulda come. Didn't get home till late.**

> *Today 7:04 AM*
> **You alive?**

> *Today 7:20 AM*
> **Hello?**

> *Today 7:32 AM*
> **I guess no gym this morning?**

> *Today 8:01 AM*
> **Still dead?**

> *Today 8:05 AM*
> **Don't forget, you promised me happy hour on Sunday when you get home. Luke said Jake has the kids, so no backing out.**

> *Today 8:30 AM*
> **I love you. I'm here for you.**

I send a bland reply, letting her know Annie and I got carried away. That I'm alright and won't bail on Sunday. As for the gym? Yeah, that's out. And who texts people at the ass crack of dawn? Kelsey, that's who, but I love her. Still, not totally sure I trust someone who's such a morning person.

That's a joke. I trust her. Our friendship is just different. I don't know how to explain it, but it works.

One from Annie.

> *Today 8:09 AM*
> **Hate you so much. But this.**

A quote from my favorite show hijacks my screen, claiming our girlfriends might be our soulmates. It's the one about the four best friends, living in New York. Blah. Fuck New York. But for real, it's a stellar series and an exceptional city.

I respond with a heart. She doesn't require any words from me.

After a few more grumbly minutes, I shower—and somehow start resembling a human again—then throw on leggings and an oversized sweatshirt. A smidge of makeup is required so I don't freak out the kids with the current Quasimodo vibe I've got goin' on.

At ten-thirty sharp, they're home.

It'll go the same as usual. Jake herds them to the house, passes off Will and Roo's stuff, says his quick goodbyes, then jets.

Doors fly open in all directions, and children pile out like it's a clown car. This army of beautiful humans we created is now programmed to hug their dad goodbye. I'm not oblivious to the hurt in the older girls' faces, though they play it off. Learned from the best. To be honest, it makes me wanna tear my heart out, and I see why so many people really *do* stay together for the kids. They're going through something on an entirely different level, something we don't know how to navigate. Neither of us had to deal with our parents splitting up.

I hold the door open, and Brynn allows me the briefest of hugs.

"Did you have a good time?" I ask, losing the battle to catch her gaze.

"Yeah, Alex. It was a magical Christmas."

Dagger.

The attitude is fun. Kind of comes with the teenage territory—we've all been there—but when we separated, it rocketed to a whole 'nother realm.

"Don't speak to your mother that way," Jake snaps after marching up with the other three in tow. I glance at him with an appreciative lift of my lips, careful not to hold eye contact for too long.

"So sorry." Brynn's teeth click together, and she doesn't look at either of us. "It was wonderful, *Mom*."

I wince when she says my name—well, one of my names—then plaster on a fake smile, letting her snide tone roll off me. I'm beyond thankful she and Jordan were at their after-school sports the day it went down. As much as I want to tell her what happened, to spill it so she knows who to blame,

I'm not going to. I will not set my girls up for a life where they distrust men and relationships.

Marriage? Potentially yes. But all men? No.

Brynn flashes an irritated glare at Jake. They resemble each other so much it's insane. He flaps his hand, signaling that's good enough, then she twirls on her heel and beelines it upstairs in a huff. To her room. That she rarely leaves.

"Hi, Mom," Jordan sings, cheery as ever. She tosses a sloppy arm around me in a pathetic imitation of a hug.

Our charismatic second child has adopted the role of peacemaker. Pay attention to the word *role*. This kid is well aware that if her sister's acting up, she can capitalize by schmoozing. It's not lost on me, but I respect it. Jordan is the one we need to keep tabs on the most. A mischievous troublemaker hidden behind a sweet and innocent smile. Another Jake clone.

"You look absolutely stunning today," she says, and I roll my eyes while she skips inside.

"Hey, Roo." I reach towards her petite body and grimace when she returns my gentle embrace with an unyielding squeeze. Our youngest daughter leans away from me, a grin dancing on her lips as if she has a secret to tell, hair unkept and knotty—that's a whole other thing. My little Ruby extends her fingers then taps her side-stretched thumb to her chin. For those of you not versed in American Sign Language, that's the sign for Mom.

She can talk. Sure can. Has a decent vocabulary these days, but she can't say *Mom*—or maybe she just won't. Dad? No problem. Not Mom. And trust me, I'm not above bribery, but if she hasn't by eleven, I don't think she ever will. Another one that took the DNA straight from Jake.

Why do we do all the work pushing these babies out so they can look exactly like their fathers?

"Mommy!" Will squeals and flings himself onto me. A louder-than-intended cry slips out, but he doesn't seem to care, just hanging on me, no biggie. I bite back any pain 'cause he's worth it. They all are.

This guy is the only one who resembles me, with his big blue eyes and light blonde hair. At least I got my stamp on one of them.

"Wish you could stay, Dad." Will shrugs, and his disappointment makes a marionette of my heart.

After the kids disappear upstairs to their sanctuaries, their bunkers stocked with electronics and toys, the two of us are left standing in the entryway.

"You okay?" Jake asks, still holding their bags, watching me as I revert to my hunchback stance. I hadn't realized he'd come inside during the commotion.

"Yeah. Fine. Just slept wrong."

His sneaker-clad feet rock over the hardwood. How's it even possible that he gets away with this ensemble? Later thirties, backwards hat, hoodie, and gym shorts. Flipping gym shorts when it's cold as balls outside. Alright, technically balls aren't cold—go with it. Also, no freaking wonder the kids won't wear the overpriced jackets they *had* to have.

"So, yesterday was…"

"Weird." I complete his sentence absentmindedly then veer my eyes from his.

It *was* weird. My head is all over the place, and I can't seem to get a handle on it. I'm not sure if it's because the holiday shot my emotions into outer space, or that my mind has been strolling down memory lane. I'd scarcely allowed myself to think about our past over the last few months, but something seems to have shifted. Well, probably just with me. But the way he looks, and the emptiness looming in his eyes, it makes me feel… bad.

And why the hell should I feel bad?

"Yeah. Weird." Jake rubs the back of his neck, and his lips bunch to the side. "I—Everyone missed you."

I swallow then glance up at him. "I missed them too." Not a lie. I did miss the people I've grown so used to seeing over the years.

A deafening silence hangs in the air between us.

"Well…" He sets down the bags then pokes a thumb over his shoulder. "I guess I should get going."

"Yeah."

"Unless…"

"Unless what?" I tilt my chin to catch the hope in his expression. His shoulders raise, and I know he's trying to play it cool, but the telltale bob of his Adam's apple gives him away.

"I could stay," he says slowly, carefully. He notices my inner gears start turning then adds a rushed, "Um, only for a little. Only to help you out."

I contemplate his olive branch. I'm so used to snapping them in half lately. Anger certainly has a tendency to skew your responses.

I let out a long sigh, but, truth is, we're gonna have to find a way to be around each other. Not to mention, some sofa surfing might come in clutch today. If he can entertain the younger ones and taxi the older girls wherever they've planned to go, it'll be a big help.

And be real. If someone offers to pitch in, you take that shit and run with it. Doesn't matter if it's the husband you're currently separated from. Minor technicality.

"Help would be… alright." My lips forge a faint smile.

He looks genuinely shocked that A: I'm speaking to him, and B: Nope, just A.

"Are you sure you just slept wrong?" His stubbled chin tips to my achy back.

I ignore his question and pad across the foyer floor.

"Jace said you and Annie were getting wild last night."

I whip my head around. Ow! Why's everything connected? And why is he so close?

"He was here for five minutes," I bite at him. "And he doesn't need to be reporting every single thing back to you."

Of course, I'd give a detailed report if the shoe were on the other foot.

Jake launches his palms in surrender, extremely aware of the eggshells he's having to tiptoe over, while I slump onto the couch.

"Sorry." I adjust myself not so gracefully. Full disclosure, it's draining to be mad, though don't mistake my fatigue for forgiveness. It's just a byproduct of my morning.

He crosses his arms, standing in the middle of the family room, not taking his cautious eyes off me.

"Honestly, yeah, we got a little off the hook, and now I'm paying for it."

This is okay. Super normal. We spent years having conversations. Millions of them. There's no reason we, or mostly I, can't be civil.

Doesn't matter that he looks more attractive than a year ago, or even yesterday. Doesn't matter that my mind and something else in my body— likely severe dopamine depletion—are waging war with each other. And it most definitely doesn't matter that he's shoving his sleeves up to his elbows.

Not at all. I'm not even looking at his forearms. Who cares about them? Why are they even a thing?

"If you remember, I'm fantastic at curing hangovers."

What?

The corners of his lips lift to a sexy smile. No! Not a sexy smile. A devious smile. A smile that, for whatever reason, spurs a chain reaction straight down to my—

"Bacon." Jake rubs his hands together as if he's trying to start a fire, cheesing like he's delivered the correct answer in *Final Jeopardy*. "My crispy bacon should do the trick."

"Right… bacon." I nod in slow-mo.

Guess I'll be getting some meat after all.

There is so much wrong with me.

6. VOLCANO GIRLS

Sore? Check. Still at it with the increased intracranial pressure? Double-check.

Sorry, medical lingo slips out occasionally. Though I'll admit, the bacon helped deescalate my affliction from severe to moderate.

Like I said, two-day minimum.

What has *not* been helping are the rigid cushions on this modern sofa I'd lobbied for last year. Jake wanted to keep our ancient sectional. It was huge and didn't match our decor, but it was the most snug-worthy piece of furniture we've ever owned.

Lots of memories made on that couch.

This is the first time I've let him come in and stay, minus opening presents yesterday morning. That was only for the kids.

Baby steps. Maybe baby steps are what we need?

He comes downstairs from whatever activity Will had him roped into, face intent on the small device we've all become addicted to. His thumbs click away, obviously responding to a text.

I automatically wonder if it's *her*. Jake said there's been zero contact since the infamous sext. Luke handles their New York business now.

But man… once you lose a bit of trust, it's near impossible to get it back.

Okay, fuck the baby steps.

"Who ya texting?" Why do I even care?

He glances up at me, and his relaxed expression morphs into one of pity. Please. I don't need that.

Why'd I ask? He knows who I'm guessing it is. He *knows* me.

"Oh… um… my mom." He clears his throat and peels his attention from… whoever.

Yeah, okay. He left his parents recently, and while his mother coddles the life out of him, I'm not convinced. Plus, she's a caller, not a texter.

Jake shifts his jaw from side to side, weighing my skepticism. "You wanna see?" He struts over and offers apparent proof.

"No thanks." My eyelids close and I sharpen my tone so icicles dangle from it. "I don't care about your phone, *Jake*. It's none of my fucking business."

Chew on those words. That's exactly what he'd said to me the day I saw the damning message—*none of my fucking business.*

Love that line.

I open my eyes to see him hovering over me. He needs to move away, because he's within striking distance, and there are a plethora of conflicting thoughts tap-dancing in my head.

"Are you sure you're okay, Alex? Seems like something's wrong." Ignoring my razor-sharp tongue, he frowns, and my immediate reaction is a *what the fuck* glare.

Everything is awesome. Are guys really *this* clueless?

Truth is, this has become our M.O. Jake takes all our cumulative shit, sweeps it under a rug, then walks over it as if it's not there.

I often park myself in the passive-aggressive lane. That behavior's not healthy, I'm aware, but flaws are legit—no one's exempt.

"I'm fine. I have a killer headache and need coffee." The first is my default response these days. The other two are facts. It's the safer answer because this pounding brain can't handle an argument. And the sooner caffeine hits my veins, the better. For everyone involved.

It'll end the same anyway—we won't get anywhere. And I'm not fighting, not with the kids upstairs.

"I'm gonna run B and Jord to their friends' houses. I'll take Roo and Will so you can relax." Jake flips off his hat, smoothing his dark hair before returning it to his head. He needs a haircut, and he looks like such a kid in his snowboard-brand hoodie.

Yup, still boards after all these years. We spent so many weekends hitting the slopes before we had Brynn.

We used to have so much in common.

Now, he takes the kids with him as often as he can. Which isn't very often.

Navy gym shorts hang from his waist, showing off toned calves and tan skin. I have a bit of a strange infatuation with them—the shorts! They seem to defy gravity, barely staying up, hanging so low, revealing every defined etch and groove leading to—

"Are you alright with that plan?"

Snap back to reality.

"Sounds great." I shake the vision of his half-naked body from my head. Why is this even happening?

Jake calls for the kids while trying to figure me out. Best wishes. The four of them clamber down the stairs, noisier than a herd of elephants.

"Brynn, you're behind the wheel." He chucks his keys at her, and she beams, her entire demeanor a one-eighty from earlier.

"Could you please pay attention and make sure she drives safely?" Yes, I'm annoying—I say it on the reg.

Cue the eye roll. Brynn has it perfected, does it better than me, and I thought *I* was the pro. She has her permit, and Superdad lets her drive all the time. Nothing can prepare you for the tsunami of anxiety once one of your kids is operating a motor vehicle. Especially when they're more concerned about the music than staying in the right lane.

It's no big deal for Jake, who's consistently calm and even-tempered. He simply grabs the wheel and guides her to where she needs to be.

"We better get our helmets." Jordan cracks up, her comment aimed at the younger two, who follow her to the garage.

"Rest up. We'll be back soon."

I flinch when Jake's lips brush over my skin. Damn forehead kisser. I fight the urge to open my eyes. He's so close, his warm breath feathers my face. Oh my God, he smells so good.

No, Alex, don't do it! That shit'll get you twenty to life. And I've already served one sentence.

"Habit," he mumbles, taking my lack of response as an invitation.

His hand covers mine, and I can predict what's coming next, even though it's been weeks since he said it in person.

"I really am sorry, Alex."

I gulp down the emotion and confusion and conflict clogging my throat. "I know."

I do know he's sorry. But...

Words just aren't enough.

* * *

We met the day after both of us finished high school.

My friend had begged me to tag along with her to some campout grad party. They were more common than not, and code for *we are turning a blind eye while our kid and company get wasted, making them sleep outside so there's no indoor aftermath.*

Times were a little different back then.

She promised it was strictly for a booty call, and that we'd be there thirty minutes max.

The place was roaring, people guzzling beer bongs from the deck to the ground. Not my scene. A bunch of fuckboys counting down the days till college so they could rush.

It was like walking through a thick curtain of some animal-named spray, or whatever the fuck.

A few lame pickup lines, combined with offers of drinks in Solo cups— no thank you—and I was over it. I made my way to a dwindling fire at the edge of the yard. No one had started the campout part of the night yet, so I was alone. My ideal waiting spot.

And that's when *he* walked up behind me. Scared the living daylights outta me. He was a mix of preppy and skater boy and... I wasn't sure what he was. Didn't fall under the typical high school *let me classify your social group by your appearance* category.

Relaxed jeans that hugged particular spots nicely covered long legs, while a white V-neck stretched across his broad chest. His almost black hair had a deliberately tousled look without being overdone with product. He wore Vans, because *yes,* Vans are classics. I still rock them.

This guy was nothing like the popped-collar crew back at the house.

He was absolutely not my type. I was an IDGAF, straight-up man-hating bitch. I'd recently gotten out of my second long-term relationship with yet another disappointment. And by long-term, I'm talking about eight months, which was as serious as a marriage in high school.

Jake wasn't into the entire scene either. Went to the prep school to play ice hockey, got a scholarship, and was ready to leave this town. Same as me.

By not my type, I mean my usual suspects were raging douche nozzles. Not him. He was sweet and easy on the eyes.

That's an understatement. He was hot. Is hot.

Tall, dark, and handsome.

He'd asked about my goals and dreams. About my family, and the things I genuinely enjoyed in life. He hung on to every word. It was… meaningful.

Most other guys had their dicks focused on all the college chicks they'd convinced themselves would line up to bang upon arrival. Good luck with that.

Anyway, we ended up talking all night, about everything. Shared a sleeping bag, which led to a PG-13 make-out session, with some heavy over-the-clothes groping. He was respectful. Most guys that age aren't.

Since my friend ditched me, or I ditched her, Jake drove me home early the next morning and promised to call me later that day. All business. He left me with a gentle kiss on my forehead.

I decided to forget about him the second I closed that passenger door. There was no point. We were both headed out of state, several hours in opposite directions.

Only he *did* call. And he didn't stop calling.

We were inseparable for the entire summer. Did everything together. Fell stupidly, wildly, recklessly in love. We promised to make it work—to try. A four-hour car ride wouldn't be too bad. Four years wasn't too long.

The odds weren't in our favor, but we made it. Kind of.

It wasn't exactly four years.

* * *

"Got ya something." His deep voice startles me awake. I guess twelve hours doesn't cut it when you party like you're not in your upper thirties, only to have your body remind you that… yes, the hell you are. Jake passes me a to-go cup filled with my favorite seasonal latte. Yup, I'm one of those—I'll own it.

"Thanks," I reply, grimacing and groaning while getting myself semi-vertical. It's not *that* bad. Feels kind of nice to have someone take care of me.

Only because I'm letting him.

"Still no better?" He slips off his shoes and settles on the couch next to me. I guess he's planning to stay awhile. Dog hair covers his shorts. Cal and Ripley won't leave his side, ecstatic that he's back.

Traitors.

"I'm getting there. Where's Will and Roo?" A quiet house makes me a smidge nervous. Well, when the kids are here.

"Upstairs playing some game my parents got 'em."

Definite video-game addiction. They get everything, and I mean *everything*, from their grandparents. Between the four of them, there's enough electronics to open a mini Best Buy.

Jake gives attention to his canine fan club, but I can tell he's trying to tread lightly, glancing at me out the corner of his eye, wanting to maintain a more casual attitude.

Man… why does he look this way? Why am I a sucker for a backwards hat? Though I always have been. I think because it reminds me of when we were younger. When life was so easy. You know, without all the heavy shit that happens when your heart has to split itself up and invest in multiple people. Before the worry and stress of marriage, kids, and financial stability keep you up at night.

"What do you want me to do for you?" Jake asks nonchalantly, gaze locked on mine.

Several coughs stumble from my throat before I squeak, "Huh?"

New plan: do not look at him. If I sink into th ose hypnotic irises, I'm done. The mechanics that make us human are twisted. I'm horny, hungover, and clearly not of sound mind.

"Alex, how can I help? Do you need me to clean or do laundry?"

Oh… that.

I stifle a laugh. *Now* you ask. How 'bout all the times I was drowning in mountains of it, no end in sight? The years I joked about being the maid.

Spoiler—I wasn't joking.

"N-No. I'm good, Jake."

"Dad!" Will shrieks, the kid literally shrieks, from upstairs. "Dad, you still here?"

"Yeah, buddy, what's up?" He studies me as I wince at every single word. Why must they be so loud?

I space out for a minute while Jake assures Will he'll be up soon.

"Did you take something?" Concern lifts his brow when he watches me try to soothe my spine. I fail miserably because my arms are too short to reach where I need.

The worst.

"Of course I did," I snip. Obviously I know how to take care of myself. I *am* a damn nurse.

"Want me to…?" The heel of his palm ghosts between my shoulder blades. His touch is reluctant, though there's something about it that lulls me into a sense of security.

I want to say yes. I don't know why I want to say yes. But…

"What? No!"

It's a false sense of security.

He retreats, marginally, but his hand lingers while the multiple voices in my head have a heated debate about my body's response. I can't lie—it feels so good. Or maybe it just feels so comfortable?

"Alex, it's only a back rub."

Is it ever? Truth be told, I'm dying for a—cough, cough—back rub.

I have lost all control.

His skilled fingertips refuse to take no for an answer. Jake always knew how to press me in just the right way. How to diffuse a situation and make me cave. That's why I've avoided him so much.

Well, that and the fact that I was borderline homicidal at first.

I sigh but don't stop him. Does this make me weak? The cushion behind me dips beneath Jake's weight as he scoots closer, taking my tensed spine as a green light when it's a blatant red.

Okay, yellow.

To the above question of weakness, survey says… yep.

He thumbs the most painful—in such a good way—circles deep into my aching muscles, which causes an involuntary moan to slip from my lips.

Why am I even letting him touch me? Fuck my actual life right now. And fuck the holiday for making me vulnerable and nostalgic, endeavoring to thaw the edges of my ice-encased heart.

"If… uh… If you move to the floor, I can work you out better."

Bold.

After mulling it over, I give in. Because first, he's being super nice and trying to help. Second, I have absolutely no resolve. Third, *screw it.*

I lie face down on the carpet, forehead resting on the backs of my hands. Jake straddles my thighs, careful not to lower himself too far, and pushes down with mind-numbing pressure.

Light groans and whimpers escape my mouth, swiftly rising to drawn-out moans. They're high-pitched. They're suggestive. I'm aware of how this sounds, but shit, there's no stopping it. His strong hands massage me in the most glorious of ways. I swear, why do I feel like I could get off right now?

From a massage? Imagine.

The firm strokes amp up—faster, harder. I cup my palms around my eyes. Apparently, blinders are today's fashion accessory.

A combination of my pelvis angling to the floor, the jarring motion sliding me up and down, and the seam of my leggings hitting dead center over my… other seam.

Welcome to rock bottom.

My ragged breathing becomes impossible to control. The tilt, the slide, the freaking leggings—it's a perfect storm. Heat surges and blooms. Yeah, you know where. A spark I haven't experienced in quite a while ignites in my belly, or just south of there.

"Alex," Jake whispers, his voice strained. But I ignore him. This is a solitary mission… to a degree.

My hips rotate rhythmically into the carpet, and he doesn't stop. If anything, he takes it up a notch. This gives shag a new meaning.

My brain cells are deteriorating by the second.

I continue to let out moans and primal pants as his hands perform their magic. What is this even? My heart slams in my chest, and any semblance of common sense evaporates. I'm aware it's him, of course I am. But also, I'm attempting to pretend it's not.

His touch drifts to the sides of my body, and he lowers himself a bit, revealing that this *innocent* massage is having the same effect on him. Daring fingertips skim a little side-boob, and unbridled desire—for an orgasm—seizes my lungs.

"Alex." Jake halts his movements. "Should I…" I can hear him work to swallow.

"Just shut up." Yeah, that's my reply.

And he does.

Holy shit, is this going to be an *actual* happy ending?

I am grinding, shamelessly grinding, on the family room floor.

Jake's semi—okay, it's a full—grazes my ass. And this is fucking peculiar, but realizing I still turn him on gives me an immense sense of satisfaction.

"Dad!" Will calls, thumping down the stairs.

Those feverish, opportunistic movements freeze, and I cover my face with my hands.

"What's up, bud?" His raspy words come out in staccato, uneven breaths.

This kid is a blocker. What the hell? Go to your room! Play whatever for hours! No screen-time limit.

Let me have this tiny win.

"What are you doing to Mom?"

He slides his palms to rest on my upper back. "Just giving her a shoulder rub."

"Oh," Will says. "I can give her one too."

"No!" we shout in unison.

No, sweet baby boy, do not come over here to this corrupted, filthy carpet.

"C'mon, Dad. I started the game."

"Fuck," Jake mutters under his breath then reluctantly eases off me after a readjustment.

My face remains buried in the almost defiled fibers. The embarrassing epiphany that I just dry humped the ground takes a front seat in my mind.

I have nothing to say for myself, except…

What the hell am I doing?

7. BITTER SWEET SYMPHONY

The rest of the day goes by uneventfully, but I'm conscious of the perplexed looks Jake sneaks my way. So far, there's been no talk of the whole freaky back rub gone XXX. Yeah, no big. It's a *totally* normal occurrence.

Not that we've had a chance—can't get a word in edgewise. Will and Roo are soaking this shit up, demanding our complete attention with their new toys and gadgets.

I didn't tell Jake that Will's letter to Santa this year asked for Daddy and Mommy to finish their break, and for me to be happy.

He gets to have both, at least for one day.

It's perhaps more damaging than anything, pretending everything's okay. But having them smile and squeal in delight from our undivided and mutual participation makes my heart full and all that gooey stuff.

I sigh, watching Jake with them, letting the two climb over him, rolling around on the floor without a care in the world.

That used to be me. I *used* to be fun.

It's difficult to stop everything and act like a kid again. Someone has to make sure the bills get paid and groceries get bought—online and shipped directly to the door that is. One of us needs to hold down the fort and be the fucking backbone.

But right now it's nice. Even if I'm only a spectator.

Jake plops his hat on Roo's head while they're all in the midst of a laughing fit, the brim covering half her face. Dark, haphazard strands of hair peek out as she dances around, arms flailing at her sides. She hates having her hair brushed. Add that to the list of things that set her off. We keep it as short as possible.

My attention roams from the playfulness in front of me to the school portraits on the wall. I'm thankful our three girls share Jake's thick locks versus my thin mess. And that Brynn inherited her father's hazel eyes. There's nothing in the world that comes close to how amazing they are—like autumn leaves with a backdrop of evergreens.

Brynn has boys falling over themselves to date her, and it's not surprising—she's gorgeous. The major deterrent—*Jake*. He flexes his muscles and interrogates every single one who's brave enough to come near his daughter.

He's been her number one protector since the second she was out in this world.

Even before.

* * *

As we geared up for that final fourth year of college, we were ready. Ready to finish what seemed like a grueling journey.

We made it. Long distance is a walk in the park. Easy-peasy.

Bullshit.

Some days it seems like it was easy because it's often tough to recall that portion of our life. So much has filled the space in between, and time has a way of making you forget. Or not completely forget, but it diminishes the hardships, dulling the edge of the difficulties until they become a distant memory.

While I'd love to say those years we spent in a long-distance relationship were a breeze… that's not entirely the case.

We always scored better when we were together—physically. Our time off school was jam-packed with mostly fantastic memories. But as with most relationships at a young age, and even more so with the miles separating us, we had our share of jealousy and dramatics.

There were missed calls, accusations, and all that typical shit throughout those first three years, but nothing I'd deem out of the norm. Nothing we didn't get through.

While Jake had gone to school to study marketing, his main goal was ice hockey. He loved it, craved it, lived and breathed it. Spent years and years perfecting his technique. But an injury in his previous season derailed plans of having a breakout senior year. One tiny blip. An error in judgment. A twist in the wrong direction, and that dream came to an abrupt end.

He was pissed off, and rightfully so. I understood.

Of course, I was there for his surgery, held his hand, and did all the PT exercises with him over the summer.

I'll always be thankful his parents raised him to see the human beyond the athlete, to know that he had more to offer the world than just a sport. By the end of break, he seemed in a better headspace.

But something was off.

That last fall semester flew by, but the strain of a cumulative everything reared its head. We became so busy, wrapped up in the increased demands of school and our separate lives. The missed calls grew more frequent. Our connection was fading—you could sense it in our limited conversations, in the short fuses we'd both adopted for who knows what reason? The relationship was unraveling. And sometimes that shit just happens for no good reason.

Jake made the four-hour drive to visit me for my birthday, a couple of days after Christmas. I lived in an off-campus apartment. And while we both went home for the holiday, I'd come back right after to work. Sometimes *home* would spur unwanted memories. Not the actual house but the area.

I'll get to that.

He would've shacked up with me if it hadn't been for his advertising internship. And maybe this would be an entirely different story if he had.

Jake despised my roommates but wouldn't miss my twenty-first. He wasn't wrong for hating them either. When his torn ACL healed, he became active—to a safe degree—in snowboarding club and pickup hockey, getting high off the white stuff. Ice and snow. But one of my roomies introduced me to the *other* white stuff.

Yeah… I know.

I'd never dabbled with drugs before then. Alcohol was my poison of choice. I suppose the approaching transition to adulthood and change caused me to question the meaning of everything. When I look back on it, no excuse seems reasonable. But there were demons tucked so far into the corners of my mind, ones I couldn't decipher. Didn't want to decipher. They clawed their way to the surface regardless.

When I tried coke for the first time, the intrusive thoughts became meaningless jargon. It also resulted in me kissing some random guy at an Axe-ridden frat party.

Yeah.

The situation spiraled… fast. We went out for my birthday, and then we fought. Jake didn't want me doing recreational drugs—not disagreeing—and I didn't want him controlling my life. The list goes on.

We were just tired. Tired of living apart, exhausted by the amount of work a long-distance relationship required. So close to the finish line we could taste it, and we threw in the towel.

Before he left, I'd come clean about the kiss, consumed with shame and remorse. Anger brewed in his quivering eyes, but Jake was the type to splinter with his actions, not his words. He said he was sorry I was lonely enough to fuck everything up, and not much more. The last betrayed glance he gave me shattered my heart into a billion shards, and then he was gone.

I tried to call, to apologize, to anything. He refused to speak to me, and it was painful. I didn't feel like our story should've ended that way. I hated that fucking ending. But it didn't matter what I felt, because the credits were already rolling.

I thought about when we were together, and how easy it seemed. But when school was back in session, it's like we were two completely different people.

If we could've just transported ourselves back to that bonfire or our earlier days at the beach… We had the type of love that if it wasn't right up in your face, its absence destroyed you.

And it did.

My poor choices continued, only this time there was no illusion. The harsh anchor of depression smothered me and dragged me under. If it's something you've dealt with, you know what a thieving game it plays. And this wasn't my first rodeo.

After two months of no returned calls, of not answering his door when I could scrounge up gas money, the black hole widened into oblivion. Then I began getting sick all the time.

I wonder if you can guess the next part?

Birthday. Present.

Fun fact—birth control pills aren't as effective if you forget to take them now and then. I'd been religious with my regiment, but with my newfound extracurriculars, I sometimes forgot.

Also, before you judge, I'm not talking *Pulp Fiction*-style line snorting every second. I'm talking about a few times here and there before going out. It's still not okay, but it's the truth.

So… I had to figure out a way to tell Jake. At that point, it was looking like I'd have to put pen to paper.

But I couldn't.

The idea of him being trapped was more torturous than our split. He was the first person to make me truly understand that genuine love was reliant on the other person's happiness. He didn't want me to contact him. And I wanted him to be happy.

Instead, I trudged further into my bottomless pit. I'm talking lying in bed all day with the blinds clamped shut, not showering, contemplating nothingness. I'd been missing classes since the start of my final semester. Suddenly, school seemed trivial. Work? What was that? I loathed everything I'd become. I didn't know what to do. There I was, alone, and rightfully so.

On a random Wednesday, he showed up. It was as if he knew, or he could somehow sense it. He didn't understand what was happening to me—thought it was drugs. It wasn't. I stopped that nonsense the second I'd gotten the positive result. He claimed he loved me and didn't want to live without me, despite any past mistakes.

I was more important. *We* were more important. And he was happy… with *me*.

I told him nothing made sense without him… because it didn't. Told him I was sorry, sorry I'd gotten so lost. That I didn't talk to him. That I'd forgotten who I was. Who *we* were.

None of it mattered anymore. Our lives were already so intertwined, it seemed inevitable.

When I broke down and told him about the baby, he was totally fine with it. Okay, that part's a joke. No, he freaked the fuck out. We could barely take care of ourselves, survived off frozen meals, and took our laundry home on breaks for our parents to wash.

Jake promised, though, we'd get through it *together*.

The sad thing is, neither of us completed that last semester. At least, not then. He was too preoccupied with being able to support us, too worried about me and the baby. I couldn't even think about school. I couldn't function.

It took him weeks to get me out of my apartment, just to sit on a bench outside. But the nothingness didn't go away. Though he held my hand and practically tethered himself to me, the debilitating grip was stronger.

Depression follows no rules.

I was petrified to be in charge of another life when my own was in such disarray.

Every day, Jake would climb into the shower with me, arms secured around my body to stop me from falling apart. He washed my hair, dressed me, brushed my teeth, all the while assuring me of his unending devotion. That we were enough.

We'd *always* be together.

His sole mission became bringing me back to life. If that's not love, tell me what is? He promised we got this, that he'd be there every step of the way.

We moved home after another month, and another hiccup or ten. It was all we could afford. The two—soon to be three—of us had each other. We could do this.

Jake defended my pregnancy with a ferocity I hadn't seen in him before, adamant we were doing the right thing when our families voiced concerns. He squared up to my brother, who responded to the news with a swinging fist. Okay, he actually took the hit and then they moved on.

Brynn came in the middle of a hurricane, in early September. I didn't feel that motherly instinct or the extreme gush of feelings everyone says you feel. It was terrifying, as if I'd failed before she was even here.

Jake was my hand holder, my staunch supporter. He didn't panic when I screamed at him or threatened to choke him—ah, that lovely transition phase. The second Brynn entered this world, he lit up enough for both of us.

* * *

Will is begging Jake to build LEGOs with him.

I hate those tiny, plastic, sharp-edged bastards. If you've had the joy of following the whack-ass instructions or the pleasure of stepping on a piece, I'm sure you're not a fan yourself.

"Mom, can you help?" Will pouts while using his eyes against me.

I groan, but a smile spreads across my lips. I'm talking full-blown.

"Thath's all I wanted for Christhmath." He jabs his finger into one of my dimples.

"You should've asked for two front teeth." Corny. Don't tell me you weren't expecting it.

"Go grab 'em," Jake says, and Will races up the stairs.

We're momentarily alone, and his attention shifts to me while he runs a hand through his hair, side-eyeing me so hard his eye might get stuck that way.

"Can I help you?" I meant for it to come out snippy, but I missed my mark. Damn.

He leans in so close that all I see are flecks of honey scattered throughout the green of his eyes. So close that every single breath—warm, minty, and familiar—draws me to him.

I know I keep fluctuating between caving and fighting it. Maybe I shouldn't? Maybe I should? If I give in, is that telling Jake it's okay? Like when you take the kids' phones for a week, only to return them a day later. I mean, what did they learn?

Why do kids these days even have phones?

"What"—his sights drift to the tainted carpet before returning to me—"was that?"

"Hm? Not sure what you're talking about."

"Alex." His head dips to level with me, both of us now standing. "If you give me an in, I'm gonna take it."

I release a long breath, wishing for simple, aware we've never been that, and praying for clarity—but I've never had much of that either.

"You know what all I want for Christmas is?" He keeps his words low and slow, pushing his way back in.

"Oh my God, please don't say it!" I can't keep this one in, and also… deflection at its finest. "I will die laughing. Do *not* Mariah Carey me."

"Hey." He grabs my hand, his voice quiet, his expression sincere. My laughing stops. "I'm serious, Alex. I'm not joking."

He flattens his palm against the wall next to my head while earlier memories continue to swim to the forefront. His sharp jaw lowers until he invades the space between us, and his gaze falls to my mouth.

The front door flies open, and the older girls stroll in, returning from their little outing.

He drops his hand but stays close, turning to them. "Have fun?"

Brynn gives her signature eye roll, I'm sure wondering what the hell we're doing.

I don't know, kid. Feelings are confusing, even when you're old.

Jordan is wide-eyed, a shit-eating grin spanning from ear to ear. I'm betting her Christmas wish list was the same as Will's.

* * *

Several hours later, after multiple misread instructions and several battery runs—because if they were included that'd be too convenient—we nestle the little ones into bed.

"I guess I'll go." Jake's brows raise in the hope I'll ask him to stay.

I shouldn't.

"Do you guys want to watch a movie?"

The soft-spoken question comes from Brynn. We're both stunned; she hasn't asked that in years. Any movies with her were in the theater—when we paid of course—and when we mandated it, which hasn't happened for quite some time.

"Sure." I beam, failing to mask the sheer excitement that my self-exiled teen wants to hang out with me.

We agree on a Christmas classic. It's just the three of us. Jordan has a way of reading the room, so she made herself scarce. Brynn gets cozy on the couch with a rare touch of a smile on her face. She never gets one-on-one time. I suppose that's a challenge of being the oldest child—they're the only ones with something else to compare it to, assuming they remember that time.

Anyway, you know the film: Different love stories intertwined, the Prime Minister, the best friends, the young boy. I've seen it a ton; made Jake watch it.

Clearly, he never paid attention before now.

The destroyed wife reveals the discovery of her husband's infidelity, to which the husband immediately shows regret—at least to her. And when she asks what he would do if the roles were reversed, if he would stay, knowing things would never be the same… Well, it's one of my favorite lines ever. Because he sees how it made her picture herself, her life.

Jake blinks and exhales a staggered breath, shoulders slumping forward. For the first time, I think he feels the gravity of our situation.

"That's so messed up." Brynn scoffs, mouth full of popcorn. She peers over at me, and disbelief makes her lips tremble as she studies the tears I'm trying not to spill. Then she watches the ring her dad twists with his thumb while he stares at the floor, and notices what's missing from my finger.

She sees it—she sees right through all the bullshit.

And my heart just broke in an entirely new way.

8. LATE AT NIGHT

"What the fuck?" I ask myself for the first time today. Okay, more like the thousandth. The kids were off limits. We'd sheltered them from the details, and now here we are.

The three of us stay up and watch another movie. I'm not sure which one; can't seem to pay attention. Brynn glares straight ahead, eyes locked on the TV. She won't look at us—either of us.

Unspoken questions of hurt and confusion hang in a dense fog around us. Neither Jake nor I dare to budge, waiting for Brynn to make the next move, not knowing where the hell to go from here.

After what feels like years, she gets up without a single word. We both sit in silence, and eventually, Jake, who appears tattered, with dark circles beneath his eyes, drifts off to sleep on the couch.

I let him stay, covering him with a blanket and everything. Brynn will tell Jordan and probably the rest of the world, and their flawless vision of this man will crumble.

It's more painful than I could've imagined.

I toss in bed forever, failing to silence my ever-revolving thoughts, the bargaining that instinctively plays on a loop. If one thing had gone differently, if I'd opened up, if I'd been more fun, maybe we wouldn't be where we are?

Don't mistake me for being soft. I'm not. There's still no excuse for the secrets, the cheating, the potential affair. If he'd gone through with it, I'd be in jail, and we'd be in a completely different story. I would have cut it off. Zero fucks. I'm thankful it didn't come to that because I look terrible in orange—it does very little to complement my fair skin.

But I need to call my ass out for some of the shit I did wrong before we came to this. For the ways I might have altered this outcome. I should've been his number one fan and supporter, like he was mine. Should have made room for him somewhere in our slew of kids. Should have made him feel as though he could talk to me.

Here we are, back at twenty-one, about to throw in the towel, yet again.

Somewhere amongst struggling to solve world peace and contemplating what happens to us when we die, I'm lulled into an unsettled rest. Isn't it so annoying when you want to sleep, but your brain decides it's time to examine the mysteries of the universe?

I'm not sure how much time passes before I feel the mattress dip slightly, and an arm slides around my waist.

If I'm being honest here, I'll admit there's a specific arm that part of me wishes it was. But it isn't. This one's even better.

We never let the kids stay in bed with us as they got bigger. There's too many of them, and we like our sleep, dammit! Plus, sometimes things that went down were not appropriate for an audience. Thank God for locks. But in the last few months, I'd thrown that rule out the window. Will and Roo would tiptoe in on random nights to cuddle, and I didn't kick them out. They need the extra love now, more than ever. I couldn't deny them—I need it too.

This arm is the last one I expect. She snuggles close to me, and soft sobs shake her body, causing tears to sting the corners of my eyes. "I'm so sorry," is all she can choke out.

"Me too, Brynn. Me too." I stroke the hair from her face, admiring this utterly beautiful creature, amazed that I made her. *We* made her.

While she stays scooped up in my embrace, her shuddered breaths calm, falling into that steady sleeping pattern.

I'm awake off and on for the rest of the night. It's one of those where you keep checking the time and thirty minutes goes by like nothing. You know you're probably sleeping a bit but not getting the good kind your body actually requires.

My eyes don't adjust well in the dark, but I catch a shadow near the doorway in the early morning hours. When Jake sees who's lying with me, I know there's not the smallest of chances he'll mess with the moment. This is something she and I have lacked for years. As much as a part of me longs to get up and be there for him, Brynn needs me now. And when your kids need you, you have to be there for them. That shit isn't optional—at least, it shouldn't be.

Teenage years are rough. You desire independence, to be an adult without the real-world repercussions, to make your own decisions. We've all been there. But sometimes, you just need your parents. I still do. Can't wait to see them.

I did the same to my mom. Pulled away, acted like a complete asshole for years, and she took it—mostly. Once I had kids of my own, I recognized how much shit parents endure from their children. But no matter what, the love never falters.

Okay… 3 AM. Deep thoughts over.

I know Jake's destroyed by what happened earlier, by the confession the movie had made for us.

A week after we split, I promised him we would keep it between us. Kids aren't something you play around with like pieces on a checkerboard. They shouldn't have to make a choice, especially not in a situation they never asked to be part of.

* * *

Life had been going great after Brynn was born. She was the best baby, slept seven hours straight the first night we brought her home and kept it up. Couldn't have asked for better.

We refused to take anything from anyone, intent on doing this for ourselves, being adults, owning the choices we'd made. Both of us worked full-time, scrimping to get by—lots of dinners from a can—but we were in it together.

Jake landed a job selling cars and was rather good at it. Unfortunately, we weren't exactly experts at managing money in our early twenties. Things get tricky when you work solely off commission. Some months the checks would be huge, while other months there'd be nothing.

We learned our lesson pretty fast after debt collectors began ringing our phone off the hook. But we dug ourselves out of that hole. No more buying random things you don't need.

Okay, only sometimes.

I took a job as a nurse's aide, but I barely made enough to cover daycare costs. Something had to give. My original path was for a general science degree with plans for grad school. To be what? Who knows? I was decent with science and when forced to declare a major, I went with a broad scope. Some days I'm still not sure what I wanna be when I grow up.

Jake was working thirteen-hour stretches, six days a week, and even took classes on the side. I'm not sure how he did it, but a year after Brynn was born, he finally got his degree in marketing. Problem was, entry-level positions paid a lot less than the money he'd been making, and we could barely stand on our own two feet.

I took the plunge, quit my job, applied for student loans and financial aid, then set my eyes on the prize. Jake's mom and mine split the babysitting time so I could finish up, saving us from outrageous childcare fees. When I tell you these two women are heaven-sent, I *mean* it. It took me a grueling year and a half, but I did it.

The prospect of becoming a nurse had never piqued my interest before. But I had a decent amount of credits, and many of them counted towards my degree. I guess there's something about helping people feel better, making even the smallest change in a life. It's rewarding as fuck.

Then, right before my college graduation, that pukey sensation hit me again. If you've experienced it once, you know exactly what it is.

We weren't trying.

Hold up. I hate when people say that. If you're not using any method of birth control and are having sex as often as you can, you *are* trying. We're all fully aware how babies happen at this stage of the game.

Those two lines showed up, revealing a new squad member. We were both excited. There wasn't the same stress as with an unexpected pregnancy, though Brynn turned out to be one of my greatest achievements. Anyway, our shit was together, and we were crazy in love.

If you'd told me at seventeen, when I met this guy, that by twenty-four we'd be married with two kids, I would have smacked you in the face.

Did I forget to say we got married? Sure did. Not long before Brynn was born.

After the initial baby-news shock wore off, our families vowed to support us, and both our moms hinted about some additional vows. It was an easy decision.

Like I said, crazy in love.

Jake woke me up in the middle of a random night, whispering sweet words of love and promises while he slipped a simple diamond ring onto my finger. Simultaneously, we both asked the formal question we already knew the answer to. It was perfect. It was mutual.

Back to the moms.

The two of them had grand plans for a traditional wedding. Everything was over the top, and I quickly became overwhelmed. Picking out the stupid things and watching bills stack drove me insane, even though it wasn't our money. It seemed so wasteful, and I was already on edge about the impending human, struggling to keep my head in a positive place.

I never cared about a wedding. I didn't grow up envisioning myself in a fairytale dress. When I told the invitation lady what I wanted them to say, our mothers were not amused.

Alex got knocked up. She and Jake are getting hitched. Come on down to their shotgun wedding.

Where's the lie?

Turns out, we didn't need invitations at all.

Jake came home from work early one day and ordered me to pack my bags for a getaway. We could still do that spur-of-the-moment stuff because... no kids.

So we jetted to Vegas and eloped, slightly pissing off our families, but screw it. I went from Alexandra McKenna to Alexandra Everett, on what was amongst the happiest days of my life to date. We promised nothing would *ever* take us away from each other.

Fucked that up.

I nearly passed out from heat exhaustion, and here's why: Vegas is in the desert. It's hotter than a whore in church. I had my own personal heater. It was July. Cankles were in full effect.

Anyway, there we were, two-and-a-half years after being on the verge of falling apart, blissfully married with a sweet little one and another on the way.

A job offer rolled in that Jake couldn't refuse, so we packed our minimal belongings and headed north, moving a couple hours from our families, which was scary. But we got this. I could work anywhere, and as long as I had him, Brynn, and baby number two…

Everything was good.

I started working at five months pregnant, in a brand new state, with zero friends, and the most horrendous nurse training me. She was a stuck-up, snarky bitch. Mean as hell. While we were close in age, she felt her skill set and knowledge were superior to mine. If you've ever heard the saying *nurses eat their young*, it's true. It was sink or swim, and she was determined to prove I didn't have the stones. Joke was on her because I was all in. Plus, I didn't take her shit. When I stood up to her and suggested she ditch her hateful, cunty attitude, she finally gained some respect for me.

Actually, she became my best friend.

Remember Annie?

We began filling our starter house. It was nothing fancy—a cute rancher. Not a bad work commute for either of us. And we didn't just fill it with objects; we filled it with memories.

Brynn was super excited for a new baby—a brother. And in early February, we had our little boy, Jordan, named after Jake's grandfather.

Only it wasn't a boy. The ultrasound tech said she was ninety-nine percent certain, but nothing's ever guaranteed, is it? And if we had learned anything about odds by then, it seemed fitting. We still went with Jordan because… why not?

A family of four at twenty-four. Life was carefree.

* * *

I wake up ridiculously early. Brynn is still fast asleep, and I carefully peel her off me. I could stare at her face forever—at all four of their faces. Something about the miraculous concept that you created these humans is mind-boggling. Gets me every time. Jake's already up, blankets folded, shoes on, dogs out and fed.

I miss *this*.

"Hey," he says, throwing on his hat, covering his disheveled dark locks. His eyes are heavy from sleep, or lack thereof, as he glances at me with a frown.

"Hey. Sleep okay?" I ask, my voice groggy from my own minimal rest. Also, that question is sorta laughable, because I know he hates the couch.

His focus flounders around the room, landing anywhere but on me. "Yeah, wasn't too bad. You?"

Well, it's nice to know he seems to feel the same way. This is awkward. Also… coffee.

I'm still staring off into space, appreciating the moment Brynn and I shared, and a genuine smile stretches along my lips. "I did."

He fiddles with the ring on his finger. He still hasn't taken it off, clinging to the hope that we'll make it back to each other. I cover my hand, feeling a tinge guilty that I don't have my rings on anymore. I miss them. Jake scrounged up whatever he could to buy me an engagement ring. It wasn't anything extraordinary to the outside eye, and later, we could afford an upgrade, but I refused, wanting to remember exactly where we started.

I never cared about an outrageous diamond. I *cared* about an outrageous love story.

"So… I came upstairs," Jake says, attempting to break the ice, walking towards me, somehow smelling fresh. Did he swipe a toothbrush from someone?

His palms gently cup either side of my face, tilting my head to his. His eyes are full of remorse, searching mine for something, anything. It's a lot.

"I saw you."

Yeah, not sure what else to say.

"Did you want me to?"

Hell yeah! Are you kidding me, dude? What have we learned in the last twenty-four hours?

"I don't know, Jake. I'm confused. I don't know *what* I want." Why am I such a damn liar? "What I *do* know is that if I don't get some coffee in my life, someone might get hurt."

There's that boyish grin. He knows coffee is my lifeline.

Usually, this would be the part where I rest my head on his chest, my ear pressed directly to his heart.

But I can't do it.

He leans in closer, his lips hovering near mine. I just can't fucking do it. Instead, I turn my cheek. He doesn't miss a beat and places a soft peck on my forehead after a quiet sigh. Kissing to me is more intimate than sex, and as much as I want to be right back there, I'm not. Everything feels like so much. When he's not around, I'm so sure of everything—my anger, our current separation. But now, when I'm with him, *nothing* makes sense.

He drapes his muscular arms around my body, drawing me in. Okay, I'll let him have this one.

"I hate to tell you this," Jake says, his chin landing on top of my head.

"Mmm?"

"You're out of creamer."

Horror. Story.

"I'll run and get some," he offers.

Never once did he complain about going out to get whatever any of us needed, always stopping for grocery runs on his way home from work.

Feet patter—or rather, thunder—upstairs. The natives are restless, and soon they'll be in the kitchen demanding their breakfast. I know… we have to feed them too. He's the more skilled cook for sure, and if Brynn comes down, it might be better if she sees he's still here. That I let him stay.

And… I don't trust myself around him. I need to regroup.

"No, I'll go."

He leans back, quirking a brow. "Seriously? You hate the store."

"But I love coffee enough to go the distance." Ouch. Those words might hurt if he takes them the wrong way. Maybe I meant it as a tiny jab?

A brief wince narrows his eyes.

"You should try to talk to Brynn." Decent recovery, if I say so myself.

He agrees, and I slip away from him, breaking the contact that did absolutely *nothing* to help organize my sparring thoughts.

9. SHOOP

The dreaded grocery store. Not a fan. You're almost guaranteed to run into at least one person you know, usually somebody you don't specifically care to see. Hence the reason for online shopping. But this is a crisis—a coffee emergency—so I've gotta bite the bullet.

I roll through the aisles. A wonky wheel that's not even touching the ground rattles and squeaks obnoxiously while I truck it to the back of the store. Just as I'm going for my favorite creamer, a large hand shoots up, smacking into mine.

Rude.

"Excuse me!" I whip my head round to deliver my poorly rested bitch face and holy…

Silver. Fox.

Man, I've got a thing for handsome dark-haired men. Who doesn't?

"Oh, gosh, I'm so sorry." He flips his phone to the other hand after his swift apology then looks me up and down.

Talking on the phone? How annoying. I detest when people do that in public. Text like the rest of us, for real.

He is *not* ugly though, so I'll give him a pass. Maybe mid-forties, rocking short, nicely styled, salt-and-pepper hair, topped off with blue eyes that house a playful twinkle and a crisp white dress shirt displaying well-defined pecs. This stud doesn't skip gym days. He clears his throat and buttons the front of his navy suit jacket, looking like he walked out of a *GQ* page.

"I'm going to have to call you back," he says into his cell, his attention not deviating from my face.

Oh hell, I've been staring at him—more like glaring, perhaps ogling. Is that the correct word? I'm enthralled by his striking features and whinny out a weird giggle—I mean that like it sounds—trying to snap out of whatever trance I've lapsed into. It's gotta be due to lack of caffeine. I swear, not receiving your daily dose can make you get off-the-chain insane. Fuck me. Figuratively.

"Here you go." He hands me the container I was beelining for, his fingers grazing mine and making me shiver just a touch.

With my trusty Italian sweet cream secure in my grasp, I'm having a problem peeling my eyes away. He looks like he could have some Italian in him.

Ugh. Trash.

"Oh, thanks, all's forgiven, yeah," I say, barely blinking, not thinking, before shooting a finger gun at him.

A finger gun?

When he offers a smile, my lips separate over my teeth, returning his grin with extreme cheese. *God, stop it, Alex.* I roll my eyes to the ceiling and set my single item in the cart. Why'd I even get a cart? I don't know how to do this. Why can't I move? The two of us are standing here in some bizarre, potentially flirty, semi-silent exchange.

I'm not dead—window shopping is permitted.

I avert my eyes, suddenly riddled with shame. For what? For glancing at an attractive man? Well, I might have been gawking, but whatever. Not whatever. Not Jake. Not nothing. *Shut up!* I spin on the heel of my cushy boot as fast as possible to hightail it up the frozen food aisle.

"Hey," Salt-and-Pepper Fox calls after me. The name seems fitting, so I can't resist.

I halt in my tracks, not turning. My shoulders stiffen at the strange reaction my body has to his voice, to the jolt of electricity that surges down my spine. It's gotta be because it's nice for a man to notice me or look at me, or… just… or.

"Are you Alexandra?"

My brows knit, my lips pursing, and I swing round to face him. His intrigued eyes roam my five-foot-two frame, and a light chuckle quakes his suited-up torso when he lands on my feet. Oversized pink sweats tucked into years-old *ugly boots*, as Jake calls them. Yes, yes, it's a vibe.

"I believe I know you, or specifically, of you. Aren't you Jake Everett's wife?"

He's pretty. Window shopping. Cross my heart.

"Huh?" That's the best we're gonna get right now. Is it hot in here? I tug the neck of my ratty shirt as he approaches me.

"Please accept my apology." He shrugs and lifts his hands in the air, flashing an award-winning smile. "I'm a jerk. I shouldn't have been on my phone not paying attention. Personal peeve of mine."

He walks even closer, delivering full eye contact that makes my palms sweaty, my heart thumpy, and apparently my voice extremely jumpy.

"No p-problem," I respond in an overly shrill, somewhat crackly tone that passed embarrassing about two minutes ago. What am I doing? With my lips forced to a polite smile, I do a queen's wave because… what in the actual shit?

"Are you? Are you the famous Alex I always hear about?"

Oh hell.

"Who's asking?"

Dear Jesus, please make this sexy man leave me alone and allow me to enjoy the view from afar. I am vulnerable, unsteady, teetering off and on the edge of a meltdown, and he's looking like a—

"Hayden Fox."

Yeah, it's not lost on me.

I bite my lip to quell the impending laughter. Of course that would be his name. Universe, you're just having a ball, aren't you?

"Hi, Hayden. Yep, I'm Alex. Nice to meet you."

Walk away.

"Pleasure's mine." He extends his hand, which is surprisingly soft, and I shake it as firmly as possible, probably a little too firm, because he winces. I'm overcompensating, seeking to squeeze these dirty thoughts from my head.

"How's Jake? I do a fair amount of business with him."

Who doesn't do business with Jake?

"We're separated." The words slingshot from my mouth so easily. A simple phrase that I never utter—that I never thought I'd utter till three months ago—slung out like it was common knowledge.

Yup, asshole status unlocked.

"Oh." He stands taller, chest swelling beneath the suit jacket he's smoothing. "Sorry, I wasn't aware."

"Yeah." I lift a shoulder. Okay, time to wrap up this uncomfortable meeting. "Well, nice to meet you, Fox—*Hayden!*"

I bolt to get my cart of shame outta dodge. *What even?* With wide eyes, I twist my head for one more not-so-sneaky glimpse, gaining an unobstructed view of the sly smirk painted on his face.

"What the fuck?" I ask the frozen food aisle. What am I doing? And why did I turn to look at him twice more?

Clean up on aisle nine.

* * *

I head into the house and toss my keys on the counter, clutching what feels like a contaminated plastic container of creamer. Especially when Jake's attentive eyes meet mine. The dishes are done, no kids in sight, and the house is spotless. I've only been gone twenty minutes.

"They haven't had breakfast yet?" I groan and survey the clean counters. There's no way they ate. It always looks like a bomb dropped after mealtime. Kids are flipping messy.

"They did."

"How in the world…?" I motion to the immaculate room. Did he have a maid service come in? Because *what the hell?* It's even cleaner than before I left.

"Cleaned up and made the kids help." He stands from the couch without further explanation and pours me a cup of liquid life. His palm lingers over my hand, now wrapped around the steaming mug. I need this. The coffee I mean. It's gonna be a three-cupper today.

"Wow," I keep repeating, stunned, fascinated by the gleaming breakfast nook. Really, we eat every meal there—I think that's just the technical term.

"You should make them help more, Alex. You shouldn't have to do this all on your own."

He's got jokes.

I choke on a snarky chuckle. "Been saying that for years."

"Sorry I didn't help more around the house. I didn't realize how much work it was till… till I got my own place. You always did that stuff." He takes a step away, frowning, then carefully meets my eyes with an apologetic expression on his face.

"Well, now ya know," I respond with a dismissive shrug before lifting the mug to my mouth.

After a conspicuous throat clearing, obviously in tune to my lack of sympathy, Jake sighs, lips scrunching side to side, probably contemplating what to say next.

Listen, I'm glad he's had a taste of what it's like to rope it all together. To balance schedules and make everything fall in line, while ensuring each kid is clothed, fed, and that the house isn't being torn to shreds.

It's hard work.

"See anyone good at the store?" he asks.

My stance goes rigid, and I cough when my sugared-up coffee trickles into my throat. And yes, I meant throat. I sputter while my thoughts travel back to those icy blue eyes, that smoldering stare. I glance at him, shaking my head no, feeling a tinge of guilt.

Should I though?

He did some window shopping of his own. Even went so far as to try it on.

After a couple more rounds of caffeine, and jamming clothes into multiple bags, Jake helps me herd the kids and load them into the car, dogs included. My parents have a huge fenced-in yard. Whenever we come to visit, it's a package deal. All or nothing.

"Come on, Daddy," Roo pleads with him while yanking on Jake's arm.

"Can't, baby—Daddy's gotta work." His lips turn down; his entire face turns down.

"No, no, no!"

This has the makings of a tantrum.

Will grabs her hands and squeezes them with just the right pressure then bends towards her with a cupped palm. Her eyes go round with anticipation of learning whatever his secret is.

"It's okay, Rubes—Dad'll come next time. You wanna play a game with me in the car?"

This kid, man… wise beyond his years. He is a saving grace for us; knows exactly how to calm her. They're inseparable, and I couldn't be more grateful.

"'K," she says.

Yup, sometimes it's as simple as that, but not *every* time.

She climbs into the car then turns to Jake. "Next trip, Daddy. Promise?"

"I promise." He leans in and gives her a kiss. "Thanks, buddy." His hand ruffles Will's hair.

"You got it—trying to be the man of the house, like you said."

Jake tosses him a thankful smile before going in for a hug.

Jordan's next up with her awkward teenage side shoulder nudge thingy. "Love you, Dad."

Okay, Brynn hasn't spilled the movie night deets… yet.

"Love you too, Jord. Be good and don't be rude to Nana and Pop." He raises expectant brows. Neither one of us can stand when the kids act like assholes towards our parents.

To us? Well, yeah, not on the top ten list. But to the grandparents? Not a shot.

She gasps and clutches her chest. "I would never!" she exclaims with a snicker before jumping into the car. Got a flair for the theatrics, little shit.

"Bye, Brynn—I love you. Be nice to your mother and behave," Jake tells our disgruntled eldest as she trudges to the car. He reaches his arms towards her, but she huffs, denying him an embrace, and slings her bag into the trunk.

"Fuck off," she mutters under her breath.

I'm not cool with that.

"What did you—"

"Brynn." Her name falls from my mouth in a reprimand as I intentionally stop Jake from sparking a shouting match.

There is a time and place for everything. Right before a two-hour drive is not the time, and standing in our driveway, after all the stuff that's gone down in the last twenty-four hours, is not the place.

"In the car… *now*." My teeth clamp into that mom grit. You know, the one that makes them aware trifling with you is a colossal mistake. I'll handle her later.

"Jake." I shake my head, requesting he drop it. "Please let it go. I'll have a talk with her, alright?"

"You allow these kids to get away with too much—that's why they're disrespectful."

I sigh because a scream is the alternative. "Yup, I'm sure that's why she said what she said. Doubt it has anything to do with something else."

"Christ." His palms drag over reddened cheeks. "Is this how life is gonna be from here on out? I can't take any more of this shit." With his fingertips to his temples, he closes his eyes.

I hate that she said that to him. And I hate that she knows. And I *really* hate what I'm about to do next.

My arms wrap around his body, because it seems like the thing to do. Plus, if Brynn sees this, perhaps she'll cut him a break. In reality, I'm winging all of this.

"I don't know, Jake. I hope not."

"Fuck, Alex, I miss you. I miss *us!*" His proclamation is loud enough that if nosey-ass Dennis is outside, he'll hear it.

This entire situation is a mess. I miss him too. No matter what I do, what I choose, it's going to be a life sentence. But here's the deal. It's not only him and me. We have four other extremely important individuals who are watching our every move. I'm serious—I can see their spying stares through the dark tint of my car windows.

Instead of letting my brain sift through the pluses and minuses, the safe choice versus the comfortable choice, I give him an in.

"Why don't you come tomorrow?" Well, that offer's on the table. "Annie and Jace are coming with the kids in the afternoon. You could ride with them?" I lean into his soft sweatshirt, the one I used to always steal, and I wonder if he wore it since he knows how much I love it.

He pulls back from me, studying my face. "Won't that be, *um*... awkward? What about Ava? Your parents? Ashton?"

Ha. I'm convinced awkward is the new normal.

"Oh, please. You know my family likes you more than me—they'll be ecstatic. Plus, I think the kids would love it."

His face lights up, and a grin spans from ear to ear. "You sure *you* want me to come?"

It makes me happy to see him smile. Cut through all the other bullshit, and push that aside for a second. When you feel you've disappointed your own child, it sucks—massively. He and Brynn have always had a special relationship. No matter what, I will not stand by and let them fall apart.

"I'm the one asking you, Jake. Anyway, tomorrow's my birthday, so you have to do what I say." My finger jabs into his shoulder, and I wink. I miss this playfulness. And I genuinely miss being happy.

"Alright." He nods, not bothering to dull his expansive grin. "As long as you're sure?"

"I'm sure," I reply and lean into him once more, letting his familiar scent flood my nostrils as I lay my cheek against his chest. "It'll be good for the kids."

He presses a kiss to my forehead. "I'll see you tomorrow, Alex."

"See ya."

I watch him staring at us as we drive away, hands tucked in his pockets, appearing immensely happy.

Super. Also… totally normal. What could go wrong? My parents *do* love him. Ava is older than me, and while we aren't super close, my sister's always been a Jake endorser, so she'll be cool with it. My brother, Ashton, and Jake are bros, which is—or was—beneficial since we're tighter. Growing up, everyone assumed Ash and I were twins, but nope. Apparently, Mom and Dad had a crazy busy year. He was born in January, and I arrived the following December. We went to school together, same grade, hung with the same crew. After Jake and I became an item, the two of them struck up a friendship. They still board together. At least they did last season.

None of them are privy to the truth behind our split. As I said, we've been keeping it on the low. I told my fam we weren't getting along and supplied no additional commentary.

If anyone's gonna see through the act, it'll be my brother… who happens to be a Muay Thai instructor. You can catch those moves in a pleasant event called cage fighting. If he finds out, well, it probably won't be fun.

So yeah, this feels like a fantastic idea. And rather fitting, since my kindred spirit at the moment seems to be a bull. Red flags are waving everywhere, and I'm hell-bent on charging into every single one.

10. ODE TO MY FAMILY

The car ride is the usual when you have kids co-dependent on electronics—silent. With their AirPods in, the girls snap selfies every five seconds, feverishly tapping away on their devices. All kinds of weird shit like tilted chins and puckered lips is happening. At least it gives me some time to think.

Who am I kidding? Me staying in my own head is one of the worst ideas *ever.*

"Hey," I almost have to yell to pull Brynn from her phone-induced spell.

"What's up?" She plucks out an earbud, not bothering to pause the music pumping into her other ear.

"Listen." I check the rearview, making sure the others are completely immersed and not eavesdropping. Though, if Jordan is, she'd never let on. "Things aren't always black and white, kid. Don't go assuming facts, okay? Your dad loves you guys. You know he—"

"What about you?"

"What about me?" I glance over, having won her full attention, which doesn't happen often.

Her nostrils flutter like they do whenever she's mad. Brynn is so similar to Jake, it's annoying. It's not. When she was first born, the nurse told him he could never deny her. As if. Always despised that shitty comment.

"Does he love you? Because if what I'm *assuming* is correct, that doesn't seem like love to me, Mom."

I sigh, because how do I even approach this? I don't want her growing up thinking this is acceptable. But she isn't ready; nor should she have inside access to all of our business.

"Of course he does, Brynn, and I love him. He gave me you guys. No matter what, I'll love him forever for that alone. There are a lot of… moving parts. There's more to it than just one thing. Your father adores you, same as you adore him." She sniffles, and I squeeze her leg. "I *know* you do."

"Sounds like bullshit to me." She smacks back into the headrest, glaring at the ceiling.

The kid's got a point, but there truly are a lot of moving parts. And she is, for real, taking advantage of the swear words I'm—temporarily—letting slide.

"Can you please watch your mouth, at least around my parents?" Shockingly enough, I come from a semi-strict family, and they don't appreciate an expanded vocabulary. I used to get in trouble for saying *crap* when I was younger. I blame my colorful commentary on years of suppression. "Anyway, your dad is coming tomorrow. We're still a family. Please, at least, for the sake of my birthday, keep things nice. Do you think you can do that?"

Brynn clears her throat, and I peek over briefly, trying to stay focused on the road, avoiding the assholes weaving in and out like their plans are more important than mine. A fast finger attempts an inconspicuous dab beneath her eyes. I'll address the earlier F-bomb at a later time. Right now, this feels more important.

"I love you, Brynn," I whisper with an exasperated rumble of my lips, not knowing what else to say.

If I can't explain it to myself, how can I explain it to her?

* * *

We make the drive to my old hometown. The house looks the same as it usually does, though it's currently decked out for Christmas. Mom and Dad have forever been extra with the holidays. But more so, they've always worked super hard to make sure my birthday was special and celebrated separately. Tonight is for Christmas; tomorrow is for my birthday.

I park in the driveway, facing the impressive tan house, windows adorned with navy shutters that match the front door. The last time I was here was back in September for Brynn's birthday.

Only a few weeks after that, on the last day of summer, is when shit went sideways. It dawns on me that we're already a week into winter. It's been over three months—an entire season has come and gone since that day.

The dogs go ballistic, bolting from the car and gunning towards my mom as she holds the door open for them.

"Hey, guys!" she calls. She does a poor job of hiding her disappointment when she sees Brynn emerge from the passenger seat. "No Jake?" Obsessed, remember?

"No, Mom." I grab the bags from the trunk as the other three shuffle out. "He's coming tomorrow; he's busy with work stuff," I lie. It's easier this way.

Every time I talk to my mom, she says, 'You'll work it out like you always have.' The denial is strong.

"Lemme help ya, darlin'." Dad dots a quick peck on my cheek and lightens my load.

They are good peeps—I love them a ton.

"So, what's new? You guys worked everything out, right?"

Right. The beloved Jake loyalty is insane with these two. I'm not sure if I told them the absolute truth that they would even hold him accountable. He's always been some sort of miracle worker to them. I suppose because of my struggles in college, and the depression I sank further into, depression I'd battled throughout my teen years. They think he's the one who fixed me. Or at least made me stop being so broken. They'd felt like he was my saving grace back then, and, if I'm being honest, they weren't wrong.

When I was younger, I had some rough stuff happen. We won't dig too deep into that, but I'll just say, when people aren't huggers, sometimes there's a justifiable reason behind it.

Before I met Jake, I would break curfew and stay out till all hours of the night. Rules? What were they? I know, tough to imagine, right? Anyway, he did calm me down—not completely, but enough for my parents to see a difference. Enough for them to believe I was alright. Which, for any parent, can be just that… *enough*.

The truth would hurt them of course, but they would find a way to backpedal, so it's pointless. Plus, I have no clue what I want… long term.

"Working on it, Dad. Just doing the best I can." Another lie. I'm literally half-assing everything lately, but they don't need to know that.

We clamber into their house, where sparkling—not for long—hardwood floors span the downstairs. It's a *massive* open space, with tall ceilings, and curved stairs leading to the multiple spare bedrooms. Sounds nice, doesn't it? This isn't the house I grew up in. After my brother, sister, and I were out on our own, my parents upgraded from an overrun rancher to this beast of a house. Probably had a ton of money after they didn't have to pay for our stuff anymore.

My nieces bombard me the moment I step inside, not even giving me time to drop my bags. After fast hellos and swift hugs, they yank my offspring along. The entire group runs rampant, and my parents soak that shit up.

The cousin crew is almost all girls. My three, Ava's two, and Ashton's two. Will is the other golden child in this family. I love that for him.

"Allie." Ava comes in for a hug. She's a few inches shorter than me, which isn't saying much.

"Avie." I lay it on thick. This bitch hates pet names just as much as me.

"Twat."

"Snatch," I respond. Yup, cut from the same cloth.

She keeps her hair short in an edgy pixie cut, and though she has brown hair and eyes, we look strikingly similar. There's no doubt the three of us are siblings.

Ashton runs over and wraps his arms around me, picking me up and crushing me into him.

"Christ, steroids much?" I snort a laugh as he puts me down. This dude is diesel—started hitting the gym when he was fifteen and never looked back.

He smirks, letting out a soft laugh as he slides a hand through his wavy blonde hair.

"Dang, dude, you've been bulking up!" I punch him in the shoulder and it freaking makes my fist throb. He's stacked. I'd describe Jake as muscular and fit, but he's small compared to my brother.

"Gotta keep up, Al. The gym's been going crazy."

"Well, lay off the protein shakes, killer." I rub my arms dramatically from the impact of his hug.

"No Jake?"

Ah, the question of the hour. He and Ava study me with matching raised brows, waiting for my response.

"Got stuck with work—he'll be here tomorrow." I force the best fake smile I can manage. It's good enough for Ava, who heads off to see the kids and help Mom in the kitchen.

"Anything else you wanna talk about, Alex?" Ashton dips his head towards me, forcing eye contact.

"Anything *you* wanna talk about?" I pin him with a challenging expression. He's got his own issues.

After a scoff, he clicks his tongue, but I know he won't push me… too much. "Only wanna make sure my baby sister's alright."

I chuckle. "Only by eleven months, old man."

He shrugs, forever frozen in that protector role.

"I'm all good."

No shot he'll buy this; he knows me too well, was there when shit went down when we were kids. I don't think he ever forgave himself, and part of me believes he's secretly devoted his life to never letting anyone harm a hair on my head again.

* * *

When we were younger, we ran wild with a bunch of degenerates, hanging out in the woods, smoking cigarettes, pot—or possibly oregano. We were idiots. The summer that Ash was fifteen, and I was fourteen, we made the mistake of linking up with the wrong crew.

All of us were drinking whatever alcohol they had, convinced we were cool, and having fun. Then it stopped being fun. Long story short, I disappeared with two of the guys, and Ashton found me… a few minutes too late. The memory flickers like a botched movie reel, but you can probably fill in the blanks.

My parents pressed charges. But since they were minors, they got a slap on the wrist for taking something I could never get back. It's fucked how justice works—or doesn't—sometimes. I was in and out of therapy, but everything was hush-hush.

Now, don't go blaming my parents. They tried their best. Not much helped though. I withdrew, made poor decisions, chose the wrong guys to soothe some void I couldn't make sense of. Though they never did.

When Jake came along, he seemed to heal me, helped me emerge from a consistent darkness. He knows about it. I wouldn't doubt that if he *ever* found himself face to face with those two, he'd slit their throats.

Ashton devoted his life to being able to fight after that. Rest assured, he beat the hell out of them, several times. I begged him to let it go. Then once I met Jake… he finally felt like he could.

* * *

"No, Ash, please don't worry about me," I say, avoiding his concerned stare while refusing to get upset about past events I can't change. "Everything's gonna be okay."

"If you say so." His smirk is skeptical at best. "But if I find out he hurt—"

"I said it's okay! You gotta stop it. We're not kids anymore."

"Fine!" He flings his hands up. "Whatever you say, *Alex*."

Ah, this should be fun—he's gonna be on me like a hawk. Part of me is nervous for Jake, anxious that a dash of the truth will trickle out. But I know if I tell Ashton to back off, he will. I think.

We spend the rest of the day enjoying each other's company, exchanging gifts, and simply being a family. I'm lucky to have them, all of them. Wish it didn't feel like there was someone missing. If only I could flip a switch and get that trust back.

But that isn't me. And it's *never* been my design.

11. BREAK STUFF

The entire family Christmas celebration goes down without a hitch. The kids are now proud owners of more toys and gift cards than should be allowed. Ashton and Sam, Ava's husband, have been getting shit-canned on an array of disgusting craft beer. My brother has some baby-mama drama, so she's not along for this shindig, which is fine. We sorta hate the bitch. The guys keep trying to call Jake; thank God he hasn't answered—yet. Kinda makes me wonder what he's doing.

They're missing their dynamic trio. Those three love to send each other vids of themselves shotgunning beers. It's one of the stupidest events I've ever had to witness, ultra-mature. Occasionally I join in.

Our collective children are running amuck, busy wreaking havoc. Of course, the grandparents let them do whatever they want—they've earned that right. After the craziness we put my parents through growing up, I love seeing them not have to worry so much. They get to enjoy the grands, then return to owner, often with a pound of sugar circulating their bloodstreams. If Mom says no, ask Nana—that shit seriously flies here. Sometimes it makes me sad we don't live closer, though it makes our visits even more special.

I'd briefly thought about moving back here if we go through with the split. But I would never take our children away from Jake, and could never ask him to up and leave the company he's worked so tirelessly to build. He would if I pushed the issue though. He'd do *anything* for the four of them.

For the last few years, Annie, Jace, and the girls have come to stay on my birthday, so we can all hang. Mom and Dad treat them like family. They were always good at taking on more kids than their own. Never sent anyone home with an empty stomach.

Ava—who's not the going-out type—and my parents babysit, which is an undertaking that requires a group effort. This way, we can pretend we're still young and make some questionable choices.

Good times.

"You and Jake working your shit out?" Ava's lips pinch to the side as she raises her glass, failing with her nonchalant approach.

The guys are preoccupied with their chuggies, and Mom and Dad are off with the grandkids, potentially learning new text lingo. Here's hoping.

I appreciate that no one's grilled me on this yet, minus the initial attempt from Ashton. They're well aware that pressing something with me gets them nowhere fast.

"Yeah. I mean… I don't know. I think so."

Fuck.

I shift on the couch next to her as her suspicious perusal doesn't let up. She can be a real judger. Ava's the star out of the three of us. Has four different degrees, overachiever extraordinaire. Ashton and I were a different story, but my parents treated us the same.

"Who cheated?" She tosses it into the conversation like it's a casual talking point, then takes a sip of her swanky mocktail.

I cough and my eyes blow out of my skull. "What?"

"Hah, you believe anyone buys that you"—and she fucking air quotes, which I hate—"suddenly stopped getting along? How dumb do you think we are?"

I glance over, making sure the guys are fully engrossed in their conversation about hops and lactose, or whatever the hell they typically discuss. No one seems to be paying us any mind. Once I turn on the couch to face her, that prissy demeanor dissolves. I think she can see the pain in my expression.

She clicks her tongue. "Damn, Alex. I had a feeling, and so did Ashton, but… I was hoping it wasn't the case."

What? They know? I can't believe they knew this entire time, or at least suspected. After a resounding gulp, I exhale a long breath. I'm not completely sure if it's relief I'm feeling, but it's… something. Like a weight of sorts, or an ugly little secret that I don't have to hide anymore through no fault of my own.

I keep my voice low. "Do Mom and Dad know too?"

"Yeah. Well, they had an idea." Her brows cinch together, and her lips curve down a smidge. "Was hoping we were wrong."

I notice the guys seem to take a slight interest in our conversation. Ashton frowns, glancing over at me while Sam forces a neutral smile.

What is this?

It's not the reaction I'd pictured, and I'm sort of stunned. What do I even say to them? No one is talking, interrogating, or trying to squeeze out the intel. They're all sitting quietly, looking at me with sympathy.

Hold up. They're looking at me with… *judgment?*

"I can't believe you, Alex. Jake's awesome. How could you do that?" Ashton scowls, and he may as well have smacked me in the face.

"Are you…?" My back stiffens against the sofa cushion, and my temper's practically poking me in the shoulder, encouraging me to let loose. "How can you guys…"

Words are becoming difficult to formulate, and a red curtain falls like a hammer over my vision.

What the hell? Do they *actually* have so little faith in me?

Sam raises his palms and excuses himself to go… wherever. Ava takes a dainty drink from her beverage, and Ashton shakes his head, wearing a look of disappointment.

"You know what." I stand abruptly from the couch. My nostrils may as well be blowing out steam, and I'm certain I've developed a full-fledged eye twitch.

"Don't be all dramatic," Ava says, and her voice is borderline bored. "He'll forgive you. Jake's always been a saint."

Harsh breaths pour from my mouth, and heat rushes to my cheeks.

Jake? A saint? Get the fuck outta here.

My foot begins to tap rapid fire against the floor as I wrap my arms around myself, lining up for the kill shot. Because even though we said we'd keep it under wraps, that we'd seal the details for now, why the hell should *I* be thrown under a bus?

"First off," I snap, pinging a withering glare at my sister, "I'd expect you to think the worst of me, Miss High and Mighty."

Ava huffs, but deep down she knows it's true. I don't give her a chance to respond.

"But you." I grit my teeth at Ashton, who presses his fingertips to his chest like I couldn't possibly be addressing him. "You assholes wanna know the truth?" My voice has reached maximum strength without shouting, and my fists clench at my side.

"Alex?" My brother gets to his feet, and I swear, it's like looking in a mirror. His neck angles to the side, and I can almost hear the cracking of each knuckle.

Wait.

"Mom?" Brynn rounds the corner into the family room. Her eyes travel to the three of us, standing in some silent standoff. Okay, Ava's still lounging, not breaking a sweat.

My mouth opens and closes several times. I stare at Ashton, who's genuinely perplexed, then my sights land on my daughter. She looks older, like she grew up in just one damn day. I suppose she might have.

"Is everything okay?" Brynn asks, and there's something in her eyes that makes the angry tears scratching at mine shift to a different emotion.

Would I go back? Change the movie?

Fuck… I don't know.

I sniff and fix a tentative smile on my face. "Everything's fine," I tell her, though the waver in my words is unmistakable.

She takes my standard answer at face value then grabs a drink and heads back to the basement.

I swallow the damning words on the tip of my tongue, and despite wanting to vindicate myself with the facts, I choose to protect Jake instead. "You guys are right." I nod to my siblings as a numbness settles inside me.

What's the best option? To bail myself out? To offer him up for the firing squad? Does it even matter? Would the truth set me free? Would it poison their perfect image of him? Would it change the way they think of me?

"Goodnight." My palm shoots in the air, and I spin on a heel, leaving them calling behind me.

After getting my younger two settled, I close the door to my room, well, one of the spare rooms that Jake and I tagged as our own years ago. I collapse onto the bed, face down, and scream into the excessive pile of pillows spanning the top of the comforter.

Once I've gotten that out, I grab the picture of us from the night table and grind my molars to shreds, allowing the pent-up frustration and hurt to finally speak for me. I slam the frame against the wooden surface. Yeah, all about breakin' shit right now.

It lessens the blow, dulls the sting… momentarily.

It's not even Jake's fault, but I can't help but feel mad as shit at him right now. I mean, it is his fault. However, I'm mad about the judgment at the moment, not the initial crime.

Everybody sucks, and everything is fucked!

I toss and turn, lying awake for hours dissecting why I didn't just spill, concluding that it's easier this way. No matter what, I'm their blood—they can't cast me out. Well, they could, but they won't. If they knew it was him, their flawless ideal of Jake would shatter into a million pieces, and I'm not sure that's what I want.

I don't know how it'll be tomorrow once he's here. Or where we'll be when the next season rolls around.

At midnight exactly, after my anger had dulled to that familiar ache, my phone dings. A text from Jake; a standard birthday message. He always waited up every year, wanting to be the first to wish me happy birthday.

I don't respond.

* * *

Somewhere around two in the morning, I wipe the shards of glass away from the picture and stare at the baby-faced, crazy-in-love, twenty-somethings. And regardless of the current clusterfuck, I can't stop feeling disappointed we let them down, so I text Jake.

> *Today 2:05 AM*
> **Thanks, sorry, just saw this.**

I'll leave it at that—he's most likely asleep. I watch the screen for a few seconds, but right before I switch it off, those little dots appear.

Today 2:05 AM
You're still awake? What are you doing?
The guys stopped trying to call me hours ago. You okay?

I hesitate but only for a moment before responding to him.

Today 2:06 AM
Can't sleep. Birthday blues, I guess.

Ugh, why did I text that?
A reply swooshes in immediately.

Today 2:06 AM
Wanna talk?

I thought that's what we're doing? But I guess I'm wrong, because a low tone rings from my phone before I have a chance to message back.

"Hey," I say to my screen as the video springs to life. Jake comes into focus in all his non-T-shirt-wearing glory. He scrubs a palm over his face; he looks like he was in a deep sleep.

His phone never used to wake him.

"What's up? Did something happen?" He slides back to sit against the headboard. His hair's unruly up top and trimmed shorter on the sides than earlier today.

I avoid his questions. "Got a haircut?"

"Yeah." He yawns, running his damn hand through those dark locks. "I can't even see you."

It's pitch-black in here. "Trust me, I'm all kinds of haggard right now."

"Alex, you're always beautiful. Turn on the light."

Ugh. Why's he have to say stuff like that? I mull it over for several seconds. But… damn, I miss him. I wish I didn't. I wish the feelings, the tumultuous emotions, could switch on or off as fast as the lamp I just brought to life.

"Hey." Jake studies my face.

"Hey, yourself," I respond, letting myself grin like an idiot at the sight of him.

Hey, yourself? Seriously, Alex?

We stay on the phone for about an hour, mostly chatting about the kids and my family. I explain the assumption, and Jake apologizes—profusely— promising he'll come clean. I ask him not to, at least for the time being, and we leave it at that. Then, for the first time in a long time, we simply talk. Not scripted, routine words, but real stuff. We speak and listen.

See, it wasn't only my husband I lost that day… it was my best friend. So maybe we can start there, because I could really use a friend these days.

That being said, I'm *not* discounting the idea of benefits.

* * *

The kids come in like bats outta hell, waking me up far too early the next morning. Will and Roo bounce up and down on the mattress, still in pajamas, like a pair of over-energized jumping beans.

"Happy birthday," they sing in unison at max volume. The usual.

"Thanks, guys," I croak, rubbing the sleep from my eyes then calming my hair, which I'm sure is a whole new realm of messy.

Birthdays are whatever. Don't get me wrong, I'm thankful for each trip around the sun, as we all should be. But they're weird as you grow older. You begin contemplating the meaning of life and start thinking about how you want to leave your mark on the world.

Every year, on the morning of my birthday, the kids come in and wake me with breakfast in bed. One day out of the 365 that I get to sit back and not lift a finger.

Top shelf.

Jordan stands at the side of the bed with Brynn and hands me a box haphazardly covered in bold paper. At least they tried. I tear it open while four sets of eyes eagerly await my reaction.

A picture.

I quickly glimpse the remnants of the one I smashed last night and regret weighs in. I can't take it back.

My attention returns to the photo in my hands, protected by a solid pane of glass, surrounded by a silver frame. There's no stopping the smile that stretches across my lips at the memory of us on the beach last summer.

Don't you love how you can look at a picture and be transported back to that exact slice of time?

"That's from me," Jordan chimes in, evidently proud of herself.

"It's from all of us." Brynn rolls her eyes at her sister and plants her palms on her hips.

"Thanks, guys. I love it."

The birthday pile-up hug-fest proceeds.

I can't help but stare at the picture. It was such a fantastic vacation—we went down south to a beach in Carolina and fell in love with the place. Had a freaking blast. We were so happy in this picture, and it kills me. Rips my heart straight out of my chest and pierces it with a rusty, tetanus-infested blade.

Okay, that's maybe a *tinge* dramatic, but it hurts.

"Dad picked it out," Will says. "He thought you would love it."

"I do." My fingers linger on the glass as I give appreciative thanks to my crew.

And just like that, Jake weaves his way back into my heart a little more.

Moving on.

After the tornado of kids, gifts, and breakfast, my parents take them out. Mom totally comprehends the wonder of doing nothing and vegging out sometimes, knowing your kids are being cared for. She can whip those hellions together faster than anyone, forever running a tight ship.

As for me, I get to do exactly what I want this morning. I get to lie on the soft, plushy comforter for most of the day and starfish, something I've come to enjoy since having a bed to myself.

Don't get filthy-minded on me. The form of starfishing I'm referring to is when you stretch your arms and legs out as far as you can. It's a treat.

A ridiculous amount of social-media notifications wish me happy birthday as I scroll through my phone.

A text from Jake:

Today 10:29 AM
Happy birthday again. Can't wait to see you.

Six from Annie:

> *Today 9:13 AM*
> **Happy birthday, slut!**
>
> *Today 9:25 AM*
> **Ummm Jace just told me that Jake is riding to your parents with us? What up with that?**
>
> *Today 9:27 AM*
> **Hello!?!? Details!!!!!!**
>
> *Today 9:35 AM*
> **What happened after Christmas?**
>
> *Today 9:45 AM*
> **WAKE UP!!!! WTF**
>
> *Today 10:01 AM*
> **We'll be there around 2. Meeting everyone at 7.**

I respond to her with an extremely short, and mostly avoidant, explanation, stating Jake's presence is for the kids. But it's Annie, so she sees right through me and replies with a "'K." Huge peeve. Then she sends me a meme about birthday sex.

Yeah… not gonna even react to *that* one.

As for the "everyone" she mentioned in the text, it's just two friends I grew up with. We've been tight since around twelve. You know the type of friends you might not talk to much, don't even text much, but when you get together, you pick up right where you left off? That's them.

Stupid Annie and her nonstop ridiculous memes. Now all I can think about is birthday sex. So why not text Jake?

> *Today 10:42 AM*
> **Can't wait. Hope you give me a present.**

Wait, did I say give? I meant get. Okay, maybe I didn't. Could I be any thirstier?

I spend the rest of my day lounging, not taking care of anything or anyone, reading one of the trashy books I have stockpiled. The ones I can never dive into with the kids always glancing over my shoulder. It's heaven.

Now don't think I'm gearing up to forgive and forget. I know it seems like I'm wearing down. I'm not. Well, not *completely*. I won't forget it, not ever.

But shoot, it's my birthday, and I'll have fun if I want to. I'm just gonna need a decent amount of liquid courage on board for what I've got planned.

12. CLARITY

I allow plenty of extra time to get ready—which takes ridiculously long.

Dudes take a shower, maybe shave, slap on some deod, a splash of cologne, two to three mins with the hair products, and boom. Camera ready.

Pipe dream.

Speaking of shaving, I myself prefer a bit of stubble on my man's face. Helps massively with a certain thing. If yours is in the market for some facial hair, treat yourself to that. And I'm not talking bristly, scratchy nonsense but just enough so it's past that stage. Trust me, the tickle is an assistive device.

Am I referring to Jake as my man? Not gonna overthink *that* one.

Anyway, here I am, putting the appropriate adapter on the blow-dryer, so my hair doesn't do a complete frizz freak-out. I'm not even sure if it's the proper one. As for the rest of the *get yourself ready* process, it's simply not a two-to-three-minute ordeal. At least not in my experience.

If your strands are dry, you might opt to lather up that conditioning treatment, because hair masks are apparently a thing. Then it's on to the moisturizing or exfoliating face wash. That choice depends on how your skin wants to act that day. And let's not forget the chore—yes, it is a chore—of pruning the legs, pits, and whatever else you're into leaving bare. No judgment on whether less is more for a female, not a male. See above. I mean, I prefer a smooth surface on my own lady parts—that is till it grows back in and gets… uncomfortable.

And let's talk after the shower. The lotion, the brows, the—cough, cough—stash. Why not add that beast into the mix?

It's a lot of work, right?

But you know why we do it, or why we should? For ourselves.

So all the prep is done and now it's on to the makeup tutorial. A highlighter is a writing tool as far as I'm concerned. Jordan can contour far better than I can, but I still give it a go.

After I'm satisfied with the shimmery copper shadow that makes the blue of my eyes pop—Kelsey's words, not mine—I finish up with enough mascara to make me look like I've got falsies on. I'm proud of it. It's not overdone but, for sure, not my go-to, natural-ish, I'm-too-tired-to-give-a-shit everyday image.

I snap a bathroom selfie, internally cringing, and send it to Kels. She's a bit of a project person, an interior designer by trade. Her work's been featured in tons of home-style magazines, and her talent's undeniable. Besides that, she's an appearance guru who's been itching to dig her claws into me for months now. Help me get my groove back... or something like that.

She replies with multiple fire emojis, telling me to "give 'em hell," and reminding me of our plans after I get home tomorrow evening.

That's right, can't forget that one. I've ditched her one too many times lately. I've just been in such a funk. The thought of going out and having to *people* sounds like a terrible idea. But she's my friend, and effort needs to come from both sides. Plus, I'm already starting to feel like I got some groove back.

With my hair neatly straightened and smooth, makeup on point, nothing in the teeth, I'm kind of flabbergasted. In a good way. Watch out world, here I come.

My parents, siblings, and the kids get home at the same time Jake, Annie, Jace, and their girls pull into the driveway. I had a brief morning exchange with Ashton and Ava, waving off whatever that was last night, not wanting to revisit it. Car doors slam left and right, and the mayhem that comes with ten kids combined ensues.

After covering my going-out shirt with a zip-up hoodie—we must protect the hair—I meet them in the entryway. Hugs are exchanged all around amongst the mix of chattering, joyful people. It makes my heart all warm and shit.

"Hey, Livvy!"

"Hi, Aunt Alex. Happy birthday." Annie and Jace's oldest brings it in for a full embrace. She got it from her mama.

Piper, Will, and Roo give a combined squeeze, shouting celebratory wishes that make me smile. Though I'm careful not to mess up my hair or face.

Shallow? Oh well, it took work.

Annie shoots me a wicked grin, wiggling her finger after taking in my getup. "Hey. Wow. Get a load of this birthday girl."

She moves in to hug me; always says she doesn't give a damn if I hate it or not. I return her tackle with a trademark pat. Her head cocks to the side, and she examines me with a scrutinizing stare.

"I knew it," she whispers, referring to the suggestive meme she sent earlier.

I roll my eyes. "You know nothing."

She laughs, because she knows something, and her nod of approval informs me I hit my mark. A big shout-out to the hair and skin gods for their cooperation!

I search for Jake's reaction. Only because he's, for sure, not used to seeing me like this. He's tangled up in a convo with my dad, more than likely about a tech-support request. They use and abuse him for his technology-friendly ways.

A low whistle comes from Jace. "Happy birthday, Alex. Twenty-five suits you well." He nudges my shoulder with his, like we're bros. That's kind of how it is with us.

"Fuck off my best friend, you perv." Annie whacks him in the chest, but she's totally playing. She also kept her voice down because… the dreaded F-word.

"She looks hot," Jace says with a shrug.

That snags Jake's attention, and he glances my way. His neck snaps back, the double-take blatant, and he makes no secret of politely squashing the convo with Dad.

"Obviously. All my friends are hot." Annie frees her hair from the bun on top of her head with a pout. "Think you could help a girl out?" she asks me.

As if she needs any. Her features are so complimentary—chestnut hair, crystal-blue eyes, and a winning personality to boot. I gotta work a bit to balance all the fairness out for myself. But shoot, I'll take this win.

"Hey." Jake goes for a hug then stops in his tracks, probably not sure what the appropriate greeting is at this stage of the game.

Me neither, but I find myself stepping into him regardless then lifting my chin because it just feels right. There's no hiding his surprise, but he speeds through my green light like he said he would. His arms hook around my waist, and he draws me closer.

"Hi, Alex." His voice is so gentle as he drops his lips to my ear.

"Hi." I lean back, and his grip tightens on my hoodie. The silent embrace continues, and I push the potential thoughts of our onlookers to the background, not picking apart the dynamics of my decision… for now.

"Did you like your present?" he asks, a hint of a smirk on his face. He knows it was a slam dunk.

I nod while he slips a finger through a rogue strand of hair over my shoulder and let the memory swallow me whole.

The six of us were standing in the surf, waiting for Annie to take the picture. Little did we know, a wave was brewing behind us. She snapped the shot at the exact moment of impact. The kids' faces, along with mine, were hysterical, loaded with comical surprise. Then there was Jake. He didn't falter for a second, his arms secured around Will and Roo, expression deadass serious. He wouldn't let anything happen to them.

* * *

We do the whole cake, singing, celebratory shit. It's mostly for the kids. I don't even like cake. Well, unless it's by the ocean.

Yeah… I embarrassed myself with that one.

Annie gets herself together in no time, much faster than me, letting her hair hang down in perfect loose curls. She wears a cute white V-neck, with tasteful cleave, and dark skinny jeans the same as mine.

My outfit is a little something Kelsey lent me for the occasion, totally not my style, but… fuck it, it's my birthday. A black, completely lace, and overly tight long-sleeved top, with the smallest, minimally concealing tank underneath.

"Holy hell!" Annie's jaw drops when I finally gather the guts to unzip my hoodie, having kept it on for the duration of her prep. "You look like…"

Nerves have me bouncing from foot to foot, praying I don't roll an ankle in these ridiculous wedge boots. She stands there gawking, making me feel self-conscious. I start to zip it back up. I can't wear this—what was I thinking?

"Nuh-uh, Alex, take it *off*. You look amazing. Jake's gonna blow his load! You look like… like sex on a stick!"

My cheeks are on fire, but we both crack up. I love this woman so much. "Is it too slutty? I mean, I'm fucking old."

"Bitch, we're *both* old. But tonight, you are bringing it." She does some sassy finger snaps. "It's exactly what you should be wearing. Let him see what he's been missing."

* * *

We make sure the kids are as settled as they can be—Mom and Ava know the drill. I've laid out Roo's meds for them, and even though they never need a refresher course, they listen to me recite her regimen. I'm confident they've got it.

The four of us head out to our Uber, approaching our self-appointed doors. We always make Jake sit in the front because he's the tallest and most social. He'll strike up a conversation with the driver and make a new friend.

Annie punches Jace lightly on the shoulder, not doing a great job concealing her nod towards the passenger door, like they've already cooked up some sort of scheme.

"I'll sit up front!" Jace blurts out, beating the usual co-pilot to the handle and ducking into the car.

Jake throws his hands in the air. "Okay, man." His nose scrunches, and he seems a smidge confused by the change-up.

I pull open the door, ignoring the current ploy.

"Nope," Annie says, jumping in front of me. "You're the smallest, so you're riding bitch."

For those of you who don't know, she's referring to the cramped middle seat. I give her a sideways glare, because I know what she's playing at. She's on a mission to keep the quarters close.

I do our little *I see you* gesture with my fingers, and she laughs then stalls before getting into the car, arching her brows behind me. Jake presses his body flush to mine, placing a hand on each hip. And I don't stop him. The heavenly scent that's just him slithers into my nose, and any logical thoughts completely disintegrate from my brain. Man, he smells intoxicating.

Alex, stay on track.

Not intoxicating, sobering.

I dip into the car and buckle quick to avoid having to fish around under him, which is a prospect when you're jammed in the back seat. He rarely wears a seatbelt. It's something that sincerely pisses me off and sets a terrible example. His hand weasels down to the side of my ass, and I swing my head towards him.

"What are you doing?" Heat races up my neck, and I'm not gonna lie, thoughts of an innocent… massage are humping to the forefront of my mind.

Thumping! I meant thumping.

"What's it look like I'm doing?" Jake lowers his face to mine, so we're mere inches apart.

I mentally slap myself, unable to peel my eyes from his, which are practically *screaming* sex. He buckles and leaves his hand resting against my side. I'm feeling like I could jump him right now. That wouldn't be awkward. Not at all.

An extended finger ghosts over my lace sleeve. "I like this," his deep, throaty voice murmurs in my ear.

Did I say deep throaty? Yeah, I did.

His stubbled jaw grazes my cheek, making me whimper from just the warmth of his breath against my skin.

"Thanks." I can barely breathe right now. I'm literally dying. "I like yours too."

Oh, come on, this is so cheesy. Also a little uncomfortable. What are we, teenagers? Either way, I give in. My open palm grazes over the thin material of his fitted—not overly—light-blue shirt. His defined bicep, which is legit making me throb, tenses beneath my touch. With his sleeves rolled to the elbows, I trail a finger down his arm, tracing the intricate waves of his tattoo. This one is Jordan's. He has one for each of the kids' astrological signs, amongst others.

We are locked in on each other in some strange feeling up, or down, or all around, of the arms. I'm completely lost in the six or maybe seven o'clock shadow surrounding his parted lips, while his eyes, framed by long, thick lashes, sear into mine.

"Ahem," Annie says then clears her throat.

I sling my head towards her as she erupts in a rowdy laugh.

"You guys ready to go in? Or do you just… need a room?"

I blow out a breath and shake my head, snapping out of whatever lust-filled hypnosis he put me under. With a stiff smile, I straighten in my seat. Jake makes a minor adjustment himself.

"Yes… I mean no." Cue the nervous laugh. "Let's go."

13. MOVE ALONG

Shakey's looks the same as it did when we used to frequent the fuck outta here as under-agers, all of us rocking IDs that were disturbingly fake. The bartender never cared, so long as we had something to show. Sticky, faded wood floors that have never met a mop span the space. A lingering aroma of bleach and stale cigarettes permeates the air. This was the original place for poor decisions.

Side note, so glad smoking indoors is pretty much nonexistent now. The next-day hair scent wasn't cute.

Erin and Casey, my OG besties, have already snagged a high-top between the bar and makeshift dance floor. The two of them were gung-ho for a mom's night out. We greet each other with hugs—well, they toss their arms around me while I offer each of them my token pat. Their faces share the same expression at the sight of Jake behind me, his palm secured on the small of my back; when the girls eye it in unison then direct their disapproval towards him, he shoves his hand in his pocket. Aw, poor Jake, feeling the wrath of my ride or dies.

They know the story—of course they do. They know all my darkest secrets. Almost all.

"Casey. Erin." He addresses them with a slight nod in their direction, apprehensive of their matching scowls.

"Hi… Jake," Erin responds in a cool tone.

Casey gives him a flat wave, accompanied by an eye roll.

Down, kitties.

I shoot them each a teeth-clenched smile with enormous eyes, like, *I'll fill ya in, just chill.* Erin claps back with a silent, *You better spill it, and now.*

He tugs the neckline of his shirt, shifting from foot to foot. "I guess I'll go get some drinks?"

I'm very aware he's making it a point not to lean in too close to me, understanding his *every* word is being closely analyzed to use against him later. What can I say? Women are fierce and, many times, blind supporters of their friends.

"That would be great. Can you grab me my usual?" I flash him a quick smile. That's right, a nice, refreshing vodka soda for me.

"You guys, um… you ladies want anything?" Jake asks, the underlying unease apparent in his stuttered words. He tips his chin to Casey and Erin, who both deliver icy glares.

Oh no.

"I'd love that. Thanks so much, *Jake*. How considerate of you to think about someone other than yourself." Casey is game on right now.

I plead with my cinched brows for her to cut it out.

She sighs and rolls her eyes. "I'll have the same as Alex."

"Water for me… Jake." Erin enunciates the living hell out of the J, and slices right through the K.

God, this is so uncomfortable. I should have texted them to give a heads up, but it obviously wasn't the plan till yesterday.

Jake wanders over to the bar after acknowledging the somewhat venomous order.

"Really, Er? Water?" I question the former wild one of our group.

"What can I say?" She lifts a shoulder with a light chuckle. "Not trying to pump and dump. I work way too hard for the shit as it is, and anyway, I'm driving."

I can totally relate to that. If you choose to—and you can do whatever you want so long as you feed your child—breastfeeding is one hell of a commitment. It can be so tough. And she's a full-time working mom. I've done both. Neither is easy, so let's settle that debate right here and now.

"I get it." I most definitely do.

My focus strays to the guys, who are requesting our drinks. Jake's fingers tap in a high-tempo beat against the bar, eyes on mine, with a look that says *please save me.* I'm sure he's uncomfortable. The tension is happening.

"So, what's up with this, Alex?" Casey flips her wrist then points a finger at the man in question. She and Erin coordinate their angled heads and pursed lips, awaiting an explanation.

Annie scowls at them, then tosses me a frown, taken aback by their reaction to his presence. "I thought you all liked Jake?" she asks, looking like someone pissed in her cereal.

"We *did* until… ya know… what *he* did," Erin explains matter-of-factly, keeping her attention on me.

Here's the thing. Annie only knows me as Alex who's married to Jake. She's never known me a different way. Casey and Erin have been my friends since middle school. We've been through so much, and grew up together. They've always loved Jake, but they'll be loyal and protective of me above all else. Old-school girl code at its finest.

"Guys, it's just… complicated. It's not that easy."

The primary subject of our conversation glances my way, as if to ask if it's safe yet. A subtle sway of my head alerts him that the claws are still out.

"We have a lot of history. And these last months have been… tough." I pick at the napkin in front of me, avoiding the simultaneous annoyed stares.

"Listen, Al," Casey says, "we love you. We don't want to see anyone get hurt."

A little late for that.

"All I'm gonna tell you is…" Erin perches her elbow on the table, chin resting on her curled fist. "You've heard the saying." And because I've known her forever, I don't even need to listen to the words coming out of her mouth. "Fool me once, shame on you. Fool me *twice*, shame on me."

I sigh as Annie sits and keeps her mouth shut, which is ultra-challenging for her. I squeeze her hand, and she works her jaw, pretending to be interested in something else happening at the bar.

"Let's just have fun tonight." I put the conversation to bed.

Casey and Erin both agree to let it go… for now. I wink at Jake, signaling it's safe to re-approach, and he responds with a relieved smile. He and Jace come back to the table with our drinks so this night can get rolling.

Somewhere between cocktails two and three, Casey gives the cold shoulder a rest, chatting up the guys. Friendly—almost. The hostility isn't so bad anymore, though Erin still holds strong with her protest. Jake sits on the barstool next to me, and I don't object when he places his palm on my thigh. I guarantee it's noticed, but they understand when enough is enough. And they aren't living my life for me.

The only other thing that's said about the whole situation is when the guys walk outside.

"You're looking extra hot tonight, Alex." Erin raises her eyebrows in a fast wiggle. "How a mom of four can have a body like yours isn't right. I'm struggling with the baby weight from one."

"Please. You look amazing… and also need your vision checked." I shrug, head down. Why's it so hard to just take a compliment?

"*Obviously* you're trying to get it in." My old friend smirks before sipping her water.

My drink sprays from my mouth at her blunt evaluation.

"I'm just saying. Maybe don't make it… easy for him." She pops a shoulder with a click of her tongue.

"Noted." I already got a little somethin' up my sleeve.

The place is jamming and getting more and more packed by the minute. Sweat and laughter hang thick in the air, mixed with an added dash of cheap cologne. This place really does reek of bad decisions.

Jake and Jace are immersed in a deep conversation about who knows what, and Ashton still hasn't shown up. He had some stuff to handle earlier. Even so, he's almost *always* late. I'm trying to pace myself, so I can hang in there with a steady buzz and not get shit-faced. Jake's made it a point to position himself close to me. If his hand isn't on my thigh, his leg is touching mine. Or his arm. Or his fingers. You get it. I'm done fighting this—I think I've made that clear.

It's got a middle-school-dance vibe though—the girls talking about our things and the boys off in their own discussion. It works. I love when I get one-on-one with Casey and Erin. I'm so glad they accepted Annie into the crew. Everyone gels, and it's easy.

"Gonna hit the bathroom," I announce to the table as I stand.

"You want me to come with?" Casey doesn't really ask, already getting up.

It's true, we usually travel in packs. What can ya do?

We zigzag through the sea of people, some dancing, others stumbling, both of us groaning but also smiling. It transports us right back to our younger days.

"God, I don't miss this, Alex. Do you?"

"No." I chuckle, shaking my head. "I miss when life was simpler, but I don't miss all this bullshit." My hand waves around at the sloppy amateurs.

I *do* miss the excitement of spontaneity. After years of a similar routine, everything becomes programmed. Monotonous. Same old, same old. But… it always felt safe. No recklessness—well, minimal in comparison. It's a comfort and a curse, knowing what to expect each day.

And speaking of recklessness…

"Oh, for shit's sake," Casey grumbles then folds her arms in front of her chest, a snarl curling her lips.

Joey *fucking* Belter.

He was the *it* guy years ago and absolutely aware of that. The over-compensating man-whore hooked up with every single one of my friends back in the day, everyone but me—because I didn't want his skeezy self anywhere near my body. He's attractive enough, but per his internet info, he's single, likely an eternal bachelor. Not marriage material.

"Hello, ladies," he says, unabashedly examining my outfit.

Okay, he's a creep.

"Hi, Joey. Still living the slut life?" Casey asks, cracking up. No filter on this one. They dated for a hot minute in our twenties. We all warned her not to. He wasn't the committal type; he was a *fuck 'em and chuck 'em* type, the kind of person you stay away from if you have any dignity.

"Ha!" He doesn't take his eyes off me, gawking blatantly at my chest. I hug myself to block his view. "Not everyone is lucky enough to live the absolute dream of popping out a ton of kids and being trapped in a caged life. I'm sad about it."

I think it's probable that his douche status has topped the charts.

A sound bordering on a growl rises from Casey's throat. "You're a fucking loser," she says through gritted teeth while I remain silent.

The hallway leading to the bathroom suddenly feels much smaller.

"How are you, Alex?" The repulsive eye-fucking continues as he dismisses her and advances his antics with some suggestive lip-licking.

"Fine, Joey." The urge to get the hell away from him is extreme.

"Hey, it's your birthday, right? I tend to remember the date." His grin makes me feel sick. "Technically, it was the day before, but you know what I mean." He winks, and my flesh crawls at his comment.

"I need to…" I scour the packed bar, searching for any sign of help.

At this exact moment, Ashton strolls in. He's always hated this dude. Threatened him to stay away from me, and it had worked… in high school.

"Well, you are looking great." He quirks a brow that matches his short, light-brown hair. His face is clean-shaven. Clearly, he didn't get the memo that facial hair is in.

"Thanks." My teeth scrape my top lip; I'm super uncomfortable while I watch Ashton, weaving through the crowd with Jake close behind.

"It's been years, hasn't it?"

He steps closer, and I wince as he skims the side of his finger along my sleeve, squeezing my eyes shut. I swallow hard before recovering from the unwanted touch and swat him away.

"What do you want?" I grimace. Nothing good, and I mean *nothing* good, comes from this guy.

"Hey, hey!" He lifts his hands.

Casey has caught on that this is a strained exchange.

Remember the kiss in college? The Axe-ridden frat boy?

Meet Joey motherfucking Belter.

"C'mon, let's go." Casey stabs him with another dirty glare then grabs my arm and pulls me towards the bathroom.

Joey grabs my other arm, yanking me to his face. "You know, when I heard you had a baby, I always wondered…"

"What the hell are you talking about?" I spit—*literally* spit—the words at him.

"That night, when you and I hung out in college, right before your twenty-first."

A twisting, turning, churning sensation swirls in my stomach like someone has kicked me square in the gut. Ashton and Jake are only a few more people away from getting to us.

"I know you aren't up on your facts, *prick*, but you don't get pregnant from kissing someone."

His voice drops after glancing past me, no doubt noticing my brother approaching. "That's not the way I remember it."

The back of my throat burns, and I think I'm going to be sick. What the fuck is he talking about?

It was a kiss. It was *only* a kiss.

I quickly relive the night in my head. We were wasted. I'm talking heavy-duty, multiple numbing-agents, my-own-worst-enemy wasted. Upon waking in a groggy haze, it repulsed me to be lying in a bed next to him. Dignity was low on the totem pole those days. All my clothes were on, but I was even more repulsed to find the top button of my jeans undone. Self-loathing wrapped its grubby fingers around my neck, and fight or flight kicked in as I bolted from the place. I would have known though. I would have known if something else went down. Plus, I'd found it difficult to believe he was the type to redress someone.

There's no fucking way.

Two large palms shove Joey's shoulders, causing him to stumble away from me.

"Forever trying to mess with my sister. Leave her alone, asshole." My brother plants his feet next to me while Jake drags me back into him by my belt loop. There's some weird territorial pissing match going on.

Joey offers him a mocking smile. "All good, Ashton. I was just wishing her happy birthday." His hand extends. "Hey, I'm Joe. I went to high school and college with your wife."

Jake reluctantly takes his hand, barely shaking it. "Yeah, that's cool." His other hand twists the back of my jeans, while any color whatsoever drains from my face.

"Anyway, good to see you guys. It was wonderful to catch up… *Alex.*"

The way he says my name makes me wanna take a shower.

I ignore him, stepping towards the bathroom, but Jake doesn't ignore me and spins me to face him. "What's up?" He studies my appearance, my likely washed-out cheeks, and my eyes, which I'm sure are twenty sizes too big from shock and disgust. "Did he say something to you?"

Casey stands there, lips zipped. I'm not sure exactly what she heard, but I would assume she's cognizant of the new accusation on the table.

"No, Jake. No." I drop my forehead to his chest, trying to fix my face and get myself together. "I just… don't feel that great. I need a minute, okay?"

Casey provides him with a reassuring nod, and he releases his death grip on my jeans. I turn to see Joey grin and wave to me as he leaves the bar.

"What the fuck?" my friend snaps at me the second the door closes. "What the hell was that about, Alex? Did you *really* do that? I knew you kissed, but what the fuck?"

"No." I can't ignore the nauseating sensation that won't let up. "I don't know what he's talking about. He is gross, vile, and—"

"Please don't lie to me. Friends no matter what."

"Case, I'm not. I promise you I'm not. We kissed that one time, and I've always regretted it. That was it. I would never."

She accepts my clarification and lets it die, thank God.

I keep thinking of that night, replaying it like some sick movie in my head. There's no way, no fucking way. But now there's doubt where there never was before. While I know I completely blacked out, I would have never done that. He's an asshole, and if anything did happen, it wasn't something I consented to.

Jake is waiting right outside the bathroom door.

"Jesus!" I jump back and slap my palm against my chest.

"Sorry." He glides his soothing touch down my arms till his hands meet mine, then he threads our fingers together, not bothering to give me space. Space is the last thing I need, or want, from him right now.

And just like that, he steers my thoughts away from any uncertainty, reminding me to trust myself. Now I'm certain, with everything in me, I would have *never* done that.

"Alex… I got you."

He hooks his thumbs through my belt loops—apparently this is becoming a thing—dragging me flush against his body. I don't mind it. How does he always sense when I need… this?

Him.

Several rounds of beverages later and we're all a little fuzzy. Heavy petting has resumed. Joey Belter has been blocked from any forms of social media, and Jake's hand hasn't left mine since the bathroom.

Let's finish this birthday strong.

14. WOMAN

The entire ride back to my parents' we just sit and stare. The fuck-me eyes are off the chain. I know, it's so much right now, and kind of like boom… but here we are.

Alcohol courses a steady stream through my veins, leaving me tingly. Not too much that I don't have it together, but just enough that those inhibitions got checked at the door.

We file into the house as quietly as possible. Clumsy stumbles from Annie here and there; high-pitched laughter from the collective buzz. There's a note on the counter from Mom stating the kids were great, all was good, and she hoped we had fun.

We did.

The house is completely silent, minus the light—it's probably louder than we realize—noise that accompanies a group of four wandering in from a bar after a hefty tab. Sorry, Mom and Dad.

Annie raids the fridge, asking if anyone wants something to eat. I cast a suggestive glance at Jake, and he picks up what I'm putting down.

"Nope, we're good!" he exclaims, clutching my hand and making a break for the stairs.

I giggle, wishing the butterflies would settle. Why am I so nervous right now? Why am I giggling? Oh right… vodka. This is so weird. It feels different. Maybe absence does make the heart grow fonder? It, for sure, makes the hormones grow stronger.

Once we're in the room, door shut, and lock engaged, Jake walks me back until I'm against the wall.

"You're so fucking hot." His fingertips dig into my waist, and he does a methodical roll of the hips.

His touch travels upward, taking the time to explore, and when he advances from my rib cage to caress the sides of each breast, I whimper. An extreme rush of air escapes my lungs as his lips sink into the skin of my neck, then his tongue teases a fiery trail along my jawline. Heavy breaths ripple—I'm sure strategically—into my ear.

Growing excitement soars through me, and the ache of impending relief ignites a fire in my core. Jake's mouth puts in some serious overtime, greedy and fast as he continues his disarming assault. Teeth graze the outer shell of my ear, followed by a soft nip. He knows that's a panty dropper for me.

I'm still not gonna let everything be forgotten so that I can have one night of—

"Ahhh." I can't hold that one in.

He tears at the hem of my lace top and yanks it over my head, flinging it across the room. With a brief pause, he blows out a long breath as devouring eyes roam over my chest.

My palms remain flat against the wall, and I tilt my head to the side with an inpatient grin. I'm not giving him much back—I'm not giving him *anything* back. This is the plan.

Jake presses his forehead to mine with an unnerving stare. An exhilarated exhale rushes from my mouth when he traces my collarbone, his finger slipping down, lining my cleavage. I sigh—like a highly erotic sigh, if that's a thing—and a heightened sense of arousal spikes when his barely there touch causes my nipples to grow taut through my thin black tank.

"I missed these so much." His voice comes out thick and husky, rendering me helpless against the groan that accompanies the kneading of my neglected breasts.

His eyes flash to my mouth, and he wets his lips, closing in.

I turn my head. Nope. No to the kissing. I'm not fucking there yet.

With a quiet grunt, he brushes a peck against my cheek and grabs my wrist, guiding me away from the wall. Jake turns our bodies so the back of my knees connect with the mattress I fall onto. Every cell, every single receptor inside me is begging for his touch, his body—honestly, his *anything*.

Except his lips. Well, kind of.

The weight of his toned physique smashes me into the bed, and his feverish mouth marks every inch of my upper body… where I allow. My hands rove his broad shoulders, and I silently pray for my mind to stay turned off. I *need* this. I *want* this.

Jake's pelvis rocks into mine, making me ready to go—and he's *undoubtedly* ready to go.

Am I seriously going to give in? Just let this happen?

There's my brain. I knew she was still in there somewhere. Okay, so here's the plan. Do I think anyone should use sex, or lack thereof, as a weapon? Not so much. But in all fairness, he fired the first shots and ultimately left me hanging. If we are going to do this—I mean this, and *this* this—then it's going to be my way, on my terms.

Okay, enough of the overthinking.

Jake drags open-mouthed kisses up my neck. The heat of his breath ignites my skin, causing my traitorous hips to rise. I moan as his solid length—I mean it; the thing is like a rock—hits directly between my legs, rubbing, creating the perfect amount of friction to unleash a blast of endorphins and numbing my mind in a fantastic way. As he reaches my chin, I blink my eyes open to his fluttering lashes, just in time to see him close any space between our lips.

I turn my head away. Straight up *Pretty Woman* style.

No. Fucking. Kissing.

At least not these lips.

With another borderline irritated grunt humming from his throat, he continues his licking and sucking down my neck. The rough pads of his fingers slip beneath the waist of my jeans, igniting a blazing trail as his knuckles graze my abdomen. His hands roam as if they haven't already memorized every square inch of my body.

My palms remain open on the white comforter. I'm not reciprocating whatsoever—this is gonna be all me. Usually, I'm an equal opportunity player, but not this time.

He teases his way from the top of my bra, up my neck, re-approaching my lips.

Head turned. Denied.

"Really?" Jake jerks back with a grumble then straddles me. Harsh exhales lift his nostrils while his chest heaves beneath his shirt.

I raise my brows, doing my best to keep my marathon-level breathing in check, to not let him know the extent of the effect he's having on me. Not to mention I'm desperately trying to conceal that my vagina is practically screaming at me to strip him naked, right here and now, and have my way with him. But I refrain.

"It's my birthday, isn't it?"

"So… what exactly do you want? I can't kiss you?" He towers above me, and the bedside lamp spotlights the outline of each muscle tensing beneath his shirt. Jake shoves a hand through messy hair, and somewhat confused eyes shut as he gradually grinds his erection over my clothes. His clothes. Our clothes.

Damn. He is straight-up tenting it just from a little neck kissing and an over-the-clothes hump-fest? I won't lie, it's a confidence booster.

"Alex," he practically whines. "Can I kiss you… please?"

Okay, deep breaths.

I've always enjoyed a hot bedroom sesh, open-minded to trying new things. When you're with someone for so long, you kind of move in sync and don't really need to say what you want. I had always been fulfilled in that way. But now we're dealing with the new, potentially improved Alex, so I'm gonna go out on a limb.

"No, you can't kiss me… on the face."

That did, in fact, come out of my mouth.

His eyes ping open, jaw dropping as he gawks at me. Then the corners of his lips perk as his head slowly tilts in awe. "Who are you?" He laughs.

I stare back, unblinking, a smirk bunching my cheek. His choice—either do it or don't. "Well?"

Holy shit, he's not wrong. Such brazen words would *never* have flown from my mouth before. Who the fuck am I right now? Who the fuck cares? I continue with my bored expression and pretend to examine my nails.

"Alright then," Jake finally responds, returning his body to mine.

He moves down my neck, licking and kissing his way between ample cleavage—push-up bras in your thirties are a must. He glances up at me, and I raise my brows again. With a brief shake of his head and an amused smile, he gets to it, picking up the pace, his fingertips tracing the edges of my new black bra. I definitely didn't plan to wear it for any specific reason.

He stops, looking up with a sigh—I know what he wants—eyes zeroed in on my lips. Instead, he goes back to kissing anywhere and everywhere else.

His tongue laps over each peaked nipple in languid strokes after he pulls my bra down. I fight the moan threatening to escape when he gently bites, sending a charge directly downtown. The repeated efforts to weasel his way to my clasp, to free my breasts from their overpriced confines, continue.

I don't lift myself up, refusing to offer any help. We're gonna keep that on, buddy. He's always been a tit guy, so he's not getting full exposure… tonight.

Another throaty chuckle. Another shake of his head. He's onto my game plan. Jake ditches the lip service attempt and moves to undo my jeans, tugging at the zipper.

I arch my back—now *this* I'll help with.

His nails drag along the insides of my thigh. I'm already throbbing in anticipation, my heart jamming in a raging tempo against my rib cage, while my poorly executed poker face fights to mask any reaction. The second he touches me, the second his fingers, or his tongue, finally dip beneath my underwear, he's gonna know *exactly* how turned on I am.

Strong and demanding palms spread me, and his precise tongue lathers up my inner legs, stopping when he reaches the hollow of each thigh. An inch—I swear, a *single* inch—away from my most definitely revved center.

I smack my hand on the mattress. Come on, man.

He tosses me his signature Jake smirk and kneels on his haunches, reaching back to grab his collar. "This okay?"

Ha-ha… fucker! "I'll allow it." I clench my teeth to stop from cracking up, knowing damn well he's trying to play this game too. He dusts his shirt in an effortless pull and hurls it across the room. Damn, he's far more toned than I remember.

"Been working out?" Why'd I even ask that?

"Had to blow off steam somehow."

I'm sure he can tell I've been doing the same over the last three months, going to the gym way more than I ever did before. I've lost weight, firmed some flab. But Jake would never say it. He *never* body-shamed, only praised.

After each kid was born, he'd tell me I looked beautiful, and I believed him. Not once was he deterred by the baby weight that takes flipping forever to go away.

He lowers over me once again, pants still on, starting back at my neck, back at the beginning. Ugh. I huff out a frustrated grumble, only to be met with a laugh.

"You're impatient," he says. "I'm *trying* to take my time, Alex. I missed this."

The smile spanning my lips dissolves, and he sees it. He missed this? There's a reason for that. The wheels are turning. What am I doing? I clamp my legs together, and he knows it's now or never. I'm about to shut him out.

Frantic kisses travel down from my neck and there's no stopping, not even as he passes my lacy bra, which requires a heavy dose of restraint. Because, like I said, definite tit obsession. I turn my brain off. That bitch is way too neurotic as it is.

He yanks my panties down, then goes straight to work. My head falls onto the pillow while he sucks the smooth skin at the top of each leg like he's in a race. Then his tongue, his glorious fucking tongue, drives as far inside me as it can. His mouth is hot and wet and devouring.

My hips rise, and he glides a finger through my arousal. I can't help letting a groan of pure ecstasy escape as he pulses the pointed tip of his tongue against my clit.

I grip him by the hair, urging, encouraging his eyes to meet mine. I'm mesmerized by the green and amber speckled together, his thick lashes, and his heady gaze.

Holy shit! *I* missed this.

"Oh God." I faintly breathe the words—or rather the praise.

This is a calculated move. Once you put the idea into a guy's head that he's doing so well, god-like, it only makes him ramp it up a notch.

Try it out.

He pumps two fingers inside me, beckoning, tapping that toe-curling spot as his tongue draws heavenly circles. I twist my fists into the blanket, arching off the bed. No more mentions of God, so now he's gonna work harder.

He alternates his fingers and tongue, making sure to press on… well, I think you know. Third finger in and that's all it takes. He flicks and sucks as

I gasp for air. The tension winding in the pit of my stomach coils tighter and tighter.

I struggle to grab a pillow and make it right in time to cover my face, suffocating the moans of unbridled relief that consume me in insane waves of pleasure. My legs go limp as I give in to the crazy convulsive state.

Hallelujah! Holy shit! I'm dead.

Jake rises from the bed, undoing his zipper. I can barely make out the satisfied smirk on his lips through the blurry clusterfuck I'm currently residing in.

With a blissful hum, I roll to my side and pull the blanket over my partially naked body. My lids lower and I smile to myself. "Thanks. Goodnight."

"Are you… *serious?*"

"Yup." I don't open my eyes.

Mm-hmm, I'm a motherfucker.

15. CHASING CARS

I wake up in a sweaty, entangled mess of hair in my face. Jake's arm is snug around my waist, his leg draped over mine as if he was afraid I'd ditch him in the middle of the night. His breaths stream in warm, steady patterns on the nape of my neck… causing something else to get a tinge warm.

I feel bad about what I did last night.

Nah, not really. I mean, a little sexual frustration might go a long way. And if I'm going to consider moving past this, Erin was right. I *can't* make it so easy. Sex, or whatever, won't solve our problems. I'm fully aware.

But it might be a good time.

It feels so nice, so comfortable having someone—having Jake—lying next to me.

You don't realize how much you miss it till you're in that bed all by yourself.

***

I was just far too fucking angry right after, and I didn't want him anywhere near me. The idea of Jake even touching me put me on edge.

He begged, and when I say begged, I *mean* it. Hands, knees, the works. I didn't wanna hear it. I didn't want to *hear* that he loved me. Those three words shouldn't be thrown around so loosely. And *fuck* the words. I didn't feel like he meant them.

It was *only* a kiss.

That lovely phrase has made its rounds. And I do believe him; that it was, for real, only a kiss. But again, there was a plan in place. So if you're lining up to commit a crime and get busted before carrying it out, are you innocent?

You tell me.

After about a month of slamming the door in his face, screaming at him to leave me alone, the bright red dulled a bit. The anger faded, and it turned into something else. It turned into real—scary real—sadness. Darkness even.

I felt like our life together was a lie. The perfect Monet: from far away it appeared amazing, but up close it was one gigantic mess. You can thank *Clueless* for that analogy.

The two of us got it together, at least somewhat. We didn't have a choice; we have kids. We've gotta make sure they survive this ordeal, though who knows if we will.

Jake had suggested going to a marriage counselor. Because I'm a stubborn bitch, I refused. I thought if I gave an inch, he would take the entire yard. And I was in the mindset that I'd *never* move beyond, that I would *never* be able to trust him again.

I know I'm not innocent, believe me. I'm fully aware of my shortcomings and dwell on them daily. But the last thing I want is for someone to sit in front of us and jot notes on a piece of paper and tell us what the hell we should do about it. I've been examined and advised by my fair share of shrinks, yet here we are.

If it were her kissing him and Jake immediately pulling away, that would be one thing—I think.

I asked him *point-blank* if he would have gone through with it… and he paused. He *fucking* paused!

That blank space where he should've answered told me everything I needed to know. He eventually said no—more like stuttered it. Then he tried to explain that it wasn't so simple, that her family's business is a huge client. His own company's largest source of income, the thing that keeps our children fed. He couldn't just sever ties, because he'd potentially lose their business.

What I took from that was that he was practically whoring himself out.

I couldn't accept that answer—I *still* don't. It's not fair to put up our family as collateral.

So the months kept ticking by, as they do. The flowers and *I love you*s kept coming. And I continued ignoring them. They were empty. I was empty. Once the rings were off my finger, he stopped.

Right before Christmas, I'd overheard Jordan on the phone with a friend, telling them how much she hated being moved back and forth. But sometimes the worst part of eavesdropping, the fucking knife to the heart, is hearing the unguarded truth. She told that same friend she was relieved not to have to hear us argue, at least not all the time, not anymore.

It's true. Before any of this, we'd fight over the stupidest nonsense. But what couple doesn't… am I right?

As a mom, at times, it can seem as though you're shackled to your household. Don't get me wrong, I love my kids something fierce—touch a hair on their head and I will end you—but it's truthfully hard sometimes. Anyone who says different is a liar. And I'm not trying to say that men don't feel this. I'm sure they do. They probably have their own list of things that keep them up at night. I can only speak from my experience.

When Jake would come home from work, I'd tap out. I was done, finito, exhausted… I had nothing left. Nothing to give. I was so drained and overwhelmed dealing with the appointments, fundraisers, sports, cleaning, laundry…

I wasn't *me* anymore. Somewhere over the last few years, the Alex that fell in love with Jake had been dwindling away.

Were we happy? I'm not actually sure if we were, or if we were so invested that keeping everything status quo was the best option.

We went through the motions, said *I love you* every night before bed, quick forehead kisses before leaving for the day and upon returning home. But the signal was fading. We paid more attention to our phones than the struggling couple in front of us. We did something we swore we wouldn't.

We forgot to take care of each other.

* * *

As if he can sense my mind is already running full speed ahead, Jake pulls me into him.

He is awake—very much awake. How can it be like this for guys most mornings? Do they just wake up and their dicks are like, *Hey, let's go?*

I asked him once how often he thought about sex. Was it true that guys think about it most of the time? He said pretty much—from the teen years on, it would pop up regularly.

Pun intended.

"Morning," I say, not turning towards him. Morning breath is a thing. Couples that wake up and go straight for it, tongues tangoing, are simply willing to take one for the team. I'm not implying morning sex *isn't* great… it's been a while. Still, I'd rather avoid the breath and put those unpolished mouths to other use.

His hand slips under my top, fingers skating lazily over my stomach and sending shivers down my spine. I'm completely dressed—still wearing my tank, with the addition of PJ pants. Jake is a redresser. Plus, gotta remember those kids. They have no concept of privacy.

"Morning." His voice is raspy and low. "Sleep okay?" He palms my breasts while his hips grind into my ass.

"Yeah." I suck in a sharp gasp, all kinds of turned on right now. Why haven't we been doing this for years, every single day? Why did the morning sex get skipped?

Kids, work, sleep… oh yeah, *that* bullshit.

Right now, it's as if the world doesn't exist outside of this room. Like we can just be whatever in here, forget about everything else… even if it won't last.

His hand coasts down my front, fingers unraveling the drawstring of my pants, while his lips brush over the back of my shoulder. He stops to press a soft kiss on each of the four inked stars that span it. He always did this when I let him. Or when it was… appropriate.

"Did you sleep okay?" I catch my lip to hold in the impending laughter.

His hand freezes, his hips thrusting into me harder. "What do you think?" He grunts and continues loosening my pants.

I won't deny him this time. His lips graze my skin, stopping to kiss and bite every so often. Not crazy biting—I'm not into that. These are gentle nips that make me wanna do bad things to him. His fingers smooth their way down, rubbing over my underwear.

He ramps up his efforts, using his other hand to sweep away my hair before nuzzling into the base of my neck. Starving lips ravage me like a lust-driven teenager, desperate for more. He traces the edge of my underwear, slipping his finger beneath. I swallow incredibly loud as he glides along my entrance. I am *so* ready for this.

Reaching back, my palm connects with the bare skin of his torso, hot and already slick with sweat, then continues the downward trend. My hand wraps around his cock, which is rock solid, if you didn't get the memo, and I slowly stroke him up and down. A muffled moan vibrates against my neck where his mouth remains fixated.

The thunderous beat of his heart drums from his chest, while staccato, impatient breaths match my own. Deep and incredibly sexy growls leave his throat as he makes his way to my ear to deliver the light nip—the panty dropper. Jake pulls his fingers from me then clutches the waist of my PJ bottoms and yanks them to my knees.

My fist corkscrews over him, moving faster, getting caught up in the moment, in the passion we've been missing for so long. My stomach somersaults, skin tingling, pulse pounding. Jake tenses behind me.

"You gotta stop." He rests his forehead between my shoulder blades, panting.

"What?"

"Been a while." He coughs out a breathy chuckle. "I'd rather get at least a minute—"

"Oh." I get it. He's not gonna last long.

Poor guy.

He slips off his pants and positions himself behind me. A rough palm separates my legs before sliding over me once more with his fingers. My hips rock along with him, both of us serenely lost in the moment, built up with anticipation.

"Alex," he says, and I hate—and also love—how beautiful it sounds coming from him. He hikes my thigh up, and we both shudder when his tip eases along my arousal.

Bang, bang, bang!

The door rattles, knob jiggling. Thank somebody it's locked. Also… fuck my life.

"No!" Jake and I whine with matching cries of annoyance.

The thuds and banging continue.

"Daddy? Daddy?"

"Shit." I jump from the bed, lifting my bottoms. It's Roo. She's not gonna stop till that door is open. Jake goes to respond, and I cover his mouth with my hand, head shaking at his widening eyes.

"Let's not complicate this right now." I'm thinking of the kids. Well, mostly Brynn. She and I need to talk. How confusing is all of this for her? Because it's *really* confusing for me.

He nods.

I offer an apologetic frown before rolling my eyes at the door, which gains me a faint chuckle in response.

"I'm coming." No, I definitely am not, but I almost was. Thanks, cock-blocker.

"I'm… yeah… I'm gonna need a minute," Jake mutters, gesturing to his… situation.

No lie, I could use an ice-cold shower right now myself.

Downstairs, the kids are awake, and the daily routine has begun.

"Good morning." Annie smiles at me over her mug before passing a cup of coffee across the kitchen island.

"Morning," I grumble, unable to hide the fact that I'm back to square one in the sexual-frustration department.

"How ya feeling?" she asks.

Annie's a griller, forever thirsty for details.

I know it killed her when we separated. She actually punched Jake square in the jaw. But she was, or is, a believer in love and thinks it can endure all things. Many people do… until they face real shit. She wants us back together in the worst way.

"I'm… fine thanks." It comes out snappy.

No, I'm not fine. I'm literally stuck between an internal struggle of body, heart, and mind—and none of those bitches can see eye to eye.

"Where are my parents?" I glance around at the clean house. Annie's somewhat of an early riser, so she must've handled it, and I'm thankful for that. Brynn, Jordan, and Liv are lounging on the couch at the other side of the large room, submerged in their screens, making videos, or doing whatever it is they do. A movie on the TV preoccupies the rest of our gang.

Jake comes bopping down the stairs in sweats and a T-shirt, capped off with a massive grin. Brynn keeps her stare glued to her phone, but I see her dark eyebrows raise. Shit. Maybe I shouldn't have let him sleep in the same room. I need to talk to her—like a serious, sit-down conversation.

His hair is spiked up top from several swipes of a towel. Well, at least one of us got that cold shower in. Didn't get much of anything else in. I sigh. He looks much more relaxed. I guess he got everything… handled.

"They're at church," Annie responds, only once Jake's in earshot.

Oh, right, my parents. I'm too busy now thinking of my older girls, contemplating how I'm going to fix this situation. No disapproving scowls from either of them—that's a surprise. Brynn must've kept the revelation to herself.

Annie clears her throat, wanting our undivided attention. Jace sits on a stool with a stupid grin on his face, head down, pretending to mind his own business.

"Can I help you?" I plant my palm on my hip, blinking at Annie.

"You like church, right?" Her eyes flicker from me to Jake, gleaming with mischief as they peek over her coffee mug.

"Um… I guess," he says with a shrug, looking around like he's not sure what he's missing.

"We all know Alex does." She directs an overly exaggerated wink at me.

Ugh. I know this chick, and she's up to no good. I shoot her a warning glare, poking a thumb at the kids camped out across the room.

"Just saying." She lifts a casual shoulder with a smirk. "I heard a specific biblical name mentioned last night." Thankfully, her voice is so soft only the three of us can make out her words.

Jace explodes into a throaty chuckle, head shaking. It's obvious she was itching to whip that one out. Probably cooked it up last night and just couldn't wait to hit us with the punchline.

Jake bites his lip and nudges into me.

All I can do is laugh and roll my eyes. Oh God!

16. BRICK

Annie and I formulate a plan to switch up the whole driving home arrangement. There are some shopping outlets on the way, which is the perfect bait to lure Brynn into some one-on-one time.

If I try to talk to her in the car, she'll shut down. She'll hear me but won't listen. And I might throw her stupid AirPods out the window. I hate to think that I'm bribing her with shopping, so I'm gonna view it as more or less a positive reinforcement.

Yeah… *that* sounds better.

I give my friend a modified recap about the movie we watched together two days ago, then I appease her by revealing exactly how church went down last night. I get a high five for the last bit. No matter her feelings, or what she wishes the future will bring, she appreciates a solid burn. But above all else, she knows I'm in desperate need to get some time alone with Brynn.

We both understand the gravity of raising these young ladies, molding them into strong, smart, confident women; not accepting being treated like trash, or left on their own to try to understand the messed-up elements of the world. Their brains aren't fully developed yet. How can they even begin to comprehend circumstances, especially if we can't make sense of them as adults?

Everything right now seems so permanent, particularly for Brynn, who's having difficulties with her own relationships. First off, teenage girls can be downright brutal, and don't even get me started on the boyfriend drama. I wouldn't go back to sixteen for shit.

Jake's fine with the plan of course. Anything for the sake of the kids. He'll ride home with Jace, Piper, Will, Roo, and the dogs, dropping the pups at my house before taking the kids to his. Annie, Liv, Jordan, Brynn, and I will go together.

Before we take off, he asks if I want to stick around and hang out for a bit when I bring the girls to his place. Obviously, I say yes. We have some unfinished business.

Okay, that's not the only reason. These past few days have been… something. But being near him, talking to him, remembering who we once were, sparks the tiniest bit of hope. Maybe there is enough there? And maybe it's worth trying to save?

I throw him a bone, asking him to schedule an appointment with the marriage counselor he'd brought up months ago. That face, man… he takes it as a win. I tell him not to overthink it though—let's just take it one day at a time. We still aren't above water. I'm keeping us under, not quite ready to let either of us surface, yet.

* * *

Back when I found out I was pregnant with Brynn, you may remember I was seriously down in the dumps. Freaked out, panicked, and scared out of my mind. Not only the whole pushing a human out of your vagina, which, yeah… it's extreme, and the endurance test of your life. But the main thing I was terrified about was screwing up this child.

I was so afraid to bring a baby into this world. Into a world I didn't love, one that I believed to be cruel. My own issues with being depressed and not having my shit together were hanging over my head. How was this fair? How could I do it?

I couldn't.

As I said, Jake totally flipped at first, but he was there for me. Whatever I wanted to do, he swore to stick by me, no judgment. He continuously promised he could support us, that it would be great—the eternal optimist.

I'd call myself more of a realist. The glass isn't half empty or full. It just has water in it.

I couldn't help but panic. How would it work? We scraped by on minimum wage. We'd only recently gotten back together. I was hanging by a thread.

Even though Jake showed up—not just showed up, but majorly stepped up—and even though I knew he loved me more than anything else, I didn't think it would ever be enough. I was young. I didn't want my life to end, and that's how I felt—like it would be over.

God, I was so incredibly wrong.

I made an appointment, and not a prenatal one. This was a different one. Before you judge this, I will say, I adamantly believe in the right to whatever the fuck you choose. I wasn't for or against anything, and it's impossible to have a legit opinion about something if you've never been in a situation where you actually have to make a choice.

I didn't see any other way.

We went to the clinic. Jake wasn't happy about it, but he tried his best to be supportive—he'd never let me go through it alone. He choked back tears when I signed myself in.

I didn't have any.

When the nurse called my name and instructed Jake to wait there, he hugged me, telling me he'd love me forever, not bothering to mask the emotion on his face. And then he walked outside.

There I was, lying on the exam table, seeking to shut off my mind, struggling not to be physically sick. I tried to imagine being with Jake, gazing into those hazel eyes ever again after this was over.

The nurse detected the faintest whoosh of a heartbeat and made me lie there, listening to it. I understood that this was only to aid in solidifying my decision. To help me be sure of my choice before it became permanent. It was only for a handful of minutes, but it felt like an eternity. I knew then and there that if I went through with this… a couple things.

I would never, *ever* forgive myself. And I could never be with Jake again. I'd never be able to look at him without returning to *this* moment. The resentment I knew I'd feel—directed mostly at myself—would never go away. There'd be no moving past it.

I respect anyone's choice on this matter. It's so much more common to judge, and I try my best not to do that. Only walkin' in my own shoes here.

The nurse gave a sympathetic smile and told me it happened often. She unhooked me, wished me the best, and sent me on my way.

I found Jake waiting in the parking lot. This young, attractive, physically and mentally strong twenty-one-year-old man was doubled over bawling when I walked out. Wouldn't touch me, wouldn't hug me, wouldn't even look at me. He thought I'd gone through with it. He had the same feelings I did.

If after all these years together, we felt like this was something we *couldn't* get through, then what was it all for anyway?

With dry eyes, I slipped into the passenger seat of his car. He didn't wipe his face or conceal the grief streaming down his cheeks. He was already in love. And if I hadn't been confident in my decision before, I absolutely was then.

My palm rested on his forearm, ensuring he couldn't turn over the engine, and after a deep breath, I told him the truth. That I couldn't do it. That he… *we* were going to be parents. And he was gonna be the best father this world had ever seen. We could do this. Together.

Relief flooded the space between us, and Jake reached over, scooping me straight out of my seat, then buried his wet face in the crook of my neck.

He looked me in the eye and told me he loved me. Us. Said *I got you.* There wasn't a doubt in my mind about that. With his thumbs soothing my cheeks while his fingers slid into my hair, he insisted *I* would be the greatest mother this world had ever seen. And you better believe those nonexistent tears made their debut.

He embraced it. Every single pee-in-a-cup, prenatal visit. He was in it for the long haul.

I wasn't.

In the beginning, I did my best to fake it, to act like it was all going to be okay, slapping a phony smile on my weary and slightly anemic face.

Our parents took it surprisingly well. There were freak-outs; a few bouts of tears, as I've said. They wanted more for us. Well, I shouldn't say more. Brynn was the first niece, grandchild, child, you name it. The shining light of the family—on both sides. But they didn't want to see us struggle. No parent wants that for their children, so they vowed to be supportive and to love us.

All three of us.

Love and the best support system in the world literally surrounded me.

The problem was, I didn't have the love and approval from the one who mattered most.

Myself.

I was drowning in guilt for the choice I'd almost made—I still do sometimes. I couldn't get over it, couldn't move on.

Jake tried to help. He fucking lived and breathed for me and the baby. I stumbled through the motions, ate well enough, took the horse-pill vitamins, but I was spiraling downward, and it wasn't easing up.

He had to call in the big guns. My mom took over at that point, while Jake was barely treading water. I'd pulled him down with me. He continually missed work, because he felt like he couldn't leave me alone in the sketchy little apartment we struggled to afford. He didn't know what to do anymore. Mom had already gone through this with me, and she took me back to the psychiatrist I'd seen a few years before. Nice enough lady, understanding… I guess. Quick to write a prescription.

Antidepressants for the win.

I'm not ashamed of it. No one should be. We shouldn't shy away from talking about these things because they might make people uncomfortable. It's the not talking about it that makes them worse.

Anyway, it kept me feeling happy enough. I wasn't quite cured, because it doesn't work that way. But I could function and was able to maintain a steady minimum-rate job. It helped Jake sleep at night. And like I said, he lit up for all of us. He *undoubtedly* was the star cheerleader of our team. I knew it was scary for him too, but he never complained. The focus was always on me. No one ever asked how he was doing.

Brynn didn't have a single complication around withdrawal from the meds. My doctor had assured me the benefits of taking them while pregnant outweighed the risks. I was so thankful she came out healthy, free of any complications, especially given my anxiety about the other things I'd done before I even knew I was pregnant.

I held my breath for months.

They say something changes in you, the second your first baby is born. That the love you feel is insane. My mom convinced me of this, well aware I wasn't having the same emotions many pregnant women have. She understood I was scared there wouldn't be a bond.

Why should this tiny little human look at me with overwhelming love if I didn't feel the same?

Well, the insane love happened… for Jake. He was a mess that time and every other—took one glance at her and was a goner. He fell completely in love with Brynn.

I loved her of course. But as I've mentioned, I was detached and didn't experience those overwhelming emotions. I was sick and sore.

I faked it; I've always been good at that. Fake it till ya make it.

Jake would stare at her for hours, a miniature face that mirrored his.

When Brynn was three weeks old, I tripped carrying her on the stairs at my in-laws. We tumbled down almost the entire flight and landed with a loud smack against the tile floor.

Something happened in those few seconds.

My body somehow instinctively twisted itself completely around her, shielding her from any harm. When we hit the bottom, there was a snap—a loud snap. My arm was undoubtedly broken, though there wasn't an ounce of pain. All I felt was tremendous fear that my little girl was hurt.

Frantically, I'd inspected the still sleeping baby Brynn for any injuries. There were none. She was peaceful and utterly perfect, her tiny nostrils flaring as she smiled. This flawless and pure child I… we created had complete faith and absolute trust in me.

It was at *that* moment I knew it.

I *felt* it.

The unmatched and overwhelming love that makes your heart want to beat out of your chest. Because that's what children are. Your heart, existing beyond the safe confines and protection of your body. It's wonderful and extremely terrifying in the same breath.

I loved this child with every single fiber of my being. It wasn't solely Jake who was my saving grace… it was also Brynn. She gave me true meaning, purpose, and I'd almost denied any of us from ever experiencing the chance.

So… do I have some guilt issues with this daughter of mine?

You're goddamn right I do. promised myself from that day on, I'd stop watching my life play out from the sidelines. And that's what I did. I threw everything I had into being the best mom I could be. It wasn't perfect, never is, but you can bet your ass it's *me* who lives and breathes for us now.

17. DAUGHTERS

We'd wandered into several of the stores, letting the girls pick out a few novelties. I'm not a huge in-person shopper. I prefer all the items delivered, avoid the assholes. But you can get some bangin' deals here, so might as well.

Annie had convinced Liv and Jordan to get their second piercings. Such a great wingman. She knew Brynn wouldn't be tempted, because that kid already has various hoops and studs lining her ears.

People say stuff about it, how they can't believe we let her do that. Be real, there are plenty *worse* things she could do at sixteen than pierce her cartilage. Move along with that pretentious garbage.

"You wanna grab something to eat?" I ask Brynn, my voice a tinge unsteady. Honestly, I have no clue what to say to her. I'm trying, but aren't we all just winging this whole mom thing?

"Nah, I'm not hungry."

Um, next plan.

"How 'bout a smoothie?"

That one works. She can't resist. It's like coffee for me, and I'll follow that glorious beverage anywhere. Her face lights up, and I get a glimpse of the deep dimples that crease her cheeks when she grins. That perfect genetic imperfection that was handed down by me and my mom. We end up in the food court, and she orders a random concoction from the menu while I mull over the words in my head, the way I'm going to approach this subject with her.

With her drink in hand, she follows me to sit at a table slightly secluded from the lunch crowd, and I stare at her long enough that my eyes *will* her to look at me. She's reluctant, I get it. She knows damn well this is a setup—kids see through so much. Not everything, but more than we give them credit for.

"Listen, Brynn." A lengthy sigh escapes my mouth. "I realize this is a lot for you right now, and I know things are messed up. We're trying to work it out."

Her attention shifts from side to side, looking anywhere but at me, though a minuscule twitch of her lids gives her away. She's listening. And despite her indifferent facade… she's upset.

My heart.

"I don't want you to think… *or feel* a certain way about your dad. If you wanna be upset with *anyone*, let it be me. I made him move out, okay?"

She raises her head, and her hazel eyes slice right through my soul while tears pool in them. "Why did he do this, Mom?" Her fist slams against the tabletop with an abrupt thud, and multiple heads swing in our direction.

I get it. The sadness, the confusion, the anger. Yeah, it's a whirlwind.

I draw in a deep breath. "It's not what you're thinking, honey. It's not *that* bad." Did I actually say that out loud? But is it as bad? I mean, as bad as an outright affair?

Fuck! I'm wearing down.

Maybe it's not. I'm not excusing his behavior—I don't think I ever will—but this is for the sake of my child's heart.

Her brows knit, and her lips curve to a frown. "Wh-What do you mean? I thought…" Her face contorts with hurt; hurt that we allowed to be projected onto her.

"I'm sorry you thought anything. And I'm sorry that I didn't talk to you, *really* talk to you, sooner."

She sits there looking puzzled. "Dad… he didn't… cheat on you?"

Those eyes, *ugh*, those eyes I can't lie to, but I can't tell her everything.

"There's a woman he did some business with. She was… umm… she flirted with him, and he didn't stop it. He wasn't sure what to do." That's enough—enough for now. It's not the *complete* truth, but it's not an absolute lie.

"Oh!" She jolts back, and her scowl makes an appearance, along with bared teeth. "So you… so *that's* why you split up? That's it? We're being shuffled around, living out of suitcases, and our lives are ruined because you can't get over being jealous?"

My scorned teen jumps up from her chair, screeching it across the floor, then makes a break for it. Several concerned glances spin in our direction.

"Brynn, it's not that simple." I follow behind her, not giving a rip about the dozens of eavesdroppers fixating on our drama as she sprints for the exit.

"How's it not? I don't understand! What's not simple?" Her cheeks flush, and her eyes are wide and unforgiving. The temper is for real.

"Brynn," I plead, grabbing her hand and staring at my beautiful child, who I would die for, on the spot, without a single thought. "Look at me." I move my head from side to side until she does.

The hurt… Man, it's doing me in.

Her chin wobbles. "You should've never gotten married in the first place."

"What?"

After shoving the door open, she begins speed-walking out onto the sidewalk. I catch her arm, turning her towards me. Tears run down her face, her bottom lip quivering. "I know you guys *only* got married because of me. I wish you didn't."

All the bags of meaningless stuff fall to the concrete, and I wrap my arms around her, letting Brynn sob into my shoulder. I can't believe my poor baby has felt like this.

She knew we got married when I was pregnant, because we didn't hide it. But we got married because we were in love.

After a solid minute of crying, she finally calms down. I comb my hand through her wavy brown hair then wipe the tears from her reddened face. Leaning back, I study her, soaking in every single detail that embodies this flawless being that Jake and I made. Our little girl. The beating heart that exists outside of our bodies. I can't wait for the day she understands just how special she is to us.

It's not a minute task to gain her attention. So I perform a ridiculous array of funny faces, attempting to get her to look at me. I smile—not *just* smile but full cheese at her until she laughs.

"What? Mom… stop. You're so weird." She chuckles between sniffles and shuddered breaths.

"Hate to tell you this, kid, but we sure as hell didn't get married 'cause of you. You think we would have done that?"

She shrugs and smacks at her cheeks.

"You were a bonus, Brynn. Icing on the cake. A cherry on top. Hate to tell you, but you were positively *not* the reason."

And that is one thousand percent true.

I'm right back there, holding that tiny infant in my arms, willing to take the pain for myself, willing to take all the blame. Anything for her not to hurt.

Doesn't matter how old any of them get, that shit will never change.

I explain that *right now* I'm fully committed to doing my best to get us through this, reassuring Brynn of Jake's undying love for her, and for all of us—though I don't make any promises that we'll get back together. It's ultra-important not to make promises, especially to your kids, if you aren't certain you can stick to them. I swear to try, then say I'm sorry I haven't shown up till now.

Sorry I let her down.

Sometimes it's not about where to put the blame, not when the kids are involved. They need stability, a common ground. We have to sit them down and work this out. Let them speak their piece and give them a say.

But it's also important to be honest—well, as *appropriately* honest— without crushing them as we can be. I get that Brynn feels the dreaded responsibility that comes with the territory of being the oldest child. The guinea pig, the leader.

I text Jake, informing him we need to talk… as in talk, not *talk*. We've gotta come up with a better plan, since this one certainly isn't working. Because as much as I want to stay mad at him, hate him forever, I just can't. My love for him runs too deep, but more than that, my love for my children runs even deeper.

We *need* to make this arrangement work—one way or another.

Thinking back to the day when I knew, for certain, this child was going to be in our lives, I can't help reflecting on all the obstacles we've overcome… *together*.

The ride home is smooth, and I even receive several smiles from Brynn. A rarity. I pull up to Jake's townhouse after dropping off Annie and Liv, and the girls run in, leaving the door open. Before stepping over the threshold, I inhale a deep breath. I've never been inside. I've never wanted to go inside.

The walls are white, bare, no decorations of any sort. Our old couch spans the living room. Jake turns his head from the sofa, flashing a smile, then entertains the girls as they show off their new digs.

I just watch them. Jordan is blissfully unaware of anything, and I'm glad. While Brynn still has the makings of a wall up, she's talking to him. And that's a positive in my book.

After they showcase their goods, they vacate the room to join their siblings upstairs, asking me to tell them when I leave.

Jake gets up and strolls towards me. He's wearing gym shorts—because it's Jake—and a plain T-shirt, because I told him the girls are getting older and sometimes it's awkward to have friends over if he's sitting there rocking *nothing* but shorts. Like seriously, dude? Not that I, myself, am opposed. He really is a sight.

He twists the front of my shirt in his palm and ushers me into the kitchen, mouth dangerously close to mine. His sole concentration is on my lips. Everything about him—corded, ink-clad forearms, the sincere glow in his charming stare—is intoxicating. The smell; his smell, soap and mint and *holy...*

I push him back. Ugh. Resolve, stick with me. "We need to talk."

"Alright," he rasps, wetting his lips. Still far too close.

"About the kids." That'll do the trick. Sexual tension now off the table—sorta.

"What about them?" he grumbles and stands up straight.

"We have to sit down with them again. We need to listen to them and get a better plan in place." I work hard to keep my eyes on his. Not on his lips, his arms, and especially not his—

"The kids are alright."

Of course he'd say that.

"No, Jake, I don't think the kids are fucking *alright.*"

That got his attention.

"I could move back in. We can get beyond this, Alex." He clutches my hand with a persuasive expression.

Give an inch, take a yard.

He draws me closer. My brain is screaming *no.* My body is screaming *hell yes!* And my heart is hurting and doesn't want to be involved.

"I'm serious." I press a palm to his chest, and he sighs but goes along with my request.

We sit the kids down at his table. They don't want a day here, a day there. We settle on alternating three and four, and agree to eat some dinners together, spend some time together. However… no fucking movies together.

Everyone seems happy—at least happy enough for right now. I tell Jake he needs to talk to the girls about stuff. That was always more my department. When I was younger, I'd divulge most things to my mom, but she was around all the time. I wasn't in this position.

His lease is up at the end of March. We're going to give it the full three months. Do the work, meet with someone. We encourage the kids to come to us with concerns, about *anything*. And of course, we stand firm—because it's the truth—this isn't their fault.

Kelsey had texted during our sit-down and told me if I ditched her again, she was coming for me. I totally forgot. No matter what's up, unless it's emergent, you gotta make time for your friends.

I say my goodbyes to the kids after checking out their rooms. Will and Roo are super proud of their bunks. The girls are, of course, engrossed in their phones. I ask them both to text me, call me, whatever, whenever.

Walking back downstairs, my ears perk when I hear Jake talking on the phone. Only he's not talking, he's whispering. "Next week? I don't know. I'm not sure if I can make it work. We have a different arrangement now."

What the hell?

I storm into the kitchen, ready for blood, but quickly remember the words we just dished out. Relax, it's probably nothing. But *damn*, am I gonna feel like this whenever he's on the phone? Like I can't ever trust him? Is my mind automatically going to speculate on the worst? No. I need to stop, put a bit more faith in him. We are trying to move on.

He holds up a finger and mouths, "Jace."

Okay, *phew*, that's normal enough. Here I was jumping the gun, assuming things.

And then I hear it. Just barely through his cell, but I undoubtedly hear it. He's silent, staring at me.

A woman's voice.

18. HOLLABACK GIRL

I'm pissed! No, pissed is too tame a word right now. I'm *livid!*

I fling open the front door, hearing Jake yell my name from inside. Why am I such an idiot? Like anything's ever gonna change.

Fool me fucking twice. Shame on me.

I run to my car then jam the key into the ignition. Jake books outside as I slam it in reverse.

"Wait, Alex, wait!"

My closed windows muffle his voice, and I crank the radio volume up. I'm talking *way* up. I don't wanna hear it. He tries to get in front of the car. Bad idea 'cause I'm about to run your ass over, dipshit. I punch it into drive, then I remember orange isn't my color. Plus, I'm only mad. I don't actually want to kill him.

Well…

Okay, no, haven't reached maximum psycho mode—yet.

Fuck! I smack the steering wheel so hard my palms sting then grip the leather as violent breaths fly from my nostrils. I contemplate laying on the horn. Nope, that'll draw too much attention. We just fixed the stuff with the kids. I don't want them snooping out the windows, seeing this standoff in motion.

The looming sense of danger seems to kick in, and Jake cautiously walks to the driver's side window, hands raised, with a perplexed look. He's so full of shit. I can see his face in my periphery, and his lips are moving. But I refuse, *refuse* to turn towards him.

Could it have been anyone? Could it have been someone other than *that* cunt? Of course it could've. That's not the point though, is it? He lied.

He *lied*.

I wasn't able to make out the voice clearly. But I know, without a doubt, it wasn't Jace, unless he's re-entered puberty.

I struggle to channel my inner Zen… is that even a thing? Inhale through my nose, exhale from my mouth. I try to chill, to slow my rattling heart, calm my churning stomach. And because I'm a sucker… I lower the window.

"Would you *just* listen?" he asks, out of breath, swiping a palm across his forehead before dragging it along his stupid face.

Nope. I don't wanna hear it. And I'm not onboard with a squabble right now. I'm gonna go meet Kelsey, forget about this, and, more than likely, get fairly numb.

"No, Jake. I'm not going to listen. You're a fucking liar, and I'm sick of it."

He opens his mouth to reply, but I cut him off. "I'll be here to pick up the kids Wednesday morning. I'll let Brynn and Jordan know to text me if any of them need anything. Please don't go to Annie's for New Year's. I don't want to see you there. And I don't want to listen to *anything* you have to say right now." I'm impressed that my voice has remained relatively calm—albeit quivering—given the circumstances.

"I'm never going to win with you, am I?" He throws his arms out to the sides, exasperated. I grit my teeth, my eyes narrowing, while fire plagues my cheeks. Jake crosses his arms over his chest, his jaw ticking. We've perfected this childish tit-for-tat dance over the years. I'm tired of it.

"Would you just let me—"

"Fuck. You." I hit the gas, leaving him standing there, barefoot, in the middle of the road.

I don't care about any explanation—there isn't one. Why wouldn't he be honest? See, this is what I meant by give an inch, take a yard. I let him in a teensy bit, and he pulls this. He took the tiny shred of whatever we got back and shattered it.

Nobody wins here; we both lose. We *all* lose.

I zip around my house, speedy as ever, because I don't need him on my trail. Feed the dogs, change into some jeans and a top, a dab of makeup— ten minutes, and I'm outta there. I've never gotten ready so fast in my life.

Thirteen missed calls, and you know who they're from. Messages chime left and right. Delete.

I don't care.

I text Brynn and tell her to call Kelsey if she needs me. My phone is about to die, and I don't have time to charge it.

And because I can't let it go, I also message Jace to get his take, but a text pops up, interrupting my mission for an answer I already know. It's from Jake, informing me he's on his way. Hell to the no! He must've convinced Brynn or Jordan to watch the little ones. I figured it was only a matter of time, but I need to be as far away from him as I can at the moment.

I'm mad right now. I'm *severely* mad. And when I'm like this, it's best to stay away. I've got a long track record of saying words I don't mean when I'm angry.

Should I hear him out? No thanks. I think the fuck not! I'm pretty sure I've done my fair share… at least for one day.

I make it to The Still, a local watering hole. The food is sub-par, service is so-so, but the drinks… the drinks are delish—their menu sports a substantial variety of Martinis.

Kelsey's already camped at the bar, jacket and purse sprawled over the chair next to her, saving me a seat.

"Hi, honey." She stands to greet me, putting a hand on my shoulder and pecking me on the cheek. Yeah, it's always a little uncomfortable. She's a cheek kisser. What can you do? It's her way.

"Hey. I'm so glad we finally got together." I feel bad even saying that. We would have gotten together *a lot* sooner, but I bailed on her. I bailed on everything. On everyone. Minus the times she and Annie popped over unannounced, I haven't really hung out with either of them, besides the last two days.

She is ultra-fancy, consistently dressed to impress—her green eyes lined with precision, her dark complexion radiant, her makeup on point. Gold twisty earrings dangle from her ears, while jet-black hair cascades down her back.

Kelsey's tiny, so everything is flattering on her. She's always sporting cleavage, and her purple V-neck sweater plunges, showing off more than enough. She paid for them, so she might as well show them off. No judgment—she looks great. Her black pants and tall heels scream high society.

Meanwhile, I'm in my usual jeans with a plain white shirt, gray leather jacket, and an old pair of lace-up boots. That's me. Not fancy. My light-blonde highlights are so grown out that my hair is a botched version of an ombre these days.

"Took you long enough."

Her nose scrunches. I'd say she scowls, but there's not a single visible wrinkle on that beautiful, clear, airbrushed-looking face. How, might you ask? A lovely fountain-of-youth injection. Don't knock it—she's happy. And truthfully, I've been considering it. I've got a *what the fuck* line between my brows, and that sucker is a valley.

"I know, Kels. I'm sorry, I've just… you know."

She frowns and places her hand over mine. "Yeah, I get it."

And you know what? She *does* know. She had a cheating husband herself. Full-blown affairs—yes, plural—with a pregnant mistress in the mix. She left him about fifteen years ago. Found Luke and the two have been a power couple since.

She's the person you'd think would be Team Alex all the way, but she had the opposite reaction when everything came to light. Kelsey backed Jake… to a point. Said the difference was he was sorry. And that the slut was preying on a married man, using her position of power in her family's company to help with her dirty work.

I'd expected her to be in my corner and was duly taken aback. She said she'd support me no matter what I chose. Though, in her opinion, the difference between Jake and her ex is that Jake's a genuinely good guy. He was sorry—sorry for the act and the plan, not *only* sorry he got caught— and this was an isolated mistake, not a string of random affairs.

I didn't feel the same way. The plan, the pause, the poison that distrust injects into a relationship—it's like an illness. It spreads and festers; seems to clear up with the proper treatment, only to relapse with one little miscalculation.

Distrust is a debilitating disease, and I promise there *isn't* a simple cure.

She didn't condone what he did. Not at all. But she thought it was worth sticking it out, especially because we have kids; thought I reacted too harshly.

Everyone has different opinions about how much is too much.

She's pro-us, and wants Jake and me together. That hope seems to be trending right now. But cut through all of that, Kelsey is a good friend and wants everyone to be happy. She's one of those people who finds the positive in everything, convinced there's always a silver lining, even if you can't see it at first. One of those people who's beautiful, intelligent, and sincerely kind. You just *can't* hate her. And even though I was frustrated at first—pissed is probably a better adjective—I'm a fan of anyone who can voice their opinion and not follow along with the popular view. That's hard to do these days.

We catch up on randomness, my kids' happenings, what she's got going on at work. This Birthday-Cake Martini I'm drinking is funneling down a smidge too fast.

"What was up last night?" Kelsey asks, waggling her brows minimally— the 'tox. She rocks an overly enthusiastic grin.

"I don't wanna talk about it." Another sip of the sweet, thick liquid burns a bit as it descends to my stomach, sizzling into my bloodstream and providing me with that slight tingle in my arms.

"Well, you don't have a choice, because I'm old and boring and in desperate need of excitement." Her eyes are wide as she awaits any scrap of juicy details. She's seven years older than me but looks late twenties. I'm not kidding. The bitch. I'm kidding with that.

"We were getting somewhere—I mean, *really* getting somewhere."

She straightens in her chair, giving me her undivided attention. "Oh, more, more."

After laughing, I huff out an overly dramatic exhale. "Then he lied to me."

Her shoulders slump, and the cheery expression melts from her face as she groans. "What do you mean, he lied? What did he lie about? I told him he had to be honest if he—"

"What?" I study her face, and her eyes shift to her manicured hands, now tapping against the varnished surface of the bar. "You've been talking to Jake? About… us?"

No thanks. I know we're a fifty-fifty split with the friendship, but that's a violation of the code.

"Hey, relax," she responds to my stank face.

Don't get me wrong, she may be nice and sweet, but she'll spit words right back at me if I let 'em fly. Clearing her throat, Kelsey runs a finger along the outside of her glass.

"Did you talk to him today? On the phone?" I ask.

"No."

Mother. Fucker.

I heave an outraged breath. "I knew it." My tongue clicks. "He *is* a liar."

"What…?" Before reclining back in the chair, she quiets my jumping knee. "What did he lie about?"

"What *didn't* he lie about?"

"Do you wanna tell me why I would be on the phone with him?"

I roll my eyes but then shake my head, turning it down a notch. "No. It doesn't matter."

Kelsey takes a drink then wipes her lips. "He's lost, Alex."

"It's his fau—"

She whips up a silencing hand. "Hear me out."

I nod and take a sip of my cocktail. If I'm telling the truth, I'm somewhat scared of Kelsey. She's the momma of the group and you know—you don't talk back to momma.

"He's been asking for advice, stuff he can do, ways he can try to make things better."

My gaze travels blankly around the crowded place, but I'm listening.

"I told him being honest is the best way. *That* and of course helping with the kids, paying attention to details, being there for you. But transparency is key. He's clueless, Alex. He's like most of the men out there. Though he just so happens to have made a massive mistake. He loves you, and I think you know that." She searches my eyes.

I nod and chew the inside of my cheek, thinking about all the reminiscing I've done lately. The anger I feel starts to fade, but only a little.

"You know what? I'm texting him." She reaches into her purse—which probably cost as much as my car; okay, that's excessive, but it's swank—and pulls out her cell before swiping away. "Holy shit, Alex. Where is your phone?"

I tap my coat pocket. "Dead," I mumble. Same as my heart. Wow, dramatic much? The booze is beginning to think for me.

"Jake's been looking for you. He wants to know where you are."

"No," I say, throwing her a stern scowl that she knows not to defy.

Kelsey sighs. "I don't want to be in the middle of anything." Staring reluctantly at her screen, her fingers hover above the keyboard.

"Then turn off your phone and don't put yourself in the middle."

"I wish the two of you would just bang it out already. You're a bit of a bitch when you aren't getting any."

My jaw drops, maybe hitting the bar, I'm not sure. "Well, that's—"

She bumps her shoulder into mine with a spirited laugh. "I'm kidding! Since when can't you take a joke?"

Since I feel like the universe has turned against me.

"Please… don't text him. I need a minute. You know how I get when I'm mad. I need it to fizzle out a bit."

Kelsey clicks off the phone in her hand and chucks it into her purse. "Deal."

The conversation is light and easy. Casually, she brings up my outgrown roots. Of course she does. This fixer-upper has been dying to do an extreme makeover—Alex edition. I give in. Giving in seems to be my strong suit lately.

I'm not getting the kids back till New Year's Day. Sadly, I have plenty of free time, and it might be nice to change things up. Kelsey swears not to get too carried away. It's cool. Because I know one thing for sure… Blondes are *not* having more fun right now.

The bartender places a drink in front of me. Huh?

"Oh, no, sorry. I didn't order anything." I slide the deep-brown cocktail away from me.

He gestures to the side with his chin. "From the gentleman over there," he responds, pushing the glass back in my direction.

Christ, do I have a sign hanging over me that screams desperate? Seriously. Kelsey is sitting here looking like a goddess and then you've got *me*. Who would consider buying me a drink? Is that even still a thing?

My eyes sift through the crowd of buzzing people, unable to make out who my secret drink-gifter is. Then I see him.

Oh, the fucking timing.

He raises his glass, offering a silent toast, while a provocative grin curves his lips. Heat instantaneously crawls up my neck to my face.

Jake? Jake who?

There's something about this guy that's particularly appealing. This is strictly a physical reaction. Window shopping only. Can't get mad at it.

"You know him?" Kelsey interrupts our completely harmless eye-fucking. Confusion laces her voice as she watches this weird, semi-flirtatious staring contest.

"Kind of." I shrug, taking a swig of whatever this coffee liquor combination is, smirking at my admirer. Way to pay attention to detail.

"What is this called?" I flick my nail against the glass, grabbing the bartender's attention as he mixes up something in front of us.

"Well, here we call it an After-Dinner-Tini." He releases an amused chuckle, focus glued to his task.

Wow, not very inventive, but I guess there are only so many names. He *obviously* knows I have a thing for coffee after our run-in.

"What's funny about that?" Kelsey snaps, clearly perturbed.

"Um… nothing," the bartender stammers, cheeks flashing red. The typical reaction men—and women—tend to have when they're face to face with her beauty. "It… it was asked for by another name." He glances at me nervously, then down the bar to make sure no one is listening.

Hayden *fucking* Fox watches me from across the noisy venue and wets his lips. The bartender leans in to whisper in my ear, and I take a drink of my concoction, almost choking.

"What'd he say?" Kelsey insists, pulling on my sleeve after the bartender gets back to work.

"You don't want to know." I shake my head and down the drink. Screw it.

The cocktail he requested had a cute, sweet, totally innocent name. Very PG, no underlying references at all.

"Alex, do *not* go there," Kelsey says in a warning tone, her grip tightening over my forearm.

"Oh my God, would you chill out?" I groan. "I'm just looking. Is that not allowed?"

She huffs but releases my arm.

Oh, yeah… and the alleged drink name?

Sit On My Face.

Fuck my life.

19. CARRY ON

It's all flowing, but doesn't it always? The drinks, the bullshit, the poor decisions. Why is it when we get so mad, or hurt, lashing out becomes a natural instinct? Maybe it's just me? Why does payback seem like such a fantastically horrible choice?

Revenge is the *worst* thing ever. It's toxic and only ensures that everything will cycle back, returning to the beginning.

I suppose that's why I'm still here at the bar right now. Why I'd convinced Kelsey I was just staying for one more drink. She had to leave; she works early in the morning, but I have nothing to go home for, just the dogs, and they're good for now.

I get it. What the hell, Alex? A bar by yourself? Safety is a thing, I recognize that. And I'm not suggesting that something can't happen, even in your own backyard, trust me, but this is the type of place that's packed with vaguely familiar faces. For example, Will's teacher is across the room hanging out with my mailman. So there's that.

Kelsey also threatened the bartender with a death-glare warning to make sure he hooked me up with a charger, so I could dial a ride.

Regardless, she knows when I put my foot down, it's impossible to get that sucker off the floor.

I never did plug my phone in.

Anyway, I'm pretty sure that whole revenge mentality is why I'm sitting here, having another cocktail, talking to Hayden. More like listening. The guy doesn't shut up.

I know, I know. What am I doing?

I'm not gonna lie, part of me wants Kelsey to mention the gifted drink to Jake, so he experiences the vicious sting of jealousy. And it's nice to get attention from another man.

Is this healthy? Of course not. My self-esteem hasn't been booming lately, and this makes me feel like I have something left to offer.

That's a shit excuse. Really, all I'm doing is sitting here wondering who Jake was on the phone with. My temper has evened out, and I'm a bit disappointed with my knee-jerk reaction. Sadly, that's just how I am.

Maybe it was Annie? Who knows? I'd think if it was, I would've gotten a text or call from her before my battery died. I should've asked Jake, or at least allowed him to get a word in. But that's not my style. I get mad and it's gloves off.

Yeah, it's a flaw.

My temper has gotten significantly better over the years. But when it's on full tilt, it's safest—for all—to stay away.

Jake always knew how to deal with it. When he'd come home late, and I'd be seven thousand shades of pissy, feeling as if I was a single parent, he'd let me have my go and simply take it. Everything was for us, to make more money, to provide for the kids, for me. He had to attend these networking dinners and whatnot for his job. I never thought he was cheating. I still don't think he was.

I don't think?

And too bad money truly isn't the key to happiness. Some days I wish us back to that sketchy shoebox apartment.

The problem is, I often felt like a silent partner; like I was watching my life go by and wasn't even a participant. I was Mom of course and did pretty well with *that* role. But I was still alone. Like I said, I'd lost me.

"Sound good?" Fox—Hayden asks, ripping me from my choppy thoughts. His blue eyes shimmer beneath the soft overhead light. He undoes a button at the top of his collared shirt, revealing a toned chest. Then his fingers brush my arm.

"What? Um, alright." I have no clue what he said. I tuned out a while ago. He lost me at buyer's and seller's markets.

This is a bad spot. I need to go home. I can't even get an Uber with my phone dead, and I'm definitely not driving. No matter what, there is *never* an excuse to drink and drive—it's not fucking worth it.

"Alright, let's go," he says, rising from his chair then smoothing out his dark dress pants. Who wears business stuff on a Sunday? Oh, did he say he was a realtor?

"What?" I can hardly hear myself. My brain is laggy.

"To my place," he says with a presumptuous smile, as if it's an everyday thing for him.

Maybe it is?

His eyes rake up and down my body suggestively, making me feel cheap. He throws money on the bar for the drinks, claiming it's his treat, then lifts his brows, informing me I'm more than welcome to return the favor.

Is he trying to be funny, or is he an actual slimeball?

Okay, so the drinks and flirting were one thing. But his place? Not a shot. The revenge I had in mind was the same crime Jake committed—a kiss—but the more I think about getting even, the sadder I become. The more I imagine kissing someone else, the more my mind goes to Jake.

This guy is hot, sure, but he hasn't asked about my life. Not a single question directed to me. He enjoys hearing himself talk and doesn't know anything about who I am.

Who am I?

I stand from my chair, and the foggy effects of the Martini menu deliver a swift smack upside the head. The floor is like Jell-O, or could that be my legs? My bartender babysitter is busy chatting it up at the other end of the bar.

"You know what, I'm actually tired and should probably get home." I semi-slur the words, attempting to figure out how I'll get there. I can't leave with this guy.

He frowns with a scowl, disappointed. "At least let me give you a ride?"

Nah, dude. I'm good.

Why am I following him to the door? He seems like the type of man who usually gets what he wants.

Wouldn't it make me feel better? Help me get over it? Be the nail in the coffin? A way to move forward?

Nope. It would be revenge. I'd only be doing it to stay connected to Jake in some backwards way, forcing the circle to keep spinning around and around, staying stuck in the past. I learned a thing or two in therapy when I was younger.

If the events of today and my talk with Brynn did anything for me—which they did—they showed me I need to slow down and try to remain calm. I still don't wanna see Jake. I'm still afraid of what will more than likely fly out of my mouth. But I surely am *not* going home with Hayden.

He pushes the door open, holding it for me as I step out into the freezing, late December air, unsure of my game plan at this point. No chance I'm getting in his Beamer.

"Sorry, I just don't… I'm not—"

"Alexandra," he says, and I cringe. "I get it. I went through a divorce myself. It's difficult to start over."

He closes any distance between us and lowers his head to my face. I'm frozen. This doesn't feel right. But I'm not sure if it feels wrong. We aren't going through a divorce… are we?

"When you're ready, give me a call." He slips a business card, *a business card*, into my pocket.

Is this how it's done these days? I have no clue. I haven't dated since I was seventeen. This isn't dating. No, this is… I don't know what the hell this is.

And while my mind is running laps on the hamster wheel, his finger traces the contour of my jaw, and the lingering whiskey on his breath temporarily lulls me into a sense of security. Maybe because Jake doesn't drink it?

My brain shifts into overdrive when his lips meet mine, and his hand anchors to my waist. He's gentle, but not in the way I'm used to, going slow when Jake would find a steadier rhythm; keeping his body slightly away from mine, whereas Jake would invade my space, consuming every single part of me. His lips pry mine apart—but there's no teasing of the tongue in that playful manner, asking for an invitation. There's no spark, no emotion, no magic, no… *Jake.*

"Stop!" I push against his chest, and he staggers back, shock inscribed on his features.

What did I do?

I paused. It lasted maybe three seconds, but… *I fucking paused.*

My mouth gapes while I process what in the actual dumpster fire just happened.

Hayden backs away further, hoisting his hands apologetically. "I'm so sorry, Alexandra. I completely misread things."

First, it's Alex. No one calls me Alexandra, and second… fuck!

"Uh, it's okay. Sorry you thought I wanted—yeah." I avoid looking him in the eye, excruciatingly mortified and ashamed.

"I'm so sorry," he apologizes again, touching a finger to his lips while the blood drains from my face. It's highly probable I'm going to be sick.

Hayden turns towards the parking lot and appears marginally embarrassed himself, while I stand there, baffled. I fight the urge to gag, utterly repulsed with myself. Why'd I let that happen for any number of seconds? What's wrong with me? How could I do that?

Are these the same thoughts that ran through Jake's head?

"It's okay. Just forget it. Left my phone inside. I'll uh…" I pat the pocket he sank his card into, signifying I'll call him.

No, I won't.

He doesn't say a word, only nods and blinks multiple times then drops his head down and walks away.

I bolt for the door and swipe my cell from its corner bar spot, thankful no one lifted it. I'll charge it in my car—just a minute or two to get me enough juice to snag a ride.

When I step outside again, a blaring horn makes me jump. My back stiffens as I slowly turn to the top of the parking lot, just now noticing the silver SUV pulled up to the curb. When did Annie get here? I guess Kelsey asked her to come pick me up, not trusting the bartender, and rightfully so. Not that it's his job.

Swallowing the lump that's lodged in my throat, I swerve-walk to the passenger door, head hung in disgrace. The window slides down.

"Annie," I cry before glancing up, not even trying to curb the shame on my face for what I've done.

Nope. Not Annie.

It's Jace. Shit.

"Kelsey thought you might need a ride." He studies me, calm as ever. A meager half-smile bunches his cheek, but the disapproval is there.

Jace saw it. He will, without a doubt, tell Jake. I would, if the shoe were on the other foot.

I'm horrified and wide-eyed as I climb into the car. My face drops into my trembling, outstretched hands, and I let the waterworks fly.

* * *

When Annie and I met at the hospital, after my hazing was complete, we realized we had a ton in common. Far too much to let it go to waste. It was a friendship that was written in the stars.

It didn't take us long to discover we shared a powerful love for sarcasm, caffeine, memes, and cuss words. We were similar in some ways and polar opposites in others. It was easy. Still is. Of course, we disagree—that's normal. But we don't really fight; we get each other.

Annie and Jace got married at nineteen. Nineteen! That's almost unheard of these days. Not a shotgun wedding either, just big love.

We both had little girls. Brynn had recently turned three, and Liv was one. It was perfect. When we talked about our husbands, it seemed they couldn't be more different. Jace worked in construction—no fancy degree, long days, and rigorous hands-on labor. Jake was the business guy, long days for sure, but he pushed paper and dealt with numbers and schmoozing. We never expected them to hit it off like they did.

It was an immediate bromance.

They shared the same interest in music, had similar outlooks on life, and obviously loved strong, smart women. Well, sometimes strong and smart. Those two became the male equivalent of Annie and me. Like I said, it was perfect. She and I were a match made in heaven. Okay, probably hell, but we have fun. They put up with our shenanigans. Laughed with us—*at* us. But we didn't care.

The four of us formed our own individual relationships. Jace became a brother to me. He was always sweet, always ready to lend an impartial ear. He's soft-spoken, but when you have someone like Annie as your partner, I suppose you need to be so it balances out.

* * *

He pulls into my driveway, letting me bawl the entire ride home. He didn't say a word or offer advice and unsolicited opinions. Jace let me do what no one else has lately. Allowed me to *feel* the way I wanted. No objections.

"Come on." He opens my car door with a soft smile, helping me out. I'm wobbly, my brain is fuzzy, my stomach churning in protest. Gentle hands slip into mine, steadying me.

"God, Jace, I'm so sorry." With a grimace, I shake my head. I'm so sorry for taking him away from his family, my best friend, on a Sunday night when I know he has to be up early for work.

He moves the hair from my face, matted from the downpour of tears. Don't go speculating—brother status, remember? Plus, I would never, and I mean *ever*, do that.

"You don't have to apologize." He drapes an arm over my shoulder, steering me towards the front porch. "I care about you and want *you* to be okay."

"I'm not."

"I know."

After multiple tries, and limited help from me, Jace finds the correct key and pops open the door. The dogs hurricane past us like a furry shitstorm.

"Let's get you water or something." He rounds up the beasts before coming inside and settling onto the couch next to me. "You know you can talk to me if you want to."

Can I? Won't he run and tell Jake everything?

"I don't only want what's best for Jake, okay? I want what's best for the both of you; for all six of you. Annie can be… well, you know, she can be tough." He shrugs.

She can be. But if the tables flip-flopped, I'd sing like a canary. That would *never* happen though. I can't picture an Annie without a Jace… it doesn't make sense.

I kick off my shoes and hug my knees to my chest, staring at the blank TV on the wall. "So, you saw, right?" I ask as the threat of more tears burns my nose.

He moves on the couch to face me. "Yeah."

"What is wrong with me?" That's it, the floodgates are open. Tonight is the first time, in over a decade of friendship, I've let Jace see me break down. I'm talking hysterics. This isn't a sniffly, quiet, dab-under-the-eyes cry. This is a big, snotty-nose ugly cry.

"Alex, it's okay." He attempts to console me, doing an awkward shoulder pat. He knows I'm not big on the hugs, and I know he's uncomfortable. "It didn't seem like it was what you wanted, at least not from where I was sitting?"

Does that make it any better though? I placed myself in that position, let myself fall right into it. I mean, yes, I stopped it. No, it wasn't anything like I'd envisioned in my mind while window shopping. But damn, I paused.

It happened.

"It wasn't." I laugh. You ever get so sad you can't help but laugh, because you just want to stop crying? "Actually, I pictured Jake, compared every little detail to—"

Jace quickly sways his head like *I don't wanna know this shit.*

I close my eyes and bury my face in my bent knees. "I know you gotta tell him."

"Not me," he replies.

I glance up to see him frowning. "Huh?"

"You're going to have to do that one."

My stomach is somewhere around my ankles.

I nod. "Yeah, I guess so."

He sighs, elbows propped on his legs, forehead resting on his fingertips. He's in a tight spot—I recognize that.

"I will… it's just… I thought it would make me feel better, but it didn't. Actually, I'm appalled with myself. Appalled that I orchestrated the situation. I'm a *fucking* idiot."

He slides a palm down his face, stress evident in the rushed breath he exhales. "No, you aren't. You're hurt, Alex, but you aren't an idiot."

Tears sting my eyes, and my lips tremble. It's time to take the mask off.

"The problem is, despite everything, as much as I don't want to…"

Not for the sake of anyone else, but for the sake of myself, I need to admit it. Because happy or not, serious screw-ups or not, you *can't* just wipe away twenty years with someone—it doesn't work that way.

"I'm still in love with Jake."

20. JUST GIVE ME
A REASON

"Of course you love him, Alex. If you didn't, none of this would be so difficult."

That's the *only* thing Jace says, hugging me, and I allow it. Full squeeze. It's surprisingly comforting. He lets me cry for who knows how long.

It's time to stop lying to myself. I need to *really* feel and think. Stop trying to do the right thing or the wrong thing or the thing everyone wants me to do. Should I take him back? I don't know. Wouldn't that make me pathetic?

The main problem is still the same problem—I'm not sure if our love is enough. If I can get over the hurt and betrayal. And I *definitely* don't know how Jake will react when I tell him about my… whatever.

Even more than that, how's he going to accept the fact it's someone he does business with. Isn't it ironic? No chance I can wrap my skull around *this* one.

I'm not placing it in the exact same category, because I stopped it. There was no plan; it was involuntary, not first or second degree. But the crime's been committed, and someone's gotta pay.

Gandhi pegged it right—an eye for an eye *does* make the entire world blind. Oh Lord Jesus, if I'm quoting Gandhi, you *know* the shit has done headed sideways.

I feel horrible. Let the self-loathing resume. Has it ever even stopped? Now we're worse off than only hours ago. It would be super convenient if I could rewind time, because the amount of changes I'd make is insane.

The dogs go crazy, howling at the lights that flash in the driveway. It's Jake—who else would it be? Jace's lips pinch as he leans back from the hug, his hand grasping mine.

Here we go.

"I had to tell him you were okay. I'm sorry, but he's been losing his mind. You wouldn't answer anyone's texts."

"Dead phone," I respond with a sigh.

Am I that much of a risk, *that much* of a loose cannon they're all on edge if I'm upset?

I guess the past is hard to let go of, in many ways, for everyone.

Goddamn Jace. Goddamn the bro code. I get it though, and I would've done the same.

"I don't wanna talk to him right now," I say, wiping my cheeks, which seems pointless. No doubt I look a mess.

Who even cares?

"He just wants to make sure you're okay." He stands from the couch and starts pacing. A palm spears through his hair after he shoves his sleeves to the elbows. "I'll make him leave… if that's what you want."

I nod. Yes, *nothing* good is going to come of this. Love or not. Anger or sadness. The emotions are way too high right now; the whiplash is incredible.

The front door flies open, cracking into the wall, elevating the dogs' level of ape shit. They love Jake. They miss him. He struggles with the jumble of furry feet hounding him but dodges the unrestrained jumping and lethal tails, darting through the foyer.

"What the hell, Alex?" He races into the living room, voice loaded with fear, worry—maybe a combo of everything.

"She's fine. Her phone died," Jace explains calmly then reaches back to where I'm now standing behind him and offers his hand.

Jake's eyes whip to the reassuring gesture before they narrow. "Why are you here? Why is he here?"

I take a step forward, my head pounding and my heart torn to fucking shreds. My sights sway to Jace, who puts a palm against Jake's chest, barring him from coming any closer.

"Get off me." He smacks his hand away, shooting his friend a poisonous scowl.

"She needed a ride home. Kelsey asked Annie, and I was up." With a shrug, Jace blocks me again.

"What the fuck are you doing, man? Move!"

"No, Jake. You see her. She's *here* and is alright. Now you gotta go."

Jace remains firmly rooted in front of me. These two have never so much as had words in all the years they've known each other.

"I'm not leaving. This is my house!" Jake shouts. "Alex, please… please talk to me." He sounds drained and overcome with desperation. "Please! I love you."

I can't look at him. There isn't even anger anymore. Remorse is the *only* thing in this living room.

"I will do *anything*, I swear to God. I can't live without you." His deep voice cracks from the raw emotion he's pouring into the words, not giving a shit that Jace is witnessing his professions.

I'm biting the inside of my lip so hard, it may very well start to bleed. Tears spill down my face, while his eyes take on a glossy sheen. I feel guilty that he assumes these tears are because of him. They aren't right now. Right now, they're for all of us. They're for our kids.

They're for the fact that we couldn't get our filthy fucking hearts together enough to realize what we had.

"You gotta go." Jace manhandles him towards the front door.

"Get the hell off me!" Jake shoves him hard.

"She doesn't want you here."

"Don't tell me… you can't tell me what my wife wants." He pushes Jace once more.

"Stop," I barely say out loud.

The scuffling continues. Shit, this is fucked up.

"Jake, cut it out!" Jace yells. No, a yell is too quiet a description—he booms, the words rolling like thunder through the house. I've never heard his voice get that loud—ever. "This *isn't* the way, man. I'm trying to help you both. You can't act like this. You can't smother her." He snatches him by the collar.

The world stops for a second. Fucking Jace. Who knew he had it in him?

But here's the thing, this can't stain their friendship. Jace has been so awesome, and *right now*, I'm letting this argument happen. It's wrong. And maybe it's one of the only things I can fix.

"Jace…" I'm hoarse from crying. "Just let him go."

The collateral damage has got to stop somewhere.

Does it ever though? You never realize how many people are affected by only one or two lives… until something changes.

He glances from me to Jake and searches the ceiling for a moment. Jake's eyes fill with hope, hands lifted in a gesture of surrender.

After drawing in a long breath, he exhales. "Fine," Jace says evenly. "But I need to talk to you for a second." He punches a finger into Jake's chest, who then follows him to the front door, briefly turning to shoot a worried glance my way.

Maybe he's gonna tell him, or maybe he's not. Either way, he'll know soon enough.

A few minutes pass, then Jace walks in alone. I'm still frozen in my spot.

"You sure you're okay?" he asks, wrapping his arms around my neck. I surprise myself by reciprocating.

We've somehow, in a matter of minutes, gained more emotional ground than we have in all our years of friendship. He *saw* me now, saw the flaws, and doesn't care. I'm so glad Annie has him.

I search his brown eyes with a silent question.

"That's on you." He frowns, sympathetic look in place.

"Thanks again, seriously, for everything."

"If you need anything—*anything*—you can call me. You can trust me, Alex."

I nod, forcing a meager smile before he leaves the house without another word. I guess Jake's tagging in.

The floor is still shaky, or jelly, or unstable—let's go with that. Needing to sit down, I opt for the longer couch. For more space.

We all need a little more space.

Jake comes in, slowly, sadly; defeated. I would have wanted this look for him months ago. Now, I think we're *both* defeated.

He's eerily quiet, with messy hair and weary eyes. In an unexpected move, he kneels on the floor in front of me, head falling into my lap. Neither of us speaks a word. His broad shoulders rise with each breath and tremble as they lower, while pain and disappointment radiate from both of us.

I feel his heart beating against my legs and fight the urge to console him by running my fingers through his hair. How can two people live together for years, be together for years, and become complete strangers?

"I'm so sorry." Jake eventually breaks the silence. Those words are on repeat, but I'm sorry too.

There's nothing about this that *isn't* heartbreaking. Is there really any saving us now?

"It was my mom on the phone earlier. She was gonna come and get the kids next weekend, so I could take you to National Harbor. I don't know why I said it was Jace; that's something I would have said before—an innocent lie." He drags in a settling breath. "I didn't want to ruin the surprise."

Everything inside me crumbles. "Why not tell me it was your mom, Jake? I don't get it?"

Innocent lies are a thing of the past.

He looks up. Long lashes curl above the hazel irises I used to get lost in, and he stares at me as he shakes his head. The sadness is the killer here.

"Because." He winces. "I'm an idiot. I thought we were getting somewhere. That we were maybe gonna try and get back like we were."

"Okay," I respond after absorbing his words. "Well, first, get up." I scoot back into the cushions, because my mind is running rampant, and even though I'm a mess at the moment, I'm also in need of some distance—immediately.

He sits on the far end of the couch, facing me.

"The thing is, Jake, we haven't done anything to actually fix us. What happened happened. And as much as I *wish* we could go back in time and erase all of it, we can't."

No matter where we go from here, we're never going to be like we were.

He silently agrees, gripping the back of his neck. "I know, Alex. I need you to know I've regretted that fucking shit every single second of every single day. I will do *whatever* it takes. I'm so mad at myself."

That makes two of us. Two of us, mad at ourselves.

I hold up a hand to stop him from continuing. "You have to start by not lying, like not ever."

He nods fast, his eyes growing larger, maybe even optimistic.

"And I need to start by not lying either."

His nose scrunches, head angling inquisitively

* * *

I can't help but think about National Harbor, because it would have been a great time. It's beautiful there, right outside of D.C. The water and boats are picturesque, while cool shops and restaurants line the streets, making you feel you're in an old town.

After we got married in Vegas, we came back and our parents—as irritated as they were that we tossed a wrench in their plans—threw us a reception. How our moms pulled that together so fast, I still don't know.

For our honeymoon, we took a small slice of the money we got and splurged… just a little.

Jake carried me over the threshold, mammothly pregnant and all. We lounged in the posh bed for hours with nothing to do, just stared at each other, talking about the future—*our* future.

Young and, um… uneducated, we'll call it. Jake was nervous whenever we had sex, because I was so far along. I felt as though he wasn't attracted to me. He begged to differ, physically showing me I *still* turned him on. We had a long laugh—well, more like I did when the motive for his nerves was disclosed. He's doing fine in that department, by the way, but why dudes *ever* assume they can reach a baby's head… yeah… it's just funny.

All things aside, it was the ideal weekend. No lack of him talking to my belly or touching it. And now I truly am feeling a certain way that he was intending to recreate. It says at least a little something.

* * *

"What?" he snaps, bringing me out of my daydream.

It's admission time.

"Tonight…"

"Yeah?" His fingers curl into fists, knuckles prominent through his skin.

"At the bar." I'm sweaty, and the scratchiness in my throat won't go away.

Alarmed eyes bore into mine, his nostrils beginning that flicker—he knows *something*'s coming. I stare down at my hands, because it's easier to look there. It's much easier than looking someone in the eyes when you know you're about to inflict harm. Uh-huh, I'm a coward.

Did he royally screw up? Yes, obviously. But did I put myself into a sketchy situation? Did a tiny part of me want him to experience the same pain I did? Yup, if I'm being dead honest, I did.

Sometimes you get what you thought you wanted only to realize you're an asshole for even contemplating it.

I open my mouth.

"Alex, no," he says, leaning towards me. "Whatever it is, I don't need to know. If you tell me we can get through this, I don't care about anything else."

He scoots closer, his palms cradling my cheeks. I know what he's doing—I can feel it. That strange, yet wonderful, tingly feeling. Jake is lining up for that coveted kiss, wanting to make a promise, to seal the deal. He stops when we're nose to nose and sinks his heavy gaze to my mouth.

Wouldn't it be so simple? To take this momentary blemish and sweep it under the rug? Pretend nothing happened? Walk over it like it's not there?

Here's the thing about that. It would become a secret, another lie, and we'd never move forward. I have to get it out there if I'm *ever* going to have a chance of letting go.

"I kissed somebody."

His hands drop.

21. HEMORRHAGE
(IN MY HANDS)

Jake stares at me, inhaling several extended breaths, eyes growing larger by the second. I can almost see the gears turning, struggling to comprehend the last three words I said.

I kissed somebody.

It was way more difficult to say out loud than I thought it would be. But I did it—Band-Aid style—and now we need to figure *this* shit out too.

His head cocks to the side, and I shy away. But not before noticing his jaw muscle tense, and his teeth mashing together.

He jolts to his feet. *"What?"*

I shrug. I'm not sure what to say here. Would I have stayed behind at the bar, if he hadn't lied? A trivial, white lie. There's no such thing anymore. Would he have ever told me about the kiss if I hadn't discovered the evidence for myself?

"Alex?" He snarls my name, and I take in his usually handsome face, contorted with viciousness, with resentment. He squints, and his teeth crack together. "What the hell? Are you *fucking* kidding me?" He scans the room like he's searching for something or someone.

Wanna break shit? I can relate.

Okay, a bit more dramatic than I was expecting. What a hypocrite, am I right? Also, I'm suffering the aftershocks of one too many drinks, putting my processing speed at an all-time low.

"I didn't exactly kiss him. He more so kissed me." I'm a little slurry, a little lackluster, and my words seem to fall on deaf ears.

Not moving from my spot on the sofa, biting at my bottom lip, I watch as Jake paces—more like stomps furiously—across the living room.

His chest heaves, fingers bending and extending repeatedly. I'm not sure I've witnessed him this pissed… *ever*. His eyes adopt a dark and unfamiliar appearance.

I've never once been afraid of Jake doing anything to harm me. Well, not physically. But at this moment, I'm not completely certain. It's as if someone flipped a switch. And that someone is me. He appears ready to lose his actual mind.

"It was stupid. I'm sorry I let it get to that point. I don't even know why…" I'm rambling, seeking to explain myself. Part of me feels like I shouldn't have to.

Let's be brutally honest here. I know *exactly* why I put myself in that situation. At the time, it was to get right here. To show Jake two can play at this game.

But sadly, this isn't a game. This is my life, and currently, it's more of a sideshow.

His cheeks are blood red, and the vein in his neck pulses, protruding from his skin. He's glaring at me, not only with disbelief, but with borderline… *hatred?* The nostril flare is happening. Okay, double standard much? God, I'm fuzzy here, but am I *missing* something?

I stand and reach for his arm. He steps away, forcing my hand off him.

"*Wow.* So that's how it is? You expect complete forgiveness, but *God forbid* if someone glances my way? You're a—"

"How could you do that?" he spits. The anger is strong, and it is substantial. This unforgiving void in his eyes is nothing, *nothing* I've seen before. He looks like he's about to go the fuck off. I mean, I knew he'd probably be pissed but—

"*My best friend?*" he screams, balled fists flying so close to me I flinch, and when he shakes them near my face… I'm done.

My brain goes blank, and he might as well be gripping me by the throat. The air is sucked out of the room like a vacuum.

"Woah, woah, woah." He must notice the paralysis that simple action produced. "Alex, no." His fingers spread, and repentance washes away the film of anger. "I would…" After tugging his collar, he works to swallow. "I'd never hurt… would *never* lay a hand on you."

Deep down I believe that, but deep down doesn't change a natural response. And his reaction… something that might be so minor to one person yet asphyxiating to another…

Oxygen filters in through my nose as I see his remorse, and the adrenaline that accompanies fight or flight simmers. Breathing becomes routine again.

"I'm sorry," he says, "but Jace?" His tone is still on edge but much more controlled than before, putting me at ease.

Wait… *Jace?*

That's what he thinks? Because he was here?

"Oh. My. God. Jake." I cross my arms over my chest, and he huffs a sigh of relief, reading my expression. "No, not *fucking* Jace. You honestly believe I would do that to my best friend?"

Sorry, Jace, but ew is my definite thought.

"Jesus." He blows out a semi-calm breath, staring at me, his eyes the same apologetic shade they've been, filled with misery and sorrow. The anger, much like the different waves of emotion we both seem to be going through lately, has promptly morphed into something else. "Alex, I'm so sorry." He soothes my shoulder, head hanging in disappointment.

He knows touch and trust go hand in hand for me, and he already violated my trust.

"It's okay, Jake. I'm okay," I mumble as he cloaks his arms around me, his face sinking to the crook of my neck. "I'm okay," I repeat quietly as his body trembles, my skin soaked from his tears.

Why do I keep saying that? It's not okay. *I'm* not okay.

Full shutdown commence.

We've done a number on each other, huh?

I'm quite emotionless about everything at this point. It's all been too much. Too tiring. I can't continue scratching and clawing to keep my head above water. I'm drained; there's nothing left to give. My arms don't move, I don't hug him back, and Jake knows I'm falling away from him again.

Sometimes it's easier. When life gets too heavy, I just go into myself. It's not the best approach, but it's part of who I am. I don't even know all the things I should feel right now.

Remorse? Yeah, obviously. Ashamed? You bet. Sad? Beyond recognition. Numb? Not enough. Not even close to enough.

And that's a problem. One I don't act on nearly as much as I did pre-kids, but when it gets to be overwhelming, it's simpler to self-medicate than face it head-on. Yeah, I know it's not the answer or the responsible attitude, but I also know I'm not alone with this shit.

* * *

I was working at the hospital around Thanksgiving when my water randomly broke, three weeks early. Several hours later, beautiful little Ruby Jean was born. My gem. We let the girls choose her name, because Jake and I couldn't agree on one, and it just worked.

Out came this tiny five-pounder, sweet and smiley. An exceptionally wonderful baby. When she turned two, the tantrums started. They progressed from there, getting worse as Roo got older. I'm talking biting, hitting, kicking; not your typical toddler fits.

Because she's not typical.

I had to fight tooth and nail for anyone to listen. Went head-to-head with doctors that were more concerned with billing, more fixated on treating lab and test results than caring for the human being in front of them.

Total bullshit.

Jake thought I was crazy. He coddled the living daylights out of her, and so did the girls. They thought she was absolutely perfect.

I don't disagree; she *is* perfect. But I saw it from early on. The repetitive movements, the anxious habits, the lack of eye contact. Finally, after months and months of pleading phone calls, walk-ins, drop-ins, and shopping around to find a pediatric specialist who would listen, we got somewhere.

You should not have to fight that *fucking* hard for someone to take your concerns seriously.

I'm in healthcare, so obviously I'm not suggesting that no one cares. I've found plenty of people that do. Tons. But some have shifted their focus from quality to quantity, and that is flat-out sad.

Anyway, we got her into as much as we could, anything to help our baby girl. But it was a lot. We immersed Roo in all the specialties; occupational therapy, speech therapy, music therapy, play therapy, aquatic therapy, even equine therapy. No, I'm not kidding. We were hell-bent on trying *everything* to make her life easier.

But it wasn't really *we*; it was *me*. Though once we got the formal diagnosis —you know, the proof they can see on paper—insurance started kicking in and we had access to all the therapies. Anyway, it was me who made the appointments, drove miles upon miles, sat in countless waiting rooms with Brynn and Jordan, carting them along to many of them.

Jake had just left his job and started his advertising business with Luke. Had he known we'd be bombarded with a gargantuan number of appointments, he would've kept his old position and held off on the new venture. But he couldn't see the future. None of us could.

I had to put in my time at work to keep us insured at that point. I realize now that Jake probably *did* believe it'd be easier for me to stay home once he could carry our family's insurance benefits, and likely assumed he was simplifying my life. Funny how perspectives change. But at the time it was stressful. Still is. We've just gotten used to it.

No, it wasn't stressful. It was a gurgling cesspool of stress. I've sought the aid of self-help books, breathing tactics, therapy, to no real avail.

I wish I could say I never felt the urge to escape my life.

But unfortunately that's just not true.

* * *

"Alex, if I could change this, I'd do it in a heartbeat," Jake whispers in my ear, his arms still holding me. And I know he means it.

I don't say a word, because there's nothing to say. I'm partly leaning on him to keep myself vertical. There's no point in me even trying to talk to him right now. Too many drinks have happened. Typical me.

He seems to realize I'm half in the bag and emotionally damaged. "Come on." His fingers slip between mine, then he guides me up the stairs.

After pulling down the cover and helping me into bed, he removes my shoes and tucks the blanket beneath my chin. Then he lies next to me, finding my hand.

"Can I ask you something?"

His approach is apprehensive and sad. A slow thumb traces circles over my palm. He knows I'm fading. I'm one of those people, that the second my head hits the pillow, my talking time is limited.

"Mm-hmm."

"Did you do it just to get back at me?" His voice stays level, and he's doing his best to remain stoic.

"Well," I sigh. "I hung out with this guy, and I only did that because… yes, it was to get back at you. And not… not because of what you did. But because I was mad, Jake. I was mad that you lied… *again.*"

"I ran outside to tell you, because I wasn't thinking. I didn't realize how you'd feel." His gaze drifts from mine. I guess he knows now, or at least a little bit.

God, it's so childish. I'm irritated with myself. Two steps forward, two steps back.

I struggle to keep my eyes open. He frowns, inspecting our hands— these hands that are clutching on to something so tight that is all but breaking, desperate to hold everything together. It's as if little pieces of us are trying to let go while other parts are fighting like hell to hold on.

It's hard, and it is fucking complicated.

"I'm sorry." I momentarily give in to my drowsy lids and swallow my disappointment.

I wonder what Jake's was like. How sad is this? I'm giving our extramarital flings an identity. I wonder if her tongue ever made it into his mouth. Did it last five seconds? Ten? Longer? Did he eventually stop it? The curiosity about the details never tapped me on the shoulder before. But now that we're in similar boats…

Nope. I can't go there. Not tonight.

Jake presses his lips into a convincing-enough smile, but his eyes don't lie. The pain, the mere prospect of someone touching the person you thought was your everything is indescribable. It injures your soul. It cuts you open, and it's near impossible to stop the bleed.

He moves closer to me, his familiar scent filling my nostrils, strangely making me more comfortable in my bed than I have been in months. There's still a space between us.

I think there always will be.

"I… I don't know what to say." His eyes gloss over, while my view of him flickers.

Man, my seventeen-year-old self would smack me in the face. After she smacked Jake of course. Why the hell are we here, and how long has it *really* been falling apart?

"You can say whatever you want." My voice is raspy; I'm fading fast.

He brings our hands to his mouth, lips skimming over each one of my knuckles. "Who?" he asks.

This is the kicker, because I know it'll piss him off. At least his cheap trick is one I can only see via social-media stalking, and, after a few days, I stopped searching her. This is someone he perhaps sees regularly. Someone he has to cater to. Someone who helps feed our children.

"Does it matter?"

"Kind of."

"I wish I never knew her name. I wish none of this shit ever happened." And I absolutely wish I didn't have to come clean. "Hayden Fox," I say, bracing myself for the repercussions.

"Jesus Christ, Alex. I do a ton of business with that guy." He lets go of my hand and covers his face, dragging his palms to his neck.

"Sorry." It's not convincing. He knows me.

"And I can't say a word, can I? But fuck! You had to go *there*?" He exhales a long breath, closing his eyes.

This was much easier when I was just hating him, when he was the only one to blame. Now I've gone and sought to even the odds. It's so pointless. What was I hoping to gain here? If I was worried he wasn't paying attention before, I can be damn sure he is now.

"Sorry," I say again, no actual emotion in the word.

Am I regretful? Of course. Though I'm not sorry Jake got a taste of his own medicine… kind of. Call it immature or whatever you want, but in this current state of mind, I'm owning it.

Sorry will happen in the morning… like it always does.

He needs to make a choice, and it's the same as it was. Because if he writes off Hayden and his money because of this… then he better completely write off the New York trash too. I don't care that it's Luke who *deals* with her now.

I pull away, and Jake reaches to grab my hand again, the same one I'm tucking beneath my pillow. It's safer to shut down than to keep riding this wave.

"Don't do this." His voice strains in agony. "We can get through this."

I barely open my eyes. "I'm just tired, Jake."

"Me too."

Neither of us utter another word. I let myself drift, leaving both of us torn, wounded, and confused. Jake's hand finds mine, holding tight, and he kisses my forehead. His quiet words hum in my ear before sleep washes over me.

"I won't give up on us."

22. GOOD AS HELL

I wake up obscenely early. Mondays suck

The unrelenting head pounding, the sensitivity to light—I gotta get my life together. Water and coffee will be my besties today.

I replay the events from last night on a constant loop. Fixating is my go-to; I obsess about anything and everything. The idiotic flirting. The weird and seriously uncomfortable spit swap. My savior, Jace. Jake being gut-punched by my quasi-retaliation. The cycle continues. The drama is for real.

It feels like it's *never* gonna end.

Of course, the bed is empty. It's not just the two of us, so Jake had to get back to his house. The kids, remember?

I'm lying here, trying to figure out if I truly want him here, or if I'm just that lonely? I keep thinking how he said he won't give up. And I wonder if I'm going to or not.

Honestly, I can't imagine being with someone else, definitely not physically. Last night's lip-locking made that apparent. My undoubtable desire for him to be in bed with me has me painfully aware I'm still very much attracted to him. Who wouldn't be? He's aging well. But attraction isn't everything. Neither is love, I suppose. Or maybe it is? Why can't these conflicting thoughts deliberate and come to some sort of definitive answer? I guess you can't reason with emotions.

Sadly, I realize where I'm headed… the dreaded spiraling. I've been here before. Not in the same situation obviously, but I've been to the point where I feel unhinged, and adding to the destruction is second nature. Yeah… it's not a good time.

I think back to Kelsey saying Jake was lost. Aren't we all? I'm so lost, so lost in life right now; have been for a while. I'm Brynn, Jordan, Roo, and Will's mom, and I'm the boss at that. But what about me? Like, who I *really* am? Why did she get put on the back-burner?

Why did I sacrifice so Jake could work and continue playing hockey? I never complained, didn't contest it, because I didn't mind it. I was happy he was doing something he loved. He'd tell me his plans, and I said okay. I never announced where I'd be between a certain time. Not because he wouldn't support it, but because it just went that way. I'd ask if he could be around to watch the kids, *our kids*, if there was something extracurricular I wanted to do, which was infrequent.

That's life, I guess…?

The day powers on, filled with trivial nothingness. The dogs are my only company. Radio silence from Jake. A few times I begin to text but stop.

Time. Maybe *we* just need time; *he* just needs time? Maybe I need to make up my mind?

I spend my night replaying events from the last two decades. Some recent, some not. Some high, some low. I marvel at how it all slips by so damn fast and simultaneously wonder what happened to the tough Alex. The funny Alex.

Fucking *life*. That's what happened.

Kelsey shoots me a text to meet her at the fancy salon she goes to, tomorrow at noon, for my supposed birthday gift. Hair, nails, the royal treatment. I don't feel like it, but again, I've got nothing better to do, and it'll make her happy.

Annie's been messaging excessively all day, drilling me for the drama-packed details. There's no doubt my one-worded responses to her long-winded texts are annoying her. I just don't feel like talking to anyone.

Only the kids.

They video called earlier, excited to be going to the movie theater. The movie theater that houses one of our post-holiday traditions. We always spent the week between Christmas and New Year's together. When I was working full-time, I'd take it off. As would Jake. Anyway, business was dead for him during that week, because people were more focused on family than advertising. That's how it should be.

On Tuesday morning, it's the same routine. Dogs out and fed, get myself somewhat in order, and let's not forget coffee. All the coffee.

I pull into the salon a couple of minutes late. That's me—never punctual.

The place is stunning. An old stone house, the inside walls planked halfway up with gray wood, matching floors, and crisp white-brick accent walls. It looks clean, classy, and has Kelsey written all over it. I can spot her designs a mile away. They're so simple and elegant, yet effortless, a lot like she is.

As for me, well, this girl could use some effort right about now.

"Hey." Kelsey goes in for the cheek kiss.

"Hi." I eye her up as she shoots me a devilish grin.

"I got a big surprise for you today!" She smiles and rubs her palms together. "Today you get the best of the best, the owner—Monica."

"Yay," I respond, sort of monotone, and nowhere near as enthused as her.

"Humor me? Have fun. You deserve some fun."

I breathe in and slap a grin on my face.

"How'd the rest of Sunday night go?" If she has any inkling of what happened, she isn't broadcasting it.

"Not so great." My tongue pokes the inside of my cheek. "But I got home safe, so don't worry."

"Did he… did that guy—"

"Could we not do this?" My question is clipped. I'm kind of upset with her, because she made me feel like she was more loyal to Jake than to me.

"Alright." She waves her hand. See, this is where she and Annie differ. "Can I tell you something?" She tilts her head, pulling her bottom lip to her mouth.

Ugh, not if it's bad. That's what I want to say. Instead, I say, "Sure."

"I want you to know I admire you."

I nod a single time.

"That I don't want you to think I'm excusing him, excusing Jake." She squeezes the forearm of my old sweatshirt, looking me straight in the eyes. "I just want you to know… sometimes when you're outside of a situation… when you aren't in it yourself—and *trust me* I know, because I've been in a not-so-ideal one myself—but when you're looking in and see something so rare and so beautiful, and you see how much love two people have for each other… it's tough to watch them let it go."

I stare back at her and blink. Kelsey isn't usually one for poignant talks. She paints an expansive smile on her face then sweeps a rogue strand of hair from my cheek and pats my shoulder.

She sighs. "Okay, well, today is for you. You want a mimosa?"

"No thanks."

First off, I'm proud of myself for not crying. Second, no *fucking* alcohol. At least not till tonight. It's New Year's Eve, so who am I kidding?

Her phone buzzes, and she raises a finger before strutting away, leaving me to peruse some of the pictures hanging on the wall.

"I'm so sorry." She groans, returning to the smaller reception area after ending her call. "Issues at a job site—gotta jet. Mon…" She juts her chin to a woman coming out to the front, dressed head to toe in black. "Take good care of my girl."

"What? I thought we were doing this together. I thought you wanted to do this?"

"Nah." Kelsey winks. "I want you to do this." And she's out, leaving me standing here in my oversized hoodie and jeans, no makeup, hair pulled into a low pony, looking like a straight-up mom.

"Alright." I exhale as Monica guides me to a chair in the back. The place is empty, the sign on the door flipped to closed. "Wait? You're not open?" I ask, a little confused.

"Only for you." Blindingly white teeth spread into a wide beam. She's flawless—full makeup, brown hair straightened and hanging sleek between her shoulder blades, emerald eyes. "You must be very special to Kelsey. She rented this *entire* place, just for you."

* * *

You ever met someone and instantly clicked? You can open up, spill all your secrets, with no worry of judgment? As if you've been friends for years? It's few and far between—at least for me it is; trust issues for the win— but Monica, she's something else. She made me feel comfortable right off the bat. Jumped straight into a broad-spectrum conversation about life and just… *everything*.

Somewhere between a manicure and deep-conditioning treatment, I pour my heart out to this chick, and she listens. *Actually* listens. Doesn't offer too much advice; only a comment here and there.

I tell her how I've been feeling like I need more in my life, and that I'm barely staying afloat. How I don't know who I am anymore.

"Do you enjoy being a nurse?" she asks, checking the dye she scrubbed into my hair a while back. With no clue what I wanted as far as a change, I told her to take the reins.

"I love it. And I miss it… a lot," I respond. And this time, I don't feel guilty for saying it.

"Go back. I mean, why not? You said your kids are in school now, so what's stopping you?"

I explain how often I have to take Roo to appointments, how overwhelmed I get trying to take care of the house. It literally takes all freaking day to keep up with shit. The to-do list is a million miles long.

"Fuck it," she says, and I'm in love. "You can make it work. You *gotta* do you, ya know? This is the only shot any of us get. Life is too short not to be happy. To-do lists will always exist."

Wow. She's not wrong. And honestly, I've been toying with the idea of going back to work. Annie's there, and maybe it'll give me a little more purpose, a little more sense of self?

"I suppose I could bring it up to Jake." I shrug as she removes the last foil, leaning me back to rinse my hair.

"Um, Jake? If you want it, don't bring it up to him—*tell* him about it. Just because you're the mom doesn't mean you have to be the one to always hold everything down. Together or not, he can step in and help you. What I've learned from talking to you is that he seems to be a decent guy. He messed up. So did you. No matter what happens, you're going to have to work as a team."

"Yeah, I guess you're right."

She straightens the chair after wringing my drenched locks in a towel. When I catch a glimpse in the mirror, my eyebrows get lost. Holy shit, my hair is dark. I'm talking Morticia Addams dark.

Monica must sense my shock, but she just laughs. "Listen. You want a change, right?"

"I… it's, um… I didn't think it would be this…"

"I'm not talking about your hair. Though don't sweat—it'll lighten. I'm talking about *you*. Look, I haven't gone through the same things, but I've had my share of difficulties. What I can tell you is sometimes you gotta stop treading water. Take the floaties off, plunge in headfirst, and go for a swim."

I'm good at plunging, I think? Swimming though?

"Stop worrying about what everyone else wants, and what's going to make them happy. Shoot, you only came here today because you wanted to make Kelsey happy."

I open my mouth to object, and she flashes her infectious smile at me in the mirror. "I'm not wrong. But it's okay because I'm glad you came in."

"Me too," I admit. This was better than any therapy I've ever had.

"And you don't have to decide everything straight away. Let it happen. If you want to be with Jake, then do it. If you don't, then don't. And it's okay if you aren't sure right now, because some stuff you figure out as you go." She squeezes my shoulders. "Start doing the things you want to do, Alex."

"I don't know." My lips rumble with a sigh. "There's so much we need to work out." I hurt him last night. No matter what he said, I'm not sure if we can ever recover, not completely.

"You never *do* know… but from what Kelsey has told me, and what I've learned from us talking, you are amazing. Time to focus on yourself though. Time to be your own hero."

Damn. She's right.

Monica spins me around while she blows out my hair. I'm sure I'll never be able to replicate this, no matter how hard I try. That's the one thing about getting my hair done I can't stand. You can *never* make it look as good as they do.

She whips out a makeup palette and goes to town, and I reposition myself nervously in the chair.

"Don't worry, I won't get too crazy," she says, and I try to relax. Something about her makes me trust her words.

"Will he be there tonight?" she asks, putting the finishing touches on my eyes.

"I don't know. I haven't heard from him. Last I told him was not to come."

"Do you want him to?"

No. Yes. Maybe?

"I think so, yeah."

"Well… text him."

"No way." I can't break the silence first.

"Why not? You guys have stuff to iron out, but if you want to see him, then say it. Guys get nervous too, ya know. He might be hoping you drop a line."

"I guess," I respond, still not going for my phone.

She reaches over to the table to grab it and hands it to me.

"Well, you can do it, or I can. You might wanna be the one though, because if I send him a pic of you right now, he'll be over here in a second."

I snicker while she studies me proudly, admiring her handiwork before I've seen it.

"You know my favorite thing about New Year's?"

I raise my brows with a *hmm*, encouraging her to continue.

"It's all about new beginnings."

She spins the chair, so I'm face to face with a reflection I barely recognize: Rich brown hair with varying blonde highlights and lowlights, beachy waves that I can never seem to get the hang of, lighter makeup than I'd expected, but it looks… incredible. She used different shades of copper that make my eyes a crazy vibrant blue. My skin doesn't appear as washed out as it did with my full blonde, and it's blushed and highlighted to perfection.

"Holy balls, I look hot!" I exclaim, staring at myself. It isn't even myself. *This* is Alex 2.0.

Monica isn't a beautician; she's a damn magician.

23. TODAY

That was the kick in the ass I needed. Definitely a change I needed. I can't help but grin when I catch myself in the rearview. This is new and it's exciting. My entire life I've been blonde, darkening as I've grown older, but always blonde. Maybe brunettes have more fun?

Let's find out.

Monica was right. Why not do this for me? Why don't I go for it, or at least try? And it's time I get back to something that's a passion for me, more than just once every month. The kids are older now and don't need me as much.

New year, new me.

I text Jake, asking him to come to Annie and Jace's tonight. That's it, short and to the point, so the ball's in his court now. Our kids are already with his parents, who take them every New Year's.

I wonder what he's doing, and why he hasn't returned my message?

When I pull into my driveway, there's a package on the porch with silver wrapping and a navy bow. It smells like Kelsey, who lives for drive-by presents. A note accompanies it, with the words *trust me* written in her fancy, calligraphic writing. I'm afraid to open it.

But today is turning out to be a fantastic day. Today feels like the beginning of something different. Today is the day I woman up, grab this bull by the horns, and stop being sorry for myself. Or at least make a college effort.

In the box is a low-cut, V-neck top, champagne-colored with sequins, and what the what? Pleather pants? No shot I can pull this off. My style is jeans and sweats. While I'm sure it'll look good, I can't do it.

Actually, forget that. Alex 2.0, time to try it out, give things a chance. The same old, same old is stale.

Not a word from Jake. No message, nothing. Serious sighs are happening, but I can't force it. I texted, and he didn't. What can I do? Be mad? Okay, how's that gonna help me out? It won't. No overthinking. Well, there's some overthinking but… new vantage point, or at least attempting a new one. Can't change overnight. It's annoying honestly, because we should be able to have open communication. What if it was something to do with the kids? Ugh, but it wasn't. I spoke to them already and know they're good.

Allison, Jake's mom, assured me she had Ruby's seizure meds. I don't even need to ask. All our parents and siblings know exactly what to do. Every hand has been on deck as far as her epilepsy goes since the diagnosis. She has a maintenance med she gets twice a day, as well as one for emergencies, just in case. I hope we never have to use it.

* * *

I arrive at Jace and Annie's about thirty minutes late—we went over my punctuality… or lack thereof. Truth is, I'm nervous about the clothes I'm wearing, but fuck it, I put that outfit on and could see why Kelsey has a booming career designing things. It fits seamlessly. The pants are slimming and, I have to admit, pretty sexy. The shirt is lower than my norm, showing moderate cleavage… but I like how I look in this.

I feel good.

Part of me, of course, wishes Jake will be here. He's seen the same strands for years. Truthfully, I don't know how he'll react. He's not the type that voices a preference for a specific hair length or color, and he never told me how to dress. He always said I was beautiful. I could be completely haggard and he'd find something nice to comment on.

Music pours from the house. Parked cars span the driveway and overflow onto the adjacent grass. The dark blue siding and rustic wood door are picturesque, lit up with white Christmas lights, as is the tree twinkling in the window.

Jace is standing outside by the garage, having a smoke. I wish he'd give it up already. Of all the cars lined up, there's one I don't see. Yeah, it's okay, no big deal.

Who cares?

I gulp in a courageous breath, praying I don't roll an ankle in the short black wedge boots that always test my coordination skills. But they look good. Fashion is painful.

It's now or never. Annie's gonna make a scene, guaranteed. But it's people from work, mutual friends. I got this.

I trek from the furthest parking spot—my penance for being late—to say hi to Jace, literally conscious of every single step I'm taking. Feet do not fail me now!

He laughs, and his mouth forms a sizeable smile. "Um, hello."

All I can do is grin sheepishly. "Yeah, I know… it's a huge change." I cringe and close my jacket tighter over my chest. Maybe I'll keep this on.

Jace closes his mouth, but his lips remain curved. "I think change can be a good thing. You look great, Alex."

"Thanks." My nose crinkles. "I actually feel great, like… shit, man."

We both share a laugh, then I flash him a smile, a sincere one. Jace graduated to MVP status the other night, though he's always held rank. But it was nice to know that he had my back. The love is for real.

A husky, strike-a-chord-down-somewhere voice speaks behind me, and I freeze. "You sure Annie hasn't heard from her? I texted, tried to call, and nothing. My mom spoke to her; said she talked to the kids."

My eyes go wide and my throat goes dry—hello, butterflies. I stare at Jace while I'm a legit ice sculpture in the driveway. He winks and bites his top lip to stop from laughing. Jake has no clue it's me, only a few feet away, with my back to him. I'm wearing a new jacket, and pants I'd never normally wear. Plus, my altered hair… but you'd think he'd know? And suddenly I'm nervous beyond anything I've *ever* felt before.

It's not just from this fresh look, but from the decisions I made today, about wanting to get back to work, to change things up.

Jake's so close, I can smell him—fresh and minty. It's never too much. I hate when you walk by people and inhale their cologne. Too much, way too much. Nope, his is an ideal balance.

"Maybe her phone died?" Jace offers with a smirk, keeping his eyes on me. Not cool, Jace. Not cool.

"Hey," Jake says indifferently, side-glancing me. He tips a bottle of beer to his lips and slowly turns his head. His jaw drops, and he stumbles back several feet, coughing on the liquid pooled in his mouth.

"See you guys inside." Jace grins like a fool, chest shaking with a hearty laugh.

The coughing and sputtering subside, and Jake stands there, dumbfounded, gawking. Say something, dude! He opens and closes his mouth, but nothing comes out. Self-conscious Alex begins to slither in. It's too much; it's way too much.

"Holy shit." His eyes barrel up and down my body like a freight train. He reaches out and slips a finger under a dark strand by my cheek, examining it.

"I know," I blurt out, awkward as ever. "It's different. I think it's not me. I don't know, I was going for a change, but it's too…"

He drains his beer, pouring it down his throat—technically his esophagus. Ugh, overthinking! The eye-sex continues. I swear, that's what it feels like. His lips turn up, the dimple expanding in his right cheek.

"Wow."

I clasp my jacket even snugger around me. Nope. Deep breaths here, bitch. "Do you think it's too much?" I fling open the front of my coat, revealing the low-cut top underneath. I might as well treat him to the entire ensemble.

Cue the choking.

It's been a while since he was speechless.

I spin on a heel. "See ya in there, I guess."

He grabs my arm, stopping me in my tracks.

"Did you need something?" I ask with a shamelessly smug smile. I'm living in this day, at least for right now. Shoot, not even this day, but this second.

"I love it, Alex," he says, pushing a wave from my face. "Do you?" His stare is so intense right now, I swear he'd gold-medal if extreme eye contact were a sport.

"Yeah… I mean, it's a change. But I needed something… new."

He blinks rapidly, then his mouth flatlines. Sorry, Jake, truth hurts. And I'm not insinuating a change with a different guy, because that didn't help anyone feel better. I'm talking about a change for myself.

"What did you mean when you told Jace you texted me and called me? You didn't."

"I did… excessively."

What the hell?

He blatantly checks out my cleavage, closing in, then reaches into my pocket. After he frees my phone, his eyes drift back to mine. Jake's lips rumble. "You know, might help if your phone wasn't on *do not disturb*." He presses a button, and it buzzes to life with notifications.

I swear, Will could school me on the technology stuff. I'm just not tech-savvy.

"Ugh, what'd you say?" I make a move to grab it from him as he swipes his fingers across the screen. "Jake!"

He hands it over. Any messages he sent are gone. That's annoying. Probably more of the same, with him being sweet then getting shitty when he's ignored.

He grabs my wrists, tipping his chin down so our foreheads connect. I'm fresh outta words when he peels my cell from my clutches and slides it into the pocket of my pants. The back pocket. Warm breaths tingle my lips, and his nose nudges against mine.

Is it suddenly hot, out in the middle of winter?

"I meant what I said." His thumb lifts my jaw, and he appears dead serious, no shitty smirk on his face now. "I'm not giving up, okay?"

I nod. "Let's take it one day at a time, yeah?"

He frowns but agrees silently.

"Better go in before Annie puts out an APB."

We make our way to the front steps.

"After you." Jake extends an arm, licking his lips, sights set on the tight black pants highlighting the curve of my ass.

Time to get this party started… I guess.

24. RAISE YOUR GLASS

The celebration is already in full swing. Annie *always* pulls out all the stops—the decorations, food, drinks, music on point. That's how she rolls. She loves to host this kinda stuff, and I'm happy to let her. Not me. I'm the type that's cool with anyone coming over, but they need to make themselves at home. I like people being comfortable enough for that. Really, that's how all our friends are.

I ditch my coat and shake my hands out before heading to the open living room and kitchen. Why is it, even if you have a ton of space, guests always congregate in the kitchen? It bugs me—the food's not even in here.

"Woah. Yes, bitch, yasssss! Comin' in hot!" Annie screams, fucking screams, causing the forty-some people here to stop what they're doing and stare.

I'm sure my face is so many kinds of red right now. I am *not* a fan of the spotlight. If it's a few of us, no prob. But all these work peeps, all these randoms? Hells no.

Introverted extroverts exist. The struggle is real.

"Alex." She beams after giving me a drawn-out hug. "Wow. You look stunning! Do you love it? I love it." She doesn't let me get a word in edgewise, pinging her snark at Jake. "I know *you* fucking love it."

He clears his throat, leaning in closer. I can feel his subtle palm trailing over the sequins on the lower back of my top—the lower *lower* back.

It's not unnoticed.

Annie pins me with a *what the hell, where's the soap opera now?* head bob.

I reply with a *find out after this commercial break* pop of my shoulder.

The guys congregate in the living room, giving off severe middle-school-dance vibes. Doesn't matter how old we get, when it's a large-enough group, it's usually split, with dudes in one area and chicks in the other. At least that's my experience.

I struggle to maintain eye contact with whoever's speaking, avoiding the persistent glances from Jake. Carol, my supervisor at the hospital, continues grumbling about how short-staffed they are, how tough it is to find decent nurses. Keeps giving me the same pouty guilt trip she does every time I see her.

"I've been considering…" I say.

Her eyes widen and her smile matches.

"I wanted to discuss adding a more regular sched—"

"Regular what?" Jake interrupts, reaching around the front of me for a drink he could have easily gotten if he went the other way. His palm lands on my waist, and a slightly seductive grin curls his lips. He's not looking at my face. No, he's looking straight down my top. So fucking blatant—and awkward.

Also… I see you! My *entire body* sees you!

"Alex was telling me she's coming back to work full-time." Carol says the words so fast, clapping, bouncing up and down in front of us.

"What?" Jake scoffs, not enthusiastic whatsoever. "No she's not."

Hold up. Huh?

I glare at him briefly but quickly decide I'm picking my battles, and this isn't a tiff for today. "I said I've been considering it, and I have. But we'll discuss it another time, Carol. No shop-talk tonight."

Jake's visibly annoyed, but he nods.

The music is blaring with a carefully constructed playlist, varying from old-school jams to today's hits, and everything in between.

I can hear some of the work hens gossiping about us, saying they thought we weren't together. No matter how private you try to keep things, news travels. Sometimes people have nothing better to talk about, but half the individuals here have their own issues to work on, and they need to worry about themselves.

When I twirl around from the kitchen island, I almost smack into Jake, who's standing directly behind me. "Um, personal space?" I laugh nervously.

He doesn't budge. I know he hears the shit-talkers too.

"I can't stand the people from your work."

That makes two of us.

"Yeah, they aren't all that bad. They just don't know what's going on, and they're nosey." I shrug.

"What *is* going on?" His hands rest on either side of me, while my lower back presses into the countertop. "And what about going back to work? I told you, you don't have to. I make plenty. You can still stay home… no matter what."

Right. I love that he assumes it's some sort of bonus for me, as if I lie around all day and do nothing, like I'm content with just that.

Was it amazing when the kids were little? Hell yes. I loved being able to be home with Will for years. But as I said, nursing was—no, is—a passion of mine. I want to get back to it. I worked my butt off for that degree.

"Jake." I say his name with a stern edge. "We can talk about this tomorrow too."

He rolls his eyes.

"Unless you wanna dive into that now?" I snap, a bit annoyed myself.

His expression softens, and he raises his hands. He's aware we're still balancing on this unpredictable tightrope together. One false move and someone's hitting the ground.

"No, umm, it's cool. Whatever you want."

Great answer.

I duck, slinking under his arm to get around him. Sure, my body might be ready to throw down, but did I ever say I was gonna make this easy? I don't think I did.

"Jake, go hang out with the guys. We need to talk shit about you," Annie says—no shame.

An incredulous grunt slips from his throat, but he treads lightly around her, so he listens. I love that he's a little scared of her.

The house is jam-packed; it's overwhelming. "Come help me," Annie says, striding towards the garage door.

"Help with what?" I stay put. She always makes up some bullshit excuse then corners me somewhere to grill me.

"Alex! Can you just come outside for one minute so you can fill me in on all the dirty details about your life lately?" She cheeses, displaying bright white teeth over her shoulder.

Well… she says what she means. I follow her into the garage, which is warmed by a small heater. How she can pull off an extremely thin-strapped tank that's barely hanging on is beyond me.

I'm thinking double-sided tape?

Annie hands me a red cup filled with an unknown mixed concoction. No matter how fortunate we become in life, we're never gonna be too high class for plastic cups.

"What's in this?" I take an exaggerated sniff of the boozy, citrusy pink liquid.

"It's giggle juice. I made it especially for you because I enjoy seeing you laugh."

Aw, that's pretty sweet.

"Now drink the shit," she demands, clinking her cup to mine.

Okay, maybe sweet to a point.

She winks as we sip our cocktails. "You wanna dish the deets on why my husband got home so late the other night?" Her lashes flutter, but it's playful. There's no hinting at anything. She knows the girl code would never, *ever* falter with us.

"Did he not tell you?" I scour the garage, ensuring we don't have any eavesdroppers. Sometimes stragglers make their way outside.

"Told me I'd have to hear it from the source. Been a long-ass two days." She shakes her head, eyes turning up, groaning with fake annoyance.

I chew the inside of my cheek as she looks at me concerningly. "So this guy… Fuck, it was so strange." I read her reaction. There isn't one, not even a hint of judgment. This is how you know someone's your person. "Anyway, I hung out with him after Kels left, which was dumb, yes, but I—"

"You wanted to give Jake a taste of his own medicine? I get it. Go on." She takes a swig of her drink, cracking her cup against mine first. It's an unspoken rule that if you get cheers'd, you drink.

"We walked out together, and he wanted me to go back to his place."

Cue her mouth hitting the floor. "The fuck?"

"Yeah. So I was panicking because my phone died. And he fucking kissed me."

She straightens her neck, brows slamming together. "You didn't kiss him back, did you?"

"No. I mean, I was shocked, so I stood there for a couple seconds, but then I pushed him away."

I bring her up to speed on the rest of the events—Jace saving me, Jake racing into the house all crazy. My confession, his proclamation. When I told her that Jake thought it was her husband that I'd kissed, she laughed it off, said ew. I told her that was my exact thought too.

I couldn't help but feel the sting when she said she would kill him if he kissed someone else.

Yeah. Let's get back to the ever-existing double standards. You just can't know how you'll deal with things until you're going through them. But let's move on from the bullshit.

"So here we are. And really, Ann, I'm just trying to have fun tonight. I'm so exhausted and—"

"Well then, let's get this party started." She grins, tugging my low-cut shirt down even further. I swat her hand away.

"Your tits are impressive. Show those babies off." Annie sticks out her tongue, brows waggling as she walks into the house.

Hours tick by like minutes, the way they do when conversation flows, when drinks are pouring, when the tunes are excellent. The beat of the music and the buzz of excitement about a new year, a chance for a fresh start, hums throughout the house.

Everyone crowds into the living room for the countdown. The versatile playlist blares, and chatter roars so loud I can't hear myself think. Which is probably a good thing.

Less than a minute to go.

Jake's hands find their way to my hips, and he closes in behind me, moving in sync, swaying along to the music, the countdown. Our bodies remember exactly how to be with each other. No effort involved, but a shit ton of certain feelings. I think everything is standing on edge. The arm hairs, the nips, the—

He grazes the outer shell of my ear with his lips, and I wanna whimper.

"I'm so ready for a new year," he whispers, arms hugging tight around my waist, chin settling on top of my shoulder.

I'm ready, but I'm scared. Scared about what this new year will bring. Will things be better? Will they be worse? Will we move on? Will we stay together?

And while my brain—who I begged to shut the fuck up earlier—keeps going off the rails, the countdown reaches zero. The ball drops.

Jake moves to the side of me, knowing I'm feeling a specific way about the whole kissing thing. His lips gently press to my cheek, his arms still wrapped around me.

I remind myself that I'm living in the moment, even if it's a one-night-only thing.

So ya know what… to hell with it.

I turn my head, and his stubbled jaw scratches my face. While confetti is floating around us and everyone is kissing and cheersing, our lips meet.

A series of fireworks blast off on the television while his tongue teases between my lips. I part them, letting my own fireworks ignite inside my body.

Our mouths move feverishly, caressing, swirling, dancing around like they have a million times before. But there's something different about this kiss—the urgency, the pain, the promises, the adrenaline.

I grasp the back of his neck, fingers spreading, tangling into his hair. Jake's palms drift from my waist to my ass, lifting me, pulling me so my thundering chest is flush with his.

His heart syncs with my own erratic beats. My body is in full control here. She knows it's time to take over.

His grip compels my hips, and I rock into the bulge already forming in his pants.

"Dirty little freaks!"

We break from the extreme face-sucking, pain-swallowing kiss, and I turn to see we have an entire audience. Annie stands near us with her hands on her hips, crystal-blue eyes lit up and a ludicrous grin on her face.

"Happy New Year. I'd come in for a hug, but it might be uncomfortable," she jokes, eyes flitting between us.

I feel the heat rush to my cheeks. Jake's hold remains secure on my waist, keeping me in front of him, blocking his uncomfortable situation from the party-goers.

What the fuck? We just made out like horny teenagers in front of a room full of people—no big.

Yeah, I'm dying.

No one seems to notice or pay attention for any longer than a few seconds, or maybe they notice and just don't care. Not that PDA was ever our norm.

My lips swell from the fierceness of the kiss, and our eyes meet. Jake's are loaded to the brim with satisfaction.

Told you he had a way of getting what he wanted.

That felt like a promise.

My arms drop from his neck, then I remove his hands from my waist.

I can't stop her; she's running wild—my mind. Racing, shouting at me. Scolding me for breaking my one rule. Okay, there was more than one, but as of late, this was the main one.

No. Fucking. Kissing.

I'm so freaking out right now. I make a break for it, needing to go get some air or spontaneously combust or I don't know what, but I need a minute.

Heart… you wanna chime in?

Crickets.

Jake stops me, grabbing hold of my wrist before I can bolt. "Where are you going?" His voice is smooth and dreamy and how old am I right now?

"I… I need a minute. Need some air or something." I fan my face, searching for the quickest escape route.

"You want me to come with you?" Enter the Jake smirk with the lazy fingers running through his hair. His teeth sink into his bottom lip like he believes we can just bang our way through this entire ordeal.

"No." It doesn't come out convincing. "No, Jake," I repeat, much firmer this time. "Don't follow me."

I glance back before disappearing down the hall to find him staring after me.

Who am I kidding? Lead me not into temptation?

Fuck it. Follow me—I know a shortcut.

25. I WANT YOU TO WANT ME

I stare at myself in the bathroom mirror. How the hell is my hair still holding up? What am I doing?

The kiss, the *oh my God* kiss. I'd be lying if I said it wasn't invigorating. We seriously haven't locked lips like that since college. It was a fuck-me kinda kiss; pretty sure I need new underwear.

But mostly the kiss was… ugh.

See, it isn't just that I think a kiss is so intimate, which I do. It's the fact that the last woman he kissed wasn't me.

I feel like a traitor to myself for giving in. Like if I allowed him this one small victory, it was undoing the damage. Forgetting and forgiving. Letting him off the hook.

I'm sure Jake's got feelings of his own about another man's lips being on mine. It makes me wanna throw up in my mouth just thinking about it. The shit is not the same though, and we all know it.

But I'm trying, I'm *really* trying here to not let it keep eating me up, at least for this one damn night.

I snuck down to the basement about five minutes ago. I *did* need a minute. Also, this bathroom is strategically connected to Annie and Jace's guest room. So there's that coincidence. They had it renovated recently, and Annie designated it my room, as if we have sleepovers often. We don't—we're adultish; there's Uber.

I'm betting no one's ever slept in here. The carpet in the room is a plush, thick gray, with white tile spanning the bathroom floor. Clean and crisp—you'd know the designer.

Anyway, I've been in here for a while and haven't heard a thing. Not a single peep. Guess he listened for once. Can't fault him for not being the best at picking up my mixed signals. But what guy is? Maybe if I said what I meant, or even knew what I meant?

I do a quick finger fluff to the hair, swipe the smudge of mascara that's smeared below my eyes, and adjust the girls back into their front and center position. Listen, after each kid, those ladies head a little further south. It's a fact of life.

My outfit's still looking okay. Can't believe I'm wearing fucking pleather.

I regroup, fixing my face with a smile, and gearing to get back to the party. I've done a decent job of maintaining, not going overboard with the giggle juice. Only smart decisions from here on out.

I switch off the light and open the door towards me, my hot-mess self somewhat together. Immediately, I thud into a wall.

Not a wall. This halting surface smells way too good—soft shirt, chiseled torso, a faint hint of mint.

"Hey." Sharp shadows cast over Jake's face from the dim plug-in. Gotta conserve that energy.

Endless forests of green, swirled with specks of honey, zero in on me. His dark eyes rove my body with undeniable hunger, and I know he's gotta be thinking about that kiss.

Why did I give in to him? Something about that kiss was so… much.

He runs a hand down his neck, his attention falling to my completely extra cleavage. His permanent five o'clock shadow is thicker than usual, neatly edged, and honestly sexy as sin.

Wait, what? Smart decisions—only smart decisions.

"What do you want, Jake?" I play the part to a tee. I know what he wants, because it's the same thing I want. Why'd I run away and hide down here? To this specific bathroom when there are three others in the house? Where we'll be secluded from the party?

That's rhetorical.

He towers close, too close, and brushes the hair from my face. I can't help but fixate on his mouth, that perfect fucking mouth, and he doesn't waste the opportunity.

Passionate lips crash against mine, and he grabs my waist, drawing me closer. What am I doing? My body betrays my brain. I thought she was supposed to take a hike anyway? His tongue, greedy and impatient, seeks an in that I can't fight. Our hands roam wildly, hearts galloping in both our chests. Cool mint and faint traces of cigarettes invade my senses.

Was he smoking? That's usually a turnoff, but this kiss is not. And I'm in desperate need of a sex reliever—I mean a stress reliever.

What?

Plus, not like this adds another notch to my belt. This is Jake. We've done this a billion times. Probably not that many, but…

Large palms ruffle the sequins of my top till they land on my ass, per the usual. He squeezes and spreads, aware of exactly how to work me. My nails scrape along the indentations of his abs through his shirt, and I'm a goner.

"Fuck." I moan into his mouth, and Jake knows it's on.

He grips the nape of my neck, smashing me into this kiss, making me question how we're even breathing. This is fucking mouth-to-mouth. His other hand snakes beneath my shirt, fingertips tracing my spine.

The bathroom? Are we really gonna get this going in the bathroom when there's a fully functional bed—

Jake hooks my thighs and lifts me so abruptly it steals the breath from my lungs. Our lips and tongues continue ravaging like we're trying to prove who can take more from the other.

Maybe if we do this enough, we can erase the past?

He walks backwards out to the bedroom, to the door, kicking it shut and barely letting go, just fast enough to press the lock.

He knows I'm an overthinker. Let this stop for one second, allow my brain to reenter the atmosphere, and I'm a ghost.

Our tongues clash like our hips did upstairs, grinding, desperate, asking for more. Our bodies know what they want, and that answer is simple. Each other.

Damn body, always betraying me.

Shut up, brain! Don't need you for this portion of the show.

He's already hard… *hard* hard, methodically plunging his hips into me. I crave him more and more as we slide into that sync we could always find, heads angling left and right, mouth fucking like there's no tomorrow.

Jake catches my bottom lip and pulls away, letting it snap into place. His eyes blaze with lust, and his ravenous kisses work their way from my cheek to my neck. He knows I can't resist—*ahh*, a light nip on the ear.

I shudder in response, sparks flying. Scratch that. I'm soaked in gasoline, and he struck the match.

This girl is on fire.

He's about to lower me onto the bed, and why's he the one in control, the one holding the upper hand? Let's go ahead and reverse that role.

I unwind my legs from around him, and Jake's face screws up as I slink down his body, seriously about to climax just from his erection rubbing over my clothed center. Hell, it's been a while.

I turn us around, so his back's to the bed, then press my hand against his pounding chest, and he drops to the edge of the mattress.

His eyes gleam when I straddle his legs then raise my arms for him. He tears off my shirt, and the rush of coolness would make me shiver if it wasn't straight tropics between us. Pleasure brews when his thumbs trace the outline of my bra, dipping beneath to circle my taut nipples.

"Take yours off," I demand, channeling my inner dominant self. Just kidding—but potentially?

His breathy laugh is full of amusement, because he's clearly not used to me being the one to make demands about, well, anything.

"Why don't you take it off?" He arches a presumptuous brow, trying to be cute, but cute is *not* what I need right now.

I step back with a roll of the eyes, and Jake snags my belt loop, yanking me so I plummet onto his lap. "I like this," he rasps, unbuttoning his shirt and lofting it across the room before situating my legs around him.

My fingers skate up his torso, mapping the various shades of ink till I reach his neck, appreciating some of my favorite artwork. His focus doesn't leave my face for a second, his hands anchoring my hips. My eyes eventually land on his, and for a few beats, we simply stare at each other, panting, hearts jamming, adrenaline rippling through the air. And for a moment, I glimpse the man I remember.

"Tell me what you want," he all but purrs in my ear.

Um, world peace, endless supply of coffee, five-day weekends? Oh, right, what do I want him to do to me?

Why do guys always get off on the dirty talk? Just kidding, I do too. It works a treat.

I know damn well he wants me to tell him to fuck me or something of that sort. But if I'm trying to take any kind of control, I better own it.

"I want"—my hips rotate, and I whimper when his erection, strained beneath his zipper, provides me with so much stimulation I'm about to combust—"to fuck you." Yeah, I said it.

Jake growls his approval and throttles his pelvis, thrusting while guiding me to rock back and forth over him. He's like a wild animal when I unclasp my bra, allowing him unrestrained access, which he takes full advantage of.

He squeezes my breasts together and lathers them with his lips, then sucks every inch until I'm shaking over him. His tongue flicks, teeth tweak, blasting heat to where I'm definitely soaked, and reducing me to a groaning mess on his lap.

He suddenly stops. If he doesn't fuck me in the next second, I'm gonna die.

I skim a finger along his waistline, and Jake gasps when I pop his button then goes back to his worshiping. He takes his time, drawing my nipple into his mouth, sucking, swirling, gently nipping as he pulls away.

I'm dangerously close to coming in these fucking pleather pants.

I need more; my body needs more. My pelvis rotates relentlessly, begging for him. We breathe tiny moans and cries into each other's mouths, completely captivated and longing for more.

"I want to fuck you," I repeat in Jake's ear before kissing his neck. I feel like he's holding back, like he wants to make sure. Lemme see if I can spur him on. "So what"—I hit him with the ear graze—"are you waiting for?"

That'll do it. We're up on our feet and his pants are history, tossed across the room faster than I can comprehend.

I'm doing this. *We* are doing this.

"Yes," I shriek, actually shriek, when his palm cups between my legs, followed by a chuckle as he tries to wriggle a finger down my waistband. Not with these pants, buddy.

Without missing a beat, Jake unzips them, eyes unnervingly locked on mine, watching every reaction, gauging if I'm sure. I raise my brows and he drops to his knees. He slips off my shoes then peels my bottoms down along with my underwear.

After a deep inhale, he buries his face between my legs, humming and growling when his tongue spreads me and fucks me.

"Jake!" His name comes out far louder than intended, and I almost buckle at the tempo of his hot lips, lavishing, savoring, devouring me. I grip his hair to stop him, but it has the opposite effect.

His mouth latches onto my clit, and those fireworks make an encore appearance when his fingers glide through my wet heat.

But it's not enough. I need him. No, I need his body.

I stagger back, and he grins with an actual gleam on his lips as he gets to his feet. Yeah.

God, what am I doing?

Shit. I had a feeling my brain would chime in at some point.

He walks into me so we fall onto the bed, and his weight pressing on top of me puts a muzzle on my thoughts. My back arches and my legs spread, welcoming his thickness sliding against me.

But wait, I'm gonna be the one in control. I shove him off me, and Jake assists in the flip without objection, seeming to enjoy this minor power struggle, the tit for tat becoming a game. His lips curve as he sits up beneath my open thighs.

The deep face-sucking kissing continues, reminding me of our hard-core make-out sessions when we were younger, tongues moving in harmony, dying for more, swallowing each other whole.

His finger sinks inside me, and he moans into my mouth. The touch is so distant and so familiar all at once. My hands lace behind his neck, dragging him to me, determined not to break the kiss and get his cock completely inside me as fast as possible.

He understands the assignment.

Without warning, he raises my hips, slamming me down over him. I wail from the intense burst of pressure and the deliciously tight fullness. It's been a while.

"You okay?" he whispers into my hair, his breaths jagged.

I nod, keeping my eyelids pinched as tight as I can. Eye contact right now would be too much. Resting my forehead against his shoulder, I'm unable to stop my rhythmic movements, craving the friction, the feeling.

My nails score his back, and Jake sucks in a sharp breath, unmoving. I know I said I was going to be the one in charge, but ya know… I'm thinking we both gotta give a little something. My head raises to his ear, still riding. Let's get this goin'.

"Fuck me."

And man, oh man, does he respond.

He scoops me up, our bodies connected, and bolts us across the room to the dresser. It's exactly the right height.

With my ass planted on the surface, he hisses when he withdraws, only to thrust so insanely hard my head jolts back, and the symphony of slaps and groans creates our own playlist.

In and out, over and over. The tension builds, twisting deep in my stomach as we both fuck into each other, completely in tune. My muscles tense with each mind-numbing stroke, and I climb higher and higher.

Jake's finger flicks down, rubbing, grinding my clit. I'm almost there. I feel like I could pass out. God, he feels so good. No, *this* feels so good.

He fists my hair and exposes my neck, lips sinking in. The ragged breaths in my ear are everything right now.

My legs squeeze and tremble around his body, and Jake bucks his hips, knowing we're both incredibly close to coming undone. He rams into me with one last, brutal thrust, and I explode.

Waves and jolts ricochet through my body as I contract around his pulsing length, our sweaty bodies twisted together in utter ecstasy.

"Fuck. Fuck," is all he can say, though I hardly hear him. I'm still welcoming the sensation of one of the most intense orgasms I've ever had in my life as he lets go inside me, lips crushing mine, moans rising from his throat to my mouth.

I'm done—kill me now.

My cheek lies against his rocketing chest, over my favorite tattoo, as his forehead rests on my shoulder. We're both wonderfully stupefied.

Holy shit, it was amazing. I'm totally drunk right now, and it's not from any alcohol.

"I think I've got a thing for brunettes," he mumbles with a quiet laugh.

I know he doesn't mean it in this way, but here my mind goes. Because guess who else is a brunette? And I'm realizing that no matter what, in every little and big thing, there's gonna be reminders. It's *always* going to hurt.

"I love you." He chokes out the words and crushes his arms around me.

Fuck. God, please don't cry! Witnessing a man cry is one of the most painful things in the world. You can't even try to fight the tears that'll ultimately fill your own eyes. It's a chain reaction.

He loves me? I know he does. But that comment, that stupid, shitty, innocent comment, has me reeling.

Give an inch, take a yard. I knew he thought we could have sex and just go straight back, but it doesn't work that way. Did he truly think I'd admit my love and forgiveness?

Nope. This isn't makeup sex. This is *we're still married, so it doesn't count* sex.

Jake grabs my jaw and lifts my face to his.

Yup. Fuck my fucking life. Tears well in his eyes. He thinks this is the answer to it all? We aren't kids anymore.

Fighting and fucking is *not* enough.

My silence to his declaration is so loud, I might as well have shouted it.

A swallow works down his throat, and his relaxed expression transitions to devastation. When you know someone well enough, you hear things in what they don't say.

His hands fall to my knees, and he leans in close enough that I can see—no, I can feel—the pain of me not reciprocating.

I just can't. All is not going to be forgiven by some quick, easy, mind-blowing sex. That shit doesn't hold up.

He pulls away from me, head shaking, nostrils flaring. His jaw muscle ticks, and those beautiful eyes glaze with rejection.

I can't look at him, can't stand the anguish on his face from my lack of response. I'm throwing fuel on the fire this time, and this isn't a good fire. This girl is not on fucking fire anymore.

"You really don't love me?" His voice breaks. "All the times I've said it to you, Alex. You can't say it back?"

I keep my eyes fixed on his chest, on my name scrolled over his heart. I always joked about it, but it's my favorite one.

The problem is, if he promised I was always going to be the one who had his heart, why was he looking for something somewhere else?

I turn my head away, trying to fight the tears stinging my eyes. I want him to feel pain. I don't care how I do it. What the hell is wrong with me?

My eyes close tight, and my lips refuse to part.
After several seconds, the bedroom door slams.

26. HOPELESS WANDERER

Annie, being her well-planned, top-hostess self, has several pairs of extra sweatpants and T-shirts in the spare-room dresser. The same dresser that was recently violated.

It was good, *really* good, then one stupid comment later—and lack of another—and it was really fucking bad. Again.

I'm an asshole. Yeah, noted. Would it have been simpler to just reciprocate and slip back into life, pre-snafus? Who knows? Imagine being perfect and articulating things clearly, especially when you're overcome with conflicting emotions.

Goals.

Look… I'm gonna love Jake Everett till the day I die. This guy has painstakingly brought me out of the darkness more times than I can count. He's a great father, a great man, but sadly, sometimes it's easier to let words create distance for you. Whether you say them or not. I'm aware of what he misinterpreted my silence to say.

Sometimes, things seem a certain way on the outside looking in. People always gotta have an opinion on what they think's the right way, what they wish would happen. They don't always see the dark, the awful shit, the real ugly ways a person can react out of hurt—or from insane pressure. It's not something commonly talked about, because maybe if we don't talk about it, it's not real.

My demons, well, you can probably identify them. Booze is a crutch. I sometimes say or do stuff that's fucked up, that I don't mean. The truth is, when I genuinely psychoanalyze myself, I'm not sure I've ever felt worthy of anyone's love. It's messed up, but when I seriously think about it, and this is the first time I've come to this realization, it's true.

See, when something happens to you, something traumatic, a part of your soul dies. No matter how hard you fight it, how much you want to move on, how consistently you cage those demons in the dark corners of your mind, it truly is an uphill battle.

A part of me will always be fourteen years old, stuck in the woods. I've tried not to camp out there, not to let it kill me every single day, but it's not that easy. Often, I find it difficult to be open and honest about exactly what I'm feeling. I'm way better at deflecting, injecting humor into serious situations, and being sarcastic. I know—how can this be?

It's easier to pretend like you don't remember, even if you're only kidding yourself.

But I *do* remember. That's not something you forget.

I deal with it in my own way. Okay, I kinda don't. Though I've made some sort of peace. I don't have negative thoughts about sex when it's with Jake. He was the first person who didn't make me feel disgusted after. I have to admit, sometimes when we were caught up in a moment, and everything seemed completely fine, I'd flashback to those woods and pull the plug.

Jake never pushed it with me. He knew there were some fucked-up emotions there. I blamed myself for years. Why'd I wear that short dress? Why'd I hang out with them?

And that's bullshit. Nobody *asks* for it.

If Ashton hadn't found me, lying there in the woods, drifting in and out of consciousness… if my mother hadn't demanded a rape kit, I wonder if anyone would've ever known.

* * *

When it happened, at first, I assumed we were having fun, hooking up. I was going into tenth grade and… we'll call him Satan—because he doesn't deserve a name—was two years older, soon to be a senior. And not just a senior, the hottest guy in school, who all the girls drooled over.

So when he pulled me along with him to go for a walk that day, I couldn't say no. I was on cloud nine, like *holy shit*. This popular guy wanted me? Me!

When he forced himself on me, everything I thought I was… stalled.

I'd always predicted, before I was face to face with the situation, that I would've fought—*seriously* fought. But I didn't. My head was a cyclone of fear and confusion. He'd kissed me and that was fine, but before I could comprehend, his grip was terrifyingly strong on my wrists. When he wrapped his fingers around my neck like a noose, my mind went disgustingly blank.

I was paralyzed in a mound of leaves and dirt, left wondering why I'd put myself in this position. The tears flooded my face, and I stopped breathing from the sobs at one point. All the while, he assured me I was loving it.

Like I've said, it's impossible to know what you'll do in any situation. You don't know until it's your reality… you genuinely don't.

The kicker was, after he was done, he told me I wasn't bad, but let's make sure. That was when I woke up, when the fight in me finally kicked in. Turns out another one of the guys had watched the entire thing. I thank God every day that we weren't in the age of smartphones back then.

Satan's counterpart was getting off on the scene in front of him. When he laid himself on top of me, I fought with everything I had. But it wasn't enough. They held me down, and I'm thankful I eventually passed out.

As I've gotten older, I realize it wasn't my fault. I didn't provoke them to commit this heinous act. They did it on their own. Normal people don't do that kind of shit. There's a special place in hell for them, and I can't wait for the day they go.

Despite knowing it was no fault of my own, life was tough after that. They were both minors, so they only got a slap on the wrist. Though, what punishment would be enough?

Anyway, the rumor mill had decided I was dramatic and had made it up. There should never be a *side* with these circumstances.

While my parents were able to push for a restraining order, which resulted in the two transferring schools, I got a wave of hate for it.

I struggled through the next three years of high school being called a slut and a whore behind my back. The narrative was that I wanted it. That it wasn't *that* bad. People believed them—at least my peers did. And I was dead enough inside to let them suspect what they wanted. I didn't have any fight left in me.

So the drinking started, and the self-loathing. I stopped caring, and guys began lining up. Ashton threatened every one of them, but some things he just couldn't control; some things he couldn't protect me from.

I was my biggest offender.

Trust issues, touch issues, fucked-up issues… yeah, let's tick all the boxes.

So keep in mind, while you may think you know how you'd react to something, you just don't. You *never* will, unless you've been there. And I pray to God every single day that no one ever has to go through it, especially my kids, because I guarantee you one thing: I'll absolutely end up wearing fucking orange.

* * *

Here I am, at almost one in the morning, lying awake, wondering why I couldn't reciprocate the *I love you*. Is it because deep down I suppose he deserves more than this, more than me?

When Annie slipped down to check on me, I pretended to be asleep. It was so difficult not to break when she hugged me and told me the same three words I didn't say.

Around two-thirty, I wake up to banging on the door, the same door I locked to avoid what I guessed might be coming. In a sleepy haze of sheer exhaustion, I turn the handle, bracing myself, waiting for the shit and the fan to collide.

Because I can smell it.

Jake's been hanging out with Jameson, and I'm not talking about a person. When he does, it's not a positive. It's been years since he's drunk it, at least that I know of. But when he does, he's mean.

"What're you doing?" he slurs, eyes glazed over and vacant.

"Well, I was sleeping. What are you doing, Jake? What do you want?" There's no point trying to hide my annoyance.

He leans in, and I inhale the whiskey seeping from his pores. He stumbles forward, and I catch him by the arms with both hands to steady him.

"Wow, okay, how about you just sit for a minute?"

"Don't tell me what to fucking do." He's struggling to stand straight, staggering all around, tipping the almost-empty bottle to his mouth.

"That's a great idea, Jake."

He bumps into me then runs his fingers up my arm, eyes blazing into mine. "I have another great idea."

Yeah, okay. Also, he can't even stand up right now.

"No," I say firmly. I want him to be away from me.

The look on his face morphs to rage, and it's not him anymore. It's not the Jake I know. This version is angry and distraught and severely drunk.

"I think you better go." Red flags are everywhere, and I'm learning that charging into them is not the fucking way.

"You think… you think," he mumbles, gripping his hair. "It's always about what you think or what you want, right?"

"Stop it! Nothing good will come from this."

He sways closer, and I squeeze my eyes shut, practically tasting the liquor as his harsh breaths fan over my face.

"Well, you don't always get the last word, *Alex*."

I can tell he's about to spew hate. *This is the alcohol talking*, I repeat over and over to myself as he tries to get his thoughts together.

When I look at him, all I can see is a lost twenty-one-year-old in those eyes. The same one who was trying so damn hard to fix the world. The optimist, the *fucking* cheerleader. He opens and closes his mouth multiple times.

"When did you stop loving me?" he whimpers.

"Jake," I plead. This isn't the time or the place. If we're gonna salvage anything, there needs to be someone else involved. If I'm going to salvage any bit of myself, I need help. The pain has gone on long enough, and it's time for it to end.

"Don't *Jake* me." He slugs another swig. "When did I stop being enough for you?"

And because I'm me, I let out a shitty chuckle, squaring up, staring him directly in the eyes. "When did I?"

"Fuck this," he says. "I'm sick of it. Always the fucking victim." He jostles the bottle back and forth between his hands, while his words take a stab at my heart.

I step away from him, backing up almost to the wall. I'm desperate to put as much space between us as I can. I get that he's pissed, but he needs to sleep it off, and we can talk about it in—

"I wish you would have just fucked him so I could hate you as much you hate me!" He cocks his arm back and lets the bottle fly.

It smashes into the wall just a foot away from me. Glass shatters everywhere, and the minimal amount he hadn't ingested drips down the paint.

Almost instantaneously, Jake's jaw drops, and his eyes grow wide with regret.

Sometimes we do stuff when we feel so much stress, we can't explain why. But once it's out there… you can't change it. Things you can't take back—the words after they're said, the bottle after you launch it, the pain after it's been inflicted.

But you know what you can do? You can make the decision that this will not be the way anymore. You can decide that this is the day it all stops.

One way or another.

27. WONDERWALL

So, I think Tupac had one of the best lines. I know, *Tupac?*

Hear me out.

You can spend crazy amounts of energy aiming to figure things out. Overanalyze the situation. Try to force it back together. Consistently dwell on what could or should've gone down. Or… you let the shit fall where it does then move the fuck on.

And guess what? This is where we're at.

It's time to stop trying to pick up every little piece; time to stop overdoing it all. Time to stop using and abusing the glue failing to keep us together.

Sometime this morning, my heart finally spoke up. A Band-Aid on a bullet hole is just not holding up anymore.

Here we are, early on New Year's Day, on this day that promises a fresh start. But really, only if you put the work in—and it hasn't been equal. It's sadly been years of pushing and pulling and growing apart, despite being married.

Funny the stuff that can happen right under your nose while you're too busy with life. It happens though—you hear about it all the time.

Jake and I were kids when we met, who struggled and grew up together, yet separate. We were with each other of course, but we went from not living in the same state for years to instant family. We never got the in-between time, the time for us to grow as a couple.

Yes, I submerged myself into the mom role, into signing up for school fundraisers and taxiing the kids around. Jake coached what he could and killed himself to make money. The picture-perfect family. But he and I didn't spare a second for each other.

It's usually me shattering the glasses and him picking up the broken pieces. That shit is not okay, not one bit—I'm aware. I think it's my turn to do the work. Make a solid effort to change the inner-fucked-up-ness of my mind.

Maybe I *do* need to let him off the hook. And maybe I need to let myself off too.

I'm not saying throw the towel in, okay. But the towel needs some serious help, because it's tattered and torn. I've been so up and down, the emotions, the everything is just all over the place. I guess when you're at a crossroads, when you see a major life change in front of you, your feelings are bound to go haywire.

Also, no drinking, period. It's not helping, and it never has.

Most importantly, we need to make sure the kids are alright, that they don't adopt any destructive behaviors. Well… hopefully not too many— no one's without faults. Make sure they don't feel any certain way towards either of us. No matter what, we're both their parents. We gotta try to hold good on the promises that were recently made and do things as a family.

I've always admired couples who split but sustain a relationship for the kids. Every kid deserves that.

We need to make sure *we're* alright. I don't mean as a couple, but I mean as individual human beings. Because life is fucking rough.

To think, this whole thing started with a kiss…

You know how the song goes.

Thankfully, after the shit *did* hit the fan last night, or this morning, Jace was the one who came down to run interference. Annie had already gone to bed. He got Jake upstairs to the couch then came back to help me clean up the glass.

He didn't ask what happened or grill me. Jace knew his friend was upset. He understands a thing or two about tempers. All he said was that this is not okay, and I told him I agreed.

I barely slept. The clock on the wall says it's seven in the morning. Time to get outta here and start this new year, new me—it's now or never—and today might as well be the day.

I tiptoe upstairs, careful not to wake anyone. Also, it would be super fun to slip out and avoid the third degree from Annie.

Jake's sprawled over the leather couch, leg dangling off the side, hugging a pillow to his chest. He's still in last night's clothes, his face drawn into a fatigued and painfully heartbroken frown.

I stand and stare a second too long… long enough to give him the weird sense you get when someone does this. Super creepy.

Wearing sweats and a shirt from the notorious dresser, I grab my jacket and boots from my bag, looking like a room-temp mess.

I didn't notice his eyes open, peering back at me. What the hell is either of us supposed to say?

"Hey." I clear my throat, hoarse from an obvious lack of sleep, then sigh as he lifts a palm to scrub over his face.

He glances around like he's trying to orient himself to where he's at, and to what exactly happened.

"Hey… Alex," Jake responds, a little timid, a lot confused.

The spread of recognition compels his mouth to hang open. He stares, barely blinking, fingertips gouging into his temples with a soft groan.

Jameson might feel like a friend at the time, but I promise he's not. He'll do you dirt the next day.

I get the whole bottle thing. He was mad, hurt as hell. But it happened. The bottle was like so many things right now—it was easier to just smash it and walk away.

"Ugh, it's early." He grimaces, squinting from the morning sun filtering in across the living room, wincing as if he's being blinded.

"Yeah." I pull my keys from my pocket. "You need a ride?" I remember I didn't see his car, so I'm not even sure what the plan was there.

"Jace can take me, so you don't have to."

"I don't mind."

"Okay… sure, I could use one," he says, foggy as can be. Poor guy's gonna require all the water today. "I need to get some sleep before I grab the kids."

"I can get them if you want."

One, I'd always go and get them, from the ends of the earth if necessary. Two, he's probably still got some whiskey running through him, and it's better to not tempt fate.

Before getting into the car, we both glance at each other, and the word comes out at the same time.

"Sorry."

That's it. Just one single word. Sometimes one word is all there is to say.

The drive isn't too long, maybe thirteen minutes—not that I've counted. Weaving my way through a series of winding roads, I become overwhelmed with an insane urge to pee. Seriously, it's a first-thing-in-the-morning necessity. I can't do life till I go. In the rush of trying to get out of there, I skipped it. Again, after kids, when you gotta go, you gotta go.

I must be squirming in the driver's seat more than I realize.

Jake smiles. "What are you doing?"

"I have to pee. I'm about to pull over and go on the side of the road."

A series of breathy chuckles erupts as he shakes his head. "Please don't. Remember the last time you did that? Don't wanna have to bail you out again."

God, do I remember it.

* * *

We'd crashed at my brother's place at the beach for a few nights, before Jake and I had to leave for college.

Despite spending the entire summer together, our make-outs had been PG-ish. I'm talking about rating standards from multiple years ago—those have changed. We wanted to wait. I mean, it was only a few months, but still. During hormonal times when neither of us was a virgin, it felt like years.

Every night, Ashton's condo housed a ton of people, hanging out, coming and going. There was no choice but to sleep on the floor, with about five other randoms who couldn't find their way home or had come to crash the beach life.

Zero privacy.

On the first night, the party started cranking after Ash got home from work, let's say around eleven.

Oh the days when that's what time the party started. Now my ass is in bed, fast asleep by then.

Somewhere around one, we decided to take a stroll on the beach. There's something incredible about the sound and smell of the ocean at night. The waves you can barely see crashing, and the cool sand that burns your feet during the day, only to welcome them after the sun retires. It's one of my favorite places in the world.

Anyway, we wandered out to an all but abandoned beach, hand in hand, desperate for every second we could soak in before separating. Both anxious about how we were gonna make it months through our first semester, without either of us having a car at school. We didn't talk about sex, but we knew we were headed there. I suspected it would happen before we went, and the countdown was on with only a couple days left.

That night, or morning, under a sky decorated with endless stars, we had the kiss of all kisses. The hard-pressed, mind-blowing promise—a promise that we would make it. The original panty dropper.

Out on the beach, we sealed the deal. Okay, not *actually* on the beach, because sand and everything do not mix. It may seem like a grand plan, but imagine it getting in some crevices—no thanks.

We climbed the lifeguard chair, this small square wooden bench with a platform to stand on, not much to it. Heavy making out ensued, hands tangling beneath our clothes, lips about everywhere.

Jake must've had high hopes, because when he reached into his pocket then flashed a condom and an optimistic smile, I nodded. The guy had his shorts down fast as hell. Not gonna lie, I stood up on the tiny stand and dropped my underwear with equal speed.

Perhaps it was something about how our skin tasted salty from the ocean air, or the reflection of the moon on the water, but the world was on fire for us.

I know… super poetic right now. It happens when I quote Tupac in the early morning.

I lowered myself onto him, skirt hiked around my waist, and our bodies joined in one of the most beautiful, breathtaking ways. Not a single thing felt wrong or unwanted. It was sensational. *We* were sensational.

Halfway through, our gazes locked in full, soul-solidifying eye contact, and we both let the words slip out—at the same time.

The *real* promise. The I love you.

We meant it.

It was the only time I'd ever said it to a guy. I'd wanted to say it to him since that bonfire. He was so different from anyone else; so genuine.

There was no awkward *he said it, so I have to,* or vice versa.

After more of me rocking my body over him, and Jake rocking my body—literally—I experienced that ever-loving, soul-leaving-my-body, stomach-tightening, everything-tensing, legs-useless, toe-curling sensation. My first orgasm ever, and it was un-fucking-believable.

It was a morning full of firsts. *And* seconds.

Once you know that feeling, you're going back for more.

We stayed cozied up on the chair, watching our first sunrise together.

Around seven in the morning, we made our way back to Ashton's place. The door was locked, and no one would answer our repeated knocks. Jake even scaled the balcony, which, you guessed it, locked. How responsible.

Unfortunately, I had to pee so bad I couldn't hold it. As embarrassed as I was, there was no other choice. I made Jake turn the other way, and I did what I had to do, squatting between cars. I'm not proud.

Well, at that exact moment, a police car rolled down the street, catching me midstream.

A minor thing that can get you in trouble: public urination. The cop had no interest in my excuse. They were patrolling all the time to catch the drunk and disorderly, to maintain the family feel of the area. I get it.

But the only thing intoxicating me was Jake.

They took me to the station and put me in the drunk tank, along with about twenty other people, and would only release me to an adult. They refused to wait for Jake's attempt to wake the entire house and grab his ID that was inside.

He promised he'd get Ashton up, so he could get his license and bail me out or whatever. I had no clue if I was in for hard time or who the fuck knows. I hadn't made a habit of taking a pee in public.

About an hour later, I was released, the one-hundred dollar fine paid by the adult—Jake—who could barely contain his hysteria.

The moment we were out the door, he bust out laughing like a fucking hyena. I couldn't help but join in. Of all the days, of all the memories to be tainted by a disorderly conduct citation. The shit was so ridiculous it was comical.

He coined me his jailbird, joked about how the story would be funny to tell our kids… one day.

***

"Yeah," I say, glancing over as he thumbs his wedding band, twisting it around his finger. I meet his eyes and laugh. "I will *always* remember."

28. DAMMIT

We make it to Jake's in record time. I'm not a big one for speeding—no breakin' the law these days. But this is emergent.

I turn into the cookie-cutter townhouse development. Honestly, it's nice. It was shocking there was something open at such short notice. After several days on Luke and Kelsey's couch, Jake was dying to be with the kids. This was the only way. I was seeing too much red at first and couldn't let my guard down, not even for them.

I'm jumping up and down while he takes forever to get the key into the lock, constantly glancing back, doing an awful job curtailing his amusement.

"Bathroom?"

"Upstairs, on the left," he says, voice a bit flat, then shoots a pointed finger at the steps. I race up them without another word.

After I handle things, I wander around, staring at the blank walls, finding myself examining the kids'—*my kids'*—rooms. No added pictures, or decals, or glowing stars on the ceiling that are impossible to remove.

Our house—well my house, kind of anyway—is filled with colors. Mostly warm tans, greens, and blues. We did the basement in gray, but I refuse to join the current industrial, contemporary trends. I'd rather my home feel comfy than look like something out of a magazine.

This entire place consists of white primed walls, zero added touches, paint, or pictures. It smells of new carpet… and Jake. Kelsey would have an absolute field day with this blank canvas.

But I know why it's blank. It's because adding anything, personalizing it, would be another foot out the door, and I know he doesn't want that. At this exact moment, after the trials of the past week—yeah, it's only been a week since I started letting Jake back in—I'm thinking I might want these walls to stay blank too.

Maybe we can work on things better if we spend more time together? In this last week, after finally allowing myself to reminisce about all we've gone through, the odds we've defied… Well, after that, it makes me think if we do the work, the actual work, we can potentially get to the other side of this.

New year, new me, sorta, kinda.

I'm not saying move back in today. No. He has a lease till March, which seems to be more than enough space to get us to where we need to go. Get some tools, some advice, some help. Let's face it—everyone can use an unbiased opinion from time to time. I already shot off a text to one of my favorite therapists from the hospital, first thing this morning. She said she'll fit me in tomorrow.

Witnessing Jake get so upset last night was somewhat of a breakthrough. It made me open my eyes and feel—like *really* feel. It made him human again, not this villain I created, or he created. It's so crazy how your inner narrative gets so fucking sideways sometimes.

Yes, he kissed someone when we weren't separated. I haven't forgotten, and I'm also not diminishing what I did. But yes, he was amazing and such a light in so many pitch-black places. I wish I wouldn't let my emotions consistently get the best of me.

Moving parts? A ton of them.

Though no one ever promised it would be easy, we knew it wouldn't. But would it be worth it? At the end of my days, do I want *him* to be the one there beside me?

I walk downstairs to the empty living room, no Jake in sight. Okay, that's a little uncomfortable. Do I find him, or do I just see myself out? He can always text me.

"Hold up. I'll be out in a sec," he calls from another room.

I turn towards the sound of his voice. "Umm… yeah, okay." Through the open door, I see Jake standing with his back to me, towel draped around his waist. Droplets of water slide excruciatingly slowly from his hair, down his sculpted shoulders, then over the intricate black petals and vines that intertwine across his upper back. The Virgo symbol—Brynn's tattoo.

Christ, the hormones. The whore moans.

No! New year, new decisions, none of the same shit. But this isn't really the same shit though, is it? I mean, we haven't had a session like last night's in a while. You know, before…

But anyway, how did he take a shower in like a minute? Back to how unfair that is. I wanna come out lookin' ready to slay the day in sixty seconds.

It was probably about five minutes I was upstairs, snooping in the kids' rooms.

Still unfair.

The house is sparse of furniture. There's our ancient oversized sectional, and an old table in the dining area. Even the meager kitchen is plain and sad.

There's a single picture on the table under the TV. That's right outside his door, which is wide open.

I'm minding my own business, looking at the frame I picked up, *totally* not tilting my head back, staring like a sex-crazed maniac. But, if I'm honest, that's how I feel right now.

After months without the real deal, last night felt so good. The sex part, I mean. I don't know how long I can go without it now. This morning, even after all the bullshit, I had the urge to jump him on the couch. It's been a while since I felt that way.

Do I want to go without it, simply for the sake of being stubborn?

Body? *Nope.* Heart? *Probs not?* Brain? *Fuck you all!*

And with that, I'm busted.

Those magnificent eyes meet mine, and I clamp my teeth together, cheesy as fuck, glancing at the picture I grabbed. It's the same candid family beach pic Jake got me for my birthday.

He clears his throat.

I barely look at him—well, barely at his face, and that doesn't go unnoticed. My eyes flicker to the middle of the towel, hanging dangerously low, and my next move is borderline bizarre, but whatever.

With my index finger, I lure him to the doorway I'm now standing in. Then I take that same finger, hook it in the knot that's interrupting my V-line view, and lift. The towel unravels, and a swallow rolls down his neck as it lands on the floor at his feet. Jake's hair appears even darker, completely mussed and insanely on edge.

There's something else on edge… ya feel me?

I get it though. As previously discussed, something about a hangover—despite the head pounding, *what the hell did I do?* hangziety—has the body raring to go. You can search-engine that fact.

Anyway, add in the combo of the fight and the action on the dresser and we've got a recipe for disaster, cookin' right in front of us.

I need to focus. I need to work on me. This *isn't* the answer. I keep telling myself that while I unzip my coat and let it join his towel.

My eyes drift lower, over every etched groove of his lean, muscular torso, following the perfectly sculpted trail, straight to—fuck my life.

He's bigger than I remember. And he is ready.

We ultimately need to work on this side by side. But… maybe top or bottom won't hurt either.

"We need to talk," he says.

"Mm-hmm," I hum, lifting the hem of my shirt then pressing my chest to his.

Jake sucks in a sharp breath then nuzzles his stubble against the crook of my neck.

Why? Why is this a thing? And why does it make me wanna do bad things?

I don't know if it's from thinking about the beach, or the need to wanna make up for last night, or the last several years. Could it be the fact that he smells so good, or I'm so lonely, or that the sex was amazing and we need more of it? But anyway, it seems I've lost any willpower. That's something I've been holding strong to for months, and in the past week, it's been fading fast.

This feels so exciting, like old times. Not routine or out of necessity, but out of—*holy hell.*

The noise that comes from his throat is something between a whine and a growl, and it makes me groan, it's so sexy. I curl my fist around his cock, and he closes his eyes, long lashes fluttering with each of my strokes.

"Still wanna talk?" I ask, adding pressure around the base, drawing tiny grunts from him as I tug to his tip. "You want me to talk about what I'm doing? Or how fucking good you feel in my hand? Still not better than when you're inside—"

"Alex… fuck." He grins and nips my bottom lip. Damn, that was a bit out of the box for me, but hot.

His finger lines the waist of my sweats then cruises down till he glides inside me, going for two straight out the gate.

Cue the pounding heart.

It's hot in here. I may wanna ditch the rest of these clothes.

Jakes's already out of breath as he kisses my neck, rapidly finding my mouth. We lapse into that easy rhythm, but my brain—yeah… shut up already—powers up.

"Unless you wanna talk right now," I say after pulling back.

Oh my God. Common sense can pound sand.

Jake lifts his gaze, quirking a brow. "How 'bout in ten minutes?" he asks. And I'm down with that plan.

"Done."

I undo my bra then promptly fuse my lips to his, not wasting any time meshing our tongues together. My curled fist continues methodically pumping him, adding the precise amount of pressure so more baritone growls rumble from his chest.

Our hearts are already beating wildly, our breathing erratic as fuck.

Jake frees my hair from its ponytail. He's got a thing for grabbing a handful, and not in a painful way, just a gentle pull here and there.

I'm not mad at it.

Before I know it, I'm lying under him on his bed, not even bothering to think at this point. This is just gonna happen. Judge the fuck outta me. No shits are given.

He shifts his weight to his elbows, eyes flooded with desire, then scrambles furiously, clawing at the waist of my sweats before moving down my body with them.

Jake stands from the bed, eyes on me. Before I can ask or even wonder what he's doing, he grips around my ankles, yanking me right to the edge… of the mattress, that is.

His hot, wet tongue licks between my legs, in a brief check to make sure all systems are a go. They are. They *definitely* are.

He lounges onto the chair next to his bed with a cocky smirk. "You wanna do this?" Jake slaps his thighs.

I *knew* he was thinking about the beach too.

Obviously about the jail thing, but I'm talking about the lifeguard chair. Truth be told, that chair, or any chair, for that matter, is my choice spot. Obviously, it has been from the get-go.

"Yup," I reply, matching his smugness.

This may seem like *what the hell, I gotta do all the work?* But he knows this is the best position for a guaranteed O-face. I'm down. Or on.

Time to cowgirl up. I straddle his legs with my back towards him as I lower, sinking over his thick length.

Identical moans gasp out while I roll over him, circling my hips, and feeling him… everywhere.

Jake steers my movements with his palms on my waist, lifting me. His hips rise, heightening the sensation, and the sound of his pelvis smacking my ass makes me cry out with each slap.

My head lolls, so his lips can take their place on my neck, and I brace myself on the chair's arms. The pace we've set is steady enough now. His hand snakes to the front of me, thumb pressing my clit, building the unmistakable feeling while I grind over him.

He halts his upward thrusts. "Stand up," his harsher, much more demanding voice rasps, and I'm straight up, fast as hell.

I'm not one to be dominated, not totally, but when you can say what you want, on either side of the fence, I'm cool with it.

"Turn around."

Yeah, alrighty then.

Jake scoots to the very end of the chair, fingertips digging into my outer thighs, making me moan as he drags me to him. He lowers me in a single swift movement over his body.

"Look at me."

My eyes do exactly as instructed, connecting with his. The striking combination of color in his irises is so hot they shouldn't be allowed to exist. There's something off in them though. Not necessarily bad but different.

He bucks beneath me and grips my jaw, forcing my stare.

I rest my elbows on his shoulders, fingers combing through his hair, cold and wet, twisting harder as the intense rush fills me, while he's… filling me.

Maybe now is the opportune time to right my wrong from last night? To tell him that despite everything, I still love him. That I was an asshole for denying him that. To confess I'm defying the urge to jump ship. Because what I want is him. And he shouldn't doubt that I love him. Jake deserves to know.

His head falls back against the chair. No attempted kissing. Something is off.

Alright, he's still upset, but it's now or never. I open my mouth to reciprocate those three little words, to undo the damage of my silence.

Jake closes his eyes. This isn't him.

I stop moving. "What's wrong?" That's a loaded question, huh?

When he finally lifts his lids, there's an immediate distance. Another shift.

Right now, even though I'm literally on top of him, he's suddenly a million miles away.

"I can't do this."

And the only thing clenching in my stomach is my heart, which just plummeted to it.

My shoulders pinch and my back straightens. I lift myself off him, and the impulse to bolt is there. It's what I know—the easy way out.

I can't. Dammit.

That's exactly what the old Alex would've done. Left and not let him explain.

"Okay," I say slowly, trying to keep my head straight, trying to shake off the sting of rejection.

I pick up my clothes and pull them on then hand him his towel, because… clothing probably shouldn't be optional for this conversation.

Jake slouches in the chair, elbows resting on his upper legs, head in his hands. "Alex. Last night… it killed me."

"Jake… I should've told you that I love—"

He holds up a palm, cutting me off. "I know you're hurt, and I know I fucked up."

Keeping my eyes on him, not searching for an exit, not needing to bite my tongue, I wait for him to say whatever he needs to.

"That's not the problem," he says with a waver in his voice. "The problem is that I did this. I broke my own heart. You were *always* enough. I made a terrible fucking choice. But last night, when I threw the bottle, part of me… I could've hurt you. And hurting you, physically, is something I never want to do."

He reluctantly glances up, his eyes taking on a glossy sheen. My own begin to burn, and I swallow the lump in my throat.

"You wouldn't hurt me like that." I reach for the hand he withdraws.

"I never thought I would… in *any* way," he admits, head down again. "But I could have, and I can't risk that. You've been through enough."

29. THE SPACE BETWEEN

It's not the easiest thing in the world to sit down with someone and open up. Especially when you have deep-rooted pain you've been running from for years.

But I'm doing it, putting in the work. Met with Janelle, the therapist I mentioned, at her off-campus office twice a week for the last four weeks.

Yup, four weeks since the New Year's Day bang sesh turned sideways. Four weeks that Jake has barely even looked at me.

I don't get it. Instead of freaking out, or lashing out, I'm trying to exercise the tools I've learned. Trying to respect space, or boundaries, or whatever the fuck. The resolution is going strong. They say once you do something for over three weeks, it becomes a habit. So I guess I'm good.

Look at me go.

Good decisions, no destructive behavior, kids are doing great, and no alcohol. Okay, that's not true, but no more benders.

I've been hitting the gym when I'm off work, saying no to stuff I don't wanna do; I've stopped trying to make life look perfect. Shit is messy, and it's only lying to yourself.

Who cares what other people see?

The truth is, this space from Jake is actually doing me some good. I'm focusing on myself and what makes me happy, while, of course, taking care of my crew.

Janelle is understanding and effortless to talk to, which is a good thing, because that's what she gets paid to do. Seriously though, it's been so freeing to unload, to finally get the truth, the *entire* truth, out there into the universe.

The only way I'm ever gonna let it go, move forward, is to get it out. I'm utilizing the methods she's offered and learning to cope, while accepting situations for what they are.

The rest is up to me. I won't bore you with further details, plus that shit is confidential.

Anyhow, we could trace the increase in my anxiety and depression to over two years ago. I don't know why I didn't see it or think of it, but it was around the time Brynn turned fourteen. So, for obvious reasons, that age is horrifying to me. Also, Jordan's fourteenth is coming up.

Trust issues—didn't need to pay someone to be told that. She knows about Jake, but we don't talk too much about him, mostly just about me. If I brought him up, she'd let me freestyle, but she said he'd taken to fixing me too much. Again, I already knew that.

The goal now is to work on getting the chip off my shoulder. Honestly, it's too heavy to carry. I'm done with it.

Not trying to force anything is a tremendous struggle for me, or not having the upper hand, or whatever you want to call it. Because that's the way it's always been. I've always felt like I needed to have it, needed some control. I could do whatever and Jake would be the one to pick up the pieces, the one to make sure *I* was okay, the one who enabled me to be destructive.

I'm not blaming him; kinda the opposite. I know he thought he had to protect me, and now he feels like a failure. No one wants to feel that way. He shouldn't have to constantly worry about protecting me, or worry about me going off the deep end.

Life is too short to let someone else's existence consume you.

So every week, for the last three, he's bailed on our appointments with a marriage counselor. Messed up, right? And every week, I've tried my best to remain calm.

I started wearing my yoga pants to actual yoga, determined to center my chi and shit.

We held good with the kids. Janelle said being present and holding true to promises was a definite step. Twice a week we all have dinner together, alternating places. Jake is elsewhere though. He's there, but he's not, leaving me with empty kisses on the forehead. His explanation is always the same. Work's gotten too crazy, too busy.

There's something else, but I'm trying to respect whatever it is because you just can't force something if someone doesn't want it.

Anyway, here we are. I came to his place, straight from work. I haven't completely transitioned to full-time, but I might as well have. I've been picking up several shifts a week, feeling great, and standing on my own two feet.

Although it's exhausting, I'm juggling it rather well. I actually feel like an Alex I've never known before. It's been... liberating.

Tonight's meal is amazing. I swear, I miss Jake's cooking. As someone who could screw up microwave mac and cheese, having a man who cooked—and enjoyed it—has me ruined for life. When he came to my place, it was sadly takeout that I provided.

Meh. But I provided it, and that's what matters.

The dinner convo is the usual, asking the kids about their days, exchanging info about different sports and such, Will talking our ears off about video games. Brynn and Jordan do their teenage duty of not saying much, except for huffs and the occasional grunt.

I notice Roo staring more often, like she's daydreaming. That makes me nervous. Every time I catch her attention, she responds, quickly snapping out of it, which is good.

After dinner, it's the routine, silently helping Jake with the dishes, then telling the kids to get their stuff together. This is still the tough day for both of us. The day the kids swap houses. You think the break would be nice, but when it's not something you really want, I promise, it sucks.

Right after the chair situation, I tried to get him to talk, and he wouldn't. He just kept saying he couldn't do this anymore. After briefly contemplating backing out of the new me, I decided I was gonna be the change.

I was going to fix the one I didn't love. Because that's the only thing I can control at this point.

I was going to fix *me*.

Get real... if he can't do this, we can't do this. I can't make him go to these appointments. Would I even want to have to make him? Nah, no thanks.

As I said, there's been underlying stuff for years. It was like he needed the forgiveness, and when I finally gave it, or was about to, he fucking bailed.

My back's against the wall here. Maybe we nailed all the stages of grief and we're rounding into acceptance. Who the hell knows?

"Jake, have you noticed Roo staring off more? Has her teacher or Cassie mentioned anything?"

Cassie is Roo's TSS, aka therapeutic support staff. She accompanies her to school daily and comes back to whatever house three days a week to help with at-home behaviors.

She's fantastic, in her early twenties, going for her master's. We've had her for the last year, and she's incredible for Roo—for all of us.

"No," he snaps, rinsing a plate in the sink then loading it in the dishwasher. "Don't you think I would notice if there was anything?" he says quickly, getting a bit defensive from the get-go. His spine stiffens beneath the crisp white of his collared shirt.

"Hey, I'm not accusing, Jake, I'm *only* asking. I haven't noticed anything either until tonight at dinner." I lean against the fridge, arms crossed, on the opposite end of the kitchen. The space that now exists between us is substantial. It's never been like this.

At least there were emotions before, unhealthy as they were. Now it's nothing. A business arrangement, and a distant one at that.

So here's the problem with time. When you have little ones, the days feel like they last forever. But after they've grown, the years seem to have flown by. Time can ultimately put space into relationships, whether you want it to or not. The hours you let pass, not saying the things you want. The minutes you remain angry, instead of sorting out a solution. The seconds it takes to spit hateful words you won't ever get back. Time is something we all desperately want more of yet tend to manage so poorly.

It's a tricky bitch.

But for matters of the heart, at least *this* heart, the more time that goes by, the more I accept. If we aren't getting back together, it's a breakup, not a breakdown. I refuse. Biting the inside of my cheek, I try to not let this distance kill me.

No, not me—I'll survive.

"I'll get her in Friday with the neurologist, maybe after our appointment? That is, if you're gonna show this time?"

I don't think it's unfair.

The plate in his hand drops with a loud clang against the bottom of the sink, making me step back. "Do you have any clue how fucking busy I've been at work?" he snarls, not even turning.

"I mean, yeah, you've said. Whatever, Jake. This shit is tired, and so the fuck am I."

Okay, yes, I've been doing great at giving him space and trying not to press him. I don't want to look like I'm desperate here, but this all stemmed from him. Not all… but anyway.

While I may be nailing the new-me persona, I'm not losing my edge. Don't doubt that for a second.

"Sorry." He turns and presses his lips tight, stress wearing on the outer corners of his eyes that look next to me, not at me.

For someone who's always huge on the eye contact, this has been a bit much—the rejection has been hard. But I'm breathing, I'm here. I guess he doesn't complete me.

Jesus, *Jerry* fucking *Maguire?*

"Jake." Still several feet away, I search his face, seeking any sign of the kid I fell in love with years ago. Hoping to see if those eyes could still spark with a feeling or a smile.

He's gone. After years of wading through the shit, he simply seems done.

"Do you want me to stop making the appointments?"

"No!" He dries his hands then sighs. "No," he repeats, toning down his tension. "That's not what I want."

I think my jaw hit the floor. Um. What?

Alex, breathe. Count to ten; better make that one hundred. Keep the temper in check. Do *not* go off.

I suck in a prolonged, deep, simmering breath, releasing it slowly. "Then I'll see you on Friday."

Damn, I am so fucking mature right now. Also, I'm good at acting. This hurts… this *really* hurts.

The kids say their goodbyes to Jake, all hugs and love, before they pile into my car.

I walk a few steps from the house and turn around.

He stands in the doorway, resting against the side. I haven't seen him smile in weeks, but the corner of his lips curls the tiniest bit.

This next part is *not* out of spite. It isn't meant to hurt; it's meant to just say what I mean. So here goes.

"If you don't show this week"—he straightens, and the smile vanishes—"I'm *done.*"

30. BULLS ON PARADE

Friday morning rolls around fast as hell, and thank God for that because…
today's the day.

I feel a little sick about it. Been worrying and stressin' my ass off for the
last two days. I'm not overthinking, but I can't just ignore it. I need to know
what's going on.

Roo's neurology appointment is this afternoon. The fact that she's been
stable on the same med dose for a while has me thinking it's time for an
EEG and a potential increase in her medication.

Also, sometimes too much knowledge is a horrible thing. Because I
know that with different developmental changes, seizures can spike, change,
and whatnot.

There are no definitive rules with epilepsy; I wish there were. It would
be so much easier if she could tell us if something felt funny or off. But no.
When I try to ask her, she says *no, silly,* or some other name, never Mommy.
I'd even settle for the teenage version of Ma. Nope. She smiles and shakes
her head.

Roo's come so far, made so much progress in school, and I can't bear
the thought of seeing her go backwards.

Oh yeah, marriage counselor at eleven. Hadn't obsessed about that one.
Nope. Not for a second.

Okay, yeah fucking right. For the last however many hours, it's crossed
my mind about twenty times every second.

I'm hopeful though, because it's eight-thirty, and there's been no text
from Jake about calling them to reschedule. The messages have come

earlier than eight the past three times, so maybe he realizes I'm not screwing around. I legit can't believe I let it go three weeks without saying anything.

There's just enough time to clean up the shit storm that comes with school mornings then hit the gym. I dabbled with it before all this started, going randomly here and there. But as far as finding a positive outlet for any anger, sadness, or pain—it works. I've stuck to a decent schedule. And it feels good to be growing stronger all the time.

The truth is, I don't know if my little Ruby will ever be able to live on her own. She may be with us for life, and that's okay. But I need to make sure I keep my ass in the best shape I can; gotta make sure I'm good, healthy, and on this earth as long as possible… for her.

* * *

The monitor on the moving stairs from hell beeps, suggesting I check my heart rate. We're gonna skip that one. I didn't die, so I'll count it as a win. I clean the bastard machine, then use a towel to wipe my dripping face. No makeup at the gym—the shit'll melt—and a separate towel. I'm not gross.

I haven't had to deal with a single human. I'll be in and out, just how I like it. Nine AM is my preference. You miss the meathead rush, striving to pump iron before work. There's a small lull at this time of day. And the less I have to *people*, the better.

"Alexandra," a voice calls from the weight room, and I stop dead in my tracks. Please, God, why me?

I keep walking, quickening my pace towards the exit.

Fuck no, not today. I've avoided this for a month, how 'bout we make it even longer. I didn't even hear him; he could have been talking to someone else. My name's super common.

I make it to the corner, the home stretch. All that's left is the long hallway to the door. I can feel the sweat beading along my forehead from the workout—just the workout.

Please do not be behind me.

A gust of cold air blasts down the hall from the door being opened. And because life is a fickle fucker, and I'm already perspiring like a pig, trying to run from a bad choice… let's step the stress level up a notch and see if we can get my heart rate uncontrollable.

Palpitations, here we come.

Gym shorts, favorite hoodie—why? He hasn't noticed me yet. I'm literally standing at the corner. If I go forward, I gotta face one thing. If I go backward, another.

What do I do?

I somewhat compose myself and glance up. Our eyes meet, and he stops briefly then continues walking. Still with the pained, faraway look, lips pressed together, taking slow strides towards me as I'm standing at the intersection of familiar and *could we just not*. Maybe if I stay super still…

Wishful thinking.

It's no biggie; it's just Jake, though his workout time was always earlier or in the evening. Not that I know this, or plan my specific time slot around it.

"Hey." It's almost as if he softens briefly, eyes flickering with a smidge of light before they inch above my head and immediately darken. His jaw tightens, and I can tell by the way it clicks that he's grinding his teeth.

At whatever—well, whoever—is behind me.

I'm flatlined.

Suddenly we've got a what-the-fuck sandwich, and I'm the meat.

"Oh." A throat clears behind me, the voice deepening before it says, "Hello, Jake. How's it going?"

I stay frozen, my body tingling and numb. My knees wanna buckle, and it's not from leg day.

An arm reaches past me, ever so slightly brushing the side of my body. I try not to flinch. Jake's nostrils quiver as he glares down at the extended hand.

He grabs it reluctantly, out of obligation I guess, standing up straighter now, chest full-on puffed out, moving closer to me. "Hayden," he says with a tone as sharp as a razor blade.

Nobody moves.

I stare at the blue carpet because it's extremely interesting. Much more interesting than the pissing match that's happening. It would be super convenient right now if I could disappear.

Their hands drop, and Jake takes another step closer. So close I can smell the detergent on his hoodie. I can smell *him*. Any closer to me and he'll plow me over.

But I get it. Here we are with the territorial bullshit. I understand it, to a point. It's kind of funny, really, because nobody owns me.

I don't know what repercussion came from the kiss, if anything. My assumption would be like most other things, it hasn't been addressed.

"Well, gotta go." I sidestep away from Jake, not bothering to look back, because that would just be shitty. "Bye!" I shoot up a clammy palm in my uncomfortable attempt at a getaway.

My eyes stay deadlocked on the door. Get me outta here.

The hallway is about a zillion miles long and getting longer by the second.

"Alex."

Before my brain can communicate with my body—and isn't that so annoying? When you react and don't exactly want to—I spin around, chin tilting up. Only one face is looking in my direction.

Salt-and-pepper hair, slightly slick with post-workout sweat, T-shirt clinging to his toned torso, blinding smile. Did he use my nickname to get Jake riled up?

"Let me walk you out."

I swear I can see Jake's shoulder blades squeeze together, and his neck angles from side to side. For a second, I wonder if we're gonna have a full-out brawl in the gym hallway.

Not on my watch. This place is reasonable, and it includes childcare.

I keep my face as indifferent as I can, no smile, no hidden expressions that scream, *Oh yes! Please follow me and try something again.*

"No thanks. I'm good"—Jake's stance relaxes—"on my own." I spin around and do the stealthiest speed walk I can into the freezing cold air, then hop into my car.

I toss my jacket onto the passenger seat and smile at myself in the rearview. I look like I spent the day baking in the sun, but I walked outta there with a shit ton of dignity, and that's priceless. The situation wasn't too unpleasant. Not at all. I'm sure they're in there having a casual chat. No problem whatsoever. Spotting each other and yucking it up.

I pat my coat pockets, frantically searching for my phone.

So yeah. Walked out of there with my dignity. Hell to the yes. But my phone and earbuds are still sitting in the motherfluffing StairMaster cup holder.

I rest my forehead against the cold steering wheel, thumping it several times. Coming back in a solid four hours sounds like a fantastic plan to avoid any residual testosterone.

A light tap on my window snaps me back to reality. Someone take the fucking wheel. I lean back, staring momentarily at the ceiling before looking over.

Phew. Jake.

I roll down the window, my lips scrunching to the side. He frowns, standing there quietly. I know it was painful for him too.

In Hayden's defense, I told him we were separated. It wasn't like his— she *knew* he was married. At least, I'm pretty sure she did. But Jake knew we were married too. Yet it happened.

I can't even begin to imagine the psycho mode I'd enter if I ever faced the bitch. But no, not gonna happen. I'm an adult. I can be a civilized human being.

"Forget something?" He reaches into the car, passing me my phone.

"Um, yeah, thanks. I actually just realized I left it."

No matter how hard he tries to dodge my gaze when his finger touches my hand, our eyes meet. He studies my face, tugging the string of his sweatshirt, while I bite the inside of my cheek.

"Sorry."

He shakes his head. "I'm gonna have to see him. It was just weird." Jake still hasn't moved his hand from mine.

I pull away from his touch and throw my phone onto the passenger seat, feeling some kind of way that after all these weeks, he's *finally* looking at me again.

After what? After he's faced with some other guy who might be interested? It's irritating.

I shift the car into drive, and Jake steps back.

"I'll be there," he says.

I can still sense his eyes on me, but I'm focused forward. Focused on what's in front of me.

I'll believe it when I see it.

But despite my better judgment, because I'm me, I turn to look at him. "You know I'm not interested in that dude, right?"

The corners of his lip curve upward, only a tad. "Yeah…" He pauses, drawing in a breath. "I'm pretty sure he got the memo."

"Good."

"I think you left these too." He hands me the stupid headphones I poke fun at the girls about. Whatever—I had a gift card from Christmas. His brows raise while he sports a smirk.

Don't judge me, bro.

I roll my eyes, landing on his, staring for a few seconds. "Show up."

He nods, and without another word, I drive away.

31. THE DISTANCE

I get myself ready. Not too much, hopefully just enough. Hair somewhat styled—I learned how to do that whole wave with a straightener thing; thanks, Monica—light makeup, jeans, ankle boots, sweater.

I look like me. Low-key stylish. I mean, enough. My kids probably have more up-to-date clothes than I do, but that's life.

This is exactly what I would wear to meet with a marriage counselor, right?

How does one even know what to wear to this shit? I'm going hard with the relaxed *I don't care, totes casual, everyday outing* look. But the hair and nontraditional makeup says, *Yeah, okay, I totally do.*

Ugh.

At New Year's, I thought I knew what I wanted; I thought, this is it. This man that I've lived for, lived with for years, he was *still* the one. This seemingly perfect human, who I knew was imperfect, but I knew loved me, was worth fighting for.

One blip, one twist in the wrong direction, and we were back to square one.

But in all fairness… he fucked up. Okay, he fucked up, then *we* fucked up.

What I've learned, after taking a long hard look at everything, is when you don't take care of something, when you don't make sure it's okay, and when you let too much time go by without saying the things you should say…

It falls apart.

When I bit my tongue, refused to tell Jake that I loved him, I *knew* it was out of anger—anger for a comment that wasn't premeditated. I saw it for what it was the next day. I was about to tell him that despite either of us, and our issues, and our filthy hearts, that I loved him. Always have.

But then Jake said he couldn't, and he repeated it. He *kept* repeating it, then he all but disappeared.

What was I supposed to do? What would *you* do?

I've been doing the best I can, and I'm going to keep on doing it, because I'm still a realist. I'm not expecting it's gonna work out or it's not. This messy shit is what it is. There's nothing else I can do.

So I've got two choices right now. I can boohoo and dwell on the fact that life currently isn't a walk in the park. Or I can move on.

I guarantee you, I'm *currently* choosing the latter. Because for the first time in a long time, I'm alright. I'm not fixed. No one ever is. Drama and life and bullshit are ongoing. Some days you're a bug, others a windshield.

But I'm okay with me. I'm enough—with or without Jake.

I pull into the parking lot of the brick building with a minute to spare. And can we please take a moment to appreciate the enormity of me not being late for once?

When I find the door etched with the family counseling center logo, I pull it open and enter a small waiting area. Tan walls span the quiet room, pictures of landscapes covering them.

I guess they can't exactly load them up with portraits of happy couples?

Front and center is an enormous desk with a modest-looking blonde sitting behind it, maybe mid-twenties. She flashes her teeth, pleasantly smiling ear to ear.

First, does she *really* love this job? Seeing people come in when more than likely they're at their worst? Or at least at their worst as a couple?

Second, there are only four other people here—two men, two women, flipping through outdated magazines and scrolling on their phones.

Guess who *isn't* here. My ears burn.

"Alexandra Everett," I say, trying not to crack a molar. "Eleven o'clock with Doctor Gable."

She glances at her computer before looking back up at me. "Have a seat, and she'll be right out."

I chuckle to myself. Those are some famous words about any doctor. Half of them think their time is so much more valuable than ours. I see it nonstop. I laugh at the sign saying *you'll be billed if you're over fifteen minutes late.* Shouldn't we hold them to the same standards?

But enough about that. I'm sure they have their reasons.

Jake isn't even here, and he's got about thirty seconds. If he doesn't show, I'm out.

I hope he shows.

Sitting in one of the waiting-room chairs, I let my mind drift, because that's what it does. And I recall another time when I thought he wouldn't show up.

* * *

I was eight months pregnant with Will. Although we had no clue what his name was gonna be then, or even if he was a he, I believed it was another girl. It would seem fitting. Four freaking girls… why not? But since he was a surprise—and a great one at that—we made it all a surprise till the very end. No gender-reveal cupcakes or balloons or exploding golf balls.

That day, I felt like I had a stomach bug more than anything else. The same nausea and other weird stuff that comes with pregnancy had kept me company for months now, so I'd waddled into an appointment, three kids in tow, ignoring faces of pity or maybe astonishment, thinking nothing of it. It felt as if the kid could fall out, *actually fall out*. After each baby, the body remembers exactly what to do

Cue the wonderful check—not fun. The nurse practitioner freaked out, because my water had apparently broke. It doesn't always come out in a big gush, and I was dilating… fast. This baby was coming *now!* In the doctor's office.

No one could get a hold of Jake. He'd been away for work, though should've landed in time to make it to my appointment, but he was a no-show. Kelsey and Annie rushed to the rescue, Kelsey taking the girls and Annie hoisting me into her car, weaving through the streets like a goddamn race car driver to get me to the hospital.

She was hysterical. You'd think she'd be calm, but nope, anything but— running red lights, begging me not to have the baby on her leather seat. I can't even imagine.

We made it there, skidding to a stop at the entrance like something straight from a movie. This kid was ready to be out in the world, ready for the amazing role he'd play in our family.

Part of me knows when we're gone, he'll be the one who looks after Roo. He's her keeper.

I had a single push left, and Annie wasn't the best cheerleader. She was a crying, blubbering mess, but it was kinda nice to tell her to *shut the fuck up* without having to deal with any sass. Labor gets you a free pass to say a slew of unfiltered shit.

Also, it's seriously painful.

There was no time for drugs. Hell, I barely had time to get a gown on.

Seconds before the final push, the door swung open, then Jake sprinted in, out of breath, suited up with his hair a mess. Right under the gun, but he made it. A moment later, our six-pounder made his entrance. We were all floored when the doctor announced it was a boy.

Jake loves the girls, and I knew he'd be absolutely fine with another, but this was our last kid. There wouldn't be any more, and the way he beamed at the words *it's a boy* was unmatched. I couldn't have asked for anything better. Our family was completely complete.

Annie followed the nurse around, hounding her the way fellow nurses do, watching and badgering as she weighed him and performed the initial assessments. He was great, perfect even.

We were perfect.

Baby bliss captivated us. In awe, and utterly proud that we'd created yet another life, Jake swept the matted hair from my face, kissed me, and told me he loved me. He loved all of us.

Something spectacular happens when those little ones come out. It's like an outpouring of emotions that's so immense and extreme you wanna burst into a million different pieces, though it doesn't always happen initially. I'm proof of that.

Jake's flight had mechanical problems, and his phone was dead. This was back before airports had outlets everywhere and portable chargers were a common accessory. He'd had to beg several airlines to get home. He got my message when he landed and somehow made it to the hospital, just in time.

Where there's a will… there's a way.

And that is—literally—how Will got his name.

* * *

"Alex?" A woman, I'm guessing Doctor Gable, walks out, dressed in a long white blouse and tan pants.

She's going hard with the casual look, but you can tell she charges high and rakes in change. Her brown hair hangs long and curly, framing her neutral expression.

The outside door opens, and my head swings towards it.

Gray suit pants, collared shirt, and *not* Jake. I feel like an idiot.

"Yeah, sorry," I apologize, taking a second to snap out of it. Standing up, I shake her outreached hand. She smiles, and I try to return the sentiment, though I'm sure my resting bitch face is a key player right now.

She supplies a firm grip and direct eye contact; seems like a to-the-point type of woman. Maybe she can sense my hesitation.

"I'm actually just waiting for my… umm."

The fuck? This feels so strange. Husband?

"Jake's already here." Her voice is low, remaining steady, her pleasant expression unfaltering.

I can feel my face screwing up, with that harsh line creasing between my brows. What?

"What do you mean he's here?" I move back.

"Alex, please come with me to my office. He can explain everything." She raises her arm, gesturing to the door she just came out of.

Why's he already in there? What is this?

She walks ahead of me, and I follow through the frosted glass door, not sure what I'm stepping into at this point. It might not be wise to have glass in close proximity.

Jake repositions himself, clearly uncomfortable, in a chair situated against the wall. His eyes dart up at me then back down to his left hand, where he's anxiously twisting his ring.

"Have a seat, Alex," she offers, gesturing next to Jake. Her own matching brown leather chair sits directly across from it, several feet back.

I sit, looking from Jake to this lady. "I'm sorry… I'm confused here."

"I'm sure this may seem confusing, but I want you to know that this is the right place for you to be, and you will have a chance to talk. I want to make sure Jake fills you in on what's been going on first. And Alex, please call me Patricia."

Oh, for shit's sake. Sounds super, Patty.

I stare at the side of Jake's head, and try to kill the growl that's itching my throat.

"Jake, go ahead," she says as he reluctantly turns to face me. His eyes avoid mine, looking over to her for a brief nod of encouragement.

He inhales a long breath through his nose, letting his one hand trickle back through his hair, while the other keeps toying with his fucking ring.

"I haven't been *completely* honest with you."

A nauseating sensation riddles my stomach. "What?" I ask. Please tell me I heard him wrong.

"I didn't say anything to you because I thought it was the better move, but it's not. And we can't ever get anywhere if I'm not completely truthful with you." He spits the words out so fast.

My ears ring, like loud as hell, high-pitched ringing. No, not ringing, *roaring*. My heart's not even in my chest… it's on the floor.

"Before I tell you this, can you please… please promise to hear me out? Just stay calm?"

I laugh—I'm talking inappropriately loud, hysterical laughter. Because if I don't, I'm gonna scream.

My attention continually alternates from Jake to Patty, searching the room for hidden cameras or some shit, because this feels like an ambush.

So sure. I'm calm. Like a motherfucking bomb.

32. MOTHER MOTHER

Breathe.

Just. Breathe.

Count to ten. Better make it fifty. Think of a happy place.

Fuck this.

Why?

I stood up somewhere right before the full-blown bomb detonation phase and walked blankly to the door, blood rushing up my neck to my cheeks. I can't with this; I'm over it.

"You won't even listen to what I have to say?" Jake barely croaks the words.

I glance back robotically to his eyes, which are filling with tears. "I don't wanna hear it. I'm not dealing with this anymore."

I'm a little mad at myself because I'm walking away. I know I was going so hard with the new year, new me, don't react, stay Zen mentality, but I feel this is the best option... for me.

Probably for everyone.

Jake didn't do me any favors. He did whatever he thought was best and didn't include me in it. Well, until now. And ya know what... I don't even *want* his explanation.

My shaking hand grips the door handle, my knuckles blanching.

"Alex," Patricia says, eerily calm.

I know that voice, that practiced tone, programmed to de-escalate. I'm sure she's whipped it out more than once. I'm not a stranger to that tactic from my own line of work.

She rises from her chair, arms hanging by her sides, thin lips pressed to a straight line. "You have every right to be upset. Those feelings are valid."

Yeah, thanks. No shit.

"But you're here, which means, at the very least, you want to work on communication. Maybe this is the place to start." She motions back to the seat I jumped out of like it was on fire.

"Yeah," I respond after a moment or two of gritting my teeth, not releasing my hold on the door. "Yeah, I did. But I didn't think I'd be walking into some sort of…" Inhaling a long breath through my nose, I do the stupid relaxation countdown in my head until the urge to bang my skull against the door isn't as strong. "Some sort of whatever the fuck *this* is."

Placating Patricia doesn't exhibit an ounce of shock when the F-bomb flies.

"I'm sorry," Jake repeats over and over and over.

What else is new?

I close my eyes, still trying to relax, struggling to be chill. It's tough because it's not in my nature.

"Isn't this a conflict of interest?" I spin around, planting my fists on my hips, glaring Patricia down. I'm pissed that she would back me into a corner like this. And I'm undoubtedly staring at her because I *cannot* look at him.

"Yes. I've already told Jake that if you choose to continue, I'd recommend you both meet with my colleague so you don't feel I've chosen a side. I want to assure you, I have not. My only job here is to listen and offer some tips."

"I've been coming here every week!" Jake blurts out before covering his face. Then his palms slide along his jawline. "I haven't been canceling the appointments. I've been coming to them by myself."

"What? Why? Why would you go to a marriage counselor by yourself?" I laugh a few high-pitched chuckles, teetering on the edge of going off.

Jake inhales a chest-expanding breath, and raises his head. "Because, Alex…" He looks away after saying my name. "Because I needed someone to talk to."

I close my eyes.

Ten. Counting to ten.

"Okay, so you needed someone to talk to… but you couldn't talk to me?" I speak the words slowly, utterly confused.

He responds with a single nod.

"You make no fucking sense."

"I know." He keeps his focus on me, begging with a guilt-ridden stare. "I didn't plan on it. It's just… I didn't know what to do. I don't know how I can *ever* make things better with you."

Fighting looming tears, I set my jaw, swallowing the perpetual lump in my throat. I refuse to let them fall. "You can't." I tighten my arms, which are folded over my chest.

He throws his hands in the air. "See, this is what I mean. It won't ever change."

"Jake!" Patricia pins him with a stern look, and his chin drops like a reprimanded child.

If I'm being honest, that's how I'm feeling right now.

"Jake," she repeats, much calmer, "why don't you start by telling Alex why you kept coming by yourself."

"Yeah, Jake." I stress the K as hard as humanly possible. If I feel I'm being treated like a child, I may as well act like one. Okay, that's not the answer, but I'm angry. "Why don't you do that?" With cinched brows, I await his response.

He frowns, looking so lost. I don't know why we've gotten to this point in our lives where we're strangers, but it sucks.

"Because you seem to be doing so great." He bites back tears after saying the words.

I let out a much quieter, far less psychotic series of chuckles. "Oh yeah." My head nods before shaking. "Life is fucking perfect—never better." If sarcasm had a voice, it would be mine.

"Seriously." His lip slides between his teeth. Dark eyebrows draw in over defeated eyes.

Does he truly think I've been okay? I mean, I have been just that… okay, but it's taken immense work.

"Even the kids notice, Alex. You seem *genuinely* happy."

"Well, I'm not." My arms fall to my sides. "But I've been trying. What does that have to do with anything?" I let my anger dim… just a bit.

"Because it's not with me. I was dragging you down, and then I screwed up." Jake's glossy stare peels away from me. "I want you to be happy, Alex."

He draws in a deep breath, reluctantly meeting my baffled gaze. "And I realize you aren't when you're with me. You haven't been in years."

The vacancy in his eyes—a desperately empty look—and his trembling lips make my heart break all over again.

"That's not true." I step towards him, frowning. "I *was* happy with you, Jake. But I wasn't happy with *me*. I'm working on that."

After walking over to his chair, I just want to hug him, to tell him we'll be alright, and that he's wrong. He means so much to me, and I feel guilty he believes he's been the problem all along.

"I scared myself that day." He chokes out the words. "I almost hurt you."

"You didn't." I place my hands over his on the armrests and bend so I'm level with his face. His eyes are bloodshot from tears and regret. "Why didn't you talk to me? Why didn't you at least tell me you were coming here? It's not a big deal."

He searches the room, avoiding my confused questions, his thumb fidgeting with his ring. This is painful for him too.

"I mean, it's a big deal because you weren't honest, but I wouldn't have been upset. Not if I'd known you were coming here. I've been talking with someone, and I think it's a *good* thing. Trust me, I've wanted to hurt you at times. We're human." I shrug with a soft laugh. "But, Jake…" My fingertip traces gentle patterns over the top of his hand. He still won't look at me. "You just have to be—"

"I went to New York."

The words shoot through the air—it's a direct hit.

Yanking my hand from his like he burned me, because he just fucking did, I spread my palms in front of me. My quivering eyes grow wide, and I back away, unable to stop the hyperventilating breaths that have begun. A crushing weight bears down on my chest. The sheer sting of his words, the name of that fucking place, punches me square in the nose.

"I went to New York," he continues frantically. "I *had* to—they're our largest account. Luke was out of town, and there was a major issue. I tried to push it off, but it would've been a breach of contract. They could have sued us. I didn't think I would see her, but I did." He flinches and waits for me to retaliate.

No words occupy my mouth. I'm speechless.

"I saw her. Nothing happened, but I didn't know how to tell you. I knew it would hurt you. I was pissed, and confused, and a fucking mess, and I went there."

My attention shifts to Patricia, who remains sitting with her ankles crossed, an impartial expression painted on her face as she studies me for a reaction.

"Thank you," I tell her, forcing my lips to a polite-enough smile before glaring at Jake, who is staring at me and shaking his head.

"I'm sorry. It was so fucking wrong. I promise my business doesn't come before us. *It doesn't.* I couldn't tell you, because I didn't want to admit that I saw her… willingly. She tried to—"

Holding up a hand, I tune him out, doing my rehearsed calming countdown. I'm gonna be okay. I *will* survive.

"We're done." I spin to the door, punch the handle, and fling it open, not stopping when it splinters the wall. My feet move so fast, trying to get the hell out of there as quick as I can. To get as far away from him as I can.

Out in the parking lot, I continue ignoring my phone, which has been buzzing nonstop in my pocket for the last couple of minutes. It's my mom. I feel bad, but I don't have it in me today. I can't fabricate the answers to all of her questions. And I don't want to lie about how everything is unicorns and fucking rainbows right now.

"Alex!" Jake's distraught voice shouts.

I hear his hurried steps gaining on me, pounding across the pavement. I double my stride.

Right as I reach the car door, he grabs my wrist, and each muscle in my body tenses; the hair on the back of my neck prickles, jaw working overtime.

"Get the fuck off me," I seethe through gritted teeth. "How could you do that to me? To *us?*" I'm trying not to break down, not to fully lose my shit.

It's gonna be fine. *I'm* gonna be fine.

"Honestly, I was hurt. And I think, deep down, I wanted to hurt you. It's not alright. And then I didn't know what to do. I started coming here, and Patricia helped me realize…"

My phone alerts yet again.

I can't right now, Mom.

"She helped me realize that by doing that, I was intentionally trying to push you away, trying to make sure you wouldn't want to work through things."

"Well, thank fucking God for Patty!"

I pull open the door.

"Not because that's what I want. I love you, Alex. I'm going to love you my entire life. When I saw her, I realized what a terrible choice it was. I put myself in a bad situation. How could I face you after that? And then I saw you were doing so good… without me. I thought it would make it all easier for you."

I stand there for a moment, completely dumbstruck. Jake doubles down, a pained groan rumbling from his chest.

"I'm sorry. So fucking sorry. I swear, nothing happened. I'm done with her company. Luke knows. I told him that I'm never going there again. I'm sorry I lied. I'm sorry I keep fucking up."

My phone continues buzzing like crazy.

"I'm sorry you did too." Inhaling a breath so deep it burns my lungs, I look away.

I *know* he's sorry; I can tell. He is literally standing here in the parking lot with tears streaming down his face.

I know all about being pissed off and wanting revenge, and wanting to make it hurt. I know about putting myself in bad situations, whether the outcome is my fault or not.

While I'm relieved he said nothing happened, and I don't have to chop his dick off, I'm so *fucking* pissed he lied to me. I can't even think straight.

"We can't keep doing this, Jake. It's not okay."

The goddamn buzzing continues. He opens his mouth to say something, and I raise a hand to stop him.

I tap the button on my phone to end my mom's incessant calls. "Hi, Mom. I'm sorry, now isn't a great time." Minimizing. "Can I talk to you later?"

The line erupts with an excruciating sob, and I'm having trouble deciphering the words that hit my ear. Every cell in my body freezes—or implodes. My fingers splay in shock, phone slipping through my hand and smacking against the asphalt with a blistering crack.

Jake's eyes go wide, searching my face. "What's wrong?"

I'm stunned. I can't speak. My pulse races, and panic puts me in a chokehold. Bile surges up the back of my throat and I think I'm gonna throw up.

"What's wrong?" he repeats, grabbing my shoulders, forcing me to face him.

"My…" An overwhelming feeling, an insane and incomparable wave of desperation and fear washes over me. The anger is gone. "My dad."

He straightens up in front of me, head shaking. "What? What happened?"

"My dad had a heart attack."

Is this real? It's like this is happening to someone else. Did I say those words? Jake gasps. "What? Is he alright?"

"He's in surgery. They aren't sure he's gonna make it." My stomach lurches and so does my body.

I love my dad… I can't lose him.

Jake wraps his arms around my body, squeezing me tight and holding me close enough to absorb the full-blown convulsions that have begun.

"I-I have to get there. I need to go." Taking a deep breath through my nose, auto-pilot flicks on. It's time to put on my big-girl pants. Time to get it together, to be strong. I need to be there for my dad… and my mom.

He nods. "I'll drive."

I don't consciously realize I'm climbing into the passenger seat. Jake calls Kelsey the second the car is in motion, and she immediately agrees to pick up the kids after school.

"Roo's appointment!"

I can't miss it. She needs it. How do I split myself in half?

He glances with another nod. His hand hasn't left mine. Yes, I'm mad at him, but right now, this is something different. This is something bigger and more important than the two of us.

One minute later, Jake already has it set up that Annie will take her. She's more than qualified to ask the right questions and will probably do a better job than I would. I trust her.

He clutches my hand tighter. "It's going to be okay. Everything will be alright."

I breathe. That's all I can do right now.

Just. Fucking. Breathe.

33. FAST CAR

As we grow older and have kids of our own, getting preoccupied with busy lives, stuck in the never-ending rat race, we sometimes forget that our parents are growing older too.

I'm beyond guilty of not calling enough, not making time for them; these two selfless people who supported me through everything. My original cheerleaders.

Now, faced with the possibility that I might lose one, I realize I've taken them for granted.

What a strange thing in life… Our parents raise us, do everything, give so much, and we push them away. The cycle continues, though the shoe was flipped onto the other foot when I became a parent myself, caught up with the day in and day out, draining every last ounce of myself for my children, and rightfully so. But as they grow and begin to pull away, it makes me reflect.

I've gotten so sidetracked in my current life woes that I've neglected the two people who are ultimately responsible for that life.

What I realize, on this drive that's taking for fucking *ever*, is that I need them. I need my dad. I'll give anything for one of his pep talks or cheesy words of infinite wisdom. The same words I'd always roll my eyes at.

I *need* him to know I love him.

Jake drives as fast as he possibly can, navigating through the cars lining the highway, not speeding too much that I flip out, but he's pushing it. Normally, I'd have something to say, but not right now. I just want to be there.

Why did we move so far away? Why am I not there?

Ava and Ashton stayed close, but they aren't runners. Neither of them felt the need, for years, to get the hell away from our hometown. They didn't experience the suffocating weight of that place. Well, I *thought* it was the place.

I thought I could never live there and be comfortable, or feel safe. It wasn't somewhere I wanted to raise my kids.

But stuff can happen anywhere. Baggage doesn't exist in a place; it exists in a person.

It's not my fault or Jake's. Opportunity knocked. Unfortunately, it was a couple hours away, but it was, most definitely, the smartest move for us. Though, right now, I wish I could push a button and transport myself.

Jake hasn't said much. He gets that I need to be alone with my thoughts. I catch the nervous glances; the worry in his eyes, but it's his turn to be the calm one now.

We've got serious shit to talk about, or maybe not talk about? At this moment… I don't care. I feel like my heart's being ripped from my chest. I'm not even sure how it's still beating. It's been broken, run over, tossed aside, yet somehow it continues to work.

But I know why. Deep down, I know. It beats for my family, all of them. Every… single… one. And although I *really* want to punch him in the face, it beats for Jake too.

I may not have gotten the perfect husband. There were times I thought he was, and looking back, there're so many things he got right, so many ways he sacrificed his own happiness for mine, for the kids. Relationships are give and take. But sometimes, the well runs dry.

No matter what, I'll never regret him. Because above everything, he's an amazing father. That's what every child deserves, and sadly they don't all get one.

But mine did. And I did.

I'd give up anything to make sure my dad's alright, and the tough part about that is…

I know he'd never let me.

We pull into the hospital parking lot in record time. I've gotten text updates from Ava. Dad is still in surgery, and there's no news yet. I'm clinging to the hope that *no* news is *good* news.

Pushing open the dark tinted doors, I clutch my chest as the strong disinfectant scent punches my nose. It's a smell I'm typically unfazed by, but it's different on this side of the fence. We follow directions to a small waiting room, lined with old, light-blue cloth chairs and walls with sporadic pictures of flowers hanging on them. As if that helps. Several windows offer a landscape of the parking lot. Like *any* view would matter anyway.

When you're sitting there, the only views are memories, playing on a constant loop. The only sounds you hear are the begging, the pleading that they'll make it, that you'll have a chance to say the things you let go unspoken for years.

Mom's short silver hair is messy and windswept, her eyes red, puffy, and weary, lined with tension. Ava paces the room, while Ashton sits with our mother, his hand clasped around hers.

"Mom." Her name strains from my mouth, and she stands blankly, arms outstretched like they always are when she sees me. I promise myself I'll keep it together. She doesn't say a word; just forces her lips to the best imitation of a positive smile she can muster, the way any mother would.

Ashton's blue eyes flash a worried look to mine, but neither of us speaks a word. He loops his arms around my neck, and I can feel his chest quake with the unshed tears he desperately wants to let flow.

I pull back… it's too hard right now, too much, and I *will* break down.

The tough thing about being a nurse… sometimes too much knowledge is a bad thing. But I also know that people survive this shit every day—why not him? So while I'm trying to be optimistic, because I have to be, I'm bracing myself.

"Hey, Alex." Ava clicks her phone off and gives me a quick hug. "He should be out soon, and we should hear something."

I nod. She's the methodical one, the level head who keeps us in check. I'm the basket case, but I'm hanging in there. I think every sibling in a family has a specific role they play.

Jake greets everyone with quick hugs, then we sit in uncomfortable silence. What else do you do? You sit, you hope, and if it's your thing, you pray. I'm making promises left and right. I'm bargaining like crazy to whoever's listening.

The clock ticks on the wall… a pin could drop, and we'd hear it.

All we can do is wait.

The doctor walks out, removing the scrub cap from her head and looking down before she scans the waiting room. Our faces are the same, all racked with fear, exhaustion, and on edge, waiting for the words to come out of her mouth.

I feel like I can breathe again when I notice that sign. The slight gleam of pride in her eyes, not defeat—it's a win.

A satisfied grin tugs at her lips, and we stand in unison.

"My husband?" Mom cries, making a dash for her, eyes wide, her hands folded together, shaking beneath her quivering chin.

"The surgery went great."

Mom flings her arms around the neck of the surgeon, who pats her back with a smile, then finally unleashes the tears she was holding back. Because she was trying to be strong… for us.

She bawls, and I mean *bawls*. We all do. I've never felt such an intense feeling of relief and love at the same time.

I look at Jake, who glances at my mom, then back to me. This moment is such a reminder of our mortality. I can't imagine how she felt, waiting, wondering if this would be the day her husband, her partner, would involuntarily leave her side.

The doctor fills us in that he was nearly one hundred percent blocked, but because Mom had been there with him, and reacted so quickly, they got to it in time. They were able to open the blockage and replace the valve. The survival rate isn't very high for this specific type of heart attack. But he's a fighter, and he fucking made it.

We'll be allowed to visit in an hour or so. In the meantime, Jake's been keeping up with Annie. Roo's appointment went well. Her doctor agreed she should have labs drawn and some tests to rule out any seizure activity.

I tell Jake to have her wait till we get back home. Getting Roo's blood drawn is insanity. She flips her shit, and he usually has to lie beneath her to hold her down, while I pin her arm to the chair for the tech to get a sample. It feels barbaric, and I promise, it hurts me more than her. Though some things are necessary, no matter *how* much they hurt.

You'd assume when you poke and prod people for a career, it would be easy. But when it comes to my kids or any close family, I'm not a nurse.

But in true Annie style, she already wrested the alligator. The blood work is done, and there's one less thing for us to worry about. Jake's mom is headed to get the kids and will stay at his place for however long we need.

To complicate matters, because… *life,* we have ten girls coming over tomorrow for Jordan's fourteenth birthday party. But Allison said she could handle it.

Remember when I said we had the best support system? We *really* do. It takes a fucking village.

They finally call us back to see him. Dad is lying in the bed, the lights in the cold room dimmed, and he beams at us as we walk in.

Suddenly, I realize he doesn't look like the redheaded man I've always envisioned him as—his hair and beard have gone gray. His eyes and face are the same though; the hero I've admired my entire life, with just a few more wrinkles. Trademark soft smile, unwavering gleam of adoration for his wife and three kids. After all the years, that has *never* faltered.

We stand there by his bedside, everyone simmering after the initial burst of emotion. That's not Dad's style. He makes jokes about Mom not getting rid of him yet, and how he's dying for a cheeseburger when the cardiologist pops in.

He steers the conversation away from him to ask about his grandkids.

Apple meet eye.

While we give him what we know he wants, day-to-day pleasantries, I notice Dad's attention lingering on me a little longer at times. He has this way about him, always seeming to suspect when something's off, or if I need a boost, or just some smart words. But he says nothing.

After a while, we exchange our goodbyes until tomorrow—he needs the rest—and head out, leaving our parents with their hands clasped around each other.

"Alex!" Mom yells in the hallway right before we step into the elevator then promptly apologizes to everyone around her. "Your dad wants to talk to you," she says, much more quietly, when she reaches us, sliding a soft palm down my cheek. She understands that he and I have a unique bond; we always have.

Nodding, I don't give a second thought to leaving Jake, Ashton, and Ava behind. I kind of predicted this was coming. Dad's never been one to let me walk away upset. Instead, he encouraged me to face things, to charge into them. And when I couldn't, he tried to hold my hand and help me get through it.

I make my way back to the frigid room. Lines and wires and tubes connect him to the beeping monitors. He struggles to scoot himself up, but manages, then motions to a chair off to the side.

"Hi, honey." His voice is hoarse, and it makes my lips tremble.

We were just in here, yes, but that was different. Because now I know a *real* talk is coming.

"You look rough." I drag the chair to his bedside and take a seat, clearly joking.

"You should see the other guy." He chuckles and then coughs. His light blue eyes turn up, deep-set wrinkles in the corners proving a reminder of how often he smiles.

This is our way with each other—I had to inherit that sarcasm from somewhere. But our love flows deep.

He places a palm on my hand, which is resting on the scratchy white blanket. I finally look at him, and it hits me. It *all* hits me.

Tears well and stream down my cheeks. My shoulders shake while I bury my face in his blanket; all the while he soothes my hair and tells me everything's alright.

"Listen, kiddo," he says after letting me sob into his hospital bed. *His* hospital bed. "I know you don't think your mom and I always see things, or understand what's going on…"

I open my mouth, and he tuts.

"I just had a heart attack, so I get to talk."

Fair… *definitely* fair.

"I am so unbelievably blessed to be your father."

My shuddered breath echoes in the sterile room, and his palm cups my cheek for a moment.

"Seriously, Alexandra. Your mother and I are incredibly proud of the woman you've become. I know you might not always think so, but we are. You have such a fire in you. You were born with it."

It comes from him, that fight, the mentality to overcome things. To not take no for an answer, to not settle. Though, lately, I'm not sure I've been doing the best with all of that.

"I am *not* afraid to leave this world. I've lived a wonderful life." His shoulder lifts, and he curls his palm around my fingers. "What I'm afraid of, for you"—he ensures my eyes stay on his—"is for that fire to go out."

And suddenly I'm five, learning how to ride my bike, with him letting go for the first time, telling me to pedal fast. Then I'm ten, ice skating on the lake, with his hand clutching mine, so I don't fall. Thirteen, with a new horseback riding obsession, Dad was there helping me back up when I got thrown off. Sixteen, learning to drive a car—thinking I knew everything. Those years have flown by in the blink of an eye.

I see him holding my four children, only hours old, looking at them like they're miracles. They are. And they look at him the same way. And so do I.

This is it. *This* is what life is about.

"We love you so much." He gives me a tender smile. "And we love Jake."

I nod. I know they do; they always have.

"But… we love you more."

I bite my lip, unable to stop my body from shaking in the chair. Tears spill down my face, and with a gentle touch, he wipes them away.

"Life's so short, Alex, and it goes by so fast. You need to be happy. If it's *not* with Jake, that's okay. Don't worry about what people want you to do, or expect you to do. You have to look inside yourself, feed your own soul. Remember that fire. My wish for you is that your flame burns strong till the very end, because of all the things I can bear… seeing that flicker out isn't one of them."

* * *

"Everything okay?" Jake asks, eyeing me cautiously as I approach the car. I'm sure he's wondering if I told my dad about our current messy life.

"Yup." I look away from him, contemplating all the things my dad said to me.

Before I left, he told me, in my heart, I'll know what the right choice is… for me. That I need to decide if it's love or *in* love, because there's a big difference. Once I figure that out, I'll know if it's time to walk away.

I sigh, climbing into the car. You'd think with his profound words and wisdom that I'd have had some revelation. I stare at Jake but quickly turn to the window when he catches my gaze. The love runs deep, but the hurt runs deep as well.

This is my life, my decision. I wish it was an easy one.

And to quote one of my father's all-time favorite lines, the exact words he said to me, right before I left: "We are the authors of our own books."

He's right, you know—we are.

Though sometimes… we just aren't sure what to write.

34. HERE IN YOUR BEDROOM

Even though Dad said he didn't need us to stay in town, and didn't want us to miss Jordan's party, we decided to anyway, at least for the weekend. I feel like I need to be here, to put in the time. It shouldn't always fall on Ava, the oldest, to be the major support for our parents.

That tends to be how it goes. The oldest has to be the responsible one, the caretaker, the one to set an example, while the youngest gets to be wild and free. I know that's how she sees it; she's been grumbling backhanded comments for years. I just let it roll, and laugh it off. I love how she thinks my life is cheery as fuck.

Truth be told, I'm fairly certain my parents were utterly exhausted by the time they got to me, and I understand it. We let things slide a lot more with Will than we did with Brynn at the same age.

I don't love any one of my kids more or less than the other, but I see it. The way Brynn assumes a sense of responsibility for her siblings. The way she sometimes feels the need to mom them. Not that they don't have rules. We set standards—they don't get away with everything. But damn, sometimes I'm just tired.

Back to staying here. I'm not sad to miss out on a dozen gossiping girls, hell-bent on pulling an all-nighter. Jordan's actual birthday isn't until Monday, and I wouldn't miss that for the world.

I told Jake's mom to offer them money to go to sleep if they drive her nuts. She said she didn't mind; she's been empty nesting for years and relishes any time with the kids.

When Jake and I got married, I think she probably cried for months straight. Not that she didn't like me—we always got along—but because she didn't get that last chunk of time with him, before he had another woman that became everything in his world.

Will is currently my stalker, obsessed, and I love it. I'm gonna miss him when he finds a new central focus. But that's how it goes. With Brynn and Jordan, I try to give them space, try not to press them too much. I know they'll come back to me one day…

I hope.

So anyway, I chauffeured my mom back and forth to the hospital, and we shared hours of laughs, bantering, and making inside jokes with my dad. I've missed them so much.

Mom gave Jake a mile-long list of tasks to keep him busy—tech support out the ass. Don't want the poor guy to get bored. Plus, it usually falls on my brother to help, and I know deep down Jake doesn't mind. I used to feel bad when they constantly asked him to do stuff during our visits. Now… not so much.

With my dad out of the woods, I guess it's reality time. Time to face the facts. Time to address the skunt—that's one of my favorite combo words, though I save it for bitches I *really* hate.

I'm stuck in this shitty place where I wanna know the details, and I also don't. Will knowing help me move on, or will it only piss me off?

I'm trying to be so *kumbaya* right now. That was the bargain I made. If God let my dad live, I would try harder to be a good person. I would remain calm and strive to find the best in every situation. I would forgive— fuck my life—so now I gotta hold up my end. I did not, however, say I would just move on.

Forgiveness is one thing. I'm not there yet; not sure I'll ever be, but I will try for my own sanity. And I'll get right to it.

Tomorrow.

Maybe there can be one night, or a couple hours, where I pretend my entire marriage hasn't plummeted down some dark and twisty rabbit hole.

When we leave here tomorrow, we gotta go home, gotta face the music, but sometimes it's easier to pretend it's not playing.

I need a hug or *something*. I'm not an overly cuddly person, but after these last few days, I need… let's go ahead and stick with something.

There's a perfectly good *something* downstairs on the couch. Not perfectly good, kind of perfectly not good, but my current prospects are limited.

What do you want from me? I'm making the best of a situation, remember?

When you're under stress, the body reacts in weird ways. I don't know if it's to make me feel alive, or simply to make me feel, but I'm not even needing, I'm *craving* a little… you get the point.

I walk out of the bathroom, towel wrapped around me. The upstairs has a landing that overlooks the living area, where Jake happens to be lounging on the couch, looking miserable. My mom already went to bed, and my siblings have left for their homes, just a short drive away.

His head rises gradually from the television to me, and we stare at each other, sullen expressions matching. There's been nothing but small talk over the last two days; nothing about us. It wasn't the time. It's *still* not the time.

I wanna pretend for a little longer.

Letting the towel drop, I stand for maybe five seconds—they have enormous windows, and the neighbors can see right in—before turning to walk into the spare room. I climb into bed, pulling the covers over my bare ass.

And now we wait.

Please, for shit's sake, pick up what I put down. I literally dropped the towel. Not sure I can be any more direct than that.

I lie on my side in the soft-lit room for what seems like forever. I'm actually contemplating clothing at this point because I'm cold, but then I hear the door creak open.

The mattress dips next to me, and Jake rests his head on the pillow, looping an arm around me, over the covers. We both remain silent for a bit, with my back to his chest.

Where do we go? What comes next?

"We need to talk," he says with a sigh, outlining the heart on my inner wrist.

I nod. Of course we do, but right now I'm not in the mood for talking. However, there is, in fact, one thing I have to know.

"Tell me this… did anything else happen? When you went to New York, did anything more—"

"No! No, and I didn't want it to. Like I said, it was stupid. She was—"

"Enough."

For at least right now, that's all I need to hear from him.

Again with the lying in silence. Ugh… come on, man, make a move. Jake draws in a deep breath through his nose.

"You sniffing my hair?" Rolling over to face him, I chuckle.

He responds with a quiet laugh, then his lips turn down, a sad, lost look covering his face. He shakes his head, just so disappointed in himself.

I smack my palm over his mouth when he opens it to say something. His eyes light up, growing wider.

"Look. I don't wanna talk right now. And maybe this is fucked up, but we're kinda fucked up." I pull the blanket off me, trying not to freeze my tits off—it's go time.

"Jesus," Jake chokes out, eyes raking up and down my naked body.

Did he not get the towel-drop memo?

"Nah, it's Alex. Now take this shit off." I flick a finger at his shirt, beating him at his own smirk game.

He doesn't hesitate to rise from the bed, mouth gaping as he tugs his shirt over his head, hair getting nice and messy in the process.

I've never been ultra-forward before, though I have to admit, I like a smidge of the upper hand. "Those too." I motion to his pants with a nod.

Taking the dose of courage I've built up, I get to my feet, completely bare, and walk him back slowly, then shove him to thud into the wall. He clears his throat, preparing to say something.

I close my eyes with a frustrated grunt. "I swear to God, Jake, can you please shut up and let this happen?"

Um… yeah. I need this. It's not a solution—hell no, of course not—but my brain is requiring some serious oxytocin. That natural, feel-good drug.

Part of me feels crazy because I want to have sex so bad. Truth time, it's science. Stress and sex often have a common link. And who am I to mess with science?

Jake's splayed fingers comb through my hair before he pulls me to him, crushing his lips against mine. Our tongues entangle with heated passion, mixed with some gentle biting.

The weird part is, we keep stopping, lips hovering, breathing into each other, eyes locked. I guess trying to figure out who the fuck we are right now.

Who the fuck cares? Like I said, let's work on it… tomorrow.

He guides me back to the bed, where we play a little *who's on top, who's on bottom* once we fall onto the mattress. You know how this is gonna end up. Pretty sure we're on *my* terms tonight. It doesn't take much for him to give in. Plus, he's gotta know, the fact that I'm even kissing him is major. I blame the hormones. And while I'm on this power trip, or whatever it is, I may as well go for it.

Casually moving down over his body, I lick my lips, pulling his briefs along with me—*showtime.*

I'm sure he's not expecting it because, truthfully, it's not my favorite thing. But… you wanna take full possession? Sometimes the answer is to give some head.

His breath gets caught in his expanded chest, eyes intent on mine. Before my mouth is even over him, quiet moans and gasps work their way from his throat. Jake grips the bedsheets, wrenching them in his balled fists as I tease my fingertips along his length.

It's all about the proper amount of hand and mouth movement, pressure, and friction. Not that I'm an expert on blowjobs or anything.

But if you wanna achieve that *come to Jesus* moment, you've gotta add the bashful lashes and undeviating stare. He loves that shit, but it works both ways.

Try it out.

I get him right to the point where he's whimpering my name and twitching at the back of my throat, then stop. Not necessarily as punishment, but because I'm not trying to have him blow his load on my parents' sheets, and I'm in no mood to swallow.

Too much? Oh well.

He sits up and flips my back onto the mattress, where I fold my hands beneath my head, feigning nonchalance. His mouth goes straight to business as he scoots himself down my legs.

Long fingers slip inside me, pumping in and out. The tip of his tongue flicks, while he sucks and devours like he always does. If you haven't gotten the memo, Jake's obsessed with oral. The vagina abides. He amps up the twisting, curling movements, pressing against that spot that everyone should seek to become acquainted with. His other palm drifts up to my breast, and he pinches my hardened nipple, causing my hips to meet each thrust of his hand, his eyes searing into mine.

Okay, let's finish this.

I wiggle a finger, motioning for him to get the hell up here. I don't know what I'm thinking right now—maybe it's better I don't

He kisses his way up, sinking his lips to my neck, grazing my earlobe. I push against his shoulders, and Jake falls to the side with an amused grin. I don't give him a second to react. Climbing on top of him, I join our bodies, then our hands. Once our fingers are interlaced, I finally let go, both of us making the other perfectly senseless.

It's so much easier to turn my reeling thoughts off, because come tomorrow, I don't know where this mind will be. Or if it's love, or lust, or what the fuck?

Obviously, we can't have sex and slide right back into happy married life. He's gotta earn it, and we've gotta work on shit. But after the craziness and the heartache of this weekend, well… maybe if we can find some of our old fun and excitement, that'll be the spark we need? The element that gets us to the next step.

Who knows? I guess I'll think about it…

Tomorrow.

35. NOVOCAINE FOR THE SOUL

You ever wake up and wonder, *Oh hell, what'd I get into last night?* More than likely, if you're being honest, the answer's yes. I have, more times than I'd prefer to share.

But the crazy thing is, waking up with Jake's face inches from mine, his arms and legs wrapped around me, I don't feel that way.

I know precisely what went down, and I'm not mad at it. I'm not even mad at myself. It's what I wanted to do.

I've been trying to figure out what's the right thing, the wrong thing, the vengeful thing, the forgiving thing? The answer is... who knows.

No one can tell you how you feel. And right now, I'm... okay.

Jake's lips turn slightly into a smile, but he's still fast asleep. He looks the way he used to when we'd visit each other in college. Something about a good night's sleep after a mind-blowing reunion was always serene. He looks young, only much more inked, *definitely* more toned. Why's he still look this way? Or is this the only way I'll ever see him?

I carefully remove his arm from my body so I can ease out of bed. Placing it on the comforter, my fingertip traces the various sized and shaded bursts of black ink, mapping from his wrist to his shoulder. The Scorpio—Will's.

Thank God we didn't have more kids. There wouldn't be anywhere left to go. I mean, there would, because he's not completely covered, but his upper body is running low on space.

After tiptoeing to the bathroom for my morning routine, I brush my teeth then slip into bed again. Just a casual freshen up before I burrow beneath the covers, where he hasn't budged.

Also… still no clothes. Oh well.

Should lock the door though, for real.

Somewhere in the few minutes of lying awake, replaying the happenings from last night—it was good, fantastic—while secretly hoping Jake will wake up, I drift back to sleep.

The smell of mint hits my nostrils before my eyes decide to open. The same warm, soft, comfortable lips I've felt a thousand times kiss mine. But it doesn't feel the same.

Apparently, someone else brushed up. Kinda cute we're both concerned about the state of our breaths. Kinda *not* cute that I keep forgetting he's an asshole. He's not, but he did some asshole things.

Why's it all so confusing?

I can't resist him. He is the drug, the ultimate gateway. No matter how badly I want to stop this, and at this moment I don't; even if I wanted to, I'm a Jake addict.

His lips press to mine in the gentlest of kisses, then he sweeps the hair from my face before pulling back, hovering above me.

His eyes plunge into the depths of my soul. How do you look into ones like his and hold any ground? If you ever find out, please tell me.

Here we are, just staring at each other, mere centimeters away from allowing it all to be physical again.

There's something about staring into the eyes of someone who's been there for you through so much. Something about being able to carry out an entire conversation without speaking a single word. The direct contact Jake desperately seeks can be overwhelming sometimes. But at this moment, it's genuinely needed.

"I wish we could go back," I say, my arms snug around his shoulders, my fingers ruffling through his hair.

Not back to before this situation, but back years, to the beginning. Wouldn't that be so great?

Tell our young, naive selves that we needed to make certain we didn't forget about each other, that we were going to be okay. Life would be occasionally difficult and messy, but we could make it if we just focused on not hurting each other. If we paid attention. If we remembered why it all started in the first place.

I spent too many years being so consumed by everything. The house, the kids, the stress, the to-do list. I took it too seriously and forgot to enjoy the ride sometimes. Got so caught up in attempting to make this perfect life that I forgot to actually live one.

"I do too." He sighs, settling his forehead against mine. "I'll do whatever it takes, okay? We can get back there, Alex. We can get *us* back to before."

That's the problem. It wasn't all that great. If I think about it long and hard, we weren't exactly happy... *before.*

"I don't wanna go back to before."

Jake flinches at my words, his brow furrowing in confusion. I grab behind his neck and return his lips to mine. "But I'm all for trying something different."

His what-the-fuck expression shifts with my last statement. I press my lips to his, mouths opening, tongues doing their thing, while my palm admires his defined torso.

Okay, I know... sex, *seriously?* And am I saying all is forgiven? You know I'm not.

Now who's on repeat?

But after sleeping on it, after my dad, after seeing my mom and him together, and after feeling some sort of way, when I envision my life, myself at their age, it's Jake who's with me.

The soul-consuming kissing continues, my mind—for once—not racing, while we move in sync. Our lips come together and part in unison, both taking the same from each other this time.

My hips arch into his, and we find that flawless beat our bodies know how to make. Jake grows harder with each connection between my legs. His naked chest is flush with mine, our hearts pounding in unison, his captivating gaze keeping me in my intoxicated trance.

Our lips fuse, and I groan into his mouth as his fingers tease my slick center. He plunges one inside me, and my back automatically bows from the bed. Several more proficient strokes and here the fuck we are—my body, overtaken by this immense desire for him to make me feel... *something.*

Am I becoming a sex addict?

Back to the task at hand.

Our ragged pants fill the room like a euphoric soundtrack, while his hot, wet mouth trails kisses along my neck, paying attention to each breast, making me whimper. I squeeze my eyes shut.

"Look at me," Jake says in an insanely rich and gravelly voice as he braces on his forearms, face level with mine.

I reach down, grab his cock, and position him to slip inside me. Muted moans escape us both, and our hips rotate, coming together with a mutual cadence, our mouths open, literally breathing for each other.

Every time he fills me, pulses into me, pushing me to the brink, I gasp, finding it difficult to swallow the X-rated sounds. *Damn,* this is my parents' house.

Jake's nails rake my side till he reaches my thigh, hooking it around his waist. His movements are so torturously slow, almost painful. He takes his time, easing out then in. Spreading me. Stretching me. Owning me.

If you've not experienced this degree of eye contact, especially during a first-thing-in-the-morning romp, please treat yourself.

I try to muffle an erotic moan when the sensation reaches an all-time high. When he lifts my ass to deepen his angle, that wonderful awareness of impending rapture clenches at the base of my spine.

"Alex?" my mom calls outside the door.

Holy fuck!

We both freeze. Jake's eyes close, and he shakes his head. When you have as many kids as we do, you grow annoyingly accustomed to interruptions.

He tries not to laugh when I grumble, a relaxed and amused expression covering his face. He doesn't move a muscle, but I can see the corner of his lips twitching, so I press a finger over them to keep him quiet.

"Be out in a second, Mom. Getting dressed!" I yell, far too fast, so totally obvious. "Holy shit, the door isn't locked," I whisper.

Jake shrugs, calm as ever. He laps his tongue along my finger, then clamps his mouth around it, teeth lightly scoring my skin.

That's new.

Once my mom retreats from the door, he instantly ramps up the pace, leaning up and steering my ass to clash with his vigorous strokes.

What was up with that? Were we just so vanilla before? I mean… I know some people are into the finger sucking, but I honestly can't remember a time he's done that.

Maybe he has? No, I'd remember.

My hands, which were previously clawing at his arms, slacken, and my impending climax swiftly evaporates into thin air. Jake reaches his with a few more thrusts then collapses on top of me. My attention fixates on the ceiling.

Now that I think about it, even the way he kisses seems different. It seems like more.

Was this something he did… with her?

Fuck. *Fuck!*

Why? Why can't I just shut it off? Why am I thinking about this? Will I always? Will every minuscule thing constantly have the potential to take me back to that bullshit?

"Hey." Jake holds the sides of my neck, forcing me to look at him. "Where'd you go?"

I close my eyes.

"Talk to me. Just talk to me, Alex." He kisses my forehead.

"I can't." With a heavy exhale, I push him off and slink out of bed, grabbing the clothes I borrowed from my sister.

"What the hell?"

Jake sits up with the blanket draped around his waist. His head tilts, and I turn away, refusing to look at him. But I hear his puzzled scowl.

"Alex?"

Right… ugh. Okay, I know I can't close up again—dammit.

After I throw a shirt over my head, I twist to face him. His palms flip, and his jaw tenses.

I sit down on the bed next to him once I finish getting dressed, and he takes my hand.

"What's wrong? I thought… Alex…" His voice grows firm. "Don't shut down. I can't read your mind."

I stare at our threaded fingers, at the band still on his, the circle. That's what this is. It's a fucking circle.

I didn't think I wanted to know, not truly, but now it's the *only* thing I can think about.

"Why'd you do the finger thing?"

"The what?"

"The finger thing!"

"What finger thing? What are you talking about? Fingering you?"

I slap a palm to my face, groaning. Is this stupid? Am I overreacting? I can't shake it though. This time felt…

"When you sucked on my finger. It was different." Wow, I seriously feel dumb saying that out loud.

"Oh." He scrunches his nose. "Um, I don't know?"

I wriggle my hand from his, rolling my eyes with a huff, and scoot to the edge of the bed.

"Hey." He moves closer behind me and rubs his palms over my upper arms, his lips to the back of my neck.

"No." I stand. His face is so screwed up right now, same as mine.

My face, my head, my heart—fucking screwed.

"You said *different*. I don't know, I'm sorry. I was just—"

"Is that how you were…" My arms cross over my chest, and heat rushes up my face. I hate this. I hate all of it. But I'm going to finish the question this time. "With her?"

Jake scoffs. "*What?*"

Awesome.

"No, no, no." He jumps to his feet, pulls on his pants, then reaches for my arms. "No, Alex. And why do we have to keep going back to this? It wasn't like that."

Why do we keep having to go back to this? I often wonder the same thing. This is unchartered territory for me, so I guess I'm just winging this whole thing. How to cope with the fact that my husband kissed someone. That he was, just maybe, going to fuck someone. That I legit didn't dwell on this shit for several hours—a new record.

And why am I now? Because he sucked on my finger? I didn't hate it either. Actually, it was even hot, in the moment, before it made my brain kick my heart in the ass.

I release a disturbingly non-humorous laugh. "Why do we keep having to go *back* to it?" I ask through clenched teeth. "We're going to go back to it as many times as I need."

"Well, it's not something I wanna talk about."

I spin away from him, doing my countdown, trying not to listen to the devil on my shoulder.

"Tough shit. You're going to have to if you want any shot at this *ever* working." And it's true. I didn't think I wanted the details, but turns out, I'm pretty sure I need them.

If there's any chance for us to move beyond this, I have to know.

"I told you, and I promise, we just kissed." His shoulders jolt with his rough exhale.

My arms cross harder, as if that's possible, and he moves in front of me, his eyes searching mine. "That's it." He shrugs and shakes his head like it's no big deal. "It was nothing. *She* is nothing. You are—"

"It wasn't *nothing* to me."

Here we are, ladies and gentlemen. The merry-go-round continues. I *do* want to work through it, or at least try. And I recognize that to do that, I have to figure out a way to move past it. Will it ever stop? Will I ever not fixate on it at random times?

"I got over it," Jake says, both brows raising as he throws his hands up.

"What?" I snap my attention towards him. He pokes his tongue along the inside of his cheek when he takes in the disbelief contorting my face.

"When you kissed that guy."

"Hayden? I told you—"

"No," he replies in a clipped tone, "not that fucking asshole. The guy you kissed back in college. Right before, you know… your birthday. Right before you were pregnant with Brynn."

Oh. My. God.

"College, Jake? Are you kidding me with this shit? That was so totally different." My arms loft to the sides, hands flailing wildly, while keeping my voice low enough not to alert my mom.

Gross, now I'm thinking about Joey Belter, that fucking douche. I'm so glad Jake wasn't aware *he* was the guy, when we were out for my last birthday. And damn, can't believe he's been holding on to that for seventeen years.

"You're right, it wasn't totally the same. But I got past it. I didn't allow it to wreck our relationship."

"We weren't married; we didn't have kids."

"But we were in love, weren't we?" His eyelids quiver, and guilt crashes into my stomach. "It fucking hurt, Alex." A quick swipe beneath his eyes.

"I'm not putting them on a level playing field." His lips rumble. "I'm only trying to say that I knew what we had. Took me a little time, but I knew it. That there's no one else on this earth I'd rather be with."

"Jake." I grasp his hand and pull him to sit next to me. "I'm sorry—"

"You already said it." He shakes his head. "I shouldn't have brought it up."

"No," I clarify, "I mean yes, but right now, I'm sorry we didn't talk about it. Sorry that life got too hectic after that. Sorry for so much."

Shuddered breaths rack his shoulders as I lean into him. "Me too."

It was so long ago, and circumstances were absolutely different. Still… if he can't tell me how I feel, I certainly can't tell him.

"What else do you wanna know?" He fidgets with his ring before folding his hands.

I wait a handful of seconds, staring into his eyes before letting them drift to his lips. "All of it. I wanna know everything you talked about. What the kiss was like, and exactly what happened the last time you went there."

Jake drags his palm over his mouth, throwing his head back.

"Whatever it takes, right?"

"Whatever it takes."

36. CUMBERSOME

So do you think you'd wanna know? I mean, I'm sure you wanna know what he said. And I'm glad I do, kind of. But... *fuck.*

For real, it was another punch to the gut, though I asked for it. I feel like if I don't have all the facts, every last detail, then I'll never be able to chew them up and spit that shit out.

How it went down is supposedly this:

Back at the beginning of September, Jake went to New York. He was able to land a meeting to pitch a year-long contract with an enormous company—a cash cow—to be in charge of their advertising placement and whatnot. They'd never even entertained his company's calls till then, so this was a monster foot in the door. And he did, in fact, get the deal. I have no doubt he could have in a more ethical manner, but yeah.

The deal is binding. They can't just pull out of it, no matter what. I mean, they can, but lawsuits are a thing. Breach of contract is a thing. I get that.

Anyway, he was supposed to meet with some dude, Aaron, the owner. Only he sent his daughter, Angela, fuck-face, cum-guzzling—not my husband's—rot-twat in his stead. The two had a business lunch. Jake said she kept leaning in, scooting closer to him. He admitted to flirting back to an extent but thought it was simply harmless. Was playing to his audience, so to speak.

Well, after lunch they still hadn't shaken on it. She requested a drink from the bar, so they went. I get that too. In sales, you sometimes have to wine and dine, but nowhere should it ever seem open to a sixty-nine.

Bad joke. Moving on.

Okay, they're at this bar and she's all flirty with him, even more than she'd been at lunch. Jake said she asked about his life and was easy to talk to at first. And then it got a little… uncomfortable. He made her aware he was married, had four kids, but she told him she didn't care. That he could have something with her and nobody needed to know.

Serial homewreckers exist.

I'm sure he was looking hot, going in there with his hair perfectly styled, probably in his custom navy suit, or maybe his gray vest and pants with a black shirt. He's nice to look at, devilishly attractive. Either way, she wanted one thing, and he wanted the deal.

A few drinks in, they shook on it, judgment a little hazy. She weaseled her way in, and he got kinda muddled up in the moment. Said it only lasted a matter of seconds, though her tongue made an appearance in his mouth. He supposedly didn't reciprocate—freaked, threw down cash to pay the tab, then got the fuck outta there… *alone.*

She was forceful, and he wasn't used to that apparently.

Shame on me. Taking care of a house and four children, I forgot to be a lioness in the bedroom.

I asked him if that's what he wanted, and he said he wasn't mad the last few times I'd taken charge. But that wasn't the point. He was more surprised, allegedly flustered.

Okay.

She texted him after saying she wanted more, and he didn't know what to do. He explained he wasn't planning to see her again, even before I found out. Jake had told Luke about it, and both of them were at a loss. He said— and he said this shamefully—that he pretended it wasn't happening; turned a blind eye. Decided to somewhat ignore her propositions until the papers were signed.

Harmless, right?

This one-year deal solidified their company, brought in more business than they could handle, and blew up their advertisement firm, literally overnight.

As for going back after New Year's, Jake claims he was so torn up, believing I didn't love him anymore, though he knew I was full of shit. He was pissed at himself for getting so angry with me and realized it was the wrong choice. But he went anyway.

It sounded sketchy to me, though I let him continue. Also, how sad is that? He felt he couldn't tell anyone. That he couldn't tell me. What would I have done if the roles were reversed? I think back to the messages—did he *not* respond? When I saw her lewd comments, I snapped; I didn't actually check.

He repeated and repeated that she meant nothing. I wish she meant nothing to me.

I know what she looks like too, because social media sucks sometimes. She has thick black hair and green eyes. Far more enticing than a fair-skinned, blonde-gone-brown, blue-eyed, late—cough—thirties, mom. She looks airbrushed in all her pictures, no lines on her face.

You know, those pesky what-the-fuck lines. But also, none of the crinkles you get around the eyes or lips, the ones from smiling.

I tend to harp on the hardships, though truth be told, I've smiled so much in the last sixteen years, even the last twenty. Lit up in more ways than I ever thought possible. And there are five amazing reasons for that.

Of course, if we hadn't had all these damn kids, we'd be loaded. We'd always say that jokingly—c'mon. Again, they're like mini money siphons. And maybe my body would look perfect. But I'd have never known the joy of a tiny face staring at me, teaching me what true love *really* is.

Back to the tell-all.

Jake went there because they have to meet with clients every so often, and like he'd said, Luke was out of town. He knew it would be fucked up, knew I would flip my shit… but he thought that was the answer to it. The way to set me free.

He even admitted that she kept trying to touch him, legit tried to grope him, and he wasn't having it. Whether we were done or not.

After that, he shut down for real, because the guilt he was feeling was way too much.

So… you buy it?

I guess I do. I don't know. The doubt is there. Maybe it always will be? But he's telling without me having to push him to continue.

Jake's jaw muscles tense, his teeth clenching intermittently, his eyes looming with shame, regret, remorse, you name it. His hand is shaky as he runs it through his hair.

"I'm so sorry, Alex," he says without looking at me.

"I need to help my mom."

That's it, the only response I can muster right now.

He inhales a deep breath, slowly letting it roll out, shoulders slumping forward as he scoots to the edge of the bed.

I sit next to him and lay my cheek on his shoulder. He immediately straightens up.

"Thanks for being… honest. I just need to process," I say softly, not protesting when his arm slips around my back.

"It was so wrong. I hope you know, I felt nothing for her. None of it's your fault." He kisses the top of my head, squeezing my side.

I remain silent. Not gonna lie, I've got a tremendous weight sitting on my shoulders with this, or sitting somewhere. Now I've gotta figure out how to disperse it.

"I love you," he whispers, our heads touching. "I'm sorry I ruined our marriage."

For just a moment, I contemplate then face him. "I don't think that's all on you. I mean… You fucked up, yeah." He frowns, his eyes veering away. "I think we're both guilty of some things."

It's true. It takes two to tango. If everything had been perfect before, perhaps he would've come to me sooner. It might've still happened, sure, and I can't predict my reaction had he outright told me. And I'm not suggesting that I made him do this, because free will—am I right? But the foundation's been cracking for quite a while. Had we not drifted and become strangers… Well, we wouldn't be in this story, would we?

This shit is heavy, and we've each had our fair share of it. But there've been *so* many fantastic times too.

Sometimes things truly need to fall apart before they can get better.

I stand and straddle one of his legs, palms landing on his neck so he looks at me. Unrest swells in his eyes as we study each other.

"I'm willing… to try. I know you want me to say all is forgiven, and I hope we get there. But I think we've gotta gut this entire thing and start over? I actually like Patricia." Fucking Patty. "So let's go from there."

Jake drops his forehead to my stomach, and my nails massage his scalp.

"Whatever it takes," he muffles, enclosing his arms around my waist.

"You… you felt nothing… when you kissed her?"

He presses his face harder into my shirt. Several breathy laughs heat through the material. "No." He sits up with a groan, a tiny trace of a smirk on his lips.

"What's funny?"

Jake leans back further, palms to the mattress, closing his eyes as more chuckles bounce his chest. His chin dips, and my attention follows. He shakes his head before pressing his lips into a tight, uncomfortable smile at the very obvious pitch in his pants.

Oops.

"But with you, Alex, I'm hard just from you touching my hair."

I can't stop the grin stretching from ear to ear, because gotta admit, it's a compliment—or I'll take it as one.

With my hand flat on his chest, I push Jake, kind of forcefully, so he falls back on the bed.

"So… aggressive, like this?" I ask, climbing over him, bending as I grab his wrists and pin them against the mattress.

A heady, sexy groan hums from Jake's throat. I grind my hips into him, sucking his neck and teasing up to his face, using his own signature bite on the earlobe and heavy breathing against him.

"Mm-hmm." He nods quickly, exhaling sharp breaths before I smash our lips together, tongues immediately diving and caressing, exploring every bit of each other's mouth.

Jumping off, I say, "Noted." I straighten my top. "Something else we can work on."

I leave Jake in the room, chest heaving, eyes closed, but an expansive grin across his face.

So, sure, there are things Patricia is gonna have to help with, but I think we can nail the sex stuff on our own. And I don't give a damn if it's not the answer. Everything's now out in the open, and I'm doing what *I* want. As long as I never have to see the ho, I think… no, I believe that we can do this.

I help my mom with some last-minute chores around the house, then run with her to the store and get things ready for when Dad comes home tomorrow.

Jake messaged that he was going for a run. I text his mom, Allison, letting her know we'll be leaving shortly, then clean up the entire bedroom mess.

He strolls in a few minutes after I finish up, forehead slightly sweaty, dressed in a hoodie and sweats borrowed from Ashton. We came here on a whim, remember? His cheeks are bright red, and brisk bursts of air leave his mouth.

"Went hard?"

Jake shrugs. "Had to clear my head."

He walks towards me—or stalks is more like it. I already feel the impending heat from his body. This new thing, or this different thing, is exciting. Can we really start over? Move beyond this?

He grabs my jaw, lowering his face to mine. "You're the only woman I ever want to kiss for the rest of my life."

Our eyes lock, sincere, full of hope and love, and my heart finally begins beating again.

We can do this.

It's gonna take work, but I'm excited. *God*, I'm still totally turned on by him. I really took him for granted for all those years. I stopped seeing him. We stopped seeing each other.

"Just know." My lips almost touch his. "If you kiss another woman again, I think I'll—"

Before I can finish my threat, Jake's body lurches backwards, crashing into the wall. His mouth hangs open, alarm enlarging his features.

Blue eyes glower at me—Ashton.

"What the hell did you say?" His voice is enraged, his muscles flexing and tensing beneath the sleeves of his shirt, while his hands wrench into fists.

Seems tempers run in the family.

"He cheated on you?" Ashton snarls, making me cower away. When I say the dude is big, he is. And when he's mad, he's fucking scary.

We stand there in silence. Ashton in the middle, glaring, his eyes darting back and forth between us.

"It's not like that, Ash. Well, not totally. Look, we got this, okay?" I take hold of his arm and can almost feel the adrenaline sprinting through his veins.

When I hinted he was protective, I mean *insanely*.

He throws my hand from his arm, his scathing attention zeroing in on Jake. "You know, she let us all think it was her. Alex had us thinking *she* was the one that messed up." He scoffs.

Jake keeps his stare on the floor, offering a single nod.

"You remember what I told you, right?" Ashton asks, jerking his neck from side to side, cracking the knuckles in each fist.

Jake hesitantly lifts his head, nodding.

Huh?

Ashton takes a step forward, his right arm cocked back.

"Stop! Ashton, stop!"

Jake doesn't react. It's as if he's prepared to take a beat down from my brother.

What the hell?

I lunge towards Ashton's raised fist, pulling him back in just enough time that I can jump around him and place myself in front of Jake.

Everything happens in a jumbled mess. Jake's hands grasp my shoulders; Ashton's forearm extends as if it's in slow motion then rapidly switches to super speed.

One of the harshest blows I've ever felt splinters into the side of my skull. My vision instantaneously flashes a crazy bright black. If you've ever seen stars, you know what I mean.

I slump to the ground, my body landing in a heap on the floor. I hear their shoes scuffling, Mom screaming, my ears roaring. Everything is dark, and a bitter, metallic taste floods my mouth.

Another crash.

"I told you I'd kill you if you ever hurt my sister."

37. DEVIL'S DANCE FLOOR

I'm so sick of this rabbit hole, this spiral of stupid bullshit.

So the following: I've got a massive knot on my head and bit the fuck outta my tongue. Everything happened in super-swift succession after the head smack heard round my parents' kitchen.

The boys—yes, I'm referring to these two grown-ass idiots as boys—had a go at each other. Couldn't miss the sounds of their scuffle, though I didn't see it; nor did I want to. I knew once Ashton got going, he wouldn't stop.

Ain't no shot I'm pickin' a side here. How could I?

This is Jake… who do I even compare him to? But it's also my brother, my protector. The person who's adored me since day one, and the feeling's mutual.

Fuck this.

What I know for sure, in this second, is that I got hit, hard as all hell, on the right side of my head. But Ashton was lined up on the left. My parents have these metal candle thingies protruding from the kitchen wall, and I'm convinced that's what cleaned my clock.

My blurring vision blinks into focus to show me Mom screaming at them, shoving Ashton away. I'm clutching my thundering skull, relieved when I lower my palm that there's no bleeding. My mouth is a different story.

Ashton sniffs, wiping his hand along a trail of blood trickling from his nostril. A dark blotch is already forming a bruise on his cheek. Jake appears unscathed, though the veins in his neck are bulging and his face is a resounding scarlet.

"Stop," I say when Ashton shoulders past our mom, trying to swing on Jake again. He leans back, narrowly dodging the blow. My voice is hoarse, my head pounding.

"Stop!" my mom pleads when she sees me slunk down on the floor. "You hurt her." She glares between them, halting the frenzy of absurd testosterone.

"Alex, are you alright?" Her soft hands carefully replace mine, examining my head, and she uses her own shirt to wipe the blood pooling between my lips.

I nod, wincing slightly, forcing a smile to help subdue the worry in her blue eyes. As if she hasn't been through enough this weekend.

"It's okay, Mom. I'm okay," I mumble, still a bit dazed.

"*What* is going on?" she shouts at the guys.

Shit, my head is banging. I scoot back so I'm straight against the wall, not quite ready to be vertical.

"Did they…" Alarm doubles in her eyes, and if looks could kill, hers might wield the sword. "Did one of them hit you?"

Shaking my head, I glance up, shooting a pointed finger at the piece of bronze metal on the wall, so thankful I can blame *that* for the massive headache I'm about to endure.

Thank God it wasn't Jake or Ashton who hit me accidentally. It happened so fast, I wasn't even sure.

"What the fuck," I mutter.

"Language!" Mom scolds.

Told ya it was a thing.

"Sorry, Mom."

Ashton and Jake are just standing on the tiled floor, both looking over me with concern. Well, Jake's concerned, but Ashton's still in roid rage, spouting off again.

"Can you not?" My voice is scratchy and faraway sounding.

Jake takes a step towards me and scoops under my arms, pulling me to stand. The sudden jolt makes me dizzy. He closes in, hugging me so I stay upright.

"I'm sorry, Alex," he says into my ear.

Ashton slices into him with a glare so sinister, his chest barreling, his eyes like slits. "You pushed her."

Damn. But it wasn't on purpose. Shit happens.

"If I hadn't, you would've hit her. Sorry." Jake frowns at me, his eyes bloodshot. "I'm sorry," he repeats, only to me. "I would never hurt you on purpose."

A sharp grunt leaves Ashton's nostrils, and he grabs my other arm, trying to yank me towards him. Jake doesn't let go.

I can't formulate words, stuck in a gentle-enough, but ridiculous, tug of war. Poor Mom is at a loss, mouth gaping like a fish, face flushed, nose scrunched, like what the hell is going on?

"I got her," Jake growls.

Ashton barks a cruel laugh, wiping more blood from his upper lip, blue eyes cold and filled with hatred. "You never were good enough for her. You know she wouldn't be with you if—"

I snap my arm free from his grasp, delivering a backhand to his chest. Ouch! It really is comparable with a wall. I give my brother the harshest warning glare I can. Though, given my current frame of mind, it's weak.

He *knows* not to go there.

"Stop." Ash and I are in a stare down. "Enough. I need you to stop."

But he's never stopped.

It's been easier for him, I think; since I've been away, life moved on. But I worry that part of him will always be stuck out there in those woods, wrecked by the guilt he feels, beating himself up for thinking he failed to protect me.

His eyes glaze over. The problem is, he does love Jake, so I get it. Hearing that made him go into psycho mode, because above everything else, he's my big brother.

From the looks of the current scene, Jake got a solid hit in—he's a southpaw, so it makes sense. I'm not totally surprised. He's smaller, but he's scrappier, and even though he's in the old dude hockey league, they still fight every now and then.

Jake would've never initiated, but he wouldn't have just stood there either. He hunches over, clutching his side. Ashton must've got at least one hit in.

What morons.

"Ashton," my mom warns as he rocks on his feet, boiling with anger, lining up and ready to spit fire.

Jake's hand squeezes mine, grinding my knuckles together. I know he's struggling to bite his tongue.

"You're right, Mom." He whips the blonde waves from his face. "I shouldn't say the *only* reason they stayed together was because he got Alex pregnant."

"Ashton!" Backing myself away from him, I tug Jake with me. "Don't react," I say, turning to face him. "That's what he wants. And it's not true." My fingers intertwine with his.

Jake responds with a curt nod, narrowed eyes not leaving my brother's face.

"Ashton, that is a disgusting thing to say. What's wrong with you?" Poor Mom would rather live in the dark. She loves those unicorns and rainbows.

He shakes his head, emitting a throaty laugh, teeth barred. "It's disgusting. Yeah, you're right. Sorry I said what everyone in this family has thought for years."

Let's backtrack here for a second.

Ashton and Jake are—were—bros. They actually like to hang together, shoot the shit, snowboard, and chill out when we go on family vacations.

However, when I became pregnant with Brynn, Ashton was pissed, so disappointed. He felt like he'd entrusted me to the wrong person. As if that's his job. He felt Jake put my future at risk and all that bullshit, though I was the careless one.

But when I was down in the dumps, and freaking the fuck out, Ashton was who I unloaded on. He knew our relationship had tanked right before I got that positive test. Knew I'd been spiraling back then.

I know he sensed it again over the last several years, always so concerned. But I'm not a child and I don't need him to protect me anymore. Saying that in front of my mom, in front of Jake, and *especially* in front of me really is disgusting.

"What everyone's thought for years?" I ask, looking at my mom, who shakes her head adamantly.

My brother clicks from the side of his mouth with an unapologetic shrug.

"That's shit," I respond to Ashton, but honestly, I'm speaking to all of them.

Was our relationship in the dumps way back then? Sure. But we changed, made something different, something better. And if we've done it once, we can do it again.

Ashton lets out a cynical laugh, muscles flexing, shooting daggers… at Jake.

"You better stop this, Ash, or I'm—"

"Or you're what? You don't wanna hear the truth, Alex? You wanna keep living in a pretend world and be a fucking doormat? Because you know, it's once a cheater, always a cheater."

Ugh.

Mom's jaw is gonna smack the tile floor.

Jake charges forward from behind me, and I grab his arm, yanking him back to look at me. "Don't." I plead with my eyes. I know that comment hurt him. It hurt me. We're both aware that some people assumed we got married because of Brynn—damn, even she did—but it's not true.

Things aren't always the way they seem on the outside.

"My brother's an asshole," I say to Jake then glare at Ashton. Mom's allowing the bombs to fly right now. The realization she's piecing together is apparent in her frown and knitted eyebrows. "But he's *my brother*." I turn back to Jake. "Ignore him, and let's just go."

"Fucking classic."

"Enough!" our mom cries, stopping Ash from going further and reprimanding us all. She's always peaceful and soft-spoken. When her volume's up, you better listen. I don't care how old I am—if Mom yells, stuff isn't going great. "It's none of our business. That's between Alex and Jake."

Ashton shakes his head again, face-palming with an annoyed groan. "I love that you guys think Jake can do no wrong. I've always let it go, but I'm so fucking sick of it."

"Me?" Jake laughs, and it's a condescending laugh.

"Jake." I silently gesture no.

"You know it's true," Ashton says with a snide expression. "You were never, and you won't *ever*, be good enough for her."

Jake frees his hand from mine and steps into Ashton's face. I try to catch him, but my response time's delayed.

"How about you?" he spits at my brother. "You took her around a bunch of guys, and let her—"

"No!" I slap my hand over Jake's mouth. But it's too late, because we all are aware of what he was gonna say.

That's worse than any physical pain he could ever inflict on Ashton. He knows it too. He knows the guilt and internal struggle Ash has endured for years, and how responsible he feels for what happened to me.

At this, expectedly, my mom has to physically restrain my brother. Her face grows pale, completely drained, her eyelids fluttering as she tries not to cry.

"You had to go there?" I snap at Jake. Come on! Two steps forward, and a big two steps back. My fleeting attention slides to Ashton. "I love you, Ash, but I'm alright. We are working on it. I don't hold you responsible for anything." I squeeze Jake's hand so tight—his left hand; no doubt it's gotta be hurting from the punch—and he sucks in a sharp breath.

"I think you better go," Mom says to Jake.

He hangs his head, gripping the back of his neck. "Sorry, Mrs. Jo."

Yeah, we still call our parents Mr. and Mrs.—kind of a habit when you meet young. Doesn't feel comfortable first-naming them without the title, at least not to their face.

"I'm sorry, Mom."

"Are you gonna stay calm if I let go?" she asks Ashton.

The only look on his face, as he slowly nods, is one of pure defeat.

We've all played with enough fire today. Don't need any more words spewing out. I don't want to do this stupid dance anymore.

Jake storms out the front door.

I wrap my arms around Ashton, his own hanging down by his sides, not reciprocating the hug.

"You gotta forgive yourself, Ash. You gotta move on. It's not on you to save me."

He takes the protector role to an extreme. I understand it, and I love him for it. But he needs to focus on his girls. He needs to stop feeling like he's a failure.

"I love you. Jake's mad, but you know he doesn't mean it, just like I know you don't." I glance up at him. He's chewing on the inside of his cheek. "Shit happens, Ash. It happens all the time. We can't change the past, but we can use it and make the future a better place."

Damn, getting deep.

"I love you too, Alex." He closes his arms around me, resting his chin on top of my head.

"Do you even lift?"

We both laugh at my always ill-timed jokes, cutting the tension and easing through the harsh words.

He steps back and shoves his sleeves up his arms. He gets his thoughts together and leaves me with this. "If you stay with him, I can't respect you."

Let's just keep the gut punches coming. Because why the fuck not?

Ashton stalks out the back door after I tell him Jake and I are gonna try to work it out. I politely decline when Mom asks if I want to talk about it but assure her I love her. I promise to check in more often then leave the shattered pieces of us all behind on the floor.

Jake's already in the driver's seat, knuckles blanched, taking it out on my steering wheel as he glares through the windshield.

"Why did you say that?" I buckle, pinning him with a sharp stare. His eyes remain dead ahead. "Jake, you *know* how he is. You know that killed him."

"Well…" He inhales a prolonged breath. "The shit he said killed me."

So back to this mentality. An eye for an eye. Fuckin' Gandhi. We shoulda listened.

I lean into the headrest and close my eyes, beyond exhausted, trying to stop replaying the barbaric little dance we just lived through.

Words really can cut deep.

Somewhere over the next two hours, I think about how living in and dwelling on the past eats you up. We're all guilty of it. But it really *is* time to let go; time to start something new.

38. THE BONES

So... it's been four months since the incident at my parents' house.

Yeah, I know, *four fucking months.*

We're almost at the end of spring, on the first of June. Coincidentally, it's the same day Jake and I met twenty-one years ago. Insane that's how much time has passed. Insane how much has happened in the midst of those years.

Just a few more peaceful days and the real chaos begins—two words that are many parents' worst nightmare.

Summer. Break.

I love my kids, and I love the time I get with them. But after a week of togetherness, I'm a referee. That shit is absurd. They're off for eleven weeks—*eleven weeks!*

Even though I said I'd never pick between them, I guess I kinda did. Because when I left that day with Jake, Ashton stopped returning my calls and texts.

First off, we only had one car there, so come on now. Second, we have children together. We're in each other's lives forever, no matter what. Not everything is so damn black and white.

I miss him though. It sucks he feels like I let him down. I try not to think about it, but we know how that works. Jake refuses to attempt any sort of contact with him.

Shit's been a bit of a shamble with my entire family since then. The truth is out there for all to see. My mom and dad say nothing about it, though I know they have their opinions. I've been going there once every couple weeks, toting the kids along, soaking up the family time, but they don't ask if Jake's coming or what he's up to. They don't ask if we're together or what's going on with us. It hurts my heart.

I know the two of them won't judge me either way, and that they're just letting us figure it out. Ava was perturbed that I would think so low of myself to even consider healing a relationship poisoned by lies—her words, not mine. We can't all be perfect. I'm trying though. Trying my best.

Still swimming.

Ashton's made himself scarce, and refuses to speak to me when I'm there. He drops off the girls when we visit then heads out to do his own thing.

It pisses me off that I have to trade one for the other. They're both stubborn. But if we can act like adults, make sure everything's copacetic, Ashton has to find a way to deal with it.

Honestly, they both need to be fucking grown-ups and apologize.

As for Roo, my intuition was right. She'd been having an increase in seizure activity. We were lucky to catch it before they progressed into something more serious. That mom gut is almost always right. Her doctor increased her med dose, and she's been stable since.

Knock on wood.

Actually, all four kids have been thriving. Seems like you can get used to anything after a while.

The spring months are always stupid busy, with Brynn and Jordan playing lacrosse, and baseball for Will. Jake helps coach the three separate teams, which is crazy if you ask me, and I cart Roo to as many games and practices as humanly possible.

This time of year always flies by for us.

Oh, Jake and me? You wanna know?

We've been doing pretty well—thanks for asking.

He extended his lease six more months. It seemed like wasting money at first, but it made sense. We both agreed on it.

Here's the thing. Our relationship started with only seeing each other here and there, so when we did, it was always exciting, fresh, and new. We never dated or had a normal courtship, or whatever outdated term Patty used. And then we lived together, got married, had kids, moved out of state. We just hit it all, like... *boom.*

We never got to learn who the other was. You'd think after living under the same roof for so long, you would know all the details about your partner. But life gets so busy, ya get caught up. Our goal is to *genuinely* get to know one another. Ask tough questions, tell uncomfortable truths. See the other as a person and not only as their role in our family. Spend time, just us.

Let's be real here. It isn't *just* us; it won't ever be.

When we left my parents that day, after some eye-opening moments of clarity and some soul searching, I brushed the chip off. I was like, let's go! Get right back into it. Fuck it, *yolo.*

Um, okay, no. No one needs to be saying that. But I do, way more than a grown woman should.

Anyways, when we saw Patricia—the voice of reason—she recommended that spending time together *apart* could be a positive thing for us. She felt that we'd done well on our own, all things considered. Likely, my dad's heart attack was a pivotal point. We started recognizing our shortcomings as a couple—Jake with his constant apologizing, me with the self-doubt and vengeful thinking, just to name a few. Of course, it was a show at times, and we aren't exactly there with the trust—well I'm not. It's hard to shake the doubts.

Patty said if we focused on each other and eased back into it, allotting time not only for family but for just the two of us, she felt we could make it. She wouldn't recommend a separation for many people, but she made some solid points. We'd run such a high risk of falling back into old habits otherwise, because we've always been good at that.

And I know… didn't I say Patty was getting the boot? Conflict of interest and whatnot? Yeah, but I like her, and Jake does too, so we let it ride.

We're still rocky. I'm stressed about my family. They've always been a major part of my life, always in my corner, and now I've traded one strained relationship for another.

But here we are. We've ripped the entire thing apart, attempting to start from scratch; plastered the cracks in our foundation and started building something more solid.

Rome wasn't built in a day, and this shit can't be either. So we're giving it till the end of September.

I'd admitted to having lost my identity. Moms, I know you hear me on this. Jake having some time alone with the kids—feeling the responsibilities of the cleanups, lunch packing, laundry, along with keeping a house in order—was a good reality check for him.

Jake felt as though I never cared about his work. That one is currently tough for me, but I gotta get over it, I suppose, or at least show an interest. I didn't realize he felt like that. Said I could never just go with the flow. So, I try to stay chill.

Man, change is hard.

We started with our issues from the beginning and tiptoed our way up, inconvenient truths, difficult admissions, and all. But here we are, going full speed ahead, totally aware that anything can happen.

No one is promised anything in this life.

The spark is still there. Hell, the spark is *way* stronger than it's ever been. Makes it challenging to walk sometimes. I guess you don't know what you've got till it's gone.

I've been putting in more hours at the hospital. Jake tries to be sensitive about my desire to make something for myself, whether or not we need the money. He thought I enjoyed staying home.

I've also been focusing on not becoming so overwhelmed by things. For real, saying no to the stuff I don't want to do, even if one event resulted in me telling the PTO president from Will's school to twist off. My fault. I stopped letting issues elevate to boiling point.

And the main thing I think I've gotten much better at—not shutting down or running away.

Growth, friends. This really is fucking growing up.

Patricia stressed the importance of sticking to a plan, being there for each other, listening, not simply reacting, all the tools that help build trust. The biggest factor in trust, of course, is time itself.

While we were in a rush to get us back together, it was truly something that needed to happen slower.

We don't do the whole sleepover thing—technically not a lie—but we've had more sex in the last four months than in the last four years. I feel like a porn star some days—no vids though. Okay seriously, we've been getting a little more, um, adventurous? Just going for it.

In all things, not only sex.

We've both been saying what we want, saying what we mean, because if you do that, it makes everything easier. It's amazing how a dash of communication goes a long way.

We keep the booty calls low-key, sneaking in and out—how very adultish of us—hiding my car down his street. Or Jake randomly takes a run, at 9 PM—ya know, totally normal in the 'burbs—concealing our after-hours meetups from our kids. Well, kind of… not completely.

They know the end game.

They're smart. I see the little shitty, Jake-clone smirks on all four of their faces. They seem genuinely happy. When the six of us are together, it's turned into laughter and fun. We enjoy each other's company; we're not just trying to get to the end of the day but finding magic in small moments and bottling them up.

We're just riding the high of this new thing.

The occasions we've gotten to have date night—yes, date night—have been incredible. This should be a mandated thing *every* couple does, like routinely. Why didn't we do it before?

Why didn't we do a lot of stuff before?

Hindsight… that bitch is twenty-twenty. But we're lucky because we are pushing through. We get to learn from our past mistakes and make something better from it.

Not everyone does.

* * *

The girls and I are sitting on the sideline at Will's baseball game. There are numerous females congregating along the first baseline. Any guesses who the base coach is? Oh well, feast your eyes.

I try not to let it bother me and take it as a compliment.

His shorts show off the mouth-watering curve of his ass, and his sleeves are bunched to his elbows, his ink-covered arms on display for the mom squad currently creaming their pants. But every time he glances over, it's directly at the girls and me, never once at any of the cougars.

The field is named Cougar Field—I'm not kidding.

He gives high fives to every kid as they make it to the base and to each one who doesn't. He's always encouraging. They all love him. There's something about a man who's already sexy that steps up to an entirely new level when he's an exemplary parent.

His own father was usually too busy working to attend his games, much less coach, so Jake's made it his life's mission to do right by our kids, making sure he always shows up.

Neither of us are *those* parents—you know the ones I mean. The ones who get way too extra about it, screaming at a seven-year-old when they don't hit a ball, or berating a poor child when they don't execute a perfect play.

Some coaches—and even worse, parents—get way too into the sports stuff. They're kids, just let them have fun. Cheer them on, sit the hell down, and stop reliving your athletic dreams through them. No college scouts here.

Okay, sorry for getting ranty.

As the game ends, Jake taps each player on the helmet, telling them what an outstanding job they did, then struts over to us.

"Hey, guys," he says with a wink after taking off his glasses, plopping his hat on Roo's head and sliding a hand through his tousled hair. Jake asks the girls about their day.

Kids come first. They still do, no matter what.

His arm slips around my waist, lugging me into him. "And how was your day?" Dropping his chin, Jake presses a quick kiss to my lips with a panty-soaking grin. His wandering hand cruises down my back, dangerously close to grabbing my ass.

Come on, man! This is a kids' sporting event.

"Get a room," Jordan mutters.

Brynn's eye roll matches her sister's. "Seriously," she says, making a face.

Get real, they love it. Okay, maybe not the potential ass grab part, but they love seeing us together again.

* * *

We all decide on a local burger joint for dinner. Nothing fancy, just right for us.

Family dinners. Yup, they've been happening. Can't lie though, Jake's phone buzzing the entire time, him constantly holding it away from me to respond, has me irritated. He can most definitely tell. I think my sideways glares and extreme stink eye give me up.

I'm the type that if my mouth doesn't say it, you can bet my face will.

"Luke." He frowns, holding up his phone, offering proof.

Oh yeah, Luke. He denied having any knowledge about Jake's text situation with… I'm not even gonna mention her name. Jake denied his denial, then Luke eventually admitted that he advised his business partner, his friend, to go with it until they finalized the deal. He completely corroborated Jake's story. So there's that. Kelsey wasn't a fan.

Him trying to hand me his phone is simply proof the trust still isn't there. Anyone got tips for that? All we can do is keep trying. All *I* can do is believe him. I'm not willing to sabotage a good thing anymore.

39. SLIDE

We finish up our nice, calm family dinner. It was more like scantily controlled pandemonium. That's what happens when you go out with all the kids. Jake was joking—nah, he was serious—suggesting we keep the outings where food is involved to the two of us. I completely agree.

Brynn was nonstop on her phone, doing a poor job hiding her fast thumbs beneath the table. Jordan wasn't feeling burgers, so she spear-headed a ridiculously bratty protest. Neither of us gave in. She apparently decided this was the week to become a vegan. I can't keep up. Roo melted down with the tantrum of all tantrums, gaining us multiple looks and stares—like that's new. What was the cause? A drop of ketchup touched one of her fries. The horror. Then Will spilled his drink, soaking our entire table.

This is what going out to dinner looks like with a family of six. At least with *our* family of six.

Anyway, we got through it.

Jake walks us to my car, saying goodbye to the kids, then gives me the routine forehead kiss. "I think I'm gonna need to go for a run tonight," he whispers in my ear, tongue sticking out between his teeth.

"Yeah, you probably should." Eyeing him up and down, my face already burns. Jake's fingers hook into my belt loops, pulling me to him. I like the upper hand, sure do, but I do not mind when he yanks me around… sometimes.

"Would you guys hurry up and kiss so we can go home?" Will shouts from the lowered car window.

"Kiss, kiss," Roo chants next to him.

Jordan fakes a gag, but she can't uphold her performance, and a smile erupts. Brynn sits in the passenger seat, honed in on her phone, lips pressed together, though the deep dimple gracing her left cheek gives her away. And this shit makes my heart full.

I'm not saying the kids are pro-PDA, but I think it's okay for them to see us being affectionate with each other.

Jake lowers his head, lips brushing mine, very PG. They meander to my cheek, his stubble grazing my neck, just below the ear. That move isn't fair. I shiver, gasping out a breath, already feeling… well, ready.

"Later," he says before backing away.

I have to clench my thighs. "Mm-hmm."

Holy fuck, kids… what kids? He can get me from nothing to *let's go* in under a second. I'm throbbing out in the burger joint parking lot.

What the hell?

"Bye, guys. Love you." He waves to the kids before swatting my ass as I climb into the car. Then he wets his lips before a devilish grin reveals itself.

"Gross," Brynn groans.

Jordan emits a chorus of retching sounds. Of course, the other two just giggle. I lift my brows at Jake before driving away.

* * *

I settle Will and Roo in bed then get to cleaning up the plethora of random shit scattered around. It accumulates in such a short time. I swear, my heathens leave stuff everywhere—neglected socks, hair ties, all the things.

Jordan and Brynn are independent with bedtime. They don't need me to tuck them in anymore or check beneath their beds for monsters. It's rough having older kids, letting them go, giving them space.

The one thing we both do, every night, regardless of which house the kids are at, is say I love you before bed. I hear Brynn first, then Jordan minutes later, talking to Jake, even though they saw him less than an hour ago.

I love you before bed is *so* important.

I give each a kiss, tell them not to stay up too late, and remind them that at nine-thirty, the Wi-Fi gets turned off. Welcome to panic time—they can't function without it. We had to initiate this last school year, when they were up till all hours of the night, scrolling their lives away. Madness.

My phone vibrates with a text from Jake saying to meet him in the backyard in thirty minutes, no peeking.

I'm no good with surprises, the actual worst. I honestly can't deal with the thought of not knowing what's coming next. I fight the impulse to look. I have no clue where he's even going with this one.

Usually, it's a text that he's here or to open the side door, so he can sneak upstairs. I know it's silly, but hell if sneaking around doesn't make things hotter. The feeling that you might get found out amps it up a notch.

Maybe that's why people cheat? Maybe it's more of a game to see what they can get away with, to see if they can't get caught?

Okay, brain, shut the hell up! We are beyond this.

I can't help feeling a tinge of annoyance when I think of Jake's phone blowing up earlier. I'm even more annoyed with the fact that I keep obsessing over what it's about, wondering if it's normal texting, and actually Luke, or something—or even someone—else.

Jake's been forthcoming enough, but I know he catches the judgy glances from me, the lingering doubt. How could I not? I mean, for real. This stems from a kiss and some text bullshit. I think I've earned the right to be suspicious.

However, I'm trying not to be too much with it.

Look. There's been plenty of messed-up stuff at this stage of the game, especially if you take everything into account. But… moving on. Right? I'm aware I can't keep living here. I can grill Jake about who texted him, or I can choose to believe what he offers me.

Fucking trust. This shit is *not* easy.

I wait till nine-thirty sharp before going to the basement. Not like I stared at my phone ticking away the seconds. No, not at all.

After walking out the door, I survey the landscape. What is Jake even playing at? Our backyard is fairly large, fenced-in with a swing set and trampoline. Pretty stock for our neighborhood.

The potent aroma of burning wood—firewood, to be exact—hits my nose and already seeps into my hair and clothes. A stone pit sits out in the far corner of our yard, flames flickering within.

I glance around, but Jake's nowhere to be seen. I laugh to myself then trek out to it, sitting on a red-and-black checkered blanket spread over the ground. How cute.

A throat clears behind me, and I swing my head round.

"What is this?" I ask, gesturing to the blanket and the fire. Occasionally, we'd have one on a random weekend here and there, but not usually on a Monday night.

Jake settles behind me, his legs stretched out along my sides. "You know," he says, sweeping my hair away and kissing my neck, making me forget about the entire world. "Twenty-one years ago, I met this girl at a bonfire."

"Is that right?" I murmur as his hands cruise down my arms then clasp around me. Lounging back into him, I close my eyes.

Also, *damn*. He remembered.

We've never been big on anniversaries, birthdays, or bullshit holidays. But I guess maybe this is an important one. I mean, it's a long time to be with someone. My heart is thumping extra hard right now. Who is this guy?

"So, what about this girl?" I chuckle as his chin rests on my shoulder.

My nails scrape over his forearms, and I breathe in a freshly showered Jake mixed with the hint of a light run—not like disgusting, dripping sweat, but the smell of outside. I'm sorry, but it gets me going.

"Well…" His lips taunt the shell of my ear. I swear he's so in tune with what that does to me, and I hate that he keeps using it against me. Alright, no, I don't.

His feet hook over my ankles, spreading my legs, and his hand travels down leisurely till the heel of his palm hits dead center. A heavy, ultra-moany gasp slips out.

It seems I've forgotten to throw on underwear. My bad.

"About this girl." He continues rubbing over me in a way that's got my hips instinctively grinding against his touch. "She was like no one else I'd ever met. Wasn't afraid to speak her mind or to go against the popular opinion. Was never about the attention, like all the other girls I'd hung out with. She didn't give a shit about fitting in—because she was born to stand out."

"Okay, Dr. Seuss."

Jake's torso quakes with laughter against my back. "And she was funny."

"Sounds like a keeper."

He holds me tighter, nuzzling into the crook of my neck, taking me a million miles away from a few months ago.

Before, the fire had all but gone out; had been dwindling for years. Makes me kind of mad that it happens to people. That it happened to *us*. But here we are, the flames growing strong once again.

Jake unravels his legs from mine, scoots next to me, and grabs my hands, his eyes blazing. They really are. The reflection of the fire flickers in them, making him look pussy-pulsing hot. It is what it is.

"You weren't like anyone else either." I climb onto his lap, facing him.

Jake arranges my legs behind him then slides his palms beneath my shirt, massaging my lower back. We remain sitting there, melting into each other. Literally. This fire's hot. The heat it's emitting burns my cheeks. The heat from his thin gym shorts burns something else.

In a good way.

I tip my forehead to his and weave my fingers through his damp hair.

"You *aren't* like anyone else. Honestly, you scared the shit outta me when we first met." Jake's shoulder lifts.

"What?" I tilt my head back, nose crinkling. He's never told me that before.

"You seemed so free, it was addicting. I couldn't get enough. You still have that incredible energy. I'm sorry I made you feel you weren't—"

My lips cut him off, my tongue delving into his mouth, trying to recreate that scorching first kiss that we shared.

Well, *second* first kiss.

* * *

We were hanging out by that post-high-school fire, twenty-one years ago to the day, talking about everything. Hopes, dreams, you name it.

The flickering flames highlighted the dark features of Jake's face. His thick eyelashes curled over intoxicating eyes. He was smaller then but still in great shape. Really great shape. Had the same intense stare, like he could see beyond the superficial.

Somewhere between chatting about the colleges we were going to and what we wanted to be, I felt that unbridled flurry of excitement, those wild tingles shivering up and down my spine. I knew he wasn't like any other guy. I knew if I didn't take a chance, I'd regret it. Jake sat there, so relaxed.

I had to go for it.

We'd glanced at each other's lips here and there during the conversation. But you know, that first kiss… it requires some guts. I had just enough liquid courage to make a move. So as he turned his head towards me, I went in for the kill, going full-on lip service, open-mouthed and all, practically attacking his face.

Jake's eyes went wide, and his lips clamped shut, arms lofting to his sides. Immediately, I turned away, feeling rejected and confused. After fumbling to get up, I apologized, utterly mortified I'd read things so wrong. I didn't realize Jake had taken a swig from the bottle I'd so graciously shared with him. He coughed and sputtered out the clear liquor, which he hadn't swallowed before I'd laid it on him.

He chased after me and grabbed my wrist, still coughing and choking, out of breath and laughing. Without saying a word, he put my arms around his waist and cupped my cheeks, angling my head to look at him.

We stared at each other for what felt like minutes. His eyes drifted to my lips, though they never once closed. He kissed me gently at first, his fingers sifting into my hair. It was as if our mouths knew *exactly* how to move together.

That moment was amazing.

He was—no, *is*—a good kisser, like superb, knowing when to speed up and slow down. Not jabby or gag-inducing with his tongue. Interlacing our hands, he led me over to his red-and-black checkered sleeping bag.

Talk time was over.

Truth be told, I would have given everything to him that night; call it what you want. I felt a crazy type of way about him, some sort of soul connection. Guys before Jake were meaningless ways to pass the time, but now it was as if the stars aligned. We were each other's missing pieces, and he made me feel whole. But, of course, he didn't take advantage. Like I said before, he was a respectful teenage guy, and I hadn't been exposed to many of them.

He whispered in my ear as I was falling asleep, his body perfectly molded behind mine, arms cradled around me, talking about the different things he wanted us to do. Already making plans for the summer after only a few hours together. I thought it was insane, but I felt the same exact way.

Fucking love at first sight.

* * *

"This is so thoughtful," I say breathlessly, hands on his shoulders, studying those intense eyes.

"I should have done this a long time ago." Jake shakes his head. "I should've made more of an effort."

"I should have too." I lick my lips, which are still tingling, almost numb from the deep, reminiscent kiss. The fabric beneath us catches my attention, and I realize it isn't a blanket, but a sleeping bag. "Holy shit." My mouth gapes. "Is this the original?"

"Yup." His fingers trace the red-and-black checks, and he offers me a gigantic smile, dimple creasing his cheek. "Where the magic began."

I chuckle, but he isn't wrong. That night, that kiss, *all* those firsts, they were magical. Unparalleled.

My hand covers his, resting on the old sleeping bag, and my heart squeezes in my chest. I haven't seen it since that night.

"Found it at my parents'." He shrugs. "I don't know, I thought it would be nice?"

"It's perfect," I say, kissing him hard. Only this time, he doesn't stop, or cough, or sputter. His lips and tongue dance in perfect harmony with mine.

"Wanna recreate?" he asks with a suggestive wink.

My arms and legs tangle around him, and I gaze into his eyes like a lovesick teenager. He nips the bottom of my ear. Fucking sexy Jake smirk. Fucking ear. I'd say fucking panty dropper, but I'm not wearing any.

"Obviously." The smile stays plastered on my face as I feel the curve of his lips over mine.

He leans forward while I'm still clinging to him and lies on top of me, then scatters kisses along my neck. "I love you, Alex." He pauses, propping himself up on his elbows above me. "I've loved you since that day."

I nod, while a slight sting of tears hits the corners of my eyes. Not in a sad way, but in the way only a powerful memory can evoke.

A moment that defined and led to so many *other* moments.

"I know," I reply softly. "Me too."

40. EVERLONG

We stay out by the fire for a while, neither one of us ready to let go of that memory just yet. I gotta admit, this is probably the sweetest, most romantic thing Jake has ever done. Who knew he had it in him?

I rarely got flowers or anything. Though I didn't exactly strive to surprise him either. Funny how this seemingly little thing feels like a really big thing—when life gets put into perspective, you begin to recognize the genuine magic in moments. It sucks we had to take the messy way, but it's alright.

We try to be as stealthy as possible, sneaking upstairs. All seems at peace in the mostly dark and quiet house. Luckily, the dogs have gotten used to Jake's drop-ins, so they don't go completely wild anymore.

Once we're up the steps, avoiding the creak on the seventh one—you learn which areas make sounds when you're determined to fly under the radar—we sneak down the hall to the bedroom, past the other four.

Jake tickles my side, being playful, yet also in an effort to make me laugh and get us busted. I bat his hands away but ultimately allow him to fasten his grip on the back waistband of my sweats. Once he was clued in that I was going commando, it's been game on. But, as luck would have it, we both noticed a neighboring light flip while lounging in the backyard. No one needs to give that nosey next-door nuisance any further ammo.

So here we are.

As soon as we're in the safety of our tan-walled bedroom, Jake closes the door behind us. Then he pushes me against it, lips on mine, hand skimming from my neck, between my breasts, continuing the downward trend.

"Lock it?" he asks, pulling away. He pokes a thumb at the door I pushed off of before settling myself on the edge of our king-sized bed.

Let's be real, railing me against the door isn't gonna happen when the kids are home—it would be way too loud.

"Yes, lock it!" I huff but keep my voice quiet. "Have you met our children? They know no boundaries."

They don't. Even the older girls will walk straight into the bathroom on me. They don't give a shit, striking up a conversation while I'm midstream.

Privacy? What the hell is that?

Locks have become my only chance of solitude. Please, if you haven't invested in them, add it to your list. I'm pretty sure they would pop it, though, if they needed something bad enough.

After engaging the necessary lock, Jake strolls towards me, lips extra smirky amid his permanent five o'clock shadow. He pinches the back collar of his navy tee, dusting it from his body in one fluid motion. So fucking effortless.

He tilts his chin, and excitement surges through me at the sight of him. Then he balls his shirt and chucks it, pelting me in the face. I crack up laughing but inhale deeply through my nose, bathing in the scent of detergent, campfire, and Jake.

Maybe it's weird, but for me, people and places have their own specific, unique smell. A mix of different components that make up their personalized fragrance.

He saunters over to me. I swear that's what it is. It's not a march or a stroll; it's a fucking saunter, a sex stalk.

My gaze roams his inked torso and arms, drifting down to that perfect— stop and stare worthy—V, which gets lost in the shorts barely holding on to his hips. Hazel eyes, already steamy and drowned in lust, meet mine, his tongue swiping along his bottom lip.

I lean back, my palms spread over the old blue comforter, the same one we've had for years. I don't care—it's snuggly. As always, the kids get the latest, updated stuff, and we get stuck with the worn blankets, but I don't want a new one.

Anyway, I'm chilling, watching my live entertainment, and thoroughly enjoying the show. Reclining back further, my elbows prop into the mattress, legs crossing as I soak in the work of art in front of me.

Jake tsks. "We can't have that." He motions a corrective finger at my legs, batting his obscenely thick lashes.

"Hah!" I raise my brows. "I'm comfortable like this." I do my best *Basic Instinct*, uncross, spread, and recross, sweatpants and all. No doubt it would be hotter if the pants were off, but I'm not quite ready to stop having fun. I shoot him a challenging grin, with my thighs remaining together, and say, "Change my mind."

A single eye narrows, and his lips curl on one side. "What are you playin' at?" He grabs my knees, attempting to separate them. But thanks to some squats and a dash of leg presses, I'm able to keep them clamped tight.

His defined, tattoo-covered chest appears even darker in the dim light of the bedroom. He's not big into colored ink. Most of his tats are plain black. Except for one. Jake's hair is tousled and gorgeous and hanging over his forehead.

"Strip," I command, lifting a shoulder and biting my lip, trying to match his usual sly grin.

"Really?" He laughs. "How 'bout *you* strip? I only have two things on."

Satisfaction pats me on the back when I spy the growing bulge in his shorts. "I only have three," I say, sliding my gaze to his.

"Hm…" Jake squints while scratching his jaw, finger tapping his chin. "That's right. Not that I forgot you weren't wearing underwear. Still…" He flips his hand over. "You have one more than me, so you're up first." Taking a step back, he rubs his palms together, and the grin on his face couldn't get any larger.

"Tit for tat?" I ask.

He nods, seriously enthused.

"I'm in."

I sit up on the edge of our bed, clasping my shirt at the hem, my eyes locked on Jake's.

He watches me intently as I gradually peel it off, in a manner I'm hoping to make look seductive, but it's a flop. The collar snags on one of my small, silver hoop earrings, and I struggle to free myself from the fabric covering my face.

Jake seizes the opportunity, cranking my thighs apart, then rubbing his growing erection against me.

"Gotcha," he says after I finally unhook my shirt and send it sailing across the room.

"Nah." I wrap my legs around him. "They're still crossed." I squeeze him harder against me, and he leans forward, forehead to mine.

"So long as they're crossed around me."

Our lips are so close, I can feel the seductive scratch of his facial hair. But his eyes, as per usual, are on mine.

"Mm-hmm."

His fingers line the straps of my bra before slipping them from my shoulders. "Time for this to go," Jake whispers, reaching behind me.

Loosening my legs, I shove a hand to his solid chest—gotta have a little fun with this before we go for the kill—pushing him and causing him to stagger backwards.

"Hm… nope. I'm pretty sure it's *your* turn." I take a second to toss my hair into a bun, so glad it's finally grown out to the point that I can do that. Life goals.

"Fair enough." Jake turns his back to me, shoulders jarring in silent laughter, thumbs hooking on to the sides of his shorts as he shimmies—yes, shimmies—them to the ground. Tight, snug, and… *that ass*. Boxer briefs are revealed, and they have my mouth watering at first glance. He whips his head over his shoulder in a failed sexy stare that has us both busting out laughing.

"Jesus." Gesturing with both hands, he spins around, showing off the monster hard-on caged by his black briefs.

"Yeah…" I sigh. "I guess we'll have to do something about that."

He steps forward, to the edge of the bed, then grips the waist of my pants, ready to yank them down.

"Not this first?" I palm my breasts that are still covered by my bra, kneading them with a smug look.

Jake watches as I feel myself up then waves a hand. "Nah, fuck it. You can leave it on."

The sound of the doorknob jiggling stops us both in our tracks.

"Mom?"

Always with the mom shit! Also, see why I was preaching about those locks?

I take a moment to compose myself, while Jake stands up, lips folding into his mouth, quaking in silent laughter.

"Yeah, Jordan?" I try to hide the exasperation in my voice. I swear I can hear a soft snicker on the other side of the door.

"Forgot to pack my lunch."

Come on.

"No problem—I'll do it." I scrunch my nose, motioning to the door. Like, *see what I deal with on the reg.*

"Thanks, Mom. Goodnight."

"Night, Jordan," I respond. Though I know this kid, and there's an edge to her voice. She's setting something up.

"Night, Dad."

Jake shakes his head with a breathy chuckle. It's one I can't help but join in on. Busted. That didn't take long.

"Night, Jord."

We both look at each other, lips clamped, stuck in this quiet fit of laughter. Kids, man… they're smart. Her room is all the way down at the opposite end of the hall too.

"Hey, Dad," Jordan calls from outside the door. "Why don't you stay this time so you can make us breakfast in the morning? Mom's cooking lacks."

Jake climbs on the bed, where I'm still propped up, then kneels over me, kissing my bottom lip that's pouting.

"Go to bed!" he yells, before his eyes search mine. "Sleepover?"

Fuck… with the eyes. This is real life here, folks. Kids, interruptions, feelings, love, packing lunches—all of it.

I wanted to go slow, take our time, but this night has been *so* good.

"Sure, let's go for it."

Jake smiles against my lips before searing a kiss to them. I place my palm on his bare chest, over my engraved name, and find comfort in the heart beating beneath it. We stare at each other, so close I can feel his long lashes butterflying against my cheek.

"Okay, so you wanna go to bed?" I ask playfully.

He grabs my wrist, moving my hand down to land on his aching appendage.

"Let's handle this first." He tears off my pants, kind of rough. And I'm kind of okay with it. "Lie back."

Sure thing.

Jake positions himself between my legs, using his knees to spread them further after kicking off his briefs. He kisses me, starting gentle but swiftly gaining speed when my lips part for his seeking tongue, smothering each other in lung-seizing caresses.

His mouth moves across my cheek, then he slides his finger over my tingling lips and glances at me with a smirk.

Oh, okay… he wants me to do the finger thing. Might as well. I suck his inching index while labored breaths pant from him, accompanying his almost pained expression. I try not to laugh, hollowing my cheeks when he pumps back and forth, noticing his chest swell when I gag on his fingertip.

Just a little. And he likes it. Do guys picture their finger as a dick? Whatever, I'm going with it.

He slinks over me and unclasps my bra—I knew that wouldn't be staying on. Roughly cupping my breasts, Jake smashes his mouth into them, tonguing my already hardened nipple with multiple flicks that have my back arching, begging for more.

His slick finger, now firmly tucked between my legs, preps the course, forcing whimpers to tumble from my lips. Jake thrusts it inside me, pumping in and out, curling, thumb double-clicking where it counts.

He glances up at me, eyes blazing. "I'm gonna make you come in my mouth first."

Mercy.

Yep, initiated some dirty talk in our bedroom routine. If that doesn't help you slide into home, I'm not sure what will.

I groan as he gently bites my hip then kisses the inside of each thigh. He parts me with his tongue before diving inside me. My hips rise to meet his face, welcoming the heat of his mouth against me, heart hammering in my chest as I grip the blanket, twisting it in clenched fists.

"Your pussy tastes so good," he says between the fucking *holy shit* that's happening.

Also… that's hot.

Jake's eyes remain on mine while he continues with his tongue thrusting, mouth fucking, sucking, and licking every spot that brings me closer and closer to the brink. His fingers plunge inside me, moving faster and faster.

My toes are curling. I'm panting wildly, reaching, searching, desperate for anything to grab a hold of. My head plummets to the pillow—fuck the eye contact—and I pinch my lids shut. No chance they're staying open right now.

Just as I'm about to explode, he slips another finger in...

Yes. Further back.

It's a shocker, I know. Before you judge this, I strongly suggest you try it out. Maybe thank me later.

Scrounging for a pillow, I clamp it over my face and suffocate the incoherent sounds coming from my mouth. The waves of pleasure thrash and flood through my body, the blast from the feelgood sensation overtaking my brain.

This is what I like to call a *come to Jesus* moment.

Sorry, God, I apologize. But if this is what heaven is like, I'm fucking in.

I try to calm my erratic panting as Jake places a final lingering kiss over my sated core before working his way up. I continue to reside in a post-climax stupor.

"How was that?" he asks, an accomplished grin on his face.

"It was alright." I shrug, completely out of breath. Also *completely* full of shit.

"You want me to do it again?"

Um, hell yes! Five times a day, every day. But really, no. I'm not sure my body can handle that extreme measure of foreplay a second time.

"Your turn," I say, sliding down beneath him.

Jake checks his hips into mine. "Nah."

Wait? What?

His thick cock connects between my legs, drawing a gasp from my throat.

"How 'bout you do that in the morning?"

Yeah, alright.

Before I can say anything, he fuses our lips and buries himself inside me, then runs a hand through my hair—buh-bye messy bun. He clutches a fistful to expose my neck and begins his torturous assault, slamming into me with mounting force, rougher than he ever has before.

I cry out, clawing the sheets, and he freezes, eyes brimming with concern. "Is it too much?"

"No," I say, closing my legs around his back. "Harder." I cross my ankles tight and jolt him into me.

He grips my hair, continuing to drive with spine-splintering strokes. "Just tell me if it's too much, and I'll stop."

Jake's always been afraid to go too hard with this. But it doesn't trigger bad memories—when he's ramming into me, yanking my hair, scoring my shoulders, whatever, it feels amazing.

Sometimes you just need it rough.

I nod, urging him to keep the strenuous pace, scratching at his tensed arms each time his pelvis smacks against mine.

And clearly he feels the same way. Because it doesn't take long.

We stop trying to fight it. We both let go.

41. SOME KIND OF DISASTER

The sleepover was a success. I mean… *obviously*. My alarm blares at six-thirty, and Jake shuts it off, leaning over me and dotting kisses along my cheek. He tells me to stay in bed, that he'll handle the morning routine. He doesn't have to make that offer twice. I don't question it for a second, snuggling back into my pillow, relishing in the idea of nothingness.

About two hours later, a freshly showered Jake and a cup of coffee are at my bedside. Hallelujah! I could stare at this glorious, hot, dark steaming mug all day. Jake's not so bad either.

"You gonna get up?" he asks, sweeping a strand of hair from my face.

I notice he's strangely casual. You already know—random tee, comfy shorts, backwards hat. I'm confused. It's Tuesday, and he should be at work by now.

"Why aren't you dressed?" I rub sleep from my eyes then sit against the headboard and sip from my beloved unicorn mug.

"Um, I *am* dressed." His eyebrows and lips scrunch as he sits on the side of the bed. An eager palm sneaks up my inner thigh, connecting with the seam of my pajama pants, making me jolt.

"What the hell?" I release a crying type of laugh when coffee splashes onto my chest. Also, ow! "It burns!"

Jake quickly grabs the mug from me as I fling off my shirt. Yeah, the bra is gone, tits are out. I never sleep in one. Usually the second I get home, that sucker's relieved of its duties. I swear, after having kids, there's not even a single ounce of shame about them, because everyone has done seen them already.

He wets his lips. "Oh, I didn't realize we were getting naked."

"Coffee." I extend my arm, awaiting my only chance for a functioning day. Just sitting here bare-chested, again… zero fucks.

Jake stares. No, he doesn't stare; he fixates.

"Can I help you?"

"Is this how you normally drink your coffee?"

"Oh, shirtless? Yup, sure do, all the time—free dem titties." I roll my eyes.

Jake's gaze is already reading the roadmap of my body, a mischievous look on his face, smirky as ever.

Seriously? Because what oozes sex appeal more than someone who just woke up, spilled coffee on themselves, and is sipping it braless?

"In that case." He whisks off his shirt, doing a showy pec flex and making me laugh. God, the playful thing is *so* fun. I'm so glad we're back here. Why'd we ever let life dull it down?

He tries to steal my mug, wanting to get things going. I let him know that's a murderable offense.

I'm floored, though, when he tells me he took the entire day off. Well, really, he just said he wasn't going in, because it's his company. He would never have done this in the past. It was always work, work, and work

Jake informs me we're spending the day together, asking what I want to do. Honestly, how 'bout bed all day? But then I remember I have plans to meet Annie for, yes, more coffee.

I click away, sending a fast text, letting her know we'll have a plus one.

Once I drain my caffeine, I head for a shower. Jake follows, hot on my heels. Pussy-whipped much? Though I'd say I'm pretty cock-locked myself.

Unfortunately, I don't think he's going to get what he wants in here. Here's the facts about me and shower sex. The shower is too small, and he's too tall, so positioning is a real bitch. I'm clumsy as hell, not a graceful bone in this body. But you know what there is room for? Some down-on-the-knees action.

Plus, I owe him one

He scrubs shampoo into my head, massaging my scalp, making me all types of moany. I wonder if you could have an orgasm from a superb hair washing? Because I think I might be there.

Clearly, the sounds leaving my mouth are doing the trick, because I already feel a poke against my lower back.

After rinsing my hair, Jake continues to grind himself into me, while I keep on with the loud sound effects. Shoot, might as well take advantage of the rarity of no eavesdroppers. He groans, encircling his arms around me, one hand palming my breast, while the other dips and slips, gliding through the blast of heat that has my pussy a quivering mess. We're just gonna call it what it is.

Streams of water beat down on us, and I tilt my head back to his chest, allowing myself to get lost in the moment.

Yes, it appears we have a full-blown sex addiction going on. Not sure who the *main* supplier is, but I'm here for it.

Okay, equal opportunity, time to repay the favor. Halting his groping hands, I twist to face him. Water drips from his hair, over his eyes and nose, then trickles down his sharp jawline.

I link my hands at the back of his neck, lowering his head to meet mine, though I still have to go up on my toes. After I lick his lips a few times, he smiles, and I melt our mouths together, swirling my tongue around his, giving a preview of what's to come.

Pun intended.

Jake lets out a groan, and it vibrates in my throat while my palm skates down his torso. I take my time, fingertips tracing each delicious groove, before stroking him with my hand. I step back, giving his jaw-dropped self a wink before lowering to my knees.

A series of sharp gasps stagger him forward as my tongue lashes long strokes over his shaft, flicking the tip. I'm pleased by the high-pitched cry he lets out.

Fun fact if you aren't aware, the tip is the equivalent to the clit.

Anyway, with the combo of one hand on his ass, encouraging his gentle hip thrusts—no pinkie slip here because Jake's not a fan; learned that years ago—my other hand corkscrews where my mouth can't reach, and it seems we have a winner. I can already feel his body tensing and trembling.

His fists tighten in my hair, and I look up with some sorta doe-eyed, innocent expression, while he stares in awe. I know this submissive shit gets him goin'. I take as much of him as I can, urging him to pick up the pace, ramming into the back of my constricting throat, reducing him to rubble.

Tears sting my eyes, but the power that radiates through me is insurmountable, and I'm fully aware I could have him on his knees in a second.

Anyway, it only takes three more methodical bobs of my mouth before he loosens his fingers from my wet locks and braces his palms against the shower stall. Every muscle in his body flexes and clenches, and a deep, guttural moan rips from his chest, accompanying his release.

Sometimes you just gotta swallow.

I take every last bit from him and don't hesitate to lick him clean.

I do a quick rinse off and get outta there while he's still coming down from his high, before he can return the favor. I know he's more than willing, and I don't mind, but I have plans with Annie. Truth be told, I've been pushing her off these past months while we've been working on stuff. And she doesn't deserve to be dicked over—literally.

Jake lazes on our bed, peering in through the partially open bathroom door, watching me get ready. "It's so much work," he says, jutting his chin to the makeup and hair products sprawled on the vanity. "You don't need any of that."

I roll my eyes but make the mistake of letting them wander in his direction

He's lying sideways, shirtless, and I swear there's zero body fat. My gaze travels lower to the waist of his shorts. The V is a trap!

Fuck, look away. Look away. We don't have time for this right now.

Too late.

"Like what ya see?" He bucks his hips in the air, tongue hanging out. I smile and shake my head, shutting the bathroom door.

* * *

Annie's already in the small coffee shop, a little hidden gem type of place we love. They know us here, can recite our orders. The second we walk in, they whip them together.

"Got yours," Annie calls from our usual table, raising a cup in the air. Her reddish-brown hair is woven into a braid draped over her shoulder. Our outfits are comparable, consisting of loose tanks and capri leggings. You know, the workout clothes you may or may not work out in.

"I wasn't sure what you'd want, Jake." Her voice is softer than usual, her attention trained on the cup in front of her, fingernails drumming over the tabletop. She glances up at me and smiles, but I see the worry in her eyes as she shifts them nervously to Jake then back down.

Um, what am I missing here? I pull out a chair to join her. "What's up?" I ask, pretty much accusing.

Jake sets his palms on my shoulders then brushes his lips over my cheek. "I'll let you ladies talk for a minute."

"So what's new with you?" Annie sips her drink, eyes blatantly avoiding mine.

"Don't *what's new with you* me."

My pulse is pounding. You know that impending-doom, bile-raising feeling you get before someone drops a bomb on you? I'm feeling it right now.

She turns away, and her bottom teeth repeatedly scrape her lip.

"Annie!" I all but shout. "You're making me nervous." My focus pings to Jake, who's at the counter, searching the overhead menu. I swear if this has something to do with—

"Alex," she says, her eyes swimming with emotion. Finally looking at me, her fingers mesh with mine on the table. "We're moving."

My heart just dropped. She's my *only* family here, my support, my fucking person.

Swallowing loudly, I choke back tears already forming, and gape at my best friend. "What? Why?"

Annie tells me through sobs that Jace was offered a deal to massively expand his company. He is seriously a *started from the bottom now we're here* type of story. Anyway, the main headquarters will be two hours south, actually close to my parents. Apparently, he'd been offered this months ago. But... they'd been waiting.

It only takes me a second to realize what she means. They were waiting on *me*. Waiting to make sure I'd be okay.

She promises we'll see each other once a month—at least—that they'll only be a short car ride away. I know they won't be too far, but shit, I'm used to her being here.

She needs my support, not for me to be selfish and throw a fit, so I smile and agree with her that it'll all work out. This is a major opportunity for them, and I'm one to attest that when opportunity knocks, you better answer.

We have a few months; they don't settle till the end of September.

I go into the bathroom to fix my face, struggling to absorb the news that the person who's been my go-to for so long won't be living in the same state as me anymore. I know I can survive without her. Of course I do. We've barely seen each other over the last few months. But there's a difference between knowing someone is only a thirteen-minute drive away and not.

When I walk back out into the coffee shop, Annie and Jake are engrossed in some conversation that has his hands in front of him defensively. Annie's staring him up and down, her eyebrows jammed together, her lips thin, her arms clasped against her chest.

"Everything okay?" I look between them as I sit down.

"Yeah," Jake says, draping his arm over my shoulder and lugging me into him.

"Yes, Alex. I was just telling Jake that he better do his very best job at keeping my girl happy. Seems he is… right now." She offers him a teeth-baring smile then winks at me.

I can probably imagine what she's said to him. Some sort of threatening lecture.

I love her.

Later, Jake strolls out ahead of me, while I give Annie a hug. An enormous hug. A hug that *I* initiate.

"What was up with all that before? I thought you were Team Jake?"

"Nope," she responds with a click of her tongue. "I'm Team Alex, bitch. Always have been, always will be."

* * *

"So, what did she actually say?" I ask Jake once I'm in the passenger seat of his car, adjusting the air vents to help dull the near summer heat.

He grips the steering wheel, knuckles draining. "You really wanna know?"

I nod, giving him a duh look.

He draws in a breath then blows it out with a chuckle, shaking his head. "She said… if I ever do anything to hurt you, she will find me, cut off my dick, and jam it down my throat, until I meet my grueling death by choking on it. Word for word."

We both start laughing. That's my girl, always so mild with her threats.

"She's so sweet," I joke. "But for real, I can't believe they're moving. Well, at least it's near our parents, so we can visit more." I shrug. "What did you say to her?"

"I told her I won't." Jake reaches over, lacing our fingers together. He dashes pecks over my knuckles then gazes into my eyes—chill, we're at a stoplight. "I won't."

I can't help but feel like the other shoe was bound to drop at some point. Everything's been going so perfectly, and we already know... life simply doesn't roll that way. Thankfully, this isn't the worst thing that could happen. Maybe it'll put a little more pressure on Jake to make amends with Ashton. Because now, if all my favorite people are there, minus us, it's where I'm gonna want to be.

"So, what do you want to do?" Jake releases my hand, dragging his fingertips up my thigh with a suggestive tip of his lips.

"Did you take a little blue pill or something?"

This guy is insatiable right now, though me too.

"No, but I could?" He's serious, and I snort at him.

"I want to take you somewhere." I direct his turns until we make it to a tiny parking lot, mostly hidden in a wooded area.

"What is this?" he asks, stepping out of the car and following me down the path.

"It's a place I found not long after we moved here."

He gets out of the car and bolts around to open my door.

"Cheesy." I tut but take his hand anyway and grin.

I stumbled upon this hidden trail when Brynn was a pipsqueak and Jordan was fairly new, after venturing a bit further from home in an effort to lull them into nap time. I gave up, and the three of us braved the elements, traipsing along the trail with no agenda. Well, Brynn and I traipsed, while Jord was strapped in a carrier on my chest.

When we reached the view, it was overwhelmingly peaceful. I declared— in my head—that this was *my* place. The perfect area for solace and reflection. I promised myself I'd make all the points to come here regularly.

But I never did.

We make our leisurely way to the end of the trail to some large boulders that hang out, providing a front-row—albeit thrill-seeking—seat to the roaring river below.

I slip beneath the fence and walk out onto one of the rocks suspended a hundred feet or so above the river.

I did *not* bring the girls this far.

"Holy shit!" Jake basks in the view. Enormous trees surround the river, and the only sound is the rushing water below, as if civilization has simply disappeared. He sits next to me in silence.

It's amazing. You'd never know it existed if you didn't look for it. Or if it didn't find you. Maybe that's how it all goes? Perhaps these stops and obstacles get randomly tossed our way, and it's up to us to decide what to do with them.

I'm redeclaring this place as mine. And I'm glad to have Jake here with me, to show him, and share this beautiful scenery. Annie's right—I *am* happy.

Here we are. Our marriage was almost a disaster. Looking over at Jake, before lying my head on his shoulder, I feel, for the first time in a long time, that this is exactly where we're meant to be.

42. ABSOLUTELY
(STORY OF A GIRL)

We sit on my rock—yeah, it's mine—for about an hour, taking in the pictur-esque, early June day. Bright blue sky, puffy clouds, and green leaves as far as the eye can see.

Serene as fuck.

Staring out at the river, I let every thought slip from my mind, allowing it to go completely blank. Okay, that's bullshit. My mind doesn't stop… ever. It moves at light speed, all day, every day. I've been thinking about the latest news, about Annie, Jace, and the girls moving away. Damn, that day is gonna suck.

A single tear escapes my eye, but Jake's right there next to me, ready to wipe it all away. He and Annie are more similar than they realize, both feeling as if they have to protect me. I bet it's been exhausting. Ashton did it too. Like it's any of their duties to keep me safe.

My life is filled with fixers. I know that's what you do for the people you love, but they shouldn't be devoted to it. I'm determined to let them see I can handle myself.

They've all watched me fall apart so many times. That's why I'm not allowing Annie's move to break me. Even though it's devastating, this isn't the end of our story.

Trying to soak up the peacefulness, I sit here, the river ferociously surging below. Well, not so ferocious—it's mostly moving at what I'd say is a normal current. Anyway, can't lie, it's pretty scary up here if you make the unfortunate mistake of glancing down.

So… I'll go ahead and not do that.

Maybe that's why this place appealed to me the first time, because it evokes a feeling. Even if that current feeling is a lot of calm sprinkled with a splash of fear.

Jake arranged himself behind me, and this new wave of touchy-feely is still happening. I bend my knees to my chest, chin resting on top.

The entire time he's kept his legs straddling either side of me, warm palms drifting along my forearms. He alternates between pressing the side of his head against my back—swear to God, he's sniffing my hair again—and laying his cheek on my shoulder, switching it up every so often.

I *know* this is torture for him.

He's a chill sort of personality, but Jake doesn't like to just chill. He's not a stop-and-smell-the-roses type. He is a pacer, a constant go-go-goer. So at least I know him sitting here in complete silence is for me.

I appreciate it.

I wonder if he would've seen the beauty in this place… before?

The excessive vibrating of his cell finally makes me turn my head. With his left hand stretched to the side, he clicks away at the screen. So fucking annoying.

I sigh, a loud, overly dramatic, annoyed groan. Hello, passive-aggressive.

"What's wrong?" He places his phone face down and draws his arms around me, pulling me back to him.

"Nothing." I swear my eye roll can be heard out loud. Clenching my jaw, I maintain my straight-ahead stare.

"Communication, remember?"

Oh my God, is he seriously Patty-ing me now? But yeah, he's right.

"It's not a big deal, but why do you have to be on your phone?" I stay fixed on the river, the sky, wherever. I hate his fucking phone. I wish I could vaporize it, along with New York—okay, that's excessive, but you get what I mean.

"Sorry, I didn't realize it bothered you so much."

I swear my back stiffens right up. Because I've never let on that it pisses me off? For real? It's so aggravating.

Sigh.

I suck in a long breath. "Every time you're on your phone, texting or whatever, and I know this might sound stupid or crazy… but anyway, when you're on it, I can't help but think you're talking to someone you shouldn't be or hiding something."

I slouch, forehead to my knees, feeling ultra-petty, but man, he asked for it, and it's the truth. That's the way I feel.

Jake's arms drop from my sides, and he scoots himself away from me before getting to his feet. My eyes stay lowered, watching small pieces of gravel that tumble from his jarring move.

"It's just a fucking phone," he says, a tinge of agitation in his voice.

I don't look up. I get it—the argument is tired. But… communication, right? If I don't say it, it'll just get stuck inside till something makes it boil over again.

"I know." I fight the unwanted sting in my nose. Physically, it's only a phone, but it's more than that.

When you don't trust someone or something, objects and places become triggers, constant reminders. I'd say his phone is one, for obvious reasons. Plus, I can't shake this underlying feeling, no matter how much I try to cover it, fight it, and fuck it away—it's there.

Jake squats down next to me and tilts my chin with two fingers. He studies me long and hard. I hate the tears that are welling. Why is it so difficult to get over this shit? I wanna keep living in fairytale land, but it seems like every few days, the insecurities, the doubts, come creeping in.

I wish it would stop, but it doesn't. It just doesn't work like that.

He swipes the tears from my lower lids. "Don't cry." Jake's forehead presses to mine.

"I'm sorry." Shaking my head, I bite at the inside of my cheek, disappointed in my damn self that I keep circling around to this. "I'm trying not to be like this… I *really* am."

"It's a fucking phone," he repeats, jaw tensing. With a quick kiss to the tip of my nose, he stands abruptly and marches out to the ledge. In a sudden movement, his elbow pitches back, and before I realize what's happening, he lofts his cell into the air.

My mouth just hit the rock. Not actually, but holy hell! That phone is his daily companion… I can't believe he did that.

"There." He flashes a smile, dusting his hands. "Now it's gone."

Settling back behind me, Jake loops his arms around me, and I feel a smile form over my neck. "I'll be better about it, Alex."

"Me too." God, I'm cheesing *so* much right now—we are making all kinds of progress. Also, let's combine the facts that he's now deliberately breathing in my ear, his hands having disappeared beneath my shirt, with that gesture, which was honestly super sweet.

Sometimes a symbolic move is what it takes, even though we're gonna pay for it. Seriously, cell prices are horrendous.

"You know you have to get a new phone now?" I laugh as his wandering lips reach my cheek.

"I'll worry about it later." Jake shifts beside me, turning his head so we're nose to nose. The pad of his finger outlines my enormous grin. "I'll do whatever it takes to see you smile."

And just like that, my bout of mistrust and insecurity disappears, right down in the river, along with his phone.

Isn't it funny that one minor act, one thing, can be enough to let someone see what they mean to you?

If he's willing to let go of that so freely, it shows me something. My phone is my lifeline, sad but true. Can't say I'd be chucking it into a body of water anytime soon…

I would for him though.

"I want this to work, Jake."

"So do I." He cups my face with his palms, the sun making the green in his eyes overtake the brown. "Whatever it takes," he says before drawing me to him, lips feverishly connecting with mine.

It's one of those perfect, promising kisses. Molding and melting together, completely in sync; neither one of us taking too much from the other.

"Alright." I press a hand to his chest. "Enough of this sappy shit."

Jake chuckles, dimple on display with a *happy-as-fuck* sorta smile. "Just tell me when stuff bothers you, alright?"

"Deal. You know what bothers me?"

"*Damn*, something else already?"

"Why do you have so many T-shirts?" I pinch the sleeve of yet another random tee.

I'm not kidding here. This guy is like a T-shirt hoarder. I think he's even got some that date back to before we met. It's like a weird obsession, and he can't let go of them.

"Well, let's rectify that." Jake flings his shirt over his head. "I'll pitch all my shorts too, if that's what you want."

"Do what you gotta do." I shrug, unable to stop appreciating his torso. I swear, you get up in your thirties, and man oh man, does that libido come right back. At least this libido is.

Anyway, chill time is over. Gotta resume normal life. The kids will be home soon.

We slip under the fence, making our way to the dirt trail. Jake tosses the shirt over his shoulder, provocative as fuck. Also, he's like a partial nudist—ain't nobody mad at it. I wish *I* was always as comfortable in my own skin.

His hand clasps around mine, fingers twining, raising our arms. He kisses the heart inked on my inner wrist. Jake is a sweet guy, he really is. Though he's not usually outward with the sweet gestures. Today was something different. Another thing that makes me excited about the future—*our* future.

I guess the problem is, or was, that we consistently focused on fixing shit. But broken pieces can't always be mended. Sometimes you need to put your energy into building something else, something completely new.

This, taking off work, hanging out, was unheard of in the past. Just sitting with each other, not having to do anything in particular, not worrying about plans with the kids, casually chucking phones in the river.

More small things that turn out to be big things—life is full of them. Amazing what happens when you say the stuff you wanna say.

"Race you back." Jake sticks his tongue out before tearing off down the trail.

"You're on!" I don't hesitate, because sometimes it's fun to act carefree. And, for real, I can't let him win.

Sprinting forward with as much force as I can muster, knowing damn well he's faster, I shock myself by pulling ahead.

Of course, in true universe-meets-Alex fashion, the tip of my shoe snags on a tree root, causing me to lose my footing, flying headfirst towards the ground.

And in true universe-meets-Jake fashion, his broad arms swoop around me, quickly stopping my nosedive and yanking me upright.

While I don't *need* him to save me—in this instance, I'm glad he did.

"Thanks for that," I say, out of breath.

He spins me to face him, holding my body against his. "I got you."

He sweeps the crazy, messy wisps of hair from my face. I swear we aren't this sappy couple. Except, maybe we are now?

"I think you have to let me fall sometimes."

"Why's that?"

Oh Lord, I'm gonna roll with the sap.

"If we hadn't fallen apart, Jake, we'd never be *here* right now."

43. TOUCH IT

"You know what's hot?" I twist my lips into a smirk, shoving Jake against the side of the car. Not too hard but enough to let him know, it's game on. He laughs and catches his hat that tipped off, his hair looking yum.

Yum? Oh well, going with it.

"This."

"You like when I take charge, huh?" I press my body flush to his.

Jake's gaze conspicuously drifts to the added cleavage the smashed contact is producing. Enclosing my fingers around his wrists, I stop him from snaking a palm beneath my shirt, or over it, weakening my stab at dominance. He's all too aware of those little moves that make me putty.

"It makes me kinda scared," he admits, a nervous chuckle ticking from his throat. "But yeah, I like it."

I release his hands and step back. "Alright. Let's play." I tease my nails along his bare torso, prompting every muscle of his stellar six-pack to tense beneath my touch. "Anyway, what I was gonna tell you, what *I* think is hot, is when you're sweet and say the kinda shit you just said."

"Is that right?"

"Mm-hmm."

"How hot?" Jake asks.

"Hot enough to make me wanna fuck your brains out." With my hands settling on my hips, I lift a nonchalant shoulder, head tilting towards it.

"Right here?" An excited gleam flashes in his wide eyes, before he glances from side to side. He'd be about it.

It is a desolate place, but there's a road right next to the lot. No cars have driven by though. We're off the beaten path for sure, but wilderness… come on now. Poison ivy is a real thing. I don't even wanna imagine the possibilities with that one.

Anyway, I'm not going for exhibitionist status here. Well, not fully.

"Maybe." I tap into my sultry voice, knowing how that raspy tone gets things drumming up for him, same as it does for me. In a brazen move, my lips descend to his bare chest. A deep growl vibrates from his throat. That is, before my teeth graze his nipple, gently biting down.

They do it to us—fair is fair.

"Oh, God. Stop." He sucks in a sharp breath through his teeth, wincing.

"You don't like it?" I skim over the growing bulge in his shorts, wearing my best innocent look. I, myself, enjoy the love bites. Maybe it's just me?

"I… yeah, I do… kind of. I'd just rather be the one doing it to *you*."

I know he would. And that, my friends, is the reason for the following.

"Get in the car," I say, and it's an order. That door is opened at warp speed. "Shorts off."

He whips them down without question, sitting buck naked in the middle of the back seat.

I climb in, closing the door, and bend my legs to straddle him, knees sliding over the somewhat sticky leather seat. I'm not gonna think about what caused that. My palms slide up to his toned shoulders till I reach the nape of his neck, fingers weaving into his hair. Then I yank Jake's head, tilting it to mine. With staggered breaths and a pained look on his face, he whimpers lightly as my hips drive into him.

My head falls back and an erotic moan escapes my lips. The budding friction and contact with his growing erection causes tingles to surge like an electrical current up and down my spine, wet heat settling in my core.

"Well, this escalated quickly," Jake jokes before grasping at the hem of my shirt.

First off, thank God for dark, tinted windows. Second, let's not think about the fact that my kids sit here. Not just that, there are probably rogue Skittles and stuff everywhere… oh well.

I let him lift the tank over my head, revealing a blue-and-white, strappy-back sports bra—totally more for fashion than support, but whatevs.

Jake's hands travel torturously slow, from my waist up my sides, fingertips feathering my skin, leaving goosebumps in their wake. He licks a pathway along the curve of my neck, focusing on that little hollow at my collarbone, then pulls off my bra, tossing it somewhere in the front seat. Rough palms squeeze my breasts, eliciting another wanton moan before his tongue does its thing, hooded eyes gazing up at me.

I'm all types of ready for this.

Jake inhales through his nostrils, continuing to worship my chest. And suddenly I'm self-conscious.

"Ew, I'm kind of sweaty." I cringe, leaning back.

He clutches my waist, not stopping with the undivided attention.

It's not like I straight-up smell, but you know… just enough that a freshen up would *not* hurt the cause.

"I love it," Jake says, face buried between my tits, breathing in, pressing them together. Literally motor-boating.

"Okay, that's gross."

"Nah, just go with it." He glances up at me, still fondling. "I like you dirty."

I raise my brows, throwing his smirk right back at him. "Hm, do you now?"

His top teeth sink into his bottom lip, head nodding with a grin, way overeager.

Okay, in charge and dirty—I got this.

I reach for both our discarded tops, while Jake's curious attention follows my hands. Grabbing his wrist a bit aggressively, I wrap one of the shirts around it.

"Wait, what are you doing?" A flicker of alarm crosses his face, and I thrust my hips into him, temporarily dispelling any rational thoughts.

"Just go with it," I whisper in his ear, my lips lingering, causing all kinds of things to twitch.

Before I lose my nerve, I tie the shirt in a knot around the metal prong of one headrest before grabbing the other wrist and doing the same across the bench. Damn, this back seat is big. His eyes snap open, arms pinned and stretched out to the sides.

Jake tugs, attempting to free himself while I continue riding, and dry-humping, admiring my handiwork—and the fact that he can't budge. It's kinda fun, watching him squirm in his seat.

"Alex…" He tries to say my name with a warning tone, but, it comes out shaky. I remain silent, arching a brow. "They're tight!"

"Good. That's the point." My nails score down his chest and bite into his upper thighs. He inhales a breath when I curl my hand around his rock-hard cock, pumping up and down, eliciting a guttural sound from his chest.

"Do I need a safe word?" He laughs again, his chuckle still riddled with uncertainty. But the way his pelvis rises beneath me tells me—or rather *shows me*—he's loving this.

"You might."

My lips move over his pecs. I go painfully slow, darting my tongue over trails of ink like a maze. Erratic breaths escape from his mouth. I'm racking my brain, trying to come up with anything that'll make this even more dominant. I seriously can't. We're in a car, for Christ's sake. But… I'll give it a go.

My mouth is extremely close to being wrapped around him, and I work my fist, which is still tightly clasped around his shaft. His pupils are already blown.

"God, I need to fuck you." Jake groans, jaw clenching. I love it.

"I'm not so sure about that." I move off his legs and onto the hot leather seat next to him, ensuring he's watching my every move. I slip out of my shoes, then peel my leggings and underwear down. "Well, hate to break it to you"—I glance over at him, and his breath is caught in his chest, making me feel so damn attractive—"but I think it's gonna be *me* who's fucking you."

Jake heaves a grunt, but the playfulness is apparent despite his show. "Alex, you really should loosen these."

"Not gonna happen. You said you wanted me in charge, and this is it." A devilish grin stretches my lips as I grab a little bottle from the front console.

"I said it kinda scares me." He weakly fights against the homemade restraints, but he's on board.

"If you don't stop pulling at them, *this* won't happen."

His hands go slack.

Okay, this next part isn't sexy, but can we real talk for a minute? We were just outside, touching all kinds of things. Germs are everywhere, and I cannot go through with my plan without the following.

Jake's nose wrinkles. "What are you doing?"

"Sorry." I make a face, rubbing gel into my hands before flapping them in the air to dry. "You know I'm crazy with the sanitizer."

He shakes his head, busting out laughing. "Are you serious?"

"Yeah." I shrug. "I'm not gonna finger myself with grimy hands."

Cue that lovely jaw drop.

"Fuck…"

Yup.

"… me."

"I will," I respond, straddling his legs once more on bent knees.

He swallows loud, Adam's apple bobbing, nodding excitedly. His eyes are glued to my hands at this point.

I slide down so my center hovers barely an inch above his solid cock, standing at, and impatiently awaiting, attention. Gripping his shoulder, I balance myself, and slither my hand between my breasts, over my stomach, stopping right at my most sensitive spot. Fuck it, let's call it what it is—I'm about to hit the clit. And Jake's eyes are about to pop out of his skull.

He bites his bottom lip so hard the pink drains from it, while I gather my arousal, already keyed up and dying for a release.

Jake studies my actions like they're final-exam material—circling, easing in and out, nowhere near the skill set he has, but him watching coaxes that quiver. He whimpers, and I love it. I tease my soaked finger over the outline of his lips, and he captures it with his teeth then sucks every bit of my wetness, making my legs tremble.

Oh, fuck… this is next level.

I stroke his thickness, dragging out a groan with every pull, then release him before sliding my finger inside me, pulsing against my palm. All kinds of primal sounds build in his throat.

"This is so hot," Jake pants.

Each time my finger plunges inside, I swear his dick twitches. And each time I take it out, I lower myself so close to him, grazing that glorious ridge, before lifting again.

"Alex." He shoots me a stern look. "Your payback is gonna be so bad."

"Can't wait."

After about a minute or so of this fingering, teasing, and grinding the underside of his cock, I decide it's been long enough. And truth be told, he does a significantly better job at getting me off using his hands than I do myself. Now if I add in a bedroom power tool… well, that's another story.

Anyway, on with the show.

I position myself over him then sink down until he bottoms out inside me. My fingers twist in his hair, tugging at the roots. He fixates, watching, entranced by our bodies joining. The spasms and shivers start, coiling with that blinding sensation.

I ride him, rocking, thrusting, and load him up with lip-licking kisses then amp up the feverish pace, desperately chasing that thrill, that burst of incredible energy.

I'm proud of myself. Car sex isn't as easy as it seems. Maybe it'd be easier if he wasn't tied up? Oh well, here we are.

"Alex," he moans, and every growl and sound spurs me to wind faster, to take him deeper.

I press my lips to his, my tongue prying them apart. "Mm-hmm. You feel so good," I say, giving him what he wants. "I love your cock inside me." My words make him tremble beneath me.

The next minute goes like this… me telling him how much I love riding his dick, Jake saying how there's no better pussy than mine. You know, the normal professions of passion and lust at the other's anatomy.

I'm all for the dirty talk. It's not something we ever did a lot of before, but he can tell me how much he loves anything of mine *all day.*

I know he's frustrated, only because he's a toucher, and it's gotta be killing him not to be able to right now. Don't get me wrong, I'm pretty sure he'll finish, but I'm completely aware, minus the fingering myself, this may not have been his dream scenario. Well, at least we can say we did it. And if I'm gonna be fully honest, I can't wait for his payback.

After a few more minutes of grinding over him, the heat of his release fills me with satisfaction, along with the telltale groan that accompanies it.

I'm gonna be honest about another thing—I didn't have an orgasm. It just doesn't happen every single time, not in real life, at least for me. But I know he's good for it.

I quickly throw on my clothes before exiting the car, leaving Jake a naked, panting hot mess, still tied up in the back seat. I jump in the front with a wicked laugh then jam the keys into the ignition, turning the engine over.

"Alex," he says, tone laced with concern. "What are you doing?"

Shifting the car into reverse, I grin back at him.

"Alex!" My name comes out far more demanding this time.

"Just fuckin' with ya," I say with a wink as I put the car into park. I climb through the middle to the back seat and release the material from each wrist, freeing Jake's arms.

"Ow," he mutters, shaking them out. "That wasn't comfortable."

Before I can apologize—though I'm not truly sorry, because it was fun—his palms find my hips, flinging me onto the seat. He flips me to my front and pins me down, chest to my back.

I know… what? Like I said, it's a large vehicle and the back seat is spacious. When you have all the kids, you gotta have all the room.

Jake slides down my body, tugging my leggings with him, pressing against the small of my back to keep me face down. I yelp the second his teeth bite into the flesh of my ass cheek—not too crazy; just a nip—hand coasting between my legs and delivering a resounding slap that makes me glitch.

"Now it's my turn."

Is he seriously ready again already?

He lines up with my entrance, teasing over me. A strangled, needy wail rises from my chest. And right before he slams inside me, the sounds of gravel kicking up beneath tires stops his movements. Another car pulls into the small parking lot.

Right next to us.

He smacks my ass with an irritated grunt. "Your day will come."

Low-key excited.

We laugh the entire drive to our house, falling in line so easily and comfortably, making it back with time to spare before the kids get home from school.

Shit… did I say *our* house? I guess I did.

We exchange hidden smiles and laughs to jokes that'll always be inside, before I head to the kitchen, shuffling through the fridge to find something for dinner.

I think about his eyes, and how I never want to look into any other eyes and do the hot, sometimes silly, occasionally filthy acts I do with him. Then I think about his heart, and my name forever inscribed over it, and I don't want that to go anywhere either.

"Alexandra," Jake says from behind me, and my nose crinkles at his unusual full-naming.

I turn to see him slowly drop to one knee, right here in the middle of the kitchen floor.

"What are you doing?" I blink rapidly as he clutches my hand, feeling kinda nervous.

"I love you. I love you so much that every second without you was more painful than anything I could've imagined. Forever is meant for us."

I nod, and tears touch both our eyes.

"I want…" He gets choked up, and so do I. "Please let me have forever with you. I promise to never hurt you again." He sighs, staring at my hand. My *left* hand.

I watch as his thumb slides over my bare finger, my heart hammering against my rib cage, my mouth falling open.

"Will you stay married to me? Will you put your rings back on?"

44. GOOD RIDDANCE (TIME OF YOUR LIFE)

The week flies by. Don't they always? I swear, the older I get, the faster time goes. Seriously, I bitch and moan about every single Monday, because they do particularly suck.

But Fridays roll around at lightning speed, and here we are—let us rejoice. I leave work a bit early and head over to Jake's place. It's his day.

Oh, that's right… Jake.

Sorry, can't always be sketchy fingerings and dates and fucking. Sometimes I wish it could, but that's not our current life.

Anyway, guess you're wondering how the whole in-the-kitchen, down-on-the-knee thing went?

Totally forgot about it.

Well… sad to say, the rings are *not* back on my finger. I just couldn't do it. I mean I physically couldn't. I've lost some weight, and those suckers slid right off. They're being resized.

Of course I said yes—are you kidding me? How could I not? He's the entire package, and truth be told, I'm currently having the time of my life.

We've got a couple more days of the kids being in school till summer break, and I'm not trying to change up all the transportation and schedule stuff right now. It's a pain in the ass.

Jake has his place until September. We figured *that* has its benefits, but I told him to confiscate the spare keys. The last thing we need is Brynn coming to hang out here. Could you imagine having access to an occasionally vacant house at sixteen? Don't get me started.

I step inside the townhome, rest against the door once it's shut, and take a breath, tired from the workday. Sounds of mayhem drift down from upstairs—the standard noises and hustling around when you're attempting to wrangle the kids to go somewhere. It's way easier now that they're older and more dependent. But still…

Shit. Show.

I say hi to the three of our four bopping down the stairs then walk into the living room, frowning at Jake.

"What's wrong?" I ask, taking in the spent expression on his face. His hair is a mess, and he's still wearing his black suit pants, the sleeves of his white dress shirt rolled to the elbows.

He musters a smile when his eyes land on me. "Hey, beautiful. Nothing. I'm good now." He presses a rough and extended kiss against my lips.

"Oh, okay. Hi to you too." With my palms to his chest, I pull back, studying him and the pants he's clutching. Thin lines crease the outer corners of his eyes, providing evidence of his weariness. I get it.

He heaves a sigh. "Are you sure we have to go to this thing?"

Ugh, yes, the worst. A school function.

"Sadly, we do. Already rsvp'd." I grab the pants from him. They're Roo's. "She's having a meltdown?"

"Yeah, I tried to make her wear something with buttons." Jake's hand runs through his hair, before scrubbing down his face.

"Buttons?" I gasp. "How could you?"

"I know, I'm evil."

I pat his chest, and a grin splits my lips before I lean to his ear. "Go change into something more comfortable. It'll make it easier for me to strip you later." Laughing, I head for the stairs. "I got this."

So, let's take a minute to not only appreciate the kids that have their typical quirks, and talk about the ones who have something more. Sensory issues are a real thing, and they're a *real* pain in the ass.

Roo could have a freak-out at any given moment. Socks too tight, shirt too itchy, and in this instance… buttons. It's ups and downs, and ebbs and flows all the time with these remarkable babes. They can't control it, but what *we* can control is how we react to it, how much play we give it.

"Ruby?" I knock softly then push open her bedroom door. She's sitting on the floor, knees hugged to her chest, dressed in pajama bottoms and a mismatched top. "Hey, kiddo." Her dark brown hair sticks out in all directions, and she stares at the wall.

I bend down to her, and she automatically clasps her arms around my neck, brown eyes finally shifting to peer at me. There's so much more going on behind them than she can handle.

I sigh when she signs *Mom* with a small hand. "Why won't you say it, you little stinker?"

After lowering myself to the carpet, I tickle her stomach till she's wiggling around on the floor. A cute and highly contagious giggle erupts from her, filling the room. "One day…" I wink at her. "One day you're gonna say it. I can feel it."

Roo sits up, offering a slight raise of her shoulder before going full koala on me. "Love you," she says in a tiny voice, barely a whisper.

It's not what I want, but I'll take what I can get.

The pants are a losing battle. Once she makes up her mind about something, she digs in—and I mean digs.

No clue where her stubbornness comes from.

Here's the thing, if it's gonna be a fight, and she'd rather wear the stupid pajama bottoms out in public… I say go for it. Sometimes you gotta pick your battles, and this one isn't it. I do have to hold her down to brush through her tangled bob, constantly reminding her this was something she wanted to go to.

Only twenty minutes late, I've ditched my scrubs, everyone's secured in the car, and we're off to a glorious school function. Because what says an outstanding time like going to an indoor trampoline park on a Friday night? How the mighty have fallen. Oh well, the kids'll eat this up—they love that open-warehouse, bounce-fest. It's not easy to find something that piques all of their interests.

"I can't believe you let her wear that," Jake says as we sit at one of the tables, observing a swarm of children literally bouncing off the walls.

"You wanna go another round with her?" My eyebrows hitch.

With a quick shake of his head, he squeezes my thigh.

"People will stare regardless," I say. They always do.

While we're on this topic, let's keep going.

People do stare from time to time. It's hard not to, I understand. Roo looks like a neurotypical child. But when kids try to talk to her, sometimes she doesn't respond. When she gets excited, her hands flap wildly, or she makes repetitive movements and talks to herself. And with all of that going on, if she's most comfortable wearing pajamas out, you do you.

You know what's important? As in, extremely? Speaking to your own children about it. Educating them and encouraging them to be the ones who make a difference. To sit with a child who's alone at the lunch table, or help an opposing team member off the ground, or simply be the reason someone smiles. An ounce of compassion. That's what these kids *truly* need to learn about. These are the qualities that make up genuine character.

I'm proud to say—and no, not always; they're kids, for Christ's sake—mine have that.

There's something even more to be said for Brynn, Jordan, and Will. I'm sure it's incredibly difficult to be the sibling of a child with disabilities. To always feel like they have to give up for her. I don't want to say sacrifice, though that's ultimately what it is.

They do it though, every day, no questions asked.

We do our best to make sure we give them their fair share of attention. But I know Roo's always gotten the most. That's how it rolls. With all those happenings and her medical issues, she needs more from us. It was harder when they were younger, though they seem to get it.

And while I know she bugs the living daylights outta them sometimes, especially the older two, they've got her back. I always said I can mess with my brother or sister as much as I want, but sure as shit, nobody else can.

So I'm sitting here, a smidge nervous, on the bench of some bright-blue picnic-table thing, watching a group of girls. They're whispering into each other's ears, their eyes darting to Roo. She's living her best life, bouncing away on one of the various trampoline squares.

I know Jake sees it too. His forearm flexes behind me, fingers gripping my shoulder. My back stiffens, and I'm trying to gauge what the next move is.

Looking around the open building, I have eyes on all three of our other kids, the rest of her army of protectors, already fully conscious of the situation. They don't stray too far from her—they're beyond aware that their sister can sadly be a target to some.

Jordan bounces her way across with purpose, booking it towards Roo, prepared to stop the bullying or taunting before it happens.

Again, not an uncommon thing.

One of the little redheaded girls breaks off from the group, jumping towards Roo, a mischievous smile crossing her lips. I stand from the bench, prepared to hop my ass in there and save her from the words of some shitty kid, but Jake grabs a hold of my back jeans pocket, keeping me in place.

"Wait," he says calmly, knowing for damn sure I'm ready to pounce.

Jordan won't make it over in time. The girl is already up to Ruby, hands cupped and whispering something in her ear. Brynn, Jordan, and Will make their way over as fast as they can.

I take a step forward, and Jake tugs me back to sit on the bench. "What the fuck?" I whisper, teeth bared, itching to mash and gnash.

His lips begin to curve, producing a massive grin that reaches all the way up to his eyes, and he motions his chin to the girls.

I look up, just in time to see the redhead grab one of Roo's hands and jump with her, turning back to the group of vultures and flipping them the bird, her tongue sticking out.

A nervous laugh comes from the other side of me. A man, about mid-thirties, walks up to us, aware of the show.

"Micah," Jake greets him, standing and delivering one of those weird fist bumps to some guy I've never seen before in my life.

"Hey, Jake," he says before veering his attention to me. He's handsome, dressed in a suit—he obviously made a dash to get here from work—with thick dark-blonde hair, styled neatly, and kind gray eyes. He also got the stubble memo.

I get to my feet, fixating and astonished at the sight—Roo is actually engaged and playing with another child.

"Oh, sorry. Micah, Alex. Alex, Micah." Jake makes the introduction and pulls my appreciation from one of those moments that makes your heart swell.

He extends a hand and gives mine a firm shake. I'm still in awe of the entire *almost* shitty situation turned amazing.

"I'm Jake's neighbor," he says, cautiously smiling. "Sorry, that's my daughter out there with Roo. She loves her so much. Unfortunately, she has a habit of flipping people off."

Before I even know what I'm doing, my arms crash around him, and I'm hugging this total stranger.

"Oh my God. I'm so sorry." I pull back, dabbing beneath my eyes. Jake chuckles next to me, but he understands. "It's just that most kids wouldn't do that for her."

"Yeah…" He flashes a smile. "That's because a lot of parents let their kids be assholes."

I love this guy.

We spend the rest of the time shooting the breeze. Micah moved here recently with his two girls, a street over from Jake. He's got one of those infectious personalities and a pleasant demeanor that makes you wanna know him.

And solely for his daughter's significant act of kindness and acceptance, I'm already a fan.

45. CANDY SHOP

The school outing was much better than I expected. The kids are thoroughly worn out, so that's a win. Plus, Roo had a fantastic time. Seeing another child who's not related genuinely wanting to interact with her made my heart full.

We get back to the townhouse a smidge after nine, Will and Roo both passed out in the back seat. Brynn is having a conniption because Jake shut her down, refusing to allow her flavor of the month to stop over.

Some kid named Slade—sounds shady to me. Not even sure why she brought it up to her dad; he's a resounding *no* with the boyfriend thing. I constantly remind him she's only one year younger than we were when we first met.

Pretty sure that's what he's most worried about.

I think she was hoping I'd be enough of a distraction that she could go out, or at least have him come by. I keep my mouth shut and allow him to make the judgment call this time. That stuff almost *always* lands on me, so it's nice to have a break.

The kids are staying here at Jake's tonight. It's easier with the little ones already asleep.

In fact, we're all staying.

But first, I've gotta run home and check on the poor, neglected dogs. They totally aren't—Sarah, across the street, works from home and lets them out for me often. She's been immensely helpful and loves the pups. Her husband is allergic, so I think she enjoys the chance to play dog owner.

I don't want her to feel as if she's doing it all the time though, so I texted earlier, letting her know I'd be home for the bedtime run. Jake's landlord has a strict, no-pet policy, and they're huge, sheddy, retrievers—can't hide 'em.

We carry Will and Roo up to their beds. Jordan's already submerged in social-media land, making music videos or whatever. Brynn stormed off, currently mad at the world. Well, mostly Jake.

"Be back," I call from the front door, after getting everyone settled, then head out to my car.

The passenger side flings open, and Jake climbs in before I even get the keys into the ignition.

"What're you doing?" I give him a sideways glance, quirking a brow.

"Just thought I'd ride along with you." He shrugs, doing a poor job of masking some sort of scheming grin. He plucks a wrapper from a lollipop, left over from the excessive amount of candy the kids ate tonight, and pops it in his mouth. "Told Brynn she can have Slater over tomorrow if she babysits for a few."

"Slade."

"Whatever."

We get to my house, our house, the main house, after a quick two-minute drive. Cal and Ripley go supreme batshit, mauling Jake. They're forever happy when any of us return from anywhere.

My cell buzzes amidst the commotion—Mom. I haven't called her this week—I picked up some extra hours. Dad's been doing just fine, minus some hefty bitching about his low-salt diet. He gets what it's about. They've been booking the trips and seizing the day. Tough to believe that was four months ago. Anyway, with the lack of me initiating communication, she's likely perturbed.

"Hi, Mom," I answer, opening the door to let the dogs stampede outside.

"Alexandra," she says in a sharp, snippy tone.

Ugh, here we go.

"Sorry, we just got back from a school function for the kids." I feel like I always have to explain myself to her. I try to call regularly, but it's hard with the kids, work, and all the extracurricular shit.

I text her every chance I get, even if it's random. But she's old school—prefers an actual verbal conversation.

Jake hops up onto the kitchen counter, swinging his legs back and forth, heels clacking against the cabinets, still at it with the lollipop. The stick hangs from the corner of his lips, and he tosses a devious look my way.

"Stop," I mouth to him.

He lifts his hands then shrugs before letting a smirk fully take over. Mischievous eyes slowly rake up and down my frame.

Yeah, I'm sure it's a turn-on watching me sift through a stack of mail. I scrunch my nose, head shaking at him. He's up to something.

"Did you hear me?"

"Yes, I mean… no. Sorry, Mom." I shoot Jake a look. "Stop. It," I mutter through my teeth, covering the speaker.

He feigns innocence, throwing his arms to the sides. Well aware that he has at least some of my divided attention, he inspects the lollipop before his eyes flit to mine. He licks it, kind of suggestively. Not how I might suggestively lick it—not that I would do that; okay, I would—but sticking out his flattened tongue, dragging it over the hard candy then circling when he reaches the top.

I don't know—he's weird.

His white tee clings to his chest, leaving little to the imagination, hugging each defined muscle, offering shadows of the dark ink underneath. His damn hazel stare follows me around the room, eye-fucking me or something. Honestly, he's making it super difficult to concentrate on my mom, who's about to go off the passive-aggressive rails if I don't start actively conversing.

"Do you still need me to watch the kids next Friday night?" she asks, underlying irritation in her voice. She can tell I'm distracted.

"Oh, yes. Is that okay?" I swing my head away from Jake, hoping he didn't overhear. His birthday is coming up, and I wanna surprise him.

I'm shuffling around the kitchen, putting away all the random crap from the week. You know, no matter how hard you try, it's always messy. All of it. The kitchen, the hair, the life.

Jake removes his hat and places it on the countertop next to him, smoothing back his hair. His eyes stay on me, and he wiggles a finger, motioning for me to come hither or some strange nonsense.

I shake my head yet again with a scowl. Hell no, he's up to no good. But damn if he doesn't look sexy right now, arms stretched behind him, palms flat, leaning back.

"Maybe the following weekend you can all come visit?"

"Sure, Mom. We'd love to."

Jake catches me sneaking a peek. He's making it difficult not to. He tugs the bottom front of his shirt, lifts it over his head, then tosses it at me.

Apparently, that's a thing now.

"What are you doing?" I grit the words out, my hand over the phone. A raised brow and stock Jake smirk are in effect. He's just chilling on the counter, shirtless—no big. Actually, it's not totally outta the ordinary. He rotates the stick between his thumb and forefinger, his pointed tongue circling over the lollipop.

A breathy laugh leaves my nostrils and I roll my eyes, making an O with my touching fingertips. He snickers. In case you didn't get that, I'm telling him to jerk off.

"Oh… umm… Dad and I are getting ready to watch a movie," my poor mom responds to the question that wasn't intended for her.

"That's nice. What movie?"

I hand Jake his shirt, and he grabs my arm, yanking me to him while his legs trap me, winding around my back. I squirm, trying to free myself, but his calf muscles flex, increasing their hold on me and gaining him a death glare. He knows my mom is a talker. Now that she's got me on the phone, it'll be damn near impossible to pull the plug on this convo.

I have no idea what she's saying. Jake grabs my shoulders and turns me away from him, still holding me prisoner with his legs. Large palms massage over my arms, up to my neck then down my spine.

This is innocent enough.

When he bends forward, the heat from his body radiates through me, and his lips graze my ear—the one that doesn't have a phone up to it. Reaching his hand around, he tries to force the lollipop into my mouth, and I promptly smack it away.

"Ew! No, stop." I huff at him. He shakes with quiet laughter.

"Have you seen it already?" Mom asks. "It got excellent reviews."

I have no clue what movie she's talking about.

"Oh, no. Sorry." I try to escape from Jake's clutches, with no luck. His legs hook around each of mine, feet pressing flat against the cabinet between my thighs, slowly spreading them and pinning my lower body.

His strong and very opportunistic hands travel from my shoulders. The side of his finger skims between my breasts, over my shirt, heading south.

"How're things with you and Jake?"

"Fine." I swallow a gasp as he pops my button and lowers my zipper, palm drifting beneath my underwear. A louder than intended sigh slips out as his massage skills get put to further use—pressing, rubbing, numbing my mind.

"That's good. You know we only want the best for you."

"Yeah," I murmur.

A beckoning finger teases my center, and my spine arches, causing me to drop back into him. His hand glides up and down, making my knees go weak. A deep growl vibrates from him as he slides through my wetness. His other arm hooks across my chest, smashing me against him, while hot, heavy breaths tickle my earlobe.

Strength-wise, I'm no match. He's solid.

Jake continues to stroke inside me, curling just right, hitting the spot that drags a strangled whimper from my throat, reminding me that I'm on the phone... *with my mother!*

"Mom." My voice comes out in an ungodly high pitch, extra shaky. "Can I call you back?"

"Sure. Everything okay?"

"Mm-hmm," I barely squeak.

He slips another finger in while his thumb gives the external assist. I pinch my eyes shut, biting my bottom lip.

Swear to God, my hips are moving involuntarily at this point.

"Dad wants to say hi. Love you, honey."

Before I can respond or object, Jake unravels his legs, freeing me. I take a quick step forward, needing to get away from him and this whackass fingerbang phone conversation.

He jumps off the counter then tears at my jeans, pulling them down.

I almost faceplant from my bound ankles. "What the hell?" I sneer at him, jaw tensing. Though I'll admit, that's not the only thing tensing.

He moves to the front of me with a seductive grin, thick lashes curled over his ridiculously sensual irises. Grabbing my cell, he hits the speaker button and slides it across the counter, out of reach.

"Oh, no you don't!"

"Payback," Jake whispers over my lips. The faint scent of bubblegum fills my nostrils from the fucking lollipop.

Roughly gripping my waist, he backs me up, caging me against the countertop, then gyrates his naked torso into my body like this is a strip club.

What the—

"Hi, sweetie." My dad's cheery voice fills the room.

Oh my God!

"Hi Dad, how's it go—" My breath hitches as Jake loops a finger around the crotch of my panties, ripping them down and dropping to his knees.

In the kitchen.

Oh, the irony right now. Back in the kitchen, on his knees. But this is *not* sweet and innocent.

"You there?"

"Mm-hmm." I stifle a groan, my mouth falling open. He pulls my jeans and panties off one leg, kissing from ankle to thigh. Fast fingers plunge inside me. The tip of his tongue darts straight to my clit and scribes the alphabet in a billion different languages, his stubble hitting all the right places.

I stretch my arm, reaching for the phone. It's *way* too far. Jake kiboshes my feeble efforts with a commanding grip while he continues spreading me with his tongue, sucking with his lips, flickering with his fingers.

"What's new with you, kiddo?" my dad asks.

I glance down to see sinister eyes peering up at me, gleaming with amusement. He licks the apex of each thigh before devouring me, alternating his movements, drawing a breathy whimper from me that can't be stopped.

"N-N-Nothing?" I stammer.

Holy Jesus. My dad is talking and I have no clue what he's saying.

My hips involuntarily roll over Jake, over his mouth. This fucking fucker. I think my lip may fall off at this rate, given how hard I'm biting into it. The budding sensation twists in the pit of my stomach, and the heat from his precise plunges obliterates thoughts, or words, or phone calls. This feels amazing.

But... shit!

"You there, Alex?"

"Yeah, Dad. Can I call you back?" I speed talk, struggling to clear my throat or cough. Anything to cover up my voice, which sounds all kinds of whacked out.

Jake lowers himself further down to the ground, so he's sitting back on his heels. He digs his fingers into my ass cheek, guiding me over him, resulting in buckling knees. They find stability on his shoulders, and shivers throttle up my spine with every languid lap of his tongue. A fair amount of my weight is on this guy's face. Fuck my life right now.

"Please call your mother more."

"I will." My voice is shrill and panty and out of control.

He slams a third finger in, and the freefall begins—I'm about to combust when he latches on to my clit, sucking so hard, heat charges up my neck.

I'm literally grinding into him. This is a fucking mustache ride. I don't know what else to call it.

One of my hands searches for the edge of the counter, bracing myself, or just trying to stay upright, or stop myself from screaming. I *cannot* subject my parents to that. I'm actually dying right now. My other hand is guiding his head—what am I doing?—adding fuel to his calculated movements, my fingers threading in Jake's hair, seriously about to rip it out.

Clenching my teeth… Who am I kidding? I'm clenching everything. The build-up is so extreme, I'm saying yes to everything. I mean it.

Per the norm, he doesn't deviate from eye contact, gaining definite enjoyment from my scowls and jaw-dropping muted moans. This is pain and pleasure on a whole new level.

Also, it's pretty messed up.

"I'll call her tomorrow. Love you, mmm, bye!" I drop my head back, still fighting against my climax as hard as humanly possible. Just waiting for the tone to signal they've hung up.

"Love you too. Bye."

I tighten my hold on his hair, twisting and pulling, causing quiet groans to vibrate from Jake's throat. They ripple through my core, making all the blood in my body rush somewhere, because it's not in my brain anymore.

"How do you turn this thing off?" My dad's voice echoes from the speaker.

Kill me. I'm gonna kill Jake!

He thrusts his fingers, pumping in and out and smacking his knuckles into me. The slightly sloppy sounds dance in my head and muddle everything into nothing. My legs are liquified. As soon as that tone sounds out, signifying they've finally hung up, he slips another finger in—further back.

I know… holy hell, but we went over this.

This time it's not a shocker. This time it's a rocker!

I come totally unraveled. Like serious, hard-core orgasm. On Jake's face. Simultaneously I scream and curse his name, while blasts of euphoria spark and burst and explode every cell in my body. He licks and sucks until I'm gloriously drained.

Jake goes to stand, and I slump over his back. His forearm wraps around my upper thighs, and my lifeless body hangs over him.

Thoughts? Never heard of them.

Told you, I totally died with that one.

"I'm gonna kill you." My threat is empty and falls from my debilitated mouth with no resolve whatsoever.

"I bet," he replies, getting to his feet with me hoisted over his shoulder. A sharp smack stings my ass, barely drawing a vocal reaction. He chuckles with triumph. "Wasn't exactly T-shirt restraints, but I'd say we're even."

And while I'm not completely sure how I feel about the whole tonsils-deep phone conversation that just happened… I can *definitely* say it was a first.

46. LOVE SONG

It's all been going so well, what could ever happen?

Okay, fuck that. Don't you hate when people say something is going great? It's as if they're inadvertently willing the universe to mess things up. So I'm not even trying to think about it right now, simply living in the moment, or moments, and taking it day by day.

At work, if someone dares to mention how eerily quiet it is, you can guarantee it'll award them the shittiest glares ever. It will also gain them all the grunt work when the wheels eventually fall off. Because let's face it— they always do.

Right now, stuff with Jake and me seems so perfect, easy, fun, and amazing. That's because it feels new again. But *nothing* is perfect.

I used to hate it when people would *ooh* and *ahh* at our story. They thought it was sweet and rare that we were still together after all these years. I guess it's uncommon these days. But our story is so far from perfect.

I don't wanna be a pessimist. Self-proclaimed realist here, remember? I'm not saying I think Jake will cheat again, though I can't say I completely trust him. We're getting there, but it's a work in progress. And I can't say I won't fuck something up—track records don't lie. 'Cause if I'm being truthful, I already see the little habits coming back. The monotonous shit I have to nag about, like the clothes on the floor, directly next to the damn laundry basket, because that makes sense.

It's stuff that really isn't a big deal. But when you're constantly keeping after someone about it, especially a grown-ass adult, it's annoying. I reprimand him, and he apologizes, promises not to do it again, but I'm not his mom, and I shouldn't have to feel like it.

Sorry to bitch and rant. But as flawless and great as he may seem to everyone else, even me at times, Jake can be a pain in the ass.

Me too though.

Is he genuinely, deep down, a good guy? Yes. A great father, even if he gives in way too easily? Of course. A beast in the bedroom and currently other places? You fucking bet. But here's the deal. I sense normalcy creeping back in. And to be honest, I'm scared that we'll fall into that vicious cycle again.

Anyway, I'm trying not to dwell on that shit. It's all a work in progress, right?

I think that's an important subject—the work in progress. That's life. That's every single issue that happens in life. None of us are ever complete and innocent throughout. It's the same with relationships—they ebb and flow. One minute you're lost in a spine-tingling moment, getting off in the middle of your kitchen. The next you're bickering about the way the kids are disciplined, about working, about money. Real life just isn't a fairytale. And honestly, it's ugly half the time.

I guess the biggest thing is being able to stick it out through the ugly. Being able to see beyond throwing in the towel and taking the easy route. Sometimes it's probably simpler to walk away than to live with the pain day in and out.

After his phone took a swim, Jake's been much better about the texting. He had to get a new one, because I'm pretty sure it's almost impossible to survive without a cell these days. But anyway, he hasn't been on it as much. I guess telling him how I felt about it made him realize. Isn't that amazing? A little bit of communication can go a long-ass way.

Who knew?

Yeah, I'm kidding. Obviously, communication is key. But it's easier said than done. It's kinda tough to put it out there, especially if you know you might sound off your rocker.

Once again, the week flew by. We ended up spending every night together, and the kids are all happy. But here's what I've noticed since we've been back at this thing full-time: Old habits really do die hard.

As early as Monday, Jake was working late, not checking in, assuming I'd be there with the kids. Every day this week he's worked late, coming home each evening worn out. Understandable—adulting takes it out of you, and it's not like I'm not exhausted myself.

Anyway, we're back to him being super lax, goofing around while I'm the enforcer, giving Roo her iPad when she threw a fit, so I had to be the one to lay down the law. Unacceptable behavior does not earn a reward. She might not be the same as other children, but she certainly understands discipline and lack thereof.

Jake sits there, oblivious, letting the kids scream for me to help them, with the most trivial of things, when he's right next to them.

Of course, when I say something about it, he jumps in. But why do I have to say anything, like he doesn't hear them?

When it's only us, when we're alone, it's fun and easy. Throw the kids into the mix and that levels it up.

Work in progress, work in progress.

Moving on.

I have everything set up with my mom to come stay with the kids. She'll be here tomorrow, after school, and Annie's on deck in case anyone needs anything before that.

We never went on trips or did stuff, just us two. We should have. I think it's super important to take time out to be a couple. But the rat race is real. I know I'm on repeat with this, but life catches you up. Plus, it's a bit terrifying to go anywhere when your kid has a medical condition.

But I gotta start putting more faith into the people that surround me. It's not that I don't trust them. Regarding Roo, I'm sort of a control freak. It happens when much of your life is devoted to advocating for them. Shit… there isn't much I *can* control with her, so I feel like going away is abandoning her. What if something happens? What if I'm not there to stop it?

You say you're gonna do the things, take the trip, the bucket list gets full. How many times are there excuses? No money, no time off, no babysitter. But sometimes, you just gotta make it happen, and that's what I'm trying to do here.

Jake has *zero* clue what I'm up to, which makes it all the more exciting. I told him to clear his schedule Friday, and that was it. I've never surprised him with anything like this before. The last time we took a random trip somewhere, spur of the moment, was close to seventeen years ago.

Vegas.

Isn't that sad? I mean, we've gone away with the kids. The itinerary was carefully planned, and time was taken to ensure everything was in place. I griped for days leading up to it about having to pack and clean the house. Then I spent most of each vacation tidying up after everyone, making it feel as if I was still at home.

This time, it's only Jake and me. Another first—look at us go. I told him we're leaving in the morning and staying overnight, and I'd get all his stuff together. I laughed when he asked how I'd know what he'd need.

Please.

I'm trying not to let the shit that's already annoying me put a damper on these plans We'll have a few hours in the car, and I figure we can talk it out then.

Friday morning rolls around, the kids are off to school, and bags are locked and loaded. Jake's been on me, begging to spill where we're going, and I've been on my own damn self, trying to remember not to sweat the small stuff. I know I do things that annoy him too. I mean, isn't marriage all about two people bugging the living piss out of each other for the rest of their lives? I saw it on one of those wooden quote decorative things.

Feels like it at times though.

I wish it was only ever relaxed and fun.

Jake refuses my request for him to wear a blindfold once we get in the car. I can't say I blame him. Didn't suspect he'd cooperate with that one.

We talk about the stuff bothering me. Well, I talk, but he listens, promising to be better with it. I tell him I don't wanna nag, but if he'd just do shit the first time, I wouldn't have to.

It's so easy.

I say how I'm feeling, put it out there, and *boom*. Simple as that.

The fact he's realized where we're heading becomes apparent in his wide smile after an hour of me driving.

"Damn," Jake says, seeing the signs for the bridge. "We're really going back there, huh?" He squeezes my thigh then splays his fingers because… he's seriously always horny.

"Yup."

Sunglasses hide his eyes, but the full cheese is happening. I know he's thinking the same thing I am.

Back to the beach, back to the night we'll always remember. Back to the beginning.

However, no urinating outdoors this time.

We empty the car, toting our bags up the stairs to the room I've rented for the night. The distinct salty air hits my nose, instantly making me relax. It's a small efficiency, with one bedroom and bathroom, overlooking the vast Atlantic. Beachfront. What more do we need?

"Wanna get our suits on?" I ask after everything's unpacked from my bag. Well, almost everything.

Jake's sitting out on the balcony, staring at the water, a serene expression on his face—already shirtless, sporting the backwards hat that causes my salivary glands to work overtime. His cell buzzes on the dresser inside. My eyes drift.

It's Kelsey.

"Here." I hand him the phone with a sigh.

He tosses it onto the metal table like he couldn't care less, and his arm, already warm from the sun, fastens around me, pulling me to his lap. The tips of his fingers smooth wisps of hair that have escaped from my mom bun, tucking them behind my ears.

Jake inhales a savoring breath, his eyes searching mine, his thumb capturing my jaw. "I should have brought you here, Alex." He frowns and glances away briefly. "I should have planned a trip. Should have made more of an—"

"You did," I interrupt him, thinking about his attempt to surprise me, to whisk us away to the harbor, our honeymoon place. How that all got totally derailed because I thought he was talking to a woman, which he was—his mom. And then the other kiss, and the fight. It seems like a lifetime ago. "We're here now." I cuddle into him.

We can't go back. We can't continue trying to keep score and wishing things from the past would be different. It's hard, though, to retrain your mind, to not dig into the past and use it against yourself. Or someone else.

"There's a lot of things I would do different, ya know?" Jake's lips pitch to the side. He seems so far away right now; I guess caught up in the memories of this place.

"Me too. But a lot of things I honestly wouldn't change."

And I wouldn't. I know I was just complaining about the stupid stuff he does that bugs me. Sorry for the vent. But in this moment, sitting here with him, getting this glimpse of our early life before the chaos, before shit got complicated, it makes me remember to not sweat the petty things.

And never pet the sweaty—my jokes will be forever cringe.

We sit outside for a while, arms tangled around each other, not speaking a word. The sounds of the ocean are our playlist, and we bask in the breeze, enjoying the feeling of no responsibilities.

This place, for us, is the definition of nostalgia.

"Good birthday surprise?" I ask, breathing him in. The mint, the spice, the salty air. It seriously takes me back to *that* night.

"Best one yet," he replies, crushing me into him and pressing a kiss to my forehead. Dark brows dance above his eyes, and the serious expression subsides. Playful Jake is back.

"So… beach? Bathing suits?"

"Sure," he murmurs into my ear, disarming me via *that* spot. He bucks his hips beneath me. "But how 'bout birthday suits first?"

47. SEMI-CHARMED LIFE

So birthday suits… yeah, that was fun. Would hate to bore you with the details.

Oh please, like I'm one to kiss and *not* tell. Let's just say there was more of the same. We may or may not have made it known to the people in the next room that they'd be in for a noisy twenty-four hours.

Sorry 'bout that.

What can I say? You tend to let loose when you're consistently forced to keep it quiet, sparing your kids from the groany moans. If they heard, they'd investigate, as they always do. And we don't need any more of that.

It only seemed appropriate, with his birthday coming up, that a little suck and blow was in order. I'm *not* talking about the game—we're grown-ass adults.

Put it this way, the fuckery continues. And when you're legit staying on Sixty-ninth Street, it's an obligation. It feels like banging it out is all we do these days, and I'm not hating it. Though, I'm painfully aware we're still covering up some shit feelings with sex. I mean, it's proving to be a gratifying coping mechanism. It won't solve our problems, but I suppose it's a good thing we can't keep our hands off each other. The addiction is real, and it seems to be mutual.

The problem isn't that, because we're okay as far as communication goes right now. The problem is time. We sure as hell can't go back and change the past, though it feels like we harp on it sometimes. If I'd done this, or if I didn't say that. I love when people claim they have no regrets. For real? Well, if so, good for you. I've got an extended list.

And to add to the time thing, we can't skip ahead to the future either. We don't know where we'll be twenty years down the road, or where the cards will fall in the end.

Before I would even entertain stripping down, you know I had to ask Jake what Kelsey was texting about—only I didn't have to. After we sat in that serene silence for a while, he offered it up. Apparently some unimportant work thing—his words, not mine. He doesn't wanna go, and she's been bugging him because Luke's going.

It's tomorrow night.

I told him to go, or I could even see if my mom would stay one more night, so we could go together. He groaned and said to drop it, that it isn't a big deal, and he's *not* interested. End of discussion.

Whatever. If he doesn't want to, and it's not a big thing, I don't get why she's been pestering him about it. But I'm also cool with dropping it… for now.

We eventually make our way out to the beach. We didn't come all this way to stay shacked up in the room, though I wouldn't object.

Sun and my fair skin aren't exactly a match made in heaven, so I lotioned up—high SPF is your friend, ladies. First off, skin cancer is for real. Second, so are wrinkles, and I'm trying to stay ahead of the game with that mess.

Jake is looking extra hot, charcoal swim trunks hanging nice and low on his hips, while his arm drapes around my neck. The V, sculpted in stone and lovely as ever, gains plenty of attention from fellow beachgoers. Some people have no fucking shame. But he's a treat, so I'll let them look. He doesn't pay them any mind, oblivious to the attention on him, in typical Jake fashion.

We sprawl across the blanket I brought, enjoying the nothingness. After a while of relaxing, reading a book, and allowing the ocean to lull me with each wave, Jake jumps up, dusting the sand from his shorts.

"Let's go for a swim."

I shake my head. "Can't," I mumble, nose totally up in my book. "I'm at a good part." I don't know about you, but I can completely lose myself in a story and become attached to the characters. It's actually one of my favorite things.

And, for real, the ocean skeeves me out. You can't see most of the creatures lurking in there. I've tuned in to *Shark Week* way too much to be calm about it. Even when we're at the beach with the kids, I'm on edge, watching them like a hawk the entire time they're in the water, running through all kinds of whacked-out scenarios in my head.

While I'm thinking about *Jaws* and killer bacteria floating around, Jake's arm slides around my waist, lifting me, surfboard style. He doesn't even give me a chance to fix my suit. Can't be going R-rated at a family place.

Well, not till later.

Jordan talked me into this maroon swimsuit. While it's a one-piece, it barely covers my ass, and the neckline plunges ridiculously low. But she told me to rock it, and I'm trying.

"We can do this the easy way or the hard way." Jake plucks the book from my hand, and I whine when he tosses it to the blanket, losing my spot.

He pulls the sunglasses from my face, dropping them to join the hat and shades he already ditched.

"No shot." My attempt to free myself is futile. He stands me up but keeps his grip tight around my waist. "No way I'm going in there willingly." I plant my fists to my sides.

"No problem." With a smirk, he scoops me up again like I'm weightless. One arm snakes around my back, while the other hooks beneath my legs, which are thrashing. It doesn't slow him down, and he sprints straight into the water, out past the breaking waves.

"Take a breath!" he yells over the roaring ocean, a smile tugging his lips.

"Jake, don't!" I don't wanna go in. I hate this kinda shit. My nails sink into the back of his neck, as if it'll do anything.

"Take a breath," he repeats, head dipping down with a reassuring kiss.

"I don't want to. I'm scared."

He studies me, and I think we both realize, at this moment, I'm not talking about the water anymore.

I've been busy getting myself straight. I'm proud of the work I've put in. I'm still winning the mom game, or at least doing the best I can, but I'm scared to let go—*with him*. I'm afraid to completely give in, even though I know most things I can't control.

I've been this way for a long time, afraid to trust too much, afraid of getting hurt. Because when I trusted, that's exactly what happened. Jake was one of the few exceptions to that rule.

But I need to get through this. I gotta start believing that our love is enough, and one day my head won't keep coming back to this shit.

The ocean, for me, is like my life—tides that change at a moment's notice; waves sometimes out of control, other times smooth and even. All of it is *so* unpredictable, and it's scary.

"Just trust me," Jake says with a serious expression, the sun reflecting off the water and swimming in his eyes. "Please, Alex, trust me. It'll be fun. We'll be fine," he all but begs, and it's as if he can see my inner struggle.

After a quick nod, I decide to let go of his neck. Fuck it—it's only water. We both inhale a deep breath, bracing ourselves for the plunge.

* * *

On that fateful night, you know, under the stars, chillin' in the lifeguard chair, young and in love, Jake jumped down after taking one of my earrings, which I thought was extremely weird. But anyway, he asked me for it, and I gave it to him. I think I would have given him anything at that point.

When we finally left in the early morning, I saw our initials carved into the white paint on the wooden chair leg.

Forever branded.

It seems like a silly thing now, defacing property and such. But I promise you, back then, it was high up there with things that made your heart go boom. An act as simple as that is something I'll always remember.

I ran my fingertip over our initials, and Jake whispered *forever* in my ear. He meant it. We had no clue what would happen between then and now.

That's the thing when you're young—you fall so fast and so hard, and this person rotates your world. You can't see how anything would ever outrank them… till you have kids. Then you see how you can love someone else a little more than your spouse, and significantly more than yourself.

* * *

After the dip, the plunge—which wasn't even that bad—we lie on the blanket-covered sand, allowing the hot sun to dry our bodies. Jake stares at me while I finish my book.

Then we do something amazing. We relax and just talk to each other. Not about the kids or our home life but about ourselves. Sharing stuff we don't know about each other anymore. It sounds strange, I'm aware. I had no clue his favorite color is green, because it used to be blue. And he thought mine was black. While it was at some point, and the majority of my wardrobe would agree, it's actually pink now.

I still hate pizza—yeah, yeah, hang that jaw—and he still loves it.

When Jake admits to venturing out of the realm of our fave music genre, and dabbling with some twang, that's when I can't take any more. Just kidding. There's a limited number of decent songs out there I can get down with.

Little tidbits like that, things you should know about your partner, and maybe you did at some point. But sometimes those details fall through the cracks.

When we go to leave, the beach long since abandoned by everyone else, lifeguard included, I walk around to the back of the chair, mind blown that here, all these years later, it's the same one. I rented a place on the exact street, because… recreation, but never in my wildest dreams did I think it would still be standing.

All the storms that have rolled through, unforgiving winters, destructive hurricanes, multiple seasons of wear and tear, yet here it is.

Running my fingertip over the lopsided heart situated between the faded initials, I let every memory of that night come flooding back. I think about those two lovesick kids who really have come so far in life

Jake crowds behind me, palm to the top of my hand, outlining the letters along with me. I can feel his lips curve as he presses them against my temple before whispering that same word from years ago.

"Forever."

48. WHATEVER IT TAKES

The feelings are blasting, full-blown love and happy shit. This place makes me… no, I think it makes *us* feel young again. It serves as a beautiful reminder of a pivotal moment in our lives.

It brings out emotions that only a specific backdrop can provide, just like some songs do, and pictures too. They take whatever's going on and transport you elsewhere. I think our brains are remarkable in that way.

There, on the lifeguard chair, the initials remained. Despite everything it'd been through over time, it never broke down, and they didn't replace it. I'm sure it must have splintered here and there, but instead of scrapping it, tossing it aside, they put in the work.

Whoever *they* are, I'm thankful for them. If that chair is still standing all these years later, I know we can too.

We leave the beach, hand in hand, the way we did back then. My skin has that tight feel to it, how it gets after the salt and sun finish mixing themselves over you.

"Wanna get something to eat?" Jake asks, a sly smile on his face—always a perv.

Same. But I am hungry… for food.

I love the beach's *no shoes, no shirt, no problem* mantra. Because that's what's happening with him. I can't imagine not having at least a little cover-up on. Oh, how I'd enjoy having no self-consciousness. Must be nice. There isn't a stitch of clothing on his body except swim trunks and a hat.

Jake shoots me some kind of look when I tell him this day is for his birthday, so we can do whatever he wants. It might have been the wrong choice of words, but I'm gonna ride the wave.

The outdoor seating at the boardwalk dive is the same as it was decades ago—peeling, orange-painted booths, potentially dry-rotted tables, right down to the sticky plastic-covered menus.

Not to worry, I brought the sanitizer.

It's as if this place is frozen in time. But the food here was good if memory serves me, and it's a quick in and out. Because we need time for some other in and out.

See, told you I was a perv too.

So here we are, my legs slung across his lap, all cozied up in the corner booth of the sparsely crowded patio. Totally relaxed from thoroughly unwinding, and for real, totally in love. Also, totally downing my margarita—my second one.

Listen, if I'm gonna go through with what I have planned, liquid encouragement is needed.

My hair hangs a bit down my back in unruly beach waves. Jake's fingers run through it nonstop while we wait for our food. He's got a thing—touch it, pull it, you know, the norm.

Also, hair and food. It's a no for me. But… his birthday.

His palms clasp around my legs, which have been not-so-subtly rubbing over his swim trunks. They're all dry and stiff, the way they get after saltwater wreaks its havoc. With a warning glance, his grip tightens over my thighs, trying to keep them down by his knees, holding strong each time I advance towards his lap.

I get it. He's making sure nothing else gets stiff.

"So." He grins, fingertips trailing up my legs, getting extra with the PDA, but there's not much room in the booth, so it's not like he's gonna get too far. "My birthday, so we can do what I want, right?"

He slips his hand up a little too high, so I begin to move my legs, arching a brow with my own devious smirk.

Two can play at this game.

"Oh God, stop," he says, sputtering out his drink. After swiping his forearm across his mouth, he pushes my legs off him. I chuckle as he scoots away from me, adjusting his shorts.

The server chooses this exact moment to bring our food. He may or may not have witnessed the exchange.

Playful eyes flit to the sky, and Jake shakes his head at me with a broadening smile. "You're bad."

I shrug. "So you were saying?" I urge him to continue then pick up a fry and drag it along my extended tongue, keeping my eyes on his. I mean, he wanted to get all kinds of inappropriate with a lollipop, so apparently food is fair game.

Jake laughs then loops his arm around me, pulling me onto his lap. His normal fresh smell is still there but mingled with the brisk ocean air. I press a palm to his chest, and yeah... we should probably head out soon.

When we're finished picking at our plates, he gives me some serious side-eye. "I have an idea that could be fun. Wanna get a little wild?" he asks, strategically wetting his lips.

I trace the design spanning his ribcage. It's the only spot where he has a splash of color. I study the intricate shapes and lines, an arrow amongst the scrolls of black, that form the red ruby—pretty sure you can guess who this one belongs to.

"Stop." He grabs my wrist, wincing. Soft laughter falls from his lips as I tickle up his side before he pushes me off, returning me to the seat next to him.

"Put a shirt on," I respond, lifting a shoulder.

"You down?" he asks.

"Hm?"

"For getting wild?"

Okay, so there's a decent number of things that I guess I am... um... down for. There's also a list of things I'm not. So let's hear it, and then I'll decide.

"What do you have in mind?" I'm trying to be cool about this, but I'm not gonna lie, my thoughts are racing.

I'm not about a facial—no thanks. That could cause a serious eye infection. There's some other kinky shit I won't even start to dabble in. People have their fetishes, and more power to them. I'm only speaking for myself. Feet? Hell to the no. If I already had reservations about his fingers in my mouth, you can bet I'm not gonna be sucking any toes.

There's some stuff I'd get in on, but I didn't pack all the essentials. I'll spare you the list.

"So, the thing in the car made me… inspired." He turns towards me, pearly whites clamped together, his grin growing wide and hopeful.

"You want me to tie you up again? No prob. Let's go!" I say with a minor hip check.

"No, no." He laughs nervously, followed by a much more forceful, "*No!*"

I scrunch my nose, tongue sticking out between my teeth.

"You trust me?"

Well, that's a loaded fucking question.

Um… well… do I?

I don't answer yes or no, and he realizes that. Instead, with a lip-rumbling exhale, I say, "I'm in."

Besides, I have a little surprise of my own.

Jake throws some money down on the table and bolts outta there, toting me behind him.

Back in the hotel room, I politely decline a joint shower. I mean, I'm not usually opposed. But if I've got an idea, and he's got an idea, there's only so much pounding I can take if I wanna be able to walk out of here. Plus, I gotta shave and all of that fun stuff, and it's way easier to do that without an audience.

I wash myself as fast as I can because the courage is on point, kind of. Anyway, I yell out to Jake that some champagne would be a fantastic idea. This place is gonna be like a champagne room pretty soon anyway, and I need to get him out of here for a minute.

Once I hear the door click shut, I race to my bag, shuffling through it to grab my intended outfit, which is buried deep. And I use the word outfit extremely lightly considering it's a red, sheer as hell, astronomically overpriced lace bra and matching thong.

I never got the whole—hey let's pay an insane amount for something that, one, is gonna come off pretty quick, and, two, isn't keeping anything a secret. This getup leaves nothing to the imagination. But it's something Jake used to hint at, offering to buy me lingerie. I was always about the comfort, not the sex appeal, but if he's willing to do whatever it takes, then I guess I can too. Even if it means dropping some serious change on a scrap of material.

I brush my wet strands into a low tight bun, because there's no time to dry it, and let's be real, there's no point. This hair tie won't be in for long.

Dusting makeup on my face—I know he doesn't care; that part's for me—I nod to myself in the mirror. The eyeliner makes the blue of my irises pop. I study my reflection. Damn, not bad.

Adrenaline mingles with nerves, making my stomach flip when I dig the other treat from my bag.

"You got this, bitch," I tell myself in the mirror with a wink, making an *okay* sign with my fingers. Wow.

I unravel some red ribbon completely from the spool, guesstimating the middle, and wind it around my waist. Looping it multiple times, till I reach my thighs, then weaving it down my body, I bind my legs together. By about the knees, I realize I'm kinda screwed, because the bed is across the room. And… I'm running out of time.

I hop—fucking hop. A bizarre combo of dilapidated Valentine's gift meets Peter Rabbit. What even? Then I toss myself sideways onto the bed, scooching and squirming like a mummy. I swear there's nothing sexy about my current state.

I swallow the budding nerves and sit up, which involves considerable core strength. Thank you, gym membership. My hands shake as I lace the ribbon around each leg, right down to my ankles, and there's just enough material left for a pretty little bow.

I look like a mermaid, or I don't even know what. As I reach to untie the material—clearly this is a whack idea—I hear the lock click.

My head plops onto the pillow, and I yank the blanket up around my chest, arms clamped in a vise over the comforter.

Heat dashes up my neck till my cheeks are on fire. I'm stuck somewhere in a jumble of anxiousness and hysterical laughter.

Jake strolls in with a big grin, a bucket of ice in one hand and a bottle of champagne in the other. "I figured we probably don't need glasses." He makes his way over and unloads the party favors on the table next to the bed. He stares for a second, finger tapping against his chin, eyes narrowing. "Whatcha hiding under there?"

"Nothing."

He grabs the top of the blanket, but I hold it tight over me. My eyes shut, my head shakes, and I fold my lips into my mouth, squelching my laughter.

My entire face has got to be the same color as the ribbon. Why? Why did I feel like *this* was a good idea?

"Hm?" Jake bends down and presses his lips to my neck. He doesn't play fair. "Lemme see." He tugs on the cover again.

Okay, I'll give him an inch or so.

I allow him to lower the blanket to just below my breasts. He straightens up in a flash, standing next to me, taking in the lacy bra.

"Well, I like this." Jake brushes a finger over the barely there material.

I open one eye to see his chest rising and falling harder, my own heart pounding from his feathery touch.

"Don't wanna show me the rest?"

"Ugh, I can't." I groan, smacking my forehead, regretting my decision.

His lips quirk, his shoulders bouncing with amusement.

"I'm so embarrassed right now."

With a swift hand, he flings his shirt off and pounces on top of me, straddling my blanketed waist.

"Alex." He sings my name in a coaxing sort of manner, staring straight into my eyes. "Trust me." He leans down with a soft kiss to my lips before sitting back up. "You have nothing, *nothing*, to be embarrassed about. Everything about you is incredibly sexy. You do things to me that no one else can." His view shifts side to side then flickers to, well, you know, which is pointing at me.

I'm still wrecked, with a bout of shrill chuckles, though I can't fight my smile at seeing Jake bite his knuckle.

"I do love this." He cups the thin bra, thumb dragging over my nipple. You guessed it, that's rock solid too. "It looks great on you."

I'm literally pouring out of it.

He kisses his way across my chest with an inviting persuasion, glancing up in between, gauging where my resolve is. I'm still clutching the blanket, though not quite as tight.

"However." His head jerks up. "It would look even better on the floor."

Okay, deep breath. "You wanna see?"

Jake nods, extra enthused.

"Alright." I scrunch my nose, releasing a long exhale. I can do this. "Stand up."

His feet hit the floor in a second flat.

Here goes nothin'.

After I fold the blanket off my body, shock bulges his eyes, and… yeah. He blinks in rapid succession, astonished, as he examines the waist-to-ankle ribbon. I fight a snort, taking a crack at being super sexy.

"Holy…" Heavy breaths pant from his gaping mouth. His eyes grow dark, roving up and down, while a swallow works his throat.

"Here's your gift," I say, cringing between spells of laughter. "Open up."

Jake's jaw has dropped, and his stare is glued to my lower half.

"Hell yes!" He beelines to my ankles, fingers working fast, impatient to dismantle my wrapping.

"This is so…" I groan, still feeling the nerves or whatever you wanna call this.

"No. Trust me. This is a perfect birthday gift." He stops his hasty ribbon ripping, that dimple creasing his cheek with the smirk we all know and love. "I got an idea too."

He lifts the black blindfold I took out of the night-table drawer and bends a finger around the elastic strap, swinging it while his eyebrows raise multiple times.

Oh, shit.

"Whatcha say?" He continues twirling the blindfold. It's actually a sleep mask, not that it matters.

Could be fun, could get kinky. I suppose trying new things keeps that fire burning.

I stretch my arms out to the sides, hesitating before returning his naughty grin. "Whatever it takes."

49. RADIOACTIVE

Okay. I'm on board with tackling these trust issues. Sure am. What says that more than agreeing to be temporarily blinded and ravaged? At least that's what I'm hoping for. I think. I'm a little scared.

While I'm still slightly warm from the margarita, I might need a tinge more, because this is next level for me. I'm terrible with surprises. I much prefer to see things coming.

"Wait, wait, wait." I hold up a hand. "I'm about this, but I think you're gonna need to pop that bottle first." Releasing a steadying breath, I shrug, nerves on full blast.

Jake's eyes—hell, his entire face—morphed from that frisky, gobsmacked expression to unrelenting lust, thick lashes hanging over a smoldering stare, his chest heaving with anticipation.

But he nods, walking over to switch off the overhead light, leaving the bathroom one on. It casts a shadow over his face, so his features appear even darker as he stalks towards me, his heady gaze fixed on my lips. He wets his before lowering himself next to me.

And when I say stalking, I mean it. He looks as if he's ready to attack and destroy me. I'm a subscriber.

My pulse is already racing.

The last thing I see when Jake leans over me are the swirls of endless amber and green. "Trust me," he says, covering my eyes with the blindfold.

I open my mouth to sling out… something, because, well, I'm nervous. And when I get nervous, I'm a talker. Mostly random ramblings.

"I can't wait to watch you fall apart," he rasps against my ear.

Any words or thoughts vanish, and a quiet moan leaves my throat.

His slow touch drags along my bottom lip, and I tremble from the slight contact. When his thumb drifts along my neck, every inch of my skin ignites, as if even that minor touch produces a chemical reaction in my body. I guess that's a fact. My hips rise, seeking, between my legs throbbing and desperate for him.

Then nothing.

The room is silent, and I can't stand not knowing. After turning up the bottom of the blindfold, I peek over. A loud pop cracks out from the champagne bottle being opened, then Jake's eyes catch mine. He tuts, finger wiggling disapprovingly.

"Are we gonna do this or not?" he asks. And though he looks deadass serious, his lips pursed, I can see the entertainment in his annoyed stare.

The thing about us… we're both mostly playful by nature. But if we're gonna try this shit out, I guess I better shape up.

"Yes, sir," I respond with a brisk salute, gaining me a chuckle. Letting the mask fall back over my eyes, I drop my arms to the side, my head settling on the pillow.

He grabs my bound ankles, yanks me further down the bed then straddles me before roughly claiming my mouth, bruising and soul-snatching. I return his ferocity, sinking my teeth into his lips.

Jake twines his fingers between mine then raises my arms, pinning them above my head. He holds my wrists in one hand, while the other strokes the side of my face before gripping my jaw.

"This okay?"

"Mm-hmm," I reply.

His fiery tongue licks my lips, seeking access. I part for him immediately. I'd part my legs if they weren't tied together. His mouth moves feverishly against mine, exploring every corner with a deep and passionate kiss. Muffled groans of anticipation hum from both our chests.

Jake reaches back—saw this comin'—removing the tie from my hair then fists my wet strands, angling my head. We lapse into our familiar rhythm, completely face sucking… or fucking.

I writhe beneath him, unable to reciprocate a single touch, my arms anchored to the mattress above me.

"Jake!" I pant as he marks my neck with his teeth, not knowing what I want but positive I can't do a long, drawn-out tease. I'm throbbing, and aching, and a sopping mess. Literally, my legs are aching, because I tied them far too tight.

He lifts off me and releases my wrists. I lie there for what feels like an hour. Okay, it's probably ten seconds. But I'm me, so I prop myself on my elbows then tip the mask.

And again, he greets me with a disapproving scowl.

"I knew you were gonna do that." His tone is a mixture of humor and frustration.

I wanna do this. The bit of unknown is exciting, but I can't help it. How are we gonna solve this problem?

"Do something about it," I challenge him, settling back with a smirk and throwing my hands above my head, one wrist over the other. His lips pout; the mask is now up above my eyebrows.

"Hm?" He scratches his chin, trying to figure out what I'm hinting at.

I get it—his head is somewhere else. Seriously. Gym shorts don't lie.

His mouth opens, and he nods, his tongue running along the inside of his cheek. It's like an *aha* moment. He pulls the bow at my ankles and furiously rips at the material. My legs are cramped as hell, and I shake them out once the ribbon's off.

A sly expression covers his face, then he fixes the mask back over my eyes. "Lift up."

The husky demand is almost enough to make me explode.

And you bet I do exactly what he says.

After sliding the satin from under me, he wraps it several times around my wrists. The pressure from his own makeshift restraint sparks an insatiable desire that sizzles and strikes a contracting chord.

Jake grabs my thighs and drags me to the edge of the bed. Then he spreads my legs, one by one, and rubs himself against me, causing me to cry out and lurch, desperate for more. He continues grinding his thick cock over our clothes—or rather, shorts and an overpriced thong. I'm already ready; like *really* ready.

My hips, with a mind of their own, rise to meet his; I want to yank his bottoms off and have my way with him. But I gotta admit, not knowing what's coming next, not being able to make a single move to stop it, or urge it to continue, is exhilarating.

"Stay still."

I freeze, almost whining from the loss of contact. No, actual whines are coming out of me. Also… am I going to let him shout commands at me? Allow him to go straight up dominant?

You fucking bet I am.

Jake's stacked body presses over mine, muscles slick with sweat, pulse jamming and slamming into me. He unclasps my bra, sliding it up my arms, until it's stopped by the ribbon.

Each of his movements is unhurried, to an extreme, but every touch is setting off a chain reaction throughout my body. He pinches my nipples, rolling them between his fingers, drawing an erotic sigh from my throat.

There go the hips again.

Then he's gone, and the clinking sound of ice in the bucket has my thoughts scrambling. Before I can question or complain, a scorching hot— no, maybe cold—sensation meets my skin, dripping and melting over the swells of my breast.

He circles the cube over my tight nipple, and I gasp, squirming with absolute delight. I cry out when his mouth covers it, nipping, flicking, and sucking.

Jake moves my underwear to the side then glides over my unmistakable arousal. His thumb presses with so much friction, my back bows off the mattress, and goosebumps coat every exposed piece of flesh.

Then he's plunging inside me, driving in and out with abandon, palm slapping my clit in time with his fingertips tapping that earth-quaking spot, his mouth hot and heavy on my breast.

"You like that?"

"Yes," I cry eagerly, and he does it again, and again, and—fuck me— again. I ride his hand while he smears the dwindling ice over my chest, sizzling a wet trail to my other nipple. When his mouth takes its place, his fingers sink deeper into my center. My hips furiously move along with him so he's reaching further, chasing the earth-shattering climax that's already looming in my core.

"Alex," he growls while I'm moaning and thrashing. "Come on my fingers, baby."

Done.

I can't even clutch the sheets, or cover my face, or anything. The tension builds wildly, coiling in the pit of my stomach. And I don't know if it's the way his fingers are thrusting so savagely, or how he's hitting *all* the right places, or the fact that I have no clue what's coming next.

My head drops back, and I combust, a rush of unmatched elation coursing through me as I come hard and fast on his hand.

"Holy. Fuck!" Erratic breaths spurt from my nostrils.

A haughty, highly satisfied laugh rings out above me, then I hear the ice again. Oh my God, I need a minute.

"Sit up."

"Can't," I mumble. "Just died."

The mattress dips next to me as I fail to form coherent words. Jake plants a quick kiss against my bottom lip, while my mouth's still gaping. I can't think. Sensible thoughts are not happening—they're overrated anyway. He grabs the ribbon and pulls me, like a puppet, to sit.

"You want some of this?" he asks.

"I want *all* of it."

We both laugh when a cold surface meets my joined palms.

"Oh yeah, this too." Tilting the bottle up, I let it fizz down my throat. Fuck clearing my head. I'm drunk anyway, and it's not from alcohol. This intoxication is strictly his doing.

"That was… um… wow," I stutter after lowering the bottle from my lips, holding my arms in front of me, fully at his mercy.

The pad of Jake's thumb swipes along my mouth, followed by the sound of him sucking away whatever remnants it held. *All* the remnants. "That was the first part." His voice is thick, and hot, and dark, and sex. I promise you, everything about that raspy tone equals *sex*.

"The first part?"

Cue the nervous laugh.

I absolutely enjoy an earth-shattering orgasm as much as the next person. But shit gets a tad sensitive right after, and that's simply logistics. I need a solid minute of recovery before I can plow back into it.

Pun fucking intended.

He takes the bottle from my hands, and I move them to the side of my face, ready to regain my sight. His fingers clasp the satin, pulling my arms down.

"Leave it on."

"Jake," I whine. "It's pretty intense." And it really is. Something about taking away certain senses puts the rest on full tilt. I mean, I can get off from a decent finger fuck, of course. But, that easy, on any other given day, when eyesight is involved? No chance.

"That's the point, so lie your pretty ass down."

Ugh… alright.

Just kidding. I'm flat on my back in a flash.

Something wet trickles over my midsection, and I flinch, shivering from the cold racing down my body. What the fuck? This is definitely on the things-I'm-not-down-with list.

Before I can say a word in protest, his mouth is on me, tongue flat and lapping the trail of liquid—obviously champagne—teeth grazing my abdomen, cleaning up his mess.

Jake situates my constrained arms back above my head before skating a finger along the top of my underwear. Slowly, teasing, then without warning, he rips them off. I can't even control the sounds coming out of my mouth.

Going straight to work, he kisses the hollow of each thigh, palm pressed to my pelvis, halting any efforts for me to expedite this process. He begins again, taunting me, hoisting my legs over each shoulder, stopping right where I desperately want those lips to connect.

After another torturous minute or so he hits me with his specialty. You know this part. The fingers, the tongue, the lips, the mouth. Ain't no shocker anymore, but also—*that*.

It doesn't take long before my toes curl. The rush of pleasure tumbles inside of me like the waves crashing beyond our balcony door, though I'm hardly able to decipher them over my wails and moans. I fall apart beneath him… again.

"This is supposed to be *your* birthday," I mumble in my current Jake-drunk state.

He collapses onto the mattress next to me; my breathing is rapid and uneven. His fingers tiptoe up from my drenched center. "Mm-hmm. You said you were my present, remember?"

Oh yeah, that whole thing.

"Well, seems one-sided. Maybe if you undo these…" I lift my arms, which are getting real uncomfortable.

It's as if he knows exactly what I'm thinking, or what I need. Jake climbs onto me, a knee on either side, then grabs my wrists and lowers them behind his neck. The long ends of the ribbon, along with my bra, dangle over him.

His racing heart drums from his chest to mine, and he must've lost his pants at some point, because his cock slides between my legs, prompting a cry—or maybe a sigh? My brain's been reduced to mush.

But there's no rest for the wicked. He kicks my legs apart with his knees and loops an arm beneath each thigh. Air is a hot commodity, and my lungs are fighting for it. I'm in the midst of a crazy, sex-dazed trance, and I choose this over consciousness.

"I love watching you come," he says over my lips.

Whimpers cascade from my throat like a waterfall as he slips up and down my entrance, hitting that sweet spot. My hips rotate under him, and I'm seriously ready to lose it… for the third time.

"And I love *all* the sounds you make." His breath heats my neck before he pulls away.

I know I'm being a whiny bitch right now, but *fuck*. Do you know how hard it is to have all this happening, and you can't see a thing?

Also, please try it out. This shit is top shelf.

I open my mouth to beg, plead, perhaps sell my soul. Who knows? Jake grips beneath my thighs, and, without warning, he slams inside me, his pelvis smacking mine, echoing through the room along with grunts and groans. Our neighbors either loathe us or are turned on. I mean it, this is like audio-only porn.

I'm not hating it.

He continues his forceful thrusts, repeatedly filling me, stroking my walls, while he bites my shoulder to muffle his own feral sounds. I shudder and shake and take everything he's got.

Jake leans up, and I have no choice but to be pulled along with him, till we're standing. Or he's standing, and I'm wrapped around him, in more ways than one. My nails scratch into his scalp, fingers threading through his hair, hanging on for dear life.

"This okay?" he asks between uneven breaths, bouncing me over him, completely in control.

So… let's give him what he *really* wants.

"Fuck me harder, Jake. Make me come all over your cock."

And that's all it takes.

He cups my ass and raises me up, ramming me down over him while bucking his hips. Stars burst into flames beyond the black curtain of my blindfold, and my skin tingles with every repeated slam inside me. I wail—yes, wail—but his thrusts don't let up. Passion mounts and pools and has me seconds away from going nuclear as he fucks into me like we'll never fuck again.

I'm a panty, sweaty mess, and when he drops me back onto the mattress, I'm not sure if I wanna protest or be relieved.

There's no time for that. I'm flipped to my front, and he slaps my ass, eliciting a shriek of pure ecstasy before he soothes the sting.

With a firm grip on each hip, he slides me to him. I'm legit face down, ass up, and if you've learned anything about me, if you know the song, you can probably guess what I'd say next.

Jake spreads me with his hands before pounding inside me, unrestrained. He angles my waist, sinking deeper each time. Desire grabs hold of me, dragging me below the surface and soaking me in lust.

I yelp at the combined pain and pleasure when he slaps my ass again and again, my body almost violently convulsing beneath him.

"Come for me, Alex. Give me one more," he rasps.

Who am I to say no?

He drives into me a few more times, and I clench so tight, implosion is imminent.

A guttural, filthy groan vibrates from his chest to my core. I tense and tighten, feeling him on the verge of climax. When his fist wraps around my hair, and Jake thunders into me, one final and extremely rough time… that's all she wrote.

Blazing white heat crashes into me like a bolt of lightning, while I spasm and scream and drown in the pleasure of this intense climax. He jerks and pulses inside me, crying out and collapsing onto my back, until we've both taken every single last bit from the other.

There's nothing left to give.

Happy. Fucking. Birthday.

He should have birthdays more often. Though I feel like I reaped all the benefits.

Still inside me, Jake mashes sloppy kisses onto my shoulder. Both of us are trying to regain any type of normal breathing.

"Round four?" I mutter.

He lets out a breathy laugh. And like all the other things that just start working in sync, when you have such a deep connection with someone, we both say the same words in our mind-blown daze.

"That was amazing."

50. SABOTAGE

If I were to sum it up, I'd say Jake's had a fantastic getaway so far. Not so bad for me either.

Yeah, right. It's been incredible. Note to self—invest in handcuffs, because that shit's alright.

We've had moments that were super sweet, volcanically hot, and just an altogether exceptional time together.

We're standing in the shoes of those young, innocent, love-stricken teenagers. Okay, I wouldn't say either of us has ever been innocent. Maybe Jake, but whatever.

The two of us lounge across the bed for an hour, sweaty and exhausted in the best way, basking in our post-bang-sesh bliss. Synapses eventually resume firing, and we decide to go out for a nighttime stroll on the beach.

The cool sand slips between our toes, while the inky sky covers us in a blanket of bright stars. Moonlight ripples over the ocean, and the surf provides a chorus of cyclical breaking waves. Sublime.

It's *exactly* like that night. Just the two of us, made to defy the odds. Us against the world.

We're right back to that wild love. We totally nailed the whole recreation. Though it was a tad more, um, adventurous this go-round.

But that's what happens with time.

Look, unless you're a straight-up freak—and more power to you if you are—it takes a while to become truly comfortable with someone. Where you can articulate what you want. To express what feels good and what doesn't. Harder, softer, faster, more… you get the point. Because early in a relationship—and maybe it was only mine, and maybe because we were young—sex was just sex. Sorta vanilla. Once you get comfortable, once you can say what you desire, let the games begin.

So here we are on a nice June night, chilly enough that I have to throw on Jake's hoodie. You know he's never getting this one back. That's a fact. Once I adopt a sweatshirt, it's for life.

We stand together beneath the dark sky, listening to the sounds of the ocean, and a new promise is made. That we will always be able to get back here. We can always be *Jake and Alex*. The punch-drunk couple who didn't give a damn that most long-distance relationships were destined to fail, and didn't care that they'd miss out on the so-called college experience. We only ever cared about the end game.

And isn't this where we wanted to be at our age? Married for almost seventeen years? Kids, dream house, dogs, white picket fence? Actually, it's vinyl—much more durable. But for real.

We made it.

Alright, it's not identical to that night. It appears a lot more people like to hang out on the beach, or perhaps it's because the world's more populated. Also, the lifeguard chairs get tipped and dragged back to the dunes overnight, so that reenactment is off the table. Cops patrol nonstop, and I got a record. Just kidding with that—it's long since been expunged.

Yeah, the beach action will have to remain PG. Can't win 'em all.

It feels like this quick getaway, *this place* was what we needed. A reminder of who we genuinely are… together.

* * *

I wake up to a sticky, jumbled, perspiring mess. Legs clamped around mine, a palm holding tight to my tit. I swear, the obsession is so real. Soft, content breaths exhale gently from Jake's nostrils, feathering the side of my neck.

There was *no* redressing. On the rare occasion of not worrying if a kid'll walk in, who needs clothes? As far as the sticky? I'll defer to the champagne. I don't even know here. Things got outta hand.

And let's talk sleep for a minute. Sometimes, or most times, with kids, you have to be up at the crack of dawn to shuffle everyone out the door. And at least for me, this results in only a few hours of sleep for myself. Because, you know, the mysteries of the universe won't solve themselves. So, yeah, if you're away, sans kids, you better believe it's your obligation to soak that shit up.

I'm pretty sure we slept a solid ten hours. And that was just as pleasurable as the face down, ass-up bang-a-rang. Well… a close second.

I peel Jake's arm and legs off me then slip out of the bed. Muted sighs hum from his lips as he nuzzles into the pillow, hair messed up, sticking out in all directions. I check mine in the mirror. It's wild as fuck, so I'm not one to judge.

"Wake up." I smooth a hand over his jaw after allowing him to catch some more Zs. I had a phone call to make.

"Nope," Jake mumbles, voice groggy with sleep. His eyes remain closed, arms stretching out across the bed. Now that I think on it, it makes complete sense why hotels use white sheets—bleach is forgiving, and I'm sure they need tons of it.

"We gotta get going. Checkout is in an hour and we need to head back. I have a hair appointment, and supposedly Kelsey has a dress that'll work. We're going to your thing."

His eyes snap open, his hand scrubbing over his face as he quickly turns and sits up. "What?"

"You heard me. Let's move."

I head for the shower, leaving Jake, his back up against the wall—well, the bed frame—looking stunned, scared, apprehensive. All of the above.

He outright told me the reason for Kelsey's messages, and I did believe him. But it got me thinking that maybe there was a bit more to it, and I was right.

I know why he wanted to dance around it, why he tried to pretend it wasn't a thing, like he didn't wanna go. We all know.

Because *she* will probably be there. And that sucks, but I find myself at another crossroads.

Kelsey explained that Jake and Luke's company is being recognized as a rising star in the advertising world, at least for the mid-Atlantic region, and apparently, this is a tremendous deal. He *is* a hard worker—has a way with words; knows how to get what he wants. Above that, he deserves to be recognized for years of busting his ass.

And as much as I'd love to pretend that we're in this hotel room for life, that we're this neatly packaged fairytale, we aren't. Real life is right up outside that door.

So… I can let him take a massive hit for my pride, or I can let him have a massive win. A win for everything he's worked for over the years. This will put his name on the map and gain him more street cred than he'll know what to do with.

I could have him go by himself, let my imagination hamster-wheel. Or I can go with him, holding my head high, with faith and trust in our relationship, and in myself, knowing it was only a kiss.

Anyway, if push comes to shove, I'm convinced I can handle her. Trust me, I've visualized smashing her face in several times—just in the last few minutes. Not trying to go there, but if it happens, I probably won't lose sleep.

Today, this is where we're at, and if we want to move forward, we can't keep avoiding things. I'm taking a deep breath here and being the bigger person, because Jake and I are together. No matter how ugly, this is a part of our story now too.

After a shower and quick dry-off, I throw on some shorts and a tank, then dot a smidge of serum below the eyes because… come the fuck on, then we're ready to hit the road.

Jake's out on the balcony, sitting in a chair, contemplating—I'm sure the same stuff I was contemplating—while staring out at the ocean. His eyes are hidden beneath sunglasses, his hair somewhat smoothed back, and he looks effortlessly hot. It's not fair, but he's mine, so I'm good with it.

I'm sure this is highly uncomfortable for him. But he shouldn't suffer, not for life. No one wins that way. I need him to be recognized for how far he's come. If I choose him, and us, then I choose all of it. I don't ever want him to hold back. Jake deserves a cheerleader too.

I walk outside and sit on a chair next to him, laying my hand over his. "We got this, okay? Besides"—I chuckle to myself with my next choice of words—"it *was* only a kiss."

Without hesitation, he turns his head so I can see the fake enthusiasm on my face mirrored in his glasses.

He nods. "It was only a kiss."

I've already called Annie, who agreed to hang with the kids for the night and has already picked them up. I didn't want to take full advantage of Mom. Plus, Annie is all about spending as much time with them as she can before their move.

She demanded ample details after of course. But my best friend told me I could do this. *We* could do this. And if all else fails, send the skunt to the dentist.

Maybe *this* is the final thing, the last part on the path to recovery, the twelfth step. See her in person—I feel kinda sick at the thought—show her we're fine, striving, and that regardless of her efforts, she failed in wrecking at least one home.

* * *

After we get back, my day consists of typical hairdresser chat and gossip. Monica says she's proud that I'm doing this, telling me to keep my chin up, glare that bitch straight in the eye, and show her who she's messing with.

I got this.

That's a lie. No the fuck I don't—my nerves are mangled, and I feel like I wanna throw up. There's no doubt the adrenaline will spike, and I'll be a mess. But I'm gonna fake it… for Jake.

"You look gorgeous." He grins, coming up behind me in our bedroom and sliding up the zipper of my mid-length black dress.

I'm asking a lot of the two extremely thin straps on my shoulders, the neckline dipping, showing off a little cleavage—but just enough that it's tasteful. Monica worked my hair into a low sort of fancy bun, loose strands curled and wisped around my face, and my makeup is on point with golden eyelids and slightly winged liner. Jordan would be proud. It's the right amount, not over the top, but it's me. I feel good.

It was all totally effortless.

And… that's some bullshit. Spanx and double-sided tape for the win. But I look great, and I'm ready for this.

"Not so bad yourself." My eyes wander up and down his frame, letting myself completely eye-fuck him. Why not? He's doing it to me. I'm picturing how much better *his* clothes would look on the floor.

His dark hair is styled and gelled to the side, while gray dress pants hug the curve of his ass, and a black, fitted shirt—unbuttoned at the collar—offers a peek of his defined chest. A silver watch hangs on his wrist, and his sleeves are rolled to the elbows, showing off some of his ink, which he rarely does for work. But I'm glad he's being himself.

We look perfectly matched. We *are* perfectly matched.

* * *

The night is a complete success!

There are so many people here to congratulate him, and I've been introduced to countless humans. Turns out peopling… not so bad after all. We danced, ate, and had a wonderful time. I can't believe I never wanted to go to one of Jake's work things before. It's so fun. Also, this event is enormous, several hundred people deep. It really is a big fucking deal.

And guess who isn't here? At least not that I've seen.

I got myself hyped up, worried and nervous for nothing.

"The guys wanna get a drink at a bar around the corner," Kelsey says, looking stunning as ever. Her jet-black hair falls straight down the back of her white strapless dress, and her eyes are lined with precision, making the dark green of her irises resemble sparkling emeralds.

Technically, she's our driver, so it's up to her. But since the night's been great so far, we might as well keep it going a bit longer.

I agree, and we make one last quick trip to the bathroom before heading out. You know we have to go together, even if one of us doesn't actually have to go—refer to the code.

Kelsey tells me to give her a few minutes. Because, as nice as that suck-you-in underwear makes things appear on the outside, it's quite a process to get it on and off.

I wait in the adjoining room. A mirror spans one wall, floor to ceiling. This is swanky, with velvet chairs and scrolled-armed couches. You know a place is fancy as hell when there's a lounge in the actual restroom.

I reapply my lip gloss and tone the shine down with a dab of powder, just smiling at myself, relieved that I was all worked up for nothing. My cheeks are bright pink from dancing, but my face and hair are holding up pretty well.

Lost somewhere in Alex-land, savoring how comfortable life feels right now, how proud of us I am, I don't even hear the door creak open. Red material catches my eye and gets me thinking about last night. Then a throat clears next to me, and I lift my gaze to the mirror.

The flush on my cheeks drains, plummeting down past my neck to the floor, pulling my stomach along with it.

Black hair and green eyes meet mine in the reflection—but it's *not* Kelsey.

51. CRIMINAL

I'm met with the reflection of bright, whore-red lipstick surrounding blindingly white teeth, and dark curls cascading over one shoulder. She has flawless skin on an airbrushed-looking face, with tits up to her chin in some smutty, slutty, skank-ass dress that matches her lips. She looks like a model.

Of course she does.

Smiling—one of those fake, superior grins—she blinks multiple times as her eyes travel up and down, taking me in.

My heart stops. I'm pretty sure it does.

Angela *fucking* DeMarco.

You know the feeling when you see someone you specifically don't want to? Your pulse pounding in your neck, mouth going dry, respirations kicking up, and every inch of your body tingling—not in a good way. The whole fight or flight?

Yeah, I'm there.

Does she even know, by appearance, the person standing next to her? Did she see me on social media after obsessing about who I was? Desperate to put a face to a name?

I'm banking on no. If she didn't care about me when Jake said he had a wife, she probably never started caring. She wouldn't have felt the need to compare herself every fucking day. There would've been no loss, or pain, or blame. And I highly doubt there was even a moment where she harbored any guilt or shame for the fallout.

Okay, back to *this* fucking moment.

I try to steady the palm that's trembling as I place my lip gloss back into my purse. The room has suddenly gotten about fifty times smaller, the floral wallpaper closing in, threatening suffocation.

I can't tear my eyes away, and I can't move.

Barely paying any attention to me, she peers approvingly at herself in the mirror, obviously in love with her reflection.

My face never lies, and right now, it's so screwed up. My nostrils are flaring, my chest is hitting a rapid rise and fall, my arms shaking, my adrenaline fucking raging.

The second she looks over, it's game on.

"God, aren't these things the worst?" Long nails sift through her hair before she adjusts the fake-ass tits up in her dress. All the while, I'm just staring—more like gawking—at this picture-perfect woman.

She looks like someone he should be with. Like a match for him

I hate to say it, but she's beautiful and appears insanely youthful for her age, which I'm guessing must be early thirties. She looks like—

"Wait." A ditsy giggle falls from her mouth. "Are *you* here with… Jake?"

She looks like I'm about to punch her in the fucking face.

I'm frozen, paralyzed, flatlined. My flushed cheeks are back, but this time, they're not a warm shade of pink. These are sweltering, crimson, volcanic, and I'm about to blow.

Standing there like an idiot, I close my eyes, trying to count to ten—better make it a million—attempting to calm myself down. Because all I can envision is bashing her skull into the marble table in the center of the room. When I open my eyes, I only see red, and I'm not talking about her stupid fucking dress and lipstick.

I inhale a collecting breath, releasing it slowly, aware of the shuddered exhale that makes my lips tremble. Just breathe—it'll be fine; this bitch is calculated, but we're beyond this. I knew a run-in could happen. I signed up for it. I'm alright; I got this.

"Yeah," I respond, turning from the mirror to face the trash head-on. I fall several inches short of her chin, probably because of the ridiculously high heels on her feet. "I'm Jake's wife."

The fake smile stays plastered on her lips, and she extends her arm towards me. "I'm Angela."

"I know who you are." My jaw is ticking, my molars grinding to nothing, and I deliver the fiercest stare down I can manage. My hands remain by my sides, curling into tightly clenched fists.

"Oh." She releases a single, snarky laugh, her expression smug as fuck, her eyes narrowing to slits. "Well, this is… uncomfortable." Her shoulder juts forward nonchalantly.

Uncomfortable? Is she for real?

I swallow several times, focusing on stopping my breath from jumping, seeking to simmer the knuckle-cracking rush spreading through me like wildfire. And I'm *really* trying to ignore the devil sitting right up on my shoulder, encouraging me to put her in the market for some porcelain veneers.

"I do, um… business with Jake." She offers a disgustingly false, grinchy grin, the corners of her lips almost curling in. I'm sure you can picture it.

"Yeah." I draw in a deep breath. I'm not about to let her get the best of me. My head is high. She doesn't deserve to win. "I've heard *all about* how you do your business."

So… let's flip the cards for a minute. The situation is brutal, I'm not gonna lie. I knew I might see her, but here, in this moment, face to face, I'm folding. I'm feeling smaller and smaller by the second. I'm thinking the best thing, the smartest thing I can do right now, and for my own sanity, is walk away.

Is it all her fault anyway? It takes two to tango, doesn't it? Why should I go full-blown psycho on her?

I'm the bigger person.

With a slow, deep, big-girl breath, I tip my chin up. "I'd say it's nice to meet you, but it isn't."

I move past her, heading for the door. Kelsey can just come find me when she's done.

"Aww, that's too bad, but I'm not surprised." The skunt's tongue smacks over her teeth, delivering an obnoxious sound. "Sorry your feelings got hurt. I'm honestly shocked he even told you anything."

"What?" I swing my head round, my body following. An inevitable scowl slices between my pinched brows, and my lips purse as I watch her silicone chest shake with silent laughter.

Okay, so there's the answer to *that*. Yes… I can, in fact, go psycho. My face burns. Fury begins to fuel me. Is this whore seriously looking at me like I'm the joke?

"Listen… sweetie—"

"No." I step towards her. "You fucking listen, *sweetie*." I point a finger at her, wiggling it in her face, and she stares down her nose at me, like I'm inferior. "Look, clearly you have some obsession with married men, and maybe it's because you have daddy issues, or you have some fucked up self-esteem, or whatever, but I feel sorry for you."

I remain inches from Angela's face. The condescending smile disintegrates, and her lips thin so much they disappear. She glares down at me from under her long false lashes.

"I'd appreciate it if you stayed the hell away from my husband. There are millions of men out there, and I'm sure they'd fall all over themselves to get into your fake, trashy snatch. Leave. Jake. Alone."

Angela throws her head back with a haughty laugh. She turns towards the mirror, eyeing me in the reflection. "First off, *Alex*"—she says my name in a way that makes my flesh crawl, a pompous expression covering her face, but this bitch knows my name—"look at you." She chuckles. "And look at me."

I do.

I try not to let my self-esteem issues come to the forefront right now. I may not be perfect or flawless, and I might not be six feet tall. I don't look like a model, but I am a good person. Not someone who goes around attempting to break up marriages and families like it's some kind of game.

My body is trembling, my fingernails digging into my palms so hard, a blistering pain shoots up my arms. I'm sweaty, and clammy, and overall a fucking train wreck.

"Second." Her arms snap against her chest, shoving her tits as high as they can go while she glowers at me. Looking closer, I can see the makeup that's caked on her skin. She's not flawless. No, she's as fake as they come, right down to her shitty smile. "I think you need to tell Jake to leave *me* alone." Her lashes bat with mock innocence, and she shrugs unapologetically.

I think I'm gonna be sick.

I swallow the massive lump in my throat, replaying the words. It was only a kiss.

It was only a kiss.

But again, this face can't lie, and she picks up on my confused expression, not missing a beat. "I don't come seeking him out, it's quite the opposite. Aw…" She curls her bottom lip in an exaggerated pout. "Did you really think it was the other way around?"

She's getting in your head. This is her shiesty style, and this is how she rolls. I'm pretty sure my body is convulsing right now, on the verge of a meltdown. But fuck? Is she telling the truth? Was it Jake that was going after her? Was everything a lie?

What. The. Fuck?

She will *not* get the best of me. And I'd love to hit her, but assault is a real thing. I'm a thirty-eight-year-old woman—can't go around hitting people.

I suck in a sharp breath through quivering nostrils then turn to leave. I grasp the door handle, tears burning my eyes, my lips trembling, my head spinning.

"And you wanna talk about fake?" she calls after me.

My shoulders squeeze together. I know I should walk away right now, but I can't. I freeze, my back to her.

"How about you keeping him trapped? Jake could be so much more. I know all about you getting pregnant young, how he had to give up on his dreams because of that. And you just kept popping out kids, sinking your claws into him, deeper and deeper. You're fake, not me. Sorry to be the one to open your eyes, but *obviously* someone needs to. At least I don't hide behind some image of a perfect life. I could help him get so far ahead, and all you do is hold him back."

My body tenses, my breathing out of control. How dare she mention my children? They are off fucking limits. I turn gradually, not even trying to hide the fact that my hands are shaking. She has this coming.

I march towards her with a purpose.

"Face it," she snaps. "You're an obligation—that's it. He told me his sad story, the pressure he's constantly under. If you cared about him, you'd want him to succeed, not make him fail."

Right before I reach her, the door to the side of us flies open, and Kelsey comes barreling through it in a flash of white. Before I can even get close to the fucking cunt, a loud thud cracks out, followed by a disturbing crunch.

Kelsey's enlarged eyes dart to mine, her mouth gaping as she clutches her fist with her other hand—the fist that just went straight into Angela's face. Blood gushes from her nose, pouring down her arms, matching her dress.

"You'd be lucky to be one quarter of the woman Alex is!" she spits, her body quivering with anger, her teeth gnashing like a wild animal.

"I think you broke my fucking nose!" Angela cries, examining the blood coating her hands.

"You tripped, bitch." Kelsey shrugs, flinging her hair over her shoulder then smoothing the front of her white dress. "You should be more careful what you run into."

Her fingers encircle my wrist, her eyes searching mine. "Let's get the hell out of here—we don't hang around trash." She pulls me to the door.

I'm stuck in a trance, an alternate universe. My head is spinning, thoughts swirling, spiraling, and funneling fast. How could he have told her those things? How could he let someone into our lives like that? Kiss or not, I'd honestly rather Jake had fucked her a million times than tell her about my life. *Our life.*

Because it means it was emotional. And that is definitely a deal-breaker.

I plant my heels down, and Kelsey stops, turning back to me. The frown on her face mirrors my own. I shake my head, hot tears streaming down my cheeks.

"I know." Her hand slips into mine, and she squeezes it. "I-I don't know what to say."

She shifts her attention across the room to Jake. I can't look at him for longer than a second, but I see his eyes widen, his relaxed smile falling immediately.

Kelsey drags me along, booking to the exit as my sobs begin to gain attention. I can hear the loud screech from his chair, and I know he's following.

We get out to the parking lot, and it feels like a blur. Jake chases after us, yelling for us to stop. Kelsey does her best to maintain a middle-of-the-road expression, but when he tries to block me from getting in the car, she tells him he better back the fuck off.

And to be perfectly honest with you, I can't even open my mouth to talk to him. I hate him. I don't want to hear his side. He doesn't get a fucking side.

She knew details about us, and that's enough.

I'm pissed and so irreversibly gutted. I feel as though the last twenty-one years have been a lie. And as much as I'd like to keep being this bigger person, that shit is overrated. I wanna be angry. I wanna fucking rage. I want to be as destructive as humanly possible.

This ride is over. It *has* to end. I'm not even tired anymore—I'm finished.

He frantically bangs against the window, his muffled voice begging for me to talk to him, pleading from outside the car. I reluctantly roll it down.

"Jake…" I don't look at him. "I'm done." Staring ahead, through the windshield, I wipe the tears from my face.

"What do you mean… done?"

"You told her about our life? Said I was an obligation? That I held you back?"

I can see the tears form in his eyes from my peripheral vision. Mine are gone—there's nothing left.

"I never said that. *I never said that!*" His voice breaks, his tone seeping regret and desperation, but it's too late. "Alex!" Jake literally screams my name in the parking lot.

People are trickling out, beginning to stare.

He inhales a deep breath. "Please, Alex," he says, softer. "I was in a different place then. We were in a different place. I just told her… I was only talking, that's it. *Please!* We have *four* kids together!"

And I take a real deep breath for this next one. Self-destruction mode is fully engaged.

Like I said, this ride has gone on for long enough. And if I'm feeling like it's all been a lie, our entire life together, then you better believe I want him to feel the same way, the same pain. To hurt him as bad as I fucking can.

"Might only be three," I whisper so quietly I'm not sure he hears. When I look at him, his hands drop, palms squealing down the car door. He eyes me with confusion, neck cranking to the side.

"What?"

"Right before my twenty-first."

His face is expressionless, void of any color. "Alex," he warns, lips pressing together, nostrils flaring, "don't do this."

You remember the creep back at the bar? His recollection of events from so long ago? Well, yeah, let's bring that up.

"I fucked someone else."

52. GO YOUR
OWN WAY

So… *life*. It's got this kind of crazy way, am I right? One minute, things are going amazing, and then something happens, and it all tumbles straight to shit.

Repeat, and repeat, and repeat.

Life is just a series of random fucking events, and then we die.

Okay, I'm kidding here. I haven't gone totally dark. Well, not yet.

The four of us had driven to the work thing together, so you can only imagine the drive home—awkward as hell. Kelsey drove, and I sat up front under her watchful eyes. She glanced over every five seconds to make sure I was holding it together. I was. Jake sat with Luke in the back.

Crickets.

This was one of those severely uncomfortable situations where I felt bad for our friends. No one knew what to say. What *do* you say? Nobody wanted to add to the tension, which a knife couldn't even cut.

After I assured her it was okay, Kelsey dropped me off at my house. I had no words for him. No nothing. It was done, and we all fucking knew it.

Days later, after that red dimmed to a pale shade of pink, resigned to the facts, we sat down and did something I never thought we would have.

Stayed calm. Talked. Listened. Our feelings were on high alert, but we worked through it. Personal growth at its finest.

We knew what the best thing was at that point. The right decision, even if it was the hard one.

I came clean about the guy, *fucking* Joey Belter. Jake knew I said it out of anger. *He knows me.* But I told him about the doubt, about the things he'd said to me, the unzipped jeans. He admitted that he'd told the cunt stain—that's what we're referring to her as now—about his life, *our* life. But he hadn't meant it negatively, and she'd twisted it around. He said he'd never felt like we were an obligation. And obviously, he knows Brynn is his. She's the spitting image, a female Jake clone, with no paternity test required. Hazel eyes, dimples, and all.

The problem—and I think it ends an extremely high number of marriages—was our words. Okay, lying plays a part in this too. While Jake confided in someone else, I didn't confide in him. I don't even want to think about what would've happened if I had. He may not have come for my twenty-first birthday… then no Brynn, no anything. No Jordan, Roo, or Will. And no matter what, I'll never regret my kids.

Never.

But in reality, his words were apparently manipulated to be used against me. My words came out for the sole purpose of inflicting gut-wrenching pain.

Yeah, it's a problem.

It's astonishing. The average human speaks anywhere between five and twenty thousand words per day—depends what site you check. But it can take only a handful to crush someone. Shit, it can take one single word.

But Jake and I both agreed we loved each other. And that's where we left it… back in June.

* * *

The entire summer flies by. You know they always do. It's been weird and strangely calm. The six of us are adjusting to life, and we're all gonna be just fine.

I've been working a full-time schedule—four ten-hour shifts a week. It feels good. I've got a steady routine, and the kids aren't driving me too crazy. They got to go to the beach a few times over the summer. Once with my family, and twice… with Jake's.

I guess what I'm avoiding here is more than likely the topic on everyone's mind. What happened after that fateful night about three months ago? Because here we are, already a week into September.

Well, I'm pretty sure you can guess. Mistakes were made, things were said, feelings were mutilated, but we didn't fucking give up, alright? There's a stark difference between giving up and knowing when to walk away. Our hearts had been slaughtered, and we couldn't keep doing it.

We did love each other; we do. Sadly, love isn't always enough. It does *not* conquer all. Some things simply aren't meant to be. Marriages fail all the time. And trust me, it wasn't for a lack of trying. It wasn't one pushing for it, and the other pulling. We are together in this. A mutual decision—the smarter choice. Time to set each other free.

It's now become our life's mission to minimize disruption for the kids; be as amicable as possible and simply try our best to be good people. Because we were great friends—we are.

And so far, so good.

I'm not saying the feelings and emotions are gone. That'll probably take a fair share of time. But I am saying that we needed the ride to be over.

I know everyone wishes and hopes for the fairytale happy ending, but those are only guaranteed in shady massage parlors. Seriously though, life isn't always centered around a happily ever after.

Years ago, we had that crazy, consuming love, that if it wasn't right in your face, it destroyed you. And now, turns out, it was still destroying us. We *both* had to let go. Had to complete the steps, get over the addiction.

We fucked things up so royally. I've said it before and I'll say it again, hindsight is twenty-twenty.

But the past is no place to live.

The kids were disappointed. Of course they were. They've been strung along on this winding ride, and that's not okay, but no matter how hard you try, there's always collateral damage when a lengthy relationship falls apart. We talk to them and encourage them to talk to us. They're so smart, they probably see more than we do. We keep everything as real with them as we can.

I know they still hope and pray that the stars will align and, somehow, something will shift. But there are too many broken pieces. Not everything can be fixed.

Sometimes, enough really *is* enough.

The problem was, we were so busy trying to recreate, wanting to get back to our past selves, and the truth is… neither of us are those people anymore.

* * *

Late Saturday morning, I get myself ready to head to our beloved coffee shop. It's one of the last times I'll see Annie before she and Jace move.

I throw on a maroon T-shirt dress and matching Vans—Brynn's—good enough. Am I too old to steal my teenage daughter's shoes? I mean, she swipes my stuff all the time. I tie a jean jacket around my waist and give myself a once-over. The weather is so up and down here, you never know what you're in for when it's this close to a season change.

My blonde hair hangs straight down my shoulders. That's right, I went back to it. I missed it, and it feels more like me. I don't need to be someone I'm not.

Pulling open the door to Queen of Beans—that's legit the name of our place—I gesture to the barista at the counter with a brief nod.

"Annie coming?" he asks, and I nod again. "Your usuals?"

"Yes please."

Annie isn't here yet, and I can't believe I arrived before she did. But being on time is something I've been trying to get better at too.

I sit in the center of the plush oversized couch. There's no one else in here. It's a shame when the local joints don't get the credit they deserve. I'm pretty sure this particular shop stays afloat on our caffeine addiction alone.

Jake likes it here too. Years ago, we turned him and Jace off the overpriced, watered-down mainstream places and showed them what the genuine stuff is all about. It's the hidden gems that make us realize what's good.

Pictures of landmarks from around the world hang neatly on the brick walls. The dark wood floors and smell of ground coffee beans make me feel at home—this is our special spot. I'm gonna miss coming here with Annie.

"Sup, slut," she announces, loud enough to be embarrassing, after bursting through the door like a hurricane. She shoots a smile to the barista, who extends our cups over the counter. "God bless you and your mother and all that is holy."

"Well… you're welcome," he replies with a laugh.

"Was talking to the coffee," she quips with a wink. "But I guess that goes for you too."

I'm *really* gonna miss Annie.

She hands me my drink and flops down on the couch with an extended huff. "I hate packing. How are you supposed to fit your life into cardboard boxes? There's too much!"

I don't even wanna think about it.

"Damn," she says, taking in my outfit. "You look super cute, and I look like… what the fuck." She motions a hand to her black leggings and plain green top.

Her chestnut hair is pulled up on the crown of her head in a way that's strategically messy—not like the actual hot mess that happens when I do it. There's not a trace of makeup on her face. Her light eyes and the freckles that dance across her nose are more than enough. She's beautiful, inside and out. The epitome of a great friend.

"You look great. You always do." I tsk then take a sip.

"Is *he* coming?" she asks, brows raised. With a fake annoyed expression, her lips punch to her nose, and Annie's head shakes.

"Yeah, I thought you said it was okay? Thought you liked him?"

"I do, I do." She sighs, tipping the cup to her mouth. "I just feel like he's my replacement." She sticks out her bottom lip, ultra exaggerated, ultra Annie.

And in this new wave of human contact I've come to appreciate, I link my arm with hers and lean into her. "No one can *ever* replace you."

And I mean it. Plus, she's not moving hundreds of miles away, it's more like 105. I may or may not have mapped it out.

"Speak of the devil," she says, nose wrinkling, gaze rolling to the door.

I glance up, and we greet each other with adoring smiles. My eyes fix on his dark hair—dark blonde to be exact; the thick kind you can run your fingers through, only to have it rebound perfectly into place.

He removes his sunglasses, and gray eyes gleam back at us. I study the rest of him. Pink lips, surrounded by light-brown, clean-cut stubble, neatly trimmed and well-kept. Tan shorts and a polo, which looks preppy as fuck.

He and I have been inseparable lately. You know, the same guy from the school thing? The rockstar daughter?

Did I mention I've been hanging out with Micah? Oops, must've forgotten that detail.

We got paired up at a volunteer thing early in August. Some back-to-school bullshit. Anyway, he's so much fun—he makes me laugh and honestly keeps me sane. The breath of fresh air I desperately need at this stage of my life.

Turns out, he was in desperate need himself. Micah has two girls of his own. The one who befriended Roo, the rebel, the flipper-offer—Jules—she's in those preteen years, and they're a thorny bitch. His youngest is Will's age, so it works out great.

Anyway, we've bonded over advice on how to talk about periods and all that drama. If you aren't there yet, buckle up, because it's a treat.

He lost his husband a few years back. It's a sad story—cancer. But he seems to make the most out of life, always trying his best, forging onward. He's easy to talk to and doesn't judge. So… yeah, I'm in.

After Micah scoops up his order, he sits down on the other side of me, giving me a peck. He's a total cheek kisser too.

"You look nice." His eyes travel over my outfit as he takes a sip of his drink. "You too, Annie."

"Ugh, fuck off, Micah." She makes a face then laughs at herself. He joins in.

She does like him, so don't let her fool you. Actually, I think if she was around more, the two of them would be close as well.

Right now, this is where I'm at in life. And all in all, I'd say things are okay. *I'm* okay. One step at a time, one shoe in front of the other.

53. LIGHTNING CRASHES

I've always been a firm believer that life-changing moments—the real big things—happen when you aren't paying attention. When you least expect them to.

How often do we take for granted a simple, boring day? All the time. We bitch and moan when there's nothing to do. But when life goes off-kilter, when it's not dull anymore, we complain about that too.

Pretty sure that's human nature, but who knows?

It's a random Wednesday, my day off. I'm spending this supposed relaxing time cleaning the house. I stop for breaks every hour or so, catching up on the latest trashy TV craze or whatever. Just sucked into the mundane things that can make up life—the laundry, the dusting, the groceries, the rat race.

A whole lotta nothing.

It's been like this lately, adjusting to the kids not being around as much… again. It's been almost a year of it, minus the months when things were going alright. I still miss them when they aren't here, and they still annoy the piss outta me when they are.

The wonders of motherhood are legit.

But time is amazing in that way. I wouldn't necessarily say it heals all wounds, because that's kind of bullshit. But I believe that with time you become used to situations. It doesn't make them better or worse; dealing with them just becomes another habit.

The kids are all in school. They were with Jake for the first half of the week and will come back here today, fulfilling their part of the fifty-fifty.

Somewhere between cleaning the bathrooms and scrubbing smudgy handprints off the walls, I sigh. This shit is never-ending. Also, why are they so dirty? I swear my kids use soap. Well, I hope they do.

I can hear my phone rumbling against the wooden coffee table all the way from upstairs, but I don't make too much of a rush for it.

My screen displays a missed call from Roo's school—no big deal. She might've gotten sick. Sometimes she stages a protest if the lunch served is something she doesn't like. And by protest, I mean she can make herself puke on demand. Not cute. She could've had a meltdown, though she hasn't been doing that lately. She's been far more well adjusted this go round. More than likely, they want to tell me about current spiritwear sales, or some other means to make us reach into our pockets. I get multiple calls every single week, from all their schools.

Anyway, I pick up the phone to dial them back, but it lights up in my hand, buzzing once again.

"Hello?" I try my best not to sound annoyed, waiting for the auto-robot voice to tell me where to shuffle my funds next. For shit's sake, how many times do the kids need a bounce-house reward day?

"Is this Mrs. Everett?" a frantic voice blurts from the other end, causing a massive weight to form in my stomach.

You know *that* feeling? The sensation I'd equate to having concrete poured inside you? The impending doom?

"Yes?" I don't even have time to add another word before she goes off, rambling, talking a mile a minute. I can't understand what she's saying—Tina or Tracey or whoever it is. I can't understand her! She's speaking far too fast.

"Stop!" I say, already scooping up my keys from the kitchen and sprinting out to the car. I know this feeling. This is emergent, and something isn't right. Nurse mode kicks in. De-escalate. "I need you to calm down. Please take a breath and tell me what's wrong."

She inhales and exhales a few times. My keys are already in the ignition.

"Ruby had a seizure," she says, her voice shaky and high-pitched.

Okay, this happens. She has epilepsy. Seizures happen sometimes; they just do. I can hear several sobs in the background, amongst the commotion that sounds like people running around, voices yelling, shouting commands.

I'm already flying through my neighborhood. Something is *really* wrong.

"What happened?" I cry. My voice doesn't sound like mine, it's shrill and strained.

"It wouldn't stop. We couldn't stop it. We tried... we tried everything."

My heart is racing, and my palms are sweaty, gripping tight to the steering wheel. I slam the gas pedal to the floor. The massive lump lodged in my throat is probably the only thing keeping vomit down.

You know what feels all kinds of fucked up? When something's wrong with your kid, and you aren't there.

"What? What do you mean you couldn't stop it? Fuck, I need you to calm down and explain this to me." I'm trying not to lose my shit. Roo has absence seizures, which are fits of staring. What the hell is she even talking about?

Her flustered speech is replaced with a bout of uncontrollable crying. This isn't helping me.

"Put Cassie on the phone. Now!" I scream at her, but fuck it, this lady can't even speak, and I need to know what the hell is going on with my child.

"Alex?" Cassie's voice is meek and unsteady. She's the unsung hero that never gets the credit she deserves—Roo's TSS, our saving grace. She knows her so well, probably better than we do.

"What's going on, Cassie? Breathe and talk to me."

"I don't know. We were out at recess, and she was fine. Roo was running around and fell. She just fell." Her voice cracks, and so does my heart. "When I went over to help her, she got really stiff then started shaking." She fails to stop a series of shuddered gasps. "I did what you told me, Alex. I tried to keep her safe. Put her on her side." Her sobs pour out through the opposite end of the phone line.

"Okay, okay that's good. You did so good." I blink back the tears to keep my vision clear. "What happened then? Did you call 911?" I'm fighting against my own hyperventilating breaths, but I need to keep a level head right now. I need to get to my daughter. *My baby.*

"Yes," she cries.

"Are they there now?"

"Yes," she cries again. "Alex, we used her rescue med, but it won't stop."

My heart's not in my body anymore. My heart is at that fucking school with my child. Fuck! That medication is a last-ditch effort, a life-saving intervention. We've never had to use it—*ever.* But it should have been enough, and it should have stopped. It has to stop it.

"I'm almost there!" I shout into my speakerphone.

"They just left."

Fuck, fuck, *fuck!*

Holy shit, stay calm, *stay calm.* Just breathe—the universe is not this cruel. We've been practicing for this; we've always known it could happen.

"Where are they taking her?" I'm not even focused on where I'm driving. The ambulance roars past me, headed in the opposite direction, and I cut the wheel in the middle of the street. Horns blare, brakes squeal, tires skid.

"Memorial." She sounds like she's gonna throw up. That makes two of us.

"Call Jake!" That's all I say before I shift to autopilot, and everything goes blank.

You know when you arrive at a place and don't remember how you got there? I'm here.

I pull up to the ambulance bay and jump out of my car, chucking the keys at the guard. They recognize me. This is my work. The rig is haphazardly parked, lights spinning, the back thrown open, gloves and packaging strewn on the ground. Oxygen tubing lies on the floor of the ambulance, where my Ruby was, likely only seconds ago. She's already inside.

I'm in a complete haze of panic and nausea and fucking suffering.

When I tell you the pain of something happening to your child is one of the most extreme forms of torture, I mean it. It's helpless—hopeless. These beautiful, perfect humans you'd die for, whom you vow to protect and can't… It's the most excruciating form of torment imaginable. I wouldn't wish it on a single soul.

The security guard outside of Trauma heads me off before I can smack my way through the doors. Before I can get back there to help her. To save her.

I know how this goes. I've just never been on this side of it.

No family allowed—not ever. It can't happen. Shit gets ugly and tensions are high. The last thing we need while trying to work is someone screaming in our faces, watching as their loved one's clothes are cut from their body, their life vigorously trying to be saved.

I'm flailing and flipping the fuck out as the massive guard keeps his arms locked around me, stopping me from going any further. He yells for someone to get Annie.

The waiting room is filled with people who are looking at me, staring, and I don't care. I can't recognize my voice, being strangled in my throat as I try to kick and claw my way to my daughter.

"Alex!" Annie shrieks, bolting towards me. Tears stream down her cheeks as she grabs a hold of me, wrapping her arms around me so tight, her body trembling against mine.

I'm numb. My *everything* goes slack. What's happening? Like some sort of flip switches, I become incredibly quiet, my mind in a fog. I'm not even on this planet anymore. I think I'm breathing. I'm not sure? This is an awful movie playing out in front of me. This *cannot* be real life.

"Alex, she's gonna be okay," she muffles into my shoulder.

Annie begins talking, telling me what she knows. Roo had a massive seizure and went into status, meaning she just wouldn't come out of it on her own. That's the thing about seizures—they can change without warning, without notice. They're a lot like life. Calm and dormant, and then, *boom*, they blow up. Epilepsy is unpredictable, and it isn't fucking fair. She's been stable, been on new meds, yet here we are.

Jake runs in through the entrance, dressed in his suit and tie, eyes wide, face pale and terrified. He doesn't hesitate to pull me straight from Annie's arms, and she doesn't stop him. We hold each other so tight, and so anguished, his body molding around mine. This is our child, our baby. No matter what happened between us, we'll always share that love and that bond. *Always.*

Our sobs and fear become one.

* * *

We sit there in silence for a while, my hand gripping Jake's for what feels like days, centuries. In reality, it's been a few hours. Neither of us has spoken a word. They wouldn't allow Annie to go back. She's too close—I get it. Jace is already en route to make sure the rest of our kids get home safe.

My heart beats once again when the slew of doctors and nurses come out, informing us that she's been stabilized, though they don't know the full extent of the damage that might have resulted.

At the same time our parents and my siblings arrive, Carol, my boss, lets Jake and me know we can see Roo soon. She's being transferred to the Pediatric Intensive Care Unit.

My mom and dad try to protect us by keeping any physical signs of fear at bay. That's how it works, I guess, no matter how old you get. My sister and brother give devoted and supportive hugs to us both.

Ashton's hand stays on Jake's shoulder, and they look at each other. If ever there was a time to bury the hatchet, it's now. And they do just that. Both of them say two simple words to each other. That's all it takes—two words, and they forgive. Wouldn't it be nice if we could all be like that? A quick *I'm sorry* and move on.

Ashton envelops his arms around my shoulders right after, pulling me into him. "I love you," he says, regarding me for a moment, drawing his lips down. Blue eyes stare into mine. "And I'm sorry."

That's it. That's all that has to be said.

Jake and I head to the third floor, leaving our families in the waiting area, promising a swift update.

The overwhelming scent of bleach slithers into my nose and churns my stomach as we silently make our way towards the darkened glass door. Sounds of machines and equipment ring out through the otherwise quiet unit.

All eyes are on me, nervously. I'm not only a parent but one of them, and they're probably already guessing that I'll be their worst nightmare. But I won't. Something happens to me when it's my own kids, even if it's a minor scrape or cut. Nurse mode disappears, and Mom takes over. That is my most important role after all.

We walk into her room, and I immediately gasp, my hands covering my mouth. Jake's arms clasp around my waist to stop me from falling.

"She's okay," he whispers, blinking away his own tears. He brushes a hand down the side of my face. "It's going to be okay."

I nod, unable to pull my eyes from our Ruby, *our* precious gem. Her cheeks are puffy, and a tube sticks out of her mouth, breathing for her. Probes and wires cover her head and tiny body; machines beep left and right. She lies in the center of the large bed, like an angel, sleeping peacefully.

They had to put her in a coma. It was the only option. This can happen. Her brain had swollen, and this is the only way to give it a much-needed rest.

There's a vast difference between being told that and seeing it. But I'm trying here; I'm *really* trying to keep it together.

"What if she doesn't wake up?" I swallow hard, shaking my head.

"This is our child," Jake says, fingers lacing with mine. "We both already know... she can beat any odds."

* * *

The next two days pass by in a blur of exhaustion. Minimal eating. No showers. Zero sleep.

But it's okay. Roo is expected to make a full recovery, though we won't know where we're going from here. We won't know when it will happen again. We won't know if this will be another setback for her. Just one more thing to add to the list of uncertainties.

By the third day, she's breathing on her own, still being her stubborn self, remaining asleep. Though I believe she will wake up completely when her body is ready.

Jake and I, beyond tired, sit on the rigid wood-framed chairs on either side of her bed. Our arms reached out to each other, resting on small legs, hand in hand.

Whatever the current circumstances, we are in this together. Forever.

At some point, we must've fallen asleep. I wake up to a slight movement and squeeze his palm. Both of us jolt from our sleep. My face is only inches from Jake's. Our heads snap towards Roo, whose little brown eyes blink open, while a smile curves her tiny mouth.

And this next part is the one that trumps *everything*, the part that makes it all worth it. The ups and downs. The pain, the frustration, the sleepless nights. And maybe you know exactly what I mean and I'm sure you felt it too, the first time you heard *that* word come out of your child's mouth, but I sure thought I would never hear it, at almost twelve years old.

Roo's pink lips part, and she looks down affectionately at us. Her attention shifts to me, and my chin wobbles as tears flood my face.

She smiles even wider, and in the softest and raspiest of all voices, she whispers, "Mommy."

54. NOTHING COMPARES 2 U

By day four, Roo was wide awake, alert, and totally on edge. She can't stay still. Try calming a child that runs a thousand miles a minute and force them to lie in a bed. Yeah, it doesn't happen.

Jake and I are running on empty, calling the other three when we can, feeling that all-too-familiar guilt when one child needs more from you. But what can you do? You can't change these fucked-up things that happen, or these shitty conditions your child might be born with. If I had the capacity, trust me, I would. You can either roll with it, taking things as they come. Or you can let it roll over you, allowing it tear your life apart.

No one wants this. If it was optional, not a single human would choose for their child to have any problems. It means life will be harder—not normal, whatever normal is—unpredictable. We don't know what the future has in store for her, and while that's scary, we have to make the best of it.

We've already been informed that Roo will be discharged tomorrow. She's stable. All of her lab work and test results came back at baseline, and she's good to go. How a tiny body like hers can make such a miraculous recovery is beyond me. But Jake was right. She is meant to beat the odds. One more day and we're outta here to resume everyday life and wait for yet another shoe to drop.

Because guess what? It will.

There's always going to be stuff that flips your world upside down. That gives you a solid and sometimes much-needed reality check. You can pretend like it won't and live a scared life. Or… choose to boss up, knowing that when shit does inevitably hit those rotating blades again, you're ready to meet the challenge, head-on. Guns blazing, screaming, *Come at me, bitch.*

Sounds easy enough, right?

Yeah, it's not. But I'm trying. That's the best any of us can do—keep our heads up, move forward, have faith, and just continue fucking swimming, knowing that no matter what happens, we can survive it.

So far, I have a one hundred percent success rate for surviving shitty things. We all do.

Sometime early morning on the fifth day, Ashton walks into the room. Both our families paused their own lives, taking turns visiting, dropping off food, spoiling our other three, and simply offering their love.

He comes in, greeting me with a quick wave but remaining silent. A soft smile curls his lips when he takes in the sight of Jake cuddled up in bed next to Roo, both sound asleep.

They moved her from the dark, quiet intensive care ward to an obnoxiously bright, yellow room. There are pictures of cartoon characters along the walls, plenty of toys—though the iPad is her current MVP—and way more hustle and bustle.

Ashton wipes a thumb beneath his eyes, blinking and sniffling. No doubt picturing himself and his own little girls.

Eventually his gaze shifts from them to me, sitting in a chair, responding to countless messages conveying love and well wishes.

"Coffee?" he suggests in a whisper. I nod then scribble a quick note to Jake to tell him where I'm headed.

* * *

"I want to tell you something." Ash drums his fingers over the plastic tabletop, in the back of the hospital cafeteria.

We both sip subpar caffeine from cardboard to-go cups, having sat there quietly for a bit. I smile, urging him to continue.

"I've been seeing someone."

My eyebrows raise, mouth opening and forming a widening grin.

He chuckles and shakes his head. "No… not like that." He lifts a palm before picking at the paper sleeve or whatever you call the thing that stops the heat from burning your hand. "Well, kind of like that too, but—"

"Who is it?" I ask, unable to hide the excitement in my voice, going stupid cheese on him, which makes him laugh.

He waves me off. "I've been talking to… a therapist." Ashton's lips pitch to the side. "It's been good."

I reach across the table, placing a hand over his, giving it a gentle squeeze. "I think that's great, Ash."

"I want… I *need* you to know that I love you." His eyes slowly drift from the table to mine. "There has never been a moment in my life that I didn't respect and admire you."

Fuck. More tears?

"I love you too."

He nods, snagging his top lip. "The things I said to you… the things I said to Jake. Well…" He pauses and takes a swig of his coffee. "They were wrong and out of line."

I keep my hand over his, giving it another squeeze, and offer him a slight smile. "We don't need to do this." And it's true, we don't. Even if he hurt me. Even if his words stung. He's my brother.

"I know." He inhales a lengthy breath before releasing it. "But I just want to say I'm sorry… for everything."

"Hey." I pull his attention to me when it strays. Then I look him directly in the eyes and say what he's needed to hear for a long time, even if I don't believe it needs to come from me. "I forgive you."

The smallest smile touches his lips, and his head barely nods, though an unmistakable weight lifts from his shoulders. I'm pretty sure Ashton was sick of living in those woods too.

* * *

We spend a few hours together, the three of us making small talk, watching Roo video call her brother and sisters, laughing along with her infectious giggle. Ashton seems to sense our weariness and offers to stay with Roo for a while, telling Jake to get some rest and me to shower because I stink.

Always the big brother.

We both know he can handle her—all of our family can. The village is in full effect.

My parents and Jake's are at my house. I know they're making sure Brynn, Jordan, and Will are being shown an insane amount of love. They especially need it right now.

Before we leave, a med student comes into the room. He greets the four of us with handshakes. Well, three. The most Roo would give was an elbow bump, not willing to glance away from the vid she's currently engrossed with.

He tugs at an overly starched tie, glancing from her chart to the three of us. I feel bad for him. It's probably not easy to walk into a room with two brawny dudes and someone he knows he can't bullshit. I can recite her med list and history like it's my job, because it is.

He flips through some notes, asking the same questions everyone else has, going over the discharge plan. We got it. They're switching up her medications. She needs to have a repeat EEG and multiple appointments. But then he asks something that no one else did, and I don't know why I never thought of it myself. Roo getting medicine day and night is just part of our daily routine.

"And she didn't skip a dose, is that correct?"

"No," I snap, totally annoyed. I shouldn't be—he's just doing his job, but like I said, minimal sleep, and the same repetitive questions and instructions have me perturbed.

I catch Jake in my peripheral vision. He looks like he's gonna be sick. His mouth falls open. "I… I don't know," he says so quietly it's barely a whisper. "I can't remember. I'm not sure if she took it."

He glances at me, his brows pulled together, then covers a hand over his quivering lips, swallowing loud enough that I can hear it. We all can.

"What?" My nostrils are flaring, my hands curling into fists. "What the—"

Ashton places his palm on my shoulder. I jerk towards him to meet sympathetic blue eyes. "He doesn't deserve that."

I stop, blowing out a breath, then stare at my daughter, who is fine, and I nod.

Ashton is a hothead, which obviously runs in the family, but when I look at Jake, who's standing there devastated, I realize he's right.

Jake doesn't need me to beat him up about this. He's human. We all fuck up and make massive mistakes. We can't go back and change it. We can hopefully learn from it and do our best to make sure it doesn't happen again.

"It's okay," I say from across the bed.

His head drops, and he doesn't say a word.

Jake's mom took his car, so I have to run him home. The ride is uncomfortably silent. When I pull up to the townhouse, I place my hand over his forearm, literally having to squeeze it to gain his attention. The stubble along his jaw has grown out after days of neglect. His eyes are red, plagued with dark circles that match mine, and the twinkle that always lights them up is gone.

"Jake, it's okay."

He rubs a palm down his face, releasing a staggered breath.

"She's alright. Everything's alright."

He nods then slips his arm from my touch and gets out of the car, walking slowly to the front door. He turns, briefly, before going inside, and his expression is one of pure defeat.

He's *not* okay.

I sit there for a minute, not sure what to do. Where do I draw the line? Do I go in? Try to help him, talk to him, try to pick him back up? Or do I drive away?

Micah must've spotted my car in the neighborhood. He knew I was dropping Jake off.

"How's everyone doing?" he asks after jogging up to the driver's side, looking from me to Jake's front door.

"You know…" I sigh then frown at him. "Best we can."

"Jake hanging in there?"

He already knows how Roo's doing. I text him now the same amount as Annie. We've got this whole group chat going, mostly sharing funny memes and hot guy pics… shit like that. Lately, it's just been for communicating the current happenings. The continuing saga.

"No… I don't think he is."

He reaches in through the open window, rubbing a hand over my arm. "You want a little advice?"

I arch a brow.

Micah laughs, sweeping the tears from beneath my eyes. These tears are from the sadness I have for Jake feeling as if he failed. He shouldn't.

I chuckle after a moment, staring at my friend, this fresh voice of reason in my life. "Not so much, but I'm sure you're gonna give it to me."

And he does.

I know what I have to do.

No matter what, I need to be there for Jake, especially on matters of the kids. We share them forever. I can't allow him to feel like he's to blame. I felt that way for so long—that every little thing was my fault. He has to know, at least with this, we're in it *together*.

I open the unlocked front door, let myself in, then glance at the kitchen counter. Relief floods me when I see the clear medicine cup sitting on it… empty. I can't help but smile. He didn't forget, and she took it.

It was just a thing. A random thing. Not because of an error, but because stuff happens. It just does.

I make my way towards his room. The walls of his house are now coated with various shades of gray, pictures hanging on them. I haven't stepped foot in here in months. It looks like a home now.

Feeling like a bit of a creeper but knowing deep down he needs someone, I open the door to his bedroom to find clothes thrown across the floor. The water falling from his shower echoes around me.

I don't hesitate or contemplate for more than a second. Without letting my mind go through some extensive list of pros and cons, trying to figure out where the line is, or where it should be, I take off my shirt and jeans. And since I don't have any extra—I promise, that's the *only* reason—I take off my bra and underwear too. Because all I can think about, at this moment, is all those years ago, when I was in the darkest of places, it was Jake who climbed into the shower with me, washing away my pain and bringing me back to life. Now it's my turn, and I am *finally* at a place where I can do the same for him.

I open the shower door, which is fogged up with steam. His head turns to me; he's still wearing the same wounded expression, his lips, eyes, his entire face turned down.

After stepping in behind him, I wrap my arms around his body. He doesn't fight it. He realizes the significance of this. I know he'll always remember those particularly tough days. I'm sure he never thought *I'd* be the one trying to bring *him* back.

Here's this man, who on the outside is tall, dark, and undeniably handsome, with such a tough-looking exterior. And he's basically becoming a puddle in front of me.

I hold my arms steadily around him, cheek pressed to his back, allowing him to get it out. He trembles and shudders and buckles forward with soft sobs.

Nothing needs to be said. Sometimes the best thing to say is nothing at all. Sometimes when we're sad, frustrated, angry at the world, we simply need human connection. Words aren't required.

I can't count, or even start to recall, how many times I've had a solid cry in the shower. It really is the best place. The water washes away the tears and sends them down the drain. But I will *always* remember the times he came in and wrapped his arms around me, making me know we were in this together.

That's totally all this is. An extreme show of support—clothing optional.

I'm not sure how long we stay like that, or exactly who initiates the movement so we're staring at each other. Water trickles down his hair and over his face, over *both* our faces. My fingertips smooth along his clenched jaw, my eyes studying his, the twinkle somewhat restored. We just stand there, gazing at each other, while both our lips part and heavy breaths exhale from our mouths.

And before I know it, my palms clasp around the back of his neck, pulling him down to me. I rise up on my tiptoes, letting the water cascade over us, and gently press my lips to his. Just a caring kiss. A friendly sign of affection.

Okay, who am I kidding here?

I've said this before. When you're under stress or in a crazy situation… well, we all react in different ways.

I'm not sure if it's the promise of oxytocin or Jake that I'm craving, but I need it. We *both* need to take this pain away. His arms engulf me, fingers dragging down my back, his lips still on mine.

We pull apart, breathing into each other, *for* each other. And when I look at him, at his distressed expression, I'm not sure what I'm nodding for, but I am.

Our lips crash feverishly. Mouths open, tongues swirling. Here we go again with the face-sucking, pain-swallowing kisses. You know, the ones you can't seem to make fast enough, or deep enough, just trying to heal each other.

My heart beats wildly, and I press a palm to his chest, feeling his own manic pulse matching mine. He pulls me against him… hard.

It's *all* hard.

We need this. It's not right. But if this is wrong I don't wanna be right. At least not in this moment.

Not breaking our kiss, his hands glide further down my back, and he lifts me to his waist, my legs raveling around him.

Somehow, we're out of the still-running shower—water conservation be damned—and Jake walks us to the bed, arms clinging so tight to each other, drenched.

Also, secret thank you that he didn't slip on the tiled floor.

He lays me down gently, and my hair, my entire body soaks his sheets, but neither one of us seems to care. He lowers himself over me, keeping his eyes on mine. His hand skims the side of my face while my nails score into his back.

The need, the desire to ease any and all grief, is mixed with unrelenting passion and soul-connecting kissing. This is right up there with one of the most intense things I've *ever* experienced.

Heavy gasps fall from our lips when he pushes inside me. We're trembling, falling, completely lost in each other. My arms remain around his back while he holds my face so my eyes stay on his, though he doesn't need to. With our foreheads connected, he pushes deeper and soothes an ache. A million aches. Tears spill down our cheeks and speak so many words that could never be said.

This is something next level. I'm not talking about the kinky shit. I'm saying that *this* is something else.

While we've made love, this is something I'm not sure we've ever done before. We aren't consuming each other's hearts, or bodies, or minds. This time, we're consuming something different.

Right now, in this drenched bed, with our hearts beating perfectly in sync, we stare into each other's eyes and realize this isn't just sex. And I don't know what will happen now, because we were done. But with each thrust, each muffled cry, each build-up of that crazy sensation, I know we both feel it.

And nothing, I mean *nothing*, compares.

55. IF THE WORLD WAS ENDING

Well, here we are, exactly one year later, nearing the end of September, or the last day of summer to be exact.

An entire year. What—and I cannot stress this enough—a fucking ride. It's amazing how much your life can change in 365 days.

It's been a year since I saw that text. The bullshit that sent us into a tailspin; took life as we knew it and shook it all kinds of sideways.

As crazy as this sounds, and trust me, I never thought I'd be saying it, but it took that one thing—that ridiculous, stupid thing—to uncover so many others. Turns out, there were a lot. And while I'm still a believer that certain relationships have to fall apart to get better, more importantly, you yourself sometimes have to fall apart to get better. And there is *nothing* wrong with that.

This past year forced me to take a long, hard look at who I am—as you already know, given you've traveled through this song and dance with me. The playlist has consisted of highs and lows, happiness, sadness, beauty, and pain.

I'm proud of who I've become.

Perfect? Nah, not even close. But I'm not viewing life like some disaster anymore. Because it isn't. While stuff happens, and not everything goes according to plan, or the way you want or wish it to, life is a precious thing. We are lucky for every single day we get.

So, victim? Nope, not anymore. Fuck that shit. I'm okay. I complete me.

That day with Jake; the shower, the significant act of love—well, it was extraordinary. It was earth-shattering, soul-binding, beyond amazing…

But sometimes it's just too late.

Like, damn. I get it, and I think we all get it, that Jake and I have a connection that's next level. Seems meant to be. But you get that when you've known someone so long, right?

You're bound to have these leftover feelings, and shit is gonna be intense. I mean, we went through something major. Our child being so sick was unbelievably scary. It's probably only natural that we had that crazy connection for the last time.

Well, really for the first time. But also… the last time.

So what took place after that? We both lay there for a while in silence, wondering what would happen next. Was it a new beginning? Or was this the final verse? I guess we were trying to figure out where we'd go from there.

Well, Jake fell sleep. I don't blame him either. We were both just so… fucking… exhausted. And I went home.

Later that day, several hours after I'd gone back to Roo, Jake brought Brynn to the hospital. She wanted to come, and to spend time with her baby sister. Soon, she'll be out in the big, imperfect world, and I think that realization is setting in. Brynn is about to start the next chapter of her story, and we all know new chapters can be exciting but scary as hell.

Micah brought Jules to the hospital to visit with Roo. Jake was cordial with him, I guess, which was weird because I thought he liked him.

The communication just kinda died out. Anyway, not like we could talk about what had happened then and there, so I went to sit outside with Micah, mediocre coffee in hand.

* * *

"You want to fill me in? Let me know what happened?" Micah asked, brows raised and awaiting full details.

"We had sex." My shoulder lifted, lacking hard in the nonchalance realm.

"Okay…" He laughed. "And?" He was shaking his head, eyes wide, not judging, but he wanted more on the story.

"And that was it," I lied, straight through my teeth.

His groan was enough to let me know he was as sick of the nonsense as me. "Alex, I may be younger than you, but I thought I was pretty clear.

You have an extra shot here, another chance. I feel like you're letting go of something you don't want to."

Still seems the popular opinion.

I laid my head on Micah's shoulder with a sigh. His arm draped around me, hand rubbing mine, which helped with the goosebumps that had spread from the fresh chill in the September air.

"You know, Taylor and I didn't have the perfect marriage. Far from it. We fought, and we messed up... a lot. But that happens. Marriage is all about trudging through the shit with someone. It doesn't have to be perfect, because the realest, truest relationships never are."

"I know." I fidgeted with the rings on my finger, the ones I'd been so quick to take off before. For whatever reason, now, I just couldn't.

All I could think about was Jake's house, and how it was painted, and how both feet were out the door. And how we'd been alright. I'd been okay, in the last few months, without him.

"Alex, I would have fought for my husband to the very end. I wouldn't have thrown the towel in. I'd give anything to have him back. It pisses me off that Jake is still here, on this earth, and neither of you can seem to get out of your own way." Micah spat the unguarded truth like he always does.

But you see, this is the problem with stories—sometimes you only hear things, and form opinions, from one single point of view. And I think we all know, there are *always* several sides to them. My side, Jake's side, and reality.

The actual truth is likely stuck somewhere in the middle.

* * * Jake * * *

I'd walked outside of the hospital after I got my head on straight, close to two weeks ago, ready to beg. To plead, with Alex, with my wife, for one more chance at redemption. God knows she's given me too many. And God knows I've fucked up. But forever was meant for us—I believe that.

Somewhere, in the mix of years, I focused so much on making a living that I didn't make a life. Did I feel neglected? Yeah, I did. But why's it on her to handle every other human in our family and still have to look after me? That's something I hadn't even given the slightest thought to... before.

We lost each other; along the winding road I wouldn't want to travel with anyone else, her hand slipped from mine. And I fucking let it.

When I think back to that day, that bullshit day where I let attention from another woman steer me off course, I'd like to rewind and start over.

But we can't.

Alex was never emotionally unavailable to me. She was going through shit, shit she pushed onto the back burner for years, so she could ensure everyone else was okay. I cursed her for not opening up to me, but I did the same. And now it's too late.

When my eyes landed on her, I saw her—*really* saw her. I watched with such a heavy heart as my world came crashing down all over again. I knew it had to end. She doesn't deserve any more pain or turmoil. And I know she's been happy lately.

She sat on the stone ledge outside the hospital, her blonde hair whipping in the breeze, looking wild, but that's how she is. It suits her. She's always stunning, and I hate that I ever made her think differently. Her head was resting on Micah's shoulder, his arm looped around her.

It made me seriously want to hurt the guy, but I couldn't. Her body language, everything about her was so relaxed. It never seems to be that way around me, because she's always nervous or worried. And I know she'll never trust me.

I should have devoted my entire life to loving her, conveying how much she means to me, to all of us. It makes me sick that I didn't truthfully know her, didn't see her for who she was. Not the exceptional mother, the devoted wife, but for Alexandra, the woman who will forever be engraved on my heart.

To add insult, the kids seem to love Micah too. But that's important to me. They've told me he's been hanging around a lot lately, and I can't fault her for it. She deserves a happy ending. She should be allowed to move on.

Alex hasn't talked to me about him, but I'm not blind. There's a genuine connection between them. Shit, we haven't talked about anything except for the kids. But I could see it even with their backs to me, the way they were leaning into each other, the way he's there for her. She needs that.

She deserves that.

I'm certain I will *never* find another Alex, but I can't pretend like it's okay that I made her cheat on Micah. The guilt is too much.

It's all been too much.

I have to do this, or I don't know if she'll ever be happy.

Once Roo was discharged, we took her home… to Alex's house. It was the full family chaos, with both our parents, the kids, the dogs. I memorized the moment. We're focused on getting life as back to normal as we can, though I'm not sure what normal is.

After everyone had left, and the kids settled in bed, I couldn't even look at her. Those blue eyes, speckled with tiny hints of yellow, feel as though they could pierce straight into your soul. Will's are the same. I love those eyes. She always complains that she doesn't look good, and I wish she could see what everyone else sees. I wish she'd see what *I* see.

Alex is beautiful, inside *and* out. And somehow, she gets even prettier as the years go by. I should've paid more attention.

When I told her I'd be over next Monday, with the papers, I couldn't look her in the eye. I knew she'd have that little line between her brows from a scowl. Her face is the most expressive one I've ever seen.

And I'm a coward. I've been acting like a complete dick to her. One last hurt to slam the nail into the coffin.

What I wouldn't sacrifice to go back, a year ago, to tell her right then and there that I'd broken my own heart. I should've been honest and focused on communicating and telling her things before they got out of hand. I want to bare my soul to her, let everything pour out, but I can't. It's not fair, and it's too late.

I *have* to let her go.

* * *

Right, so where were we?

Oh yeah, random Monday, the last day of summer. I opted to cut down on my work schedule, just for a month, to make sure Roo is completely stable. She is—already back in school, doing just fine.

Jake had stopped over around lunchtime, handed me a stack of papers, and said he'd be back later.

It's amazing, in a totally fucked-up and sad kind of way, but if you don't want some long, drawn-out fight, and if you can be adults about it, a divorce is super easy. And like I said, it's been a year, so the formal wait time is over.

Clearly, that day in the shower didn't mean a *thing* to him. He's been a straight-up asshole since, dismissive, and I don't know, just acting like he doesn't give a shit. He's nice enough when we talk about the kids and all, but he won't even look at me.

I dig through the junk drawer for a pen and set the papers on the kitchen counter. Sifting through the pages, my heart drops when I see the signature—Jake's—scribbled across the first line. And I think about the first night we met, the bonfire, and can't help but smile at the memory.

Even though our story is ending, I will *always* appreciate the parts that truly were beautiful.

With each turn of the page, each time my pen meets the paper, each time I sign my name, I remember every single happy moment.

There have been so many.

I don't remember the bad times, only the good. I think about the last year; the people we've become. And push the bad stuff aside, because, at this point, why dwell on it anymore?

I think about the fact that our oldest daughter is the same age we were when we first met. My wish for Brynn is that she finds a man like her father, and I hope she doesn't let their signal fade over the years.

The ride has to end. It's sad, but it's true. We will always have a strong relationship—I don't doubt that for a second—and we'll continue to be the best parents we can.

I turn to the last page, the last required signature. Once my ink meets the paper, that's it. That and a quick trip to the courthouse will seal the deal.

The pen shakes in my hand, and my heart speeds up. I draw in a long breath and let one single tear fall as I stare at the blank signature line on the final page.

56. CLOSING TIME

Here's what's up. It's super easy, insanely, to stand outside of a situation, looking in, and form an opinion. It's easy to see exactly what's wrong, as well as all the things that are right. But when you're in the thick of it, I promise you, so much can be blinding. Jealousy, love, happiness, sadness, anger, grief—the twisty list goes on, and on, and fucking on.

And people can give you advice, load you up with their beliefs, but it doesn't matter. We see what we want.

Like an unspoken word that can ultimately speak volumes, maybe an unsigned signature can do the same.

With the papers clutched in my hand, I walk out onto my front porch. Everything is bright and vibrant—the deep green grass coating my lawn, the crisp blue sky; a regular late-summer day in the mid-Atlantic area.

Jake leans against the side of his car. He must've run home and changed. When he dropped off the papers earlier, he was buttoned up in his suit and tie. Now, he appears much more relaxed. He looks like himself. I smile, taking it all in. How is it possible to make a plain white T-shirt and some navy gym shorts look so damn good? Well, I don't know, but he rocks it. That's something I'll *never* want him to change.

His arms are crossed in front of his chest, still kissed from the summer sun. Dark ink swirls perfectly over his skin. With his head dipped down, he walks across the front yard. The flowers, the trees, everything in its last phase of bloom, preparing for the next season.

Jake bites his bottom lip, because that's what he does, and slowly looks up, until his gaze meets mine. He barely blinks, staring at me. Then his head tips to the side, mouth opening, eyes growing wide. That little twinkle of hope reignites when his attention shifts to my hand. To the last page.

The blank page.

"You forgot to sign." I raise a brow, letting the corner of my lips curl up, getting a little smirky.

I know this guy. He deals with paperwork day in and out—there's no chance he forgot to sign.

He didn't want to. And neither do I.

Jake runs a hand down over the dark stubble on his chin. A few gray hairs are peeking through. With his backwards hat in place, he glances over at douche czar Dennis, out watering his sidewalk or whatever he's doing. Probably scrutinizing this entire exchange. He can watch all he wants.

Unfortunately, I'm standing here in tiny black booty shorts that should probably never be worn outside and a thin-as-fuck pink tank top. Those built-in bras don't do shit! It's all hanging out.

Back to the papers.

"I didn't want to," Jake admits quietly, shifting his weight from foot to foot, kicking an imaginary rock with his shoe.

"Why then? Why'd you even bring these?"

My eye catches the platinum ring, reflecting so brightly from the afternoon sun shining down on it. The one he keeps rolling subconsciously with his thumb. The one he continues glancing at.

"I want you to be happy, Alex. I *need* you to be happy."

He looks up at me. Small creases line the corners of his eyes, and dark lashes curl over his pained hazels as he worries his lip.

And for the first time, I don't see that young guy anymore. I don't see the one who was out to fix the world, or the one who needed to fix me. I see this man, who has changed and who is totally flawed. But despite his mistakes, and my mistakes, and all the bullshit in between, he's so perfect for me, it's insane.

"And you thought this is what would make me happy?" I hold up the papers, crinkling my nose with a huff.

"I see how you and Micah are together. You care about each other. You seem to be doing great, and that's all I want."

I smack a hand over my mouth but fail at trying to contain the snorts of laughter coming out. Jake's eyes roll all over the place, full-on what-the-fuck face happening.

I pull my lips into my mouth, trying to curb my hilarity as my entire body shakes in amusement.

"How is any of this funny?" He scowls, jaw tensing.

"Okay, first off, Micah is just a friend. Seriously, Jake? Is that why?"

"It's alright, Alex, you don't have to tell me that. You're beautiful. I'm not surprised he's interes—"

"Jake."

And it really is all one big circle, no beginning or end. It's a roller coaster, and it always will be. Because that's life. There's gonna be bad times mixed in with good. It's not going to be pretty, and that's alright.

We need to let go of our past—insecurities, fuck-ups, and all. Need to realize that we *are* different people today.

I'm not saying just forget everything. Hell no, that's impossible. But what I'm saying is… we can give a nod to our past selves, those beautiful, ridiculous messed-up humans. Thank them for surviving and finally let them go.

It truly is time to turn the page. Make a new beginning, and come out stronger and better than ever before.

Marriage is a ride. But I'd rather be on this ride all day, every day. I'll stay on it till I throw up, and then some. I don't care anymore. This *entire* time I've been at war with myself.

All I know is, I constantly let my heart, my mind, or my body speak for me. But this time… I'm listening to my soul. And that beats the others.

Problems? Yup, sure got 'em. Communication is obviously not our strong suit, but we can spend the rest of our lives working on it; working on all the things. We'll probably keep Patricia—fucking Patty—in business just by ourselves. Oh well, I'm here for it.

We can do it *together*. Because I'd rather stay on this insane, unpredictable roller coaster with Jake than stand in line, or get on some lame-ass one, with anybody else.

People will have an opinion. But unless they've been in this exact spot, this same situation, they can shove it. A love story like ours is more than likely a one-time deal.

And with that, I decide it's time to take a genuine leap of faith. An actual fucking leap.

I jump from the front porch, over the steps, and launch myself at him. Maybe I should have thought about it first, because the sidewalk is concrete, and that would hurt. But ya know what? Jake caught me.

Of course he did.

I wrap my legs around his waist and slide my hands up the back of his neck, taking in the fresh, spicy, minty Jake smell. His brows knit together in confusion.

I crush my lips over his, pressing hard, and he jerks back, exhaling in heavy, short bursts, his mouth gaping open.

"I think you're beautiful too," I whisper in his ear, snagging the bottom of it with my teeth. "So does Micah."

"What?"

"Yes, you idiot!" I thought he knew? "Why didn't you just say something?"

He stands there, his face maybe an inch from mine. I can feel his heart pounding, our chests smashed together. His eyes bore into mine. "It took me so long to see things, to see you." His muscular arms squeeze around my back.

"So…" I move my lips right over his. "What do you say? Wanna spend the rest of our lives making up for it?"

My heart flutters. An overwhelming feeling of relief, and joy, and exhilaration floods through me when Jake's mouth covers mine. His tongue slides along the seam of my lips, prying them apart with a deep, hungry kiss. His palms travel down under my ass, which is hanging out.

I hoist an arm, giving dick-off Dennis the one-finger salute. He can take a pic, post it up on the neighborhood page with a full review. Zero fucks.

I feel like I could burst into a million pieces as Jake smiles, his hands roaming all over me.

My legs are still tight around his body as he walks us inside. Not exactly the storybook version of crossing the threshold, but this is *our* story. It is, and always will be, the furthest thing from a fairytale. I hope we keep this fire forever. I'm already grinding into him, and Jake kisses along my neck, trailing to my ear.

Panty dropper? Not a problem.

He lowers me onto the family room floor—may as well finish that whole freaky-ass massage thing that started all those months ago—why not, right? Then he jumps up, letting the dogs out back.

Dogs, kids, interruptions… yeah, that stuff won't change.

He throws his hat onto the couch, his dark hair nice and tousled, then his shirt meets the same fate. Nobody's mad at it. He lowers over me, lips right back to mine, then pulls away for a brief second, the biggest cheese I've ever seen rockets all the way to his eyes. Jake leans back, straddling my waist.

"So is that a yes?" I ask with a laugh.

He nods vigorously, and I situate my hands behind my head. This carpet's about to get real messy, but screw it. Messy carpet, messy hair, messy heart, messy life—I'm ready to serve this sentence.

Both our mouths open at the same time.

"Whatever it takes," Jake swears.

"Forever," I promise.

So cue that sexy Jake smirk. We are doing this. *All* of this.

I'm stubborn. Also sometimes oblivious to the shit right in front of me, but no more. Self-destruction is off the menu.

My nails scrape down his bare back, drifting to that well-defined ass, pressing him harder against me. The panting has already started, and groans and moans fill our house. But fuck it, no one's home. It's just some shameless grinding on the family room floor. No big.

His palms slip beneath my tank, every single part of me on fire as his fingers tease over my skin. He pulls my top off and yanks the tie from my hair, then stares down at me with an ear-to-ear, happy-life smile on his face.

We ditch our shorts fast as hell.

I'm already ready, if ya know what I mean. A little through-the-clothes grinding got that party started for *both* of us.

"I love you," I say. Actually, I kinda scream it as he thrusts inside me. My arms hook beneath his, gripping his shoulders, my hips rising to meet every single pound.

Jake grabs a handful of hair. You know it's his thing—but I think it might be *my* thing? Giving it a tug, he sinks his lips to my neck, his stubble tickling my skin. Then he whispers in my ear, which makes me about to lose my mind. "Alex, I fucking love you."

So… I'll spare you the rest. The kids will be home soon. We gotta get this goin', finish it up then figure out what we're gonna tell them.

Because I guarantee you this: I'm not sleeping without him. Not for one more single night.

Anyway…

I don't care where you go, but you can't stay here. Plus, there's nothing more to see.

Story's over.

So, for those who prefer their endings wrapped up in pretty pink paper, with a matching bow on top, this next part's for you.

They lived happily ever after.

Okay, bullshit on that. Of course not. There's gonna be highs and lows, fights, drama, tears, all of it. That's the way it works. Love is super messy; it's not an easy ride. Would it be worth it if it was?

I can't tell you what the future holds. Nobody knows. Marriage, just like life, is unpredictable. It truly is like the different seasons.

Winter—blizzards, dreary, sometimes lonely days, dark and cold. Spring—rain mixed with sunshine; new life, growth, and all of that nonsense. Summer—hot and bright, carefree days; the calm breeze and fun. And fall, when everything changes and prepares for a brand-new cycle. The ever-continuing circle; the merry-go-round.

What I realize is, if you can get through all that shit, if you can endure the different seasons, and if you can muddle through the gray days, stick it out, probably talk it out, then you'll be there for the sunny ones.

You *have* to take the bad with the good. It's a package deal.

So… no. I can't promise it'll be perfect. And I'm sorry it took me a year to get here. But I can promise you this.

We will never spend the fall apart again.

The end. The beginning. It's the stuff in between that *really* matters anyway.

Fuck it! Cue the Shania.

JEDAM

ACKNOWLEDGMENTS

I don't even know where to begin with this, because there are so many of you who helped me, in so many ways. First off, thank you to anyone who has picked this story up, and taken a chance on me and these characters. It's been quite the process, and there were about a million times when I wanted to give up. Trust me when I say this came from the depths of my actual soul. Your messages, words of encouragement, love for this different story, and just being supportive mean everything to me and are the reason you're even reading this right now.

To Claire, you've been at it with me from the get-go, and are a flipping rockstar. You always drop everything to help me, even when you have so much of your own stuff going on. I appreciate you more than I could ever express. Not only the countless times of reading, editing, triple-checking, making all the things, knowing when to push me and when I'm going to dig in, you never gave up on me and were with me through some rough times. This book is already successful in my mind because it brought me you.

To J, my Sagittarius sis, who also drops everything, encourages me, pushes me, and has given up so much time to help shine this baby to its highest potential, pop 23 for life. You are another amazing human I met through our little slice of the book world, and our friendship means everything to me. Thank you for being such a light to me in my dark places.

The two of you mean the fucking universe to me!

To Margarita, you are another reason this book is in anyone's hands. Thank you for the shove to follow my dreams and for believing in this story and me. To Jines, you jumped right on board when I was in a tight spot, I can't thank you enough for helping me and following behind my mad dash, picking up my errors. I'm happy to call you my friend. To Leigh, we started from hiding in the bathroom from our kids while reading, and now we're here. I'm so thankful for this journey that began with you and me in Jan 2020… Yeah, I'll never let it go. Seriously, thank you for all your help. To

L.A. Cannon, who delivered countless virtual smacks over the years and will forever be my cover guru, you're so talented, and I appreciate all you've done for me over our years of friendship. And for putting up with my obsessive ways and handling it with grace. Gold-medal status.

To Meg, for your help back when, with the blurb and so much insight, and Cheka, with your input and spreadsheets that kept me straight. To Sookie, for diving in and giving me your candid and detailed overview of my story, it is, and I am stronger because of that. To the countless people I've met over the years, who support me daily, who read this in its initial form, who share, who spread the word, and who simply brighten my day, please know that you've made me so blessed, and I seriously love every one of you.

To all the incredibly courageous babes I've been blessed to know, thank you for showing me what life is all about.

To my Annie… you already know. And you'll always be my favorite.

To my family, for encouraging a dreamer and loving me no matter what, even when it wasn't easy.

And my husband. The one who keeps me grounded when I need it, and who supports me in everything, even when my ideas are super sketch…

Thank You!

ABOUT THE AUTHOR

L.M. Wolfe is a mature—cough—writer from the East Coast. She's an avid daydreamer, coffee enthusiast, and meme recycler.

When L's not juggling her household, the kids, or putting in the extra hours at work, she's picking apart her stories.

Chock-full of snark, steam, and a lotta WTF, she's an acquired taste. And she is me because it feels weird to write about myself in the third person. Anywho… welcome aboard. I hope you have fun.

Connect with me:
www.lmwolfe.com
IG: @thewolfeofwtf
thewolfeofwtf@gmail.com